SEARCH FOR THE PROPHECY
STORIES FROM THE MULTIVERSE
AUBREY M. GOING

To My English Teacher in high school who never gave up on me and believed I could become an Author. Thank you, Mr. Daily, for believing in me and driving me to become the writer I am today. It took me a long time since my classes with you to make this happen, but it is finally here.

Christopher Sanders. Thank you so much for all your help in finding an artist for the perfect Cover Art for this project.

To everyone who ever told me I couldn't. I did it.

CONTENTS

Acknowledgement

First and foremost, I want to express my deepest gratitude to you,
Ashe Armstrong. Your encouragement and support were the catalyst
that pushed me to take the leap into the world of publishing. Without
you, my passion for writing would have remained dormant. I am truly
indebted to you.

To my beta readers, thank you for putting up with my rough writing
as I returned to writing. At the start, it was a long and bumpy road,
but I wouldn't be here without you.

Huge thanks to everyone who helped me realize this long-term dream
of mine. It's been 20 years in the making, and it finally came true.

PROLOGUE

The Multiverse, an expansive and beautiful cacophony of planets, races, species, and creatures of all kinds. It is said that the gods created life and the creatures that inhabited them out of boredom and desire for something more. Some species have existed for millions of years, some only a few thousand. Some species learn, adapt, survive, and join the many other races that comprise most of the multiverse. Others are still developing, building their first rockets, and searching for life outside their planet. Yet even evolution and the development of technology can't stop the multitude of species in the multiverse from waging war against each other.

The Spiritosk are no different. A people born with a spirit separate from themselves that holds a conscience of its own, taking the form of a single animal. When a spiritosk comes of age, they take their true form, which is neither wholly human nor animal, but a mix of the two.

Among the spiritosk are the special few that hold power over the Major Eight, the main eight bodies of elements: Fire, Water, Earth, Air, Light, Dark, Mind, and Body. That was until the dragon spiritosk race was brought into creation. Where control of the major eight had once been a rare and unique gift that only a select few had, dragons were naturally gifted with it. Because of this, those not born with a dragon spirit grew resentful, even outright hateful. This helped spur the coming war from the bat spiritosk, a race of people oppressed by the dragons for millennia. Unhappy with the racism towards their people, the bats rose against the dragons and any other races that allied with them.

For millennia, the bats had been portrayed as evil and dark under the tyranny of the dragon spiritosk. Some bat spiritosk had even been forced into reclusion, even denying having a bat as a spirit. The final strike to their kind was the lack of trade, causing a starving and weak people to grow weaker. Unable to take the treatment towards their kind anymore, a new leader took charge and sought to right a wrong. As time passed, the bat spiritosk strengthened under their new leader and started a rebellion. Allies tired of the dragons' tyranny flocked to them quickly, and soon, the dragons found themselves outnumbered in spite of their gifts.

Word soon spread across the Multiverse, causing fights to erupt between dragons and bats wherever they lived. Nowhere was safe for spiritosk wanting to avoid the war. Those who wished to leave the war behind boarded ships and left for the edges of the Multiverse, bound for a planet not yet aware of the existence of the rest of the Multiverse or the wonders it held... Earth.

As the first ship arrived, the spiritosk aboard explained their situation to the humans that greeted them. At first, the humans were hesitant, but the temptation of knowledge and advanced technology quickly changed their minds. Though met with caution, the spiritosk were eventually met with open arms and welcomed to Earth. Taking every possible precaution, the humans gave them refuge, but in the form of camps across the world. The refugee spiritosk were overseen, day and night, for their own safety and those of the humans. The humans of Earth took every precaution possible given the strangeness of the spiritosk people. To ensure that no alien diseases, viruses, or infections were transmitted to humans, they were kept under close watch and quarantined in their camps.

When that quarantine time finally ended, humans had to determine what they would do to integrate their two species. Several activist groups raised their voices in defense of the spiritosk, stating that caging them like animals in the camps was inhumane. Other activists called them animals because of how they looked and acted, going so far as calling their camps "Preserves", a term that spiritosk themselves adopted openly. Summits were held, where the world's leaders would argue on what to do with the spiritosk and their current situation. Eventually, under the agreement for the spiritosk to share their knowledge of technology and space travel, it was decided an integration test would be held.

After a decade of struggle and advocacy, the Spiritosk's long-awaited integration into human society was about to begin. The children, now teenagers, of the first wave of arrivals, were poised to step beyond the confines of their 'Preserves'. They would be the pioneers, the first spiritosk to venture into human schools, to experience the world outside their encampments. This is the story of one such teenager.

I

NEW ARRIVALS

"Kirra, are you listening to me?" Her mother's sweet-sounding voice called out softly. Kirra was staring at what was to be considered her breakfast for the morning. A reflection of black, unkempt, shaggy hair stared back at her from a pool of milk and floating pieces of cereal. She was only half paying attention to her mother while playing with the long bangs that framed her angular face, wondering if she was overdue for a trim. The brilliant green eyes of her reflection stared back at her as Kirra heard her mother call out once more, "Helloooooooo? Is my daughter in there somewhere?"

Snapping out of her trance of self-examination, Kirra finally looked up, "Hmmm? Oh! Yeah, just wondering if we should probably have someone trim my bangs." Kirra gracefully shoveled a spoonful of cold cereal into her mouth before continuing, "I just- Can I just stay home and read about The Great Fall and The Warriors of Old? I can learn so much more here than being stuck in a classroom full of earthers that are just going to stare at me like a zoo animal."

Kirra was one of many kids that had come to Earth in what they called "The Great Migration". Like many her age that grew up in the "Preserves", Kirra knew very little about her home planet. She didn't have very many memories of Spiritoski. Still, she loved reading up on the old warriors and wars from their culture, more specifically, The Great Fall, a historic event that hadn't been well documented. She'd never known anything but living on the Preserve, growing up in a camp with high walls like an animal. Kirra always wondered what her life would have been like if she had grown up like any other spiritosk child and not a refugee.

Dayla corrected her daughter, "Humans...." Cleaning the dishes from her breakfast, she pointed to Kirra's bowl, "Hurry up and stop delaying. And yes, you do, in fact have to do this. We will not be going back to Spiritoski any time soon." Dayla's own brilliant green eyes looked over Kirra.

Dayla was a woman with an immaculate appearance and attitude. Everything had a proper place and a way it had to look. She was a bat spiritosk, and her wings were almost constantly out on display, one of which flicked with annoyance at Kirra's appearance. Like Kirra, Dayla's hair was an ebony black, but instead of the messy tresses that Kirra sported, a sleek bun with neat braids adorned Dayla's head. Unsurprisingly, her daughter, who was a direct contradiction to her appearance with her baggy shirts and ripped jeans, might irk her prim and proper mother. This contradiction was mirrored further by Kirra's light-colored skin and frail-looking frame despite her taller height.

Today was one of the rare days that her mother commented on her appearance, "I would very much love it if you put more effort into how you presented yourself, Kirra."

Justin, Kirra's older brother, chuckled as he walked past Kirra, commenting, "Oh come on, Mom, it takes a long time to master the look of grunge and ripped jeans." He stopped briefly to ruffle Kirra's hair before moving on with a cackle, "It's totally radical, dude!" A glare was shot in his direction from Kirra while she attempted to fix her hair. Taking a moment to examine Kirra's appearance, he shrugged, "I mean, it's not a bad look either."

Justin bore the same familiar tanned skin, dark hair, and green eyes as their mother. The phrase wolfishly handsome fit him perfectly, as he possessed the spirit of a wolf and was currently sporting fluffy black ears and a tail at that exact moment. His hair was cut short and smoothed back on his head neatly. Even his dress attire was neat, hole-less, and well taken care of despite him wearing jeans and a light t-shirt.

With a wag of her finger, their mother stated promptly, "It's not about looking good; it's about making an impression, and that type of speech is from the wrong era, according to human lore. You should do some more studying." The wolf ears on Justin's head went down slightly in a mock pout as Dayla continued to chide her son, "Speaking of fitting in, hide your tail and ears. You're supposed to be more... humany... to fit in."

"I think the girls will like it. At least they'll know how much of a dog he really is." Kirra's snarky comment came, causing a wadded-up napkin to fly across the table at her, which she dodged with a laugh. After the fit of laughter, she turned to her mother and asked curiously, "Why do we need to hide ourselves? I mean, you and Dad look badass as spirit people. You shouldn't have to hide what you look like."

As Dayla looked over at her daughter, she began to round the table with a mischievous look in her eyes. The suburban mom look dropped almost instantly as a shroud of black fog drooled over her human form and grew. As the dark shroud dissipated, the form of the bat-like monstrosity that was her mother took its place. The creature that was her mother nearly doubled Kirra's size and had to bend over to fit inside the small house as it growled out, "You really think this is the face that people wish to see whilst we represent our kind?" Having seen her mother's full form before, Kirra wasn't shocked and only smirked up at her with a nod.

Dayla's form began to shrink to a less formidable size as that same dark shroud took her over momentarily. When she emerged this time, she was only slightly taller than her normal height but retained the features of clawed feet, hands, bat ears, and even the velvety fur-covered wings as she planted her hands on her hips and asked, "And what about now?" Kirra's response was the same, causing a defeated huff from the older bat spiritosk. With one last dark shroud covering her animalistic parts, they all disappeared except for her wings as Dayla explained, "The point is, we look intimidating no matter what form we take. So, we make ourselves look smaller, weaker, and timid. Even amongst our own kind, we hide our features. We only bring out the more violent aspects of our forms if we mean to intimidate others or need to fight. Both of you would do well to remember that. Even you, Kirra, for when you get your spirit as well."

Not requiring further instruction from his mother, Justin's ears and tail slowly started to disappear as an almost painful look crossed his face before stating disdainfully, "Ugh, I don't know how you stand to hide everything all the time. Just feels weird..." He shook like a dog before continuing, "Feels unnatural to do it. I can't hear as well and feel off balance, ya know?"

The familiar sound of their father's baritone voice filled the small kitchen, "You get used to it. Not many approve of our natural appearances, so we accommodate them with something more appealing to the eyes."

Justin turned to regard his father, Taro, as he entered. He was something akin to that of a Viking warrior who had just crawled out from your favorite fantasy novel. If it wasn't for the kind eyes and smile on his face, he could've been considered dangerous. His hair was braided on certain parts of his head and pulled half back. Kirra had asked why he styled his hair that way once, and his only response was that it was an old habit he'd never grown out of.

As he reached the kitchen counter, he grabbed the pot of dark liquid and poured it into a mug, regarding it with a frown, "I do miss the tea from home..." Much like most of the bats that had come with them, Taro also had a darker complexion, but his hair was dark brown, and his eyes were a deeper emerald than that of his wife's. After considering the coffee momentarily, he looked up and chided his children, "Better grab your bags and get going. You don't want to miss the bus on your first day. Whatever a bus is..."

Both Taro and Dayla worked with the human government of the United States, the country they lived in, though Kirra didn't know what they did. She just knew that both of them were highly respected in their Preserve, and that was saying something given both of them were both bat spiritosk. Something told Kirra that they worked with seeing to the rights of their people and were probably helping with the whole integration process.

An audible groan escaped Kirra while Justin hopped out of the chair he was perched on before racing over to the front door. Kirra, who was delaying her departure, finally pushed the empty bowl of cereal away before standing regretfully. Pausing, she found herself staring at the back of her left hand as a heavy sigh escaped her. There it stood. The egg-shaped outline that let every other Spiritosk know her spirit hadn't hatched yet. It was a symbol she was growing to hate. Every spiritosk was born with a simple, oval-shaped black line on their hand.

The weight of a hand on her shoulder drew her attention away from the marking her father as he stated, "It'll happen, hun. Just give it time, and it will hatch eventually."

A smile that didn't quite reach her eyes grew on her face as she stated, "Yeah, right..." The disbelief in her voice was strong despite the smile she'd plastered on her face.

"Hey..." Her father called out, causing her to pause and look at him as he continued, "I mean it. This might be good for you. Maybe you'll be able to make some friends there."

A sound of disgust came from her, "Ugh, I don't need friends. What I need is not to be an outcast because I don't have a spirit yet." Turning her back to him, she hurriedly put her shoes on, calling out, "I gotta go, I'm going to be late."

Attempting to remind her before she left, he called out loudly, "Don't forget to take your ..." The door slammed, leaving his last word to be sighed out tiredly, "...medicine."

As Kirra started walking from the tiny townhouse, a sound of discontent came from her as she shook her head. Thoughts started to swirl in her head, only worsening her current mood as she walked. She was tired of the constant looks of sympathy from other people or her parents when they thought she wasn't looking. She was 14 going on 15, which meant she might have missed her window to get a spirit. Kirra was the only kid her age who didn't have a spirit in the encampment yet. With her birthday coming in a few months, she was afraid she might not get a spirit and be what her people called soulless.

When a spiritosk gained their spirit, it was called hatching, given the egg on their hand cracked and grew into the shape of whatever animal spirit they were gifted. If you didn't get a spirit by the age of 15, you were considered a soulless. It was possible that a spirit could hatch earlier, but that was uncommon. It was one thing to have a spirit different from the race of your parents, like her brother, but not to have one hatch out was an entirely different affair. Being a soulless was worse than being a human, and humans weren't very high on the food chain to begin with.

Making her way towards the front entrance of the Preserve, her mind swirled with thoughts of being a burden and failure to her family. Those thoughts eventually began to fade as she approached the entrance. The sounds of angry protesters gathered just beyond the walls could be heard. Justin, who was just ahead of her, stopped dead in his path, looking a little more than concerned, while the few other teens walking to the entrance walked around him. Kirra knew he was thinking about her safety over his own since she lacked any means to defend herself. Where her brother was strong and had been training in martial arts since the day he could walk, Kirra was frail, thin, and almost sickly. For fear of her getting hurt, they kept her away from such activities.

The pair looked towards the concrete structure of the building with the words "Welcome Center" in large letters across the top of the front of the building. The Welcome Center was different from every other building in the Preserve. It was really nothing more than a large grey box where people checked in and out of the Preserve. Mostly, it was for the military that were stationed in the building and around the perimeter of the Preserve.

Ignoring that he was hesitating for her own safety, Kirra stepped forward, placing a gentle hand on his shoulder, saying, "Don't worry about me. I'm sure Mom and Dad wouldn't have sent us through this if they didn't believe we couldn't be protected."

Despite fear crawling up her throat, Kirra proceeded to get in one of the lines filled with teenagers to sign out of the Preserve. Digging through her messenger bag for the ID she had been issued, Kirra had plenty of time to look for it given the number of teens lined up before her signing out for the first time. Justin jumped in line a little after her, having been gawking at the concrete building. The process of checking out didn't take too long to get inside of the building. Once she was inside, she stopped just within, looking past the glass wall and doors behind to her brother, who fumbled about in his own bag looking for his own ID, causing her to laugh softly.

While waiting for her brother to pass through the checkpoint, Kirra examined the young faces gathered inside. Some she recognized, most she didn't. As she surveyed her surroundings, Kirra noticed several scrutinizing looks in her direction. Most of her peers were sticking to their own particular races or spirit types. As her brother finally made it through, she waved at him to get his attention, but he passed by to rush over to his group of wolf, bear, and fox friends.

A sigh came from Kirra as she watched everyone around her group up, talking excitedly about the new school, friendships, outfits, bands, and whatnot. Part of her wished she'd found a group of friends among her own kind, but she also remembered how cruel they were. These people weren't her friends. Their kind was nothing but a giant animal kingdom, with each race segregating into groups of similar spirits, Kirra being the outcast who didn't belong to any of them. She was different, frail, weak, and therefore excluded because of her weakness and the lack of a spirit.

Her thoughts were suddenly disrupted when someone suddenly collided into her, causing her to fall. As she sprawled out on the floor, she quickly got back to her feet, helping whoever had smashed into her gather their things. The entire time she was helping them, she was apologizing profusely until she looked up. Kirra's heart instantly stopped as she meekly handed the items to the girl who had run into her. The girl was slender and gorgeous, and her blonde hair seemed to glow with a golden aura. To Kirra, she looked like a golden-skinned goddess. Everything about her looked perfect: her skin, her hair, her clothes, even her body.

A strange attraction drew Kirra towards the girl as she suddenly blurted out awkwardly, "You're gorgeous." Almost instantly, Kirra's face flushed with embarrassment as she heard nearby teens giggling at the sudden outburst, causing her to try and save face, "I meant, you're pretty, like... ethereal almost..." Facepalming out of embarrassment, she tried to recover by simply introducing herself, "Hi, I'm Kirra. What I meant..."

Brushing a stray piece of hair behind her own ear, the girl interrupted Kirra with, "That you think I'm pretty. I get that a lot." The girl cocked an eyebrow at Kirra in question, "Why are you even talking to me?" More snickers erupted around them as Kirra glanced up at the girl's head and realized she'd made a grave mistake as she went on, "Aren't your parents bats?" The girl had a very particular set of antlers on her head that only meant one thing to everyone in that room.

This girl was a dragon. Not just any dragon, but a celestial dragon, which meant she was pretty much royalty in the dragon world. Kirra had just committed the equivalent of social suicide in their culture. The only reason you even spoke to a celestial dragon was if you worked for them or were a dragon yourself. Kirra was neither. She attempted to save face as she stammered over her words, "I just—I wanted to apologize to you. Y-Your things went flying all over the place s-so I..."

The weight of a hand clamped down on her shoulder as a familiar voice leaned over to whisper in her ear, "You don't have anything to apologize for. She bumped into you." As he spoke, Kirra slowly looked up towards the voice and recognized the boy as he turned to address the celestial dragon, "You bumped into my friend here. You should apologize to her."

It was the son of the leader of Bat Colony, Devin. As he stepped up next to Kirra, his red eyes flashed over the celestial dragon with cruel cynicism. Short, shaggy hair hung partially in his eyes as he looked down his nose towards the dragoness with a confident smirk on his face. The room became quiet as the two stood their ground. Though they hadn't grown up in the war, it felt as though it was in that room at that very moment.

The girl's next words were practically spat towards Devin, "I'm not apologizing to the child of a pair of murderous bats for standing in the middle of a room and not moving. It's not my fault that she was born a soulless." Kirra wanted nothing more than to disappear as she heard those words while a few nearby snickered.

Devin's malicious response came swiftly, "I heard your sister sent you here. Something along the lines of you being the sad excuse of your family. Too weak, too skinny, and you don't even have control over light like the rest of your predecessors..." Each word was like acid melting that confident armor of the dragoness. While the argument was going on, Kirra slowly lifted her bag up to hide, wishing she had the ability of invisibility in that moment.

The dragoness stepped right up to him, hissing angrily, "You take that back you—"

"What's going on here?!" A voice demanded as a few of the spiritosk teens parted for a pair of military personnel.

The pair of military officials wore normal green and black camo uniforms and armor. The most intimidating thing about them was that they were all armed with at least a side arm and rifle of some variety. All of the adults liked to claim the military was there for their protection, but Kirra didn't feel like that was the case most days. They felt like nothing more than uniformed government bullies, but they still did their job.

Kirra immediately stepped up to the approaching pair and proclaimed, "Nothing... Exactly nothing." Reaching over, she pinched Devin's arm, "Right, Devin?"

Hissing from the pinch, Devin glared at Kirra briefly before stating coolly, "Just a few words being exchanged. That's all."

Both men looked to the three spiritosk teenagers, commenting, "Separate and make sure it stays that way. Don't want your war spilling over onto our planet as well, now do we?"

As the three separated, Devin wrapped an arm around Kirra as he guided her to walk with him towards his group of friends. Almost instantly, she felt a flush come to her cheeks as she stammered over her words of protest.

Her stammering soon stopped as one of Devin's friends suddenly exclaimed, "Man, that was ballsy talking down to a dragon like that, Devin."

Kirra wanted nothing to do with that group or their conversations, but Devin's firm hold around her waist stopped her from running away. Eventually, she gave up trying to escape and instead just kept to herself. Tuning out the conversation of the gossiping teens, she looked off in the distance and spotted her brother laughing with his group of friends. She wanted nothing to do with their conversations of blaming the dragons for all of their problems. None of them knew what their home was like except Devin, and he wasn't complaining. To Kirra, it felt more like the teens wanted something to complain about and someone to blame for being stuck in the Preserves.

Just as she thought she was getting comfortable around the group of teens, that came to a screeching halt as the sound of a shrill voice called out accusingly, "Why is she here?" It was one of the girls that'd been hanging all over Devin since he'd gotten there. Dark long hair, yellow eyes, and the face of a model on the body of someone with the confidence that they looked beautiful.

Looking towards the stuck-up teen, Kirra opened her mouth to answer but was saved from having to speak as Devin defended her with, "Because she's where she belongs. And as long as she's promised to me, she'll always be welcome." The arm around Kirra only squeezed her lightly with the comment, causing an angry glare from the snobby teen that was nearly palpable.

She had been promised at an early age to Devin. It was the same as an arranged marriage to their people, and it wasn't too uncommon, especially between the parents of wealthy families or those who had influence. Despite that she was promised to Devin, her parents didn't seem to like Devin too much and tried to keep the pair separated from each other. Kirra didn't actually know that much about Devin other than he was the son of the Bat Spiritosk leader.

Ignoring the girl's hubris, Kirra kept to herself, hoping the less she spoke, the less the group would pick on her. She didn't belong in that group and always felt that way, given her lack of a spirit despite being around fellow bat spiritosk.

Something deep down inside of her told her so. It was instinctual. Sometimes, that instinct gave way to a voice, a deep rumbling growl of a sleeping beast waiting to be woke. Part of her felt that the beast inside of her responded to the actions of the world around her. A sudden squeeze from Devin caused the beast to rumble almost angrily, causing her to jump.

"Kirra, I asked you a question." Devin's whisper came in conjunction with the squeeze of her waist. He chuckled at her startled expression, causing the beast to snarl lightly before it calmed. Part of her wondered if the beast was her spirit, or perhaps, just her hallucinating.

A nervous laugh came from her, "Sorry. I didn't hear you. What did you say?" Just like that, the feeling of the beast was gone.

A chuckle came from the handsome Bat Prince, "What are your classes? Where's your schedule?" Kirra dug through her bag before pulling out the paper schedule and showing it to Devin as he sneered, "Well, that's annoying. We don't even share any classes together. What does AP stand for?"

Blushing, she explained, "Advanced Placement. The classes are just more difficult, or that's what the counselor told me when I took the placement tests." Kirra shrugged, "I think it means I'm ahead of my age group realistically."

He spoke out to her with a smile, "Huh. Interesting. I'm not going to lie. My dad made me come here more out of wanting to ensure you were protected. It sucks that we don't have any classes together. We could've spent more time getting to know each other." Kirra's face flushed at his words.

"Listen up!" A booming voice called out, saving Kirra from having to reply. The room grew quiet as a man in the center of the room stood on a step ladder so he was visible to everyone in the room. He wore the same military uniform as all the soldiers and spoke with confidence and authority, "I don't like repeating myself, so can everyone hear me?"

The murmur of teens in the room caused the man to call out, "I can't hear you, so that must mean you can't hear me..." Somehow, he managed to get even louder as he yelled, "Can everyone hear me?!"

There was an almost unison-sounding affirmation as everyone in the room made a point of calling out loudly back at him this time.

"GOOOOOD!" After the sarcastic confirmation, he said in a more serious tone, "Now then. The lot of you will be split up into three different schools evenly amongst your...." He searched for a word to not come across as insulting, "... species. Three different buses, three different schools. All of you will more than likely be split up from your normal little cliques." A sound of confusion ran through the group of teens as they looked around, not quite believing the soldier.

Despite the confusion his previous comment caused, he continued explaining, "At the top of your schedules should be the name of the school you are attending. Next to the school's name is the number of the bus you are assigned to. This bus number will never change unless there is a security concern. There are going to be people that bully you. They will try to goad you into starting a fight. If you throw a single punch, claw, or bite, you are out of the program." As this registered with the group of young teens, several of them looked around with trepidation, "Here are the rules!"

Pulling out a sheet, the man proceeded to read, "1. No interspecies fighting. We don't want your war on our planet, so keep it civil. 2. No copulation with humans. You can date and become friends, but no bumping uglies." There were a few snickers in the crowd, causing Kirra to cover her face when the man mentioned the topic before continuing, "This isn't a joke. We don't know what consequences could happen if one of you gets a human pregnant or vice versa. The last thing you want is to be the first to pass on space AIDs and get someone killed... or one of you contract something and find out it's deadly to you." The last caused the group to grow quiet.

With a throat clear, the man proceeded, "3. You are allowed to participate in sports and explore the towns at your own risk. A shuttle will take you to and from here with a schedule and route attached. The last shuttle arrives back here at 2300 hours, that's 11 p.m. If you miss that shuttle, you will be in trouble, and trust me, you do not want to be in trouble." There were some excited mumbles about being able to get out and explore.

The man continued to speak but in a louder tone over the excited chatter of the teens, "4. If you need to spend a night out from the Preserve, you are required to submit a formal request three days prior to the date requested. There are forms at the check-in point." The man gestured to the side, where another uniformed personnel waved behind a glass window. This news caused even more excited chattering from the teens.

As the man waited for the excitement to die down, he started back up with, "You do not have to wear your badges once you have scanned in or out of the checkpoint. All you need it for is scanning in or out. If you **LOSE** your badge, you can get a new one but lose it too many times, and you're out of the program. In case you didn't hear me..." He paused, held up the sheet he was reading from, and waved it around, "There are printed-out instructions that will be handed to you as you get on your assigned bus. These instructions will also be sent to your parents and/or guardians to ensure you follow them. Now, form an orderly line out the door and proceed to your assigned buses."

After the soldier stopped speaking, the chatter from the teens started back up, but most seemed hesitant to move from where they were. The grouping around Devin and Kirra were all peering out the windows and seemed too afraid to move first. Deciding to leave the possessive coil of Devin's arm, Kirra strode forward. She was more eager to get out of the stuffy building than anything.

She wasn't first, but she was near the front of one of the lines that led outside to bright yellow metal machines. From the corner of her eye, Kirra caught a glimpse of the celestial dragon that had run into her earlier. The beast inside of Kirra roiled and rumbled as though it caught the scent of something familiar. The feeling caused Kirra to pause and stare at the girl as she felt one brilliant blue eye open lazily. These hallucinations weren't uncommon with her, but it usually was the sign she needed to take her medicine soon.

"*Half-Blood...*" However, the deep rumbling from the beast was something that she had never experienced as it spoke with a note of disapproval.

Confused, Kirra mumbled to herself aloud, "Half-blood?"

"What did you just say?!" The celestial dragon girl hadn't been looking at her originally, but clearly, she had heard Kirra as the girl rounded on her suddenly. She had gone so far as to step out of her own line over into Kirra's, cutting in front of another teen as she stared down at Kirra.

Backing up from the girl, Kirra waved her hands frantically, trying to look small. An impressive feat for Kirra, given she was almost 6 feet tall. While attempting to back up from the girl, Kirra bumped into someone behind her who shoved her, making her stumble back in her own line. This made the girl laugh as she mumbled something to a couple of her friends, causing them all to laugh. Pulling the hood of her jacket over her head, Kirra kept her head down, letting out a little whimper of embarrassment. The sound of a throaty chuckle from the beast reverberated in her head before going silent.

All around her, Kirra could hear the teens laughing and joking about what happened. She'd already been pulled from the school on the Preserve, and her parents did their best with her at home, but now she couldn't hide anymore. She was going to try her hardest to find a group of friends and fit in at the new school.

She was certain things couldn't get much worse.

2

OUTSIDERS

The moment Kirra stepped outside, she was greeted with a blinding light from the rising sun, forcing her to raise an arm to block the sun. The roaring sound of angry protesters battered her ears while her eyes adjusted. When they finally adjusted, what lay before her made her pause.

Everywhere she looked, there were armed military guards wearing some sort of armor with shields that looked to be made out of plastic. Opposite the military guards were angry protesters who sat behind flimsy, metal waist-high fences that seemed more for show than actual protection. The protesters were screaming vulgarly at the teens, raising signs with racist slurs, and even threatening their lives. On another side, behind fences, were those there in support of the spiritosk and their rights.

The only reason she moved from her spot at all was because of someone shoving her forward out of their way. Kirra seemed to be the only person who was concerned. The others whispered about flying back or just using their spirit's strength if they needed to defend themselves. Kirra didn't have such protection. No spirit to protect her, fly away, use their strength, speed, or abilities. She would be left completely at the mercy of the angry crowds.

23

At a soldier's urging, Kirra managed to find the courage to look for her bus and started heading towards it. As she got on, they double-checked that she was where she needed to be, handed her a form, and rushed her on the bus. Finding a seat at the back of the bus, that tightening in her chest finally calmed as she clutched her bag tightly. She sat quietly in the very back of the bus, staring hard as people screamed and hollered and those boarding. Though it didn't take long, to Kirra, it felt like hours passed as she sat still.

A sudden thud right next to her head caused her to gasp and jump as something red and juicy sprayed over the side of her window. Several more thuds were heard before the sounds of fighting broke out just beyond the windows of the bus. The armed military guards were pressing back protestors as things got out of hand, and the guards began shooting what appeared to be cans of gas into the crowd, causing Kirra to cling to her bag more tightly.

Fear welled up in her, tightening her throat as though a hand was squeezing the life from her. The feeling of a hand clapping down on her shoulder caused her to let out a squeak of fear and jump. With a knee-jerk reaction, she wound a hand back before blindly slapping at the potential threat next to her.

Another hand caught her wrist, halting her attack. When Kirra looked up, her voice caught in her throat as Devin looked at her with worry etching the lines of his face, "Sorry, I didn't mean to scare you." He slowly let go of her wrist and removed his hand from her shoulder before sitting down next to her, asking, "Are you okay? I was going to sit somewhere else, but I saw you were alone when the fighting broke out."

Relief swept through Kirra as she let her head fall back and took a few calming breaths, "I'll be fine." Relaxing some, she turned to him in question, "You're not afraid of them?"

The laugh that came from him hinted that he thought she was joking before he looked at her seriously, "Oh, you're serious." He cleared his throat, shaking his head, "Nah, they don't scare me. I was trained from before I could even walk on how to defend myself and fight. Having a spirit helps as well..." He grew quiet as she only clutched her bag closer, causing him to add, "I forget sometimes that you don't have a spirit yet." He nudged her with a wink, "Don't worry though, I won't let anything happen to you. They'd have to go through me first to get to you." The frown on Kirra's face gave away the fact that his words were only making her feel worse, so he quieted down.

That quiet stretched for some time as she stared down at her hands as her fingers clung tightly around each other before she finally gathered the courage to speak, "It's kind of hard to forget with everyone reminding me about it all the time." A nervous laugh came from her with her attempt at humor before she sighed and quieted down once more.

Devin let out a soft laugh before he asked sincerely, "Feel better?"

The question caught her off guard. Kirra nodded her head shyly before turning to look out her window as she watched the trees passing. The landscape was a lush green haven. Rows of trees lined the length of the black asphalt road. Beyond the tree tops, a clear blue sky with just a smidge of clouds that looked soft as wool. Her mind drifted freely at the beautiful sight of nature not seen from over the top of her high-walled enclosure.

Devin was a surprisingly good bus companion. He wasn't outright annoying or attempting to fill the silence of the ride with excited chittering like the other teens. He was just enjoying the peace and quiet in the seat next to her. There were no attempts to showboat or impress her, just a calming quiet that surrounded him as he relaxed back with his eyes closed.

The peace didn't last forever. The sound of a beeping alarm on her watch went off. It was her reminder alarm to take her medicine. However annoying the alarm was, it was a necessary reminder for her. Shutting it off, she dug through her bag for the pill bottle, pulled it out, and took one of the small white pills sighing out afterwards.

Devin looked on curiously with an arched brow, "Everything okay?"

Kirra seemed hesitant but eventually explained, "I have a severe allergy to something in the air here. The medicine helps me from keeling over and just dying from merely breathing." An awkward laugh escaped her.

Curiosity got the better of Devin as he held a hand out and asked politely, "Can I see?" Not used to having someone being curious about her allergy, she hesitantly placed the bottle in his open hand. Spinning the bottle, he examined the label, reading over everything before he pulled one of the tiny pills out. His brows furrowed with confusion as he stated, "This isn't allergy medicine."

Initially, Kirra scoffed, stating firmly, "That's crazy. I've been on them for a long time." Kirra immediately snatched at the bottle, but Devin didn't immediately relinquish his hold.

Eventually, he let go of the bottle, asking seriously, "How long is long?"

"As long as I can remember..." Kirra stuffed the bottle away before shrugging, "All I know is that I start hallucinating, which is the sign that I'm about to have an allergy attack."

"Hallucinate how?" The question came so immediately that it took her off guard.

She'd never had anyone so interested in her allergy before, so she had to think on how to word her response, "I... start hearing things."

"What kinds of things?"

There was clear reluctance in her voice as she felt slightly wary at his sudden interest in the topic, "Like... a beast rumbling inside of me; like it's going to rip me apart from the inside out."

Devin seemed to be considering not asking his next question, but it came in that same firm tone, "Have you ever considered not taking your 'medicine'?"

Kirra's eyes widened at even considering such a thing, "Um, no. Considering it's the only thing keeping me alive on this planet? Yeah, no. Not a chance." The thought had never truly crossed her mind.

The subject seemed to drop as Devin went silent briefly before he proclaimed, "Don't take them."

Almost immediately, she looked at Devin as though he'd lost his mind, "What?! No. You're absolutely crazy."

"Okay, sheep." His statement earned him a glare to which he responded, "You follow what your parents tell you to do like a good little sheep, so I called you a sheep."

As though he didn't hear her the first time, she reiterated, "If I don't take the medicine, I will die."

He slowly faced her and tried to clarify his point, "Hear me out. You've never **not** taken them before, so how would you know?"

Kirra found herself running a hand over her face as she very pointedly explained once more, "Because I don't want to **die**..."

After a few moments of the pair staring at each other, Devin turned to face the front of the bus with a shrug, "Just food for thought... What if the medicine was actually preventing you from getting your spirit?" Despite Devin seeming to know something Kirra didn't, he didn't press her further and let the matter drop.

Once he stopped pestering her about the medicine, the pair eventually started up some small talk. Mostly, they spoke about his time in Spiritoski, given that Devin only recently arrived on Earth in the last year. Being curious about life on Spritoski, Kirra had quite a few questions. Devin didn't know that much about their home world, given he spent the majority of his time training in Bat Colony. He did, however, mention that most of the bat spiritosk lived in Bat Colony, a massive cave carved out of a mountain.

Their chatter started to die out as Kirra saw signs for the school coming up on road signs and markers. It wasn't just Kirra that had started to quiet down. The rest of the bus grew quiet as other teens started staring out the window and looking towards the school as it came into view. Finally, the bus lurched to a stop, and everyone started to get out of their seats, moving down the narrow aisle toward the exit.

Being one of the last off the bus was a bit eye-opening for Kirra. Most of the teens from the Preserve stuck out like sore thumbs. The combination of colorful hair, eyes, and overall ethereal strangeness set them apart from the rest of the humans. It didn't help that some, like that celestial dragon girl, bore horns or other parts like fangs, slightly pointed ears, or animalistic eyes. The confidence the teens had seemed to have melted away the second they stepped off the bus and were getting stared at by the school's regular students.

Kirra, on the other hand, mostly blended in. While the human students out front were milling about, catching up, or staring at the new spiritosk students, Kirra decided to use the distraction and slip into the crowd unnoticed. Wandering the halls, she looked down at the sheet she was given and attempted to find her locker. She was even surprised when a boy saw her struggling to get oriented and volunteered to help her find it.

Surprised at the kind gesture, she accepted the help gratefully. He even helped her to locate her first class even though she was a bit awkward about the entire interaction. Watching the kids interact in the classroom, she went to a seat that wasn't taken and just watched the other teens for the moment. All of their topics of discussion were confusing to her since she didn't know much about current human interests. Something told her she should have paid more attention to the news or television at home.

Her first class of the day was rather boring. It was what they called Calculus. She was far ahead of the rest of the kids, and as she'd found out, all of the teens in the room were a few years older than her. Mostly it was just introductions to the class and what they'd be going over. To Kirra, though, the class didn't have much to offer as she was far ahead of them.

History was going to be a bit harder. It was all based on the history of Earth. She remembered her parents telling her that it was an optional class in Spiritoski. They preferred much more relevant topics like teaching survival, combat, politics, finance, and overall general education to get by in the world. Despite how important the Spiritoski history was in their culture, it was up to each individual to pursue further education independently or go into the world and find what drove them.

As the bell rang, Kirra looked at her schedule and noticed it was lunchtime. As interesting as it was to be stuck in English Composition, learning how to write in a language she already knew, Kirra was thankful to be free from the class. Rushing through the halls, she followed the crowd of students, all seeming to move to the cafeteria like a herd of cattle.

Pale fluorescent lights bathed the room with artificial lights. The room was large, and most of it was consumed by long grey tables and benches that were spaced for walking room in between. No windows graced the room or basked it in natural light. The room itself was painted in that same depressing grey paint, where it looked to be peeling in some places. The room gave off a depressing feeling despite the excited chatter of students as they made their way in small groups to tables, forming their cliques. To her, it seemed as though there were more tables than students, almost overwhelmingly so.

Immediately seeing a line of students moving through a room on one side of the cafeteria, Kirra made her way in as she guessed that was where they served the food. A look of disappointment came to her face the moment she stepped inside. Every one of the foods in the line was greasy, fattening, downright disgusting looking, or looked inedible.

She mumbled to herself softly, "How do humans eat this garbage."

A girl standing in line just behind Kirra piped up, "Oh, it's all as terrible as it looks, but there are items that you can always buy that at least taste good." Kirra doubted the girl's words before she pointed out, "The mozzarella sticks are always good. I know it's just bread and cheese, but it'll fill you up, and it's edible... mostly."

Looking behind her at the teenager, Kirra was met with a pair of wiry glasses, thin pin-straight brown hair, and lightly tanned skin. The girl looked about the same height and build as her, which made her seem less imposing.

That friendly voice continued, "If you have certain things you prefer to eat, it's probably better if you pack your own lunch or get your parents to make it. Everything else is pretty much inedible or the consistency of cardboard." Surprised at her kindness, Kirra remained quiet as her green orbs took in the scrawny teen, "I'm Sam, by the way. You can sit with us if you'd like to."

Looking around to see if it was a prank, Kirra finally answered, "Yeah.... I uh- um. Sure. I think that would be kinda cool. I'm Kirra." Sam scooted past Kirra to grab a couple of items, making sure to point out the Mozzarella sticks to her as she did so. After the pair paid for their food, Sam led the way to one of the long tables near a wall and sat down with a small group of people. The table itself was mostly empty, save for the small group. All the teens looked up as Sam approached and smiled brightly as the pair joined them.

The group was about as mixed-looking as one social group could get. All of them sat close save for one girl with wavy brown hair and baggy clothes who was scribbling in a notebook. Bruises marked the girl's arms, which others probably couldn't see, and were visible to Kirra, given her improved vision. The girl was the only one at the table that didn't greet Sam and Kirra when they joined.

Unable to contain her excitement, Sam immediately chirped, "It's so cool that you guys get to come to school with us now." Taking a bite of a mozzarella stick she continued, "I've tried talking to a few of the other spiritosk, but they all look at us like we're food or something. Then I saw you on your own and figured, why not give it another shot?"

A nervous laugh escaped Kirra's chest, "I kind of don't fit in with the rest of my kind, so I don't sit with them. I was actually pulled out of our school on the Preserve because of all the bullying that was happening to me..." Kirra went quiet, a little embarrassed at bringing it up

The girl sitting off on her own suddenly spoke up, "You? Got bullied?" As Kirra nodded affirmatively at the girl, she replied, "H-How? You're really pretty and not to mention not socially awkward. I can't see how anyone would bully you." A long, awkward pause followed as the girl looked around at the others before apologizing for the outburst, "Sorry, I didn't mean to interrupt. I just... ya know... didn't think you guys had bullies given that you are all more advanced than us, but then I forgot that you're here because of a war, and I'm shutting up now." With a couple of nervous laughs, the girl suddenly found that her notebook was very interesting and avoided eye contact after her awkward outburst.

After a few moments, Kirra finally said, "I don't really like talking about it a lot, but since I'm getting to experience your human culture, I guess I can share some of mine. The uh big reason I get bullied is because I'm not like the others my age. I haven't uh...developed any uh, animalistic features, so it makes me a bit weird to them."

Since everyone at the table was staring at her like she'd spoken a different language, Kirra explained again, "So, like... when we're born, we're born with a mark on our hand in the shape of an egg. And when our spirit hatches... it grows into a larger mark. That mark is what spirit you take on, and that's considered hatching a spirit." Knowing she was doing a terrible job at explaining, she quickly finished up, "And I don't have mine yet, so I get made fun of and bullied by everyone for it."

The silence at the table was thick enough to cut with a knife. Thankfully, Kirra heard the awkward girl speak up once more as she reiterated, "So you're born with a birthmark in the shape of an egg?" Kirra nodded, "And then that egg becomes something else, and that's called hatching?" Another nod, "And your spirit is the thing that causes all of this, and it's basically your guys' version of puberty?" Kirra nodded, but the others at the table seemed lost as the girl looked at the rest of the group and said, "Basically, she's a late bloomer, and they bully her because of it."

Almost in unison, the group called out, "Ohhhhhh." Almost immediately, a few of the members spoke up and insisted they would never do that to Kirra. Once the initial awkwardness faded, the group started up their normal conversations, mostly around smaller worries about what teachers they had and who was dating whom. It was refreshing for Kirra just to be a part of a group at all. When the chatter suddenly stopped, Kirra looked about and saw most of the group staring at something behind her, causing her to turn.

Devin was standing there and asked after Kirra turned and noticed him, "You wanna come sit with us?"

Looking to where Devin gestured, she noticed the "us" was a small group of primarily female spiritosk glaring in her direction. The idea of sitting with them didn't sit well with her, "I uh— I don't think I should. Your uh— friends don't seem too fond of me."

Turning just enough to peek over his shoulder, Devin realized why she might be hesitant as he commented, "It'll be fine. They'll be nice. I promise."

Glancing between the group of spiritosk and Devin, she shook her head again, "I *really* don't think it's a good idea..."

Just as Kirra turned to face her newfound group of friends, she felt the bench shift lightly. Devin sat beside her with a smirk, "Guess I'll have to join you then." He looked towards the group of humans and smiled, nodding his head at them, "Sup?" Almost immediately, the table devolved into a fit of giggles except for the one girl with the note-book, who stared for a moment before returning to her scribbling.

It was only then that Sam finally started to introduce everyone in the group, "I'm Sam; these are my band friends, Aubrey and Crystal," She pointed at the girl that was scribbling in her book, indicating her to be Aubrey. Aubrey gave a single wave before resuming her drawing, though Kirra noticed even through the baggy clothing that she looked quite muscular despite her small stature. Crystal, on the other hand, looked like a tall and thin goddess next to Aubrey. Dark, thin hair draped down her narrow frame, which only accentuated her lighter grey eyes. Sam continued to point to each person as she continued introductions, "Katrina," A rather tall and awkward-looking girl sitting next to Crystal, rather plain in the face and average looking with brown hair and doe eyes that hid behind large framed glasses. "And finally, last but not least, Tyler," He was a boy on the smaller side with dark, short hair that swept across his face.

Once She was finished giving introductions, she added with a laugh, "We're all kind of band nerds, well... except Tyler."

Tyler was quick to explain, "Yeah, I gave up in 6th grade. Kind of sucks playing a brass instrument with braces." Smiling brightly, he showed off the metal on his teeth, making Kirra grimace and wonder why there was metal on his teeth at all. It caused both Devin and Kirra to share a look with each other momentarily to which Devin just shrugged in confusion while the group of human teens laughed.

Not noticing the awkwardness between the spiritosk, Sam continued on, "Anyway, this is our little group. Sometimes, we hang out after school when we're not too busy with band practice or, in Aubrey's case, work, band, sports, homework, and chores."

The group talked for a while, chattering about one thing or another, more curious about the two spiritosk teens than anything. Aubrey, however, took no part in engaging with them as she sat off on her own, seemingly scribbling in her notebook. After some time, she got up without saying a word and left. Once she left the table, the others commented about her being the weird one. Apparently, it wasn't uncommon for her to just get up and leave without saying anything.

Shortly after her sudden dismissal, the sound of books clattering on the ground could be heard, followed by teens laughing. As the group turned to look at the sound, they saw a disheveled and downtrodden Aubrey splayed out on the ground after seemingly having tripped. The group of friends near Kirra snickered at Aubrey's mishap while Kirra looked on with dismay. Kirra's brother, Justin, ran over to help Aubrey with her things, but she shrugged him off. Out of concern of looking like a misfit, Kirra stayed out of it as she had enough problems of her own back on the Preserve.

It was only after the group finished snickering and Aubrey had quickly exited the cafeteria that the group explained the anomaly that was Aubrey. It appeared that she was heavily bullied at school, and most of it was encouraged by her own family. The group hung out with her as often as they could stand and indulged in her weirdness and the horror drawings that she often scribbled, but some were just so creepy that it often scared them. Although Kirra felt this was wrong, she didn't speak up as this was only her first day. For once, she was probably going to be able to make friends, and she didn't want to ruin her chances by jumping to conclusions.

3

Breaking the Rules

T he first few days of school were very rough. If the spiritosk teens in the integration program weren't dealing with angry protesters, they were dealing with racist teachers who purposely marked down their grades. Even after a few weeks, racism was still prevalent, but it wasn't as obvious as when they first started.

As weeks turned to months with fall arriving, the protesters stopped coming to the Welcome Center altogether. Kirra found herself staring out the windows, watching the colorful leaves drop from the trees in wonder. There weren't any trees on the Preserve. All she'd seen growing up were buildings and tents as the Preserve progressed. From beyond the high walls of the Preserve, she could barely manage to see the tips of the trees. All of it was alien and new as she finally got to see what lay beyond the Preserve for the first time.

From what she had read growing up, the biology of their planets was largely similar except for their seasons. While Earth was on a tilt as it spun around the sun, Spiritoski was not, which allowed for its seasons to remain the same. Most parts of the planet were basked in the sun, while a small portion of the planet did not receive hardly any light. While Earth had one moon, Spiritoski had three. This meant that the temperature variances caused were strictly based on location. Had it not been for her fascination with the seasonal differences, Kirra would have never noticed the shadowy figure standing under the tree she was examining.

Under the tree was a rather sizeable black, shaggy dog that appeared to be staring towards her very classroom. After a moment of looking at the large shaggy dog, the alarm on her watch went off. Sighing out, she groaned as she remembered her medicine dosage had changed with her increased hallucinations. She now had to take her medicine one more time during the day which changed the times she took it.

Once she took her medicine, she looked back out the window and tried to find the dog again, but saw it trotting away from the tree and around the back of the school. Squinting at the retreating form, she noticed that the animal's size was larger than a normal dog and narrower in the chest. The realization hit her that it wasn't a dog but a wolf, which looked oddly like her brother in his full form. The question was, why was her brother taking his full form to keep an eye on her? Kirra decided from then on, that she was going to be more vigilant with her surroundings because it was too coincidental that her brother had disappeared right after she took her medicine.

To confirm her hypothesis, she started to keep an eye out for him during all of her classes, confirmed that he only appeared before the alarm for her medicine at the one class, and left after taking it. Seeing that her hypothesis was correct, she started taking in her surroundings only during the times that she took her medicine since it was taken more periodically throughout the day. If he was keeping a close eye on her during the other time at school when she had to take her medicine, her hypothesis would be confirmed.

Sitting down where she usually ate her lunch, she casually looked around as though looking between her friends only to find Justin in a group of his own friends not sitting too far away but not too close. He was also facing towards her general direction so he could see her rather easily. Like clockwork, her alarm went off on her watch, and she reset it after taking her medicine. She noticed him watching her as she did. The moment she took the pill, he ignored her completely and paid attention to the conversation his friends were having. Her parents had always trusted her to take her medication, so why now was he making sure she was taking it? She didn't know if it was because of her birthday coming up or something else, but something seemed off about the entire thing.

The conversation Devin and her had at the beginning of the year flitted through her mind. What if he was right about the medicine? What if it wasn't medicine at all? The question was how Devin knew about her medicine if he was correct. Kirra needed to test her next hypothesis further before jumping to conclusions.

To test out her hypothesis, she left her pills at home a few different times, first in a few obvious places, then in not-so-obvious places. The first few times she had left the bottle behind, her father called her back to retrieve it. It wasn't done maliciously but rather out of concern for her own well-being. Another day, she hid them in a location she knew they wouldn't find. Miraculously, Kirra was called to the office and there was a fresh bottle of medicine at her disposal. Sensing something was definitely off about the entire thing, Kirra figured it was time she approached Devin and finally questioned him about the issue.

Under the guise of going to a friend's house, she made plans to meet up with Devin and have him explain things. Devin lived in a single apartment on the second floor of the building by himself. Moving up the steps, she kept an eye out, wondering if anyone saw her visiting him. Mostly, she didn't want anyone jumping to conclusions about her visiting him.

The sound of a door opening caused her to turn. Instead of words coming out, Kirra found herself staring wide-eyed. Before her stood Devin with nothing but a pair of shorts on and a toothbrush idly hanging from the side of his mouth. A slow flush crept up Kirra's neck and face as she found herself staring.

Devin hadn't been lying when he said he had been training since before he could walk, and it seemed he continued to do so. Before her stood the years of work and training that was his sculpted physique on show right before her very eyes. It would have been enough to make any girl her age drool, so it was no surprise that she caught herself staring a little longer than expected.

Snapping out of her trance, She turned and hid the flush on her face as frustration filled her voice, "Can you put on a shirt or something?!"

Noticing the hint of a blush along her neck and the part of her face that wasn't hidden, he looked down and realized he was making her uncomfortable. Sighing out, he stated softly, "Come in and I'll put a shirt on."

As he moved to the side to let her in, she quickly scooted by him, keeping her eyes low so she wouldn't be caught staring. Keeping her back to him, she stayed like that until he gave her the okay.

Stepping up behind her, he softly said, "All good now..."

Turning around, she saw how close he was to her, which made her step back away from him as she cleared her throat, "Sorry, just not really used to seeing people like that." The flush on her face remained, though it was fading slowly.

With a shrug, he said, "It's fine. Just wasn't expecting company." His eyebrows furrowed in question, "What are you doing here? Not that I mind your company, but I'm certain your parents wouldn't be thrilled at the idea."

Kirra quickly fired back, "I don't do everything my parents say..." Before adding, "They actually don't know that I'm here. I told them I was at a friend's house."

Surprise brightened his eyes before mischievousness twinkled in the red hues. He closed the gap, making her back up against a wall. He leaned in and commented, "Oh? Breaking the rules now, little sheep?" He leaned in and whispered the next, "What did you come here for then?"

Face hot from embarrassment at his proximity; she finally whispered, "I wanted to talk about my medicine..."

A stillness entered his form before he pushed off of the wall and spoke to her frankly, "We've already been through this song and dance. I told you that your medicine isn't what you think it is, and you blew me off." He crossed his arms, arching an eyebrow at her in question, "What changed your mind about it?"

There was a moment of hesitation before Kirra explained, "My brother has been watching me when I'm supposed to be taking my 'medicine'. I started leaving it behind on purpose, and then I was either being reminded or brought an entirely new bottle. I realized at that point that everything was related only to the medicine, and I don't feel comfortable bringing it up to them. I think they would lie to my face and say that he's just keeping an eye on me or something along those lines."

He stood there considering her words for a long moment before finally saying, "Alright."

A look of confusion crossed Kirra's face, "Alright?"

Devin was already moving into a different room as she heard the rustling of clothes while he spoke, "You know the saying, 'Seeing is Believing'?"

He walked past her, now wearing pants instead of shorts, still waiting for an answer as she responded, "Yeah?"

Emptying out his backpack on the bed, he moved through the room, lightly pressing her to the side when she was in the way as he started to put a few items in the bag, explaining, "I'm going to show you rather than explain since it's easier." He turned towards her, stating, "There's a problem though..." After putting on a knee-length black jacket, he paused and swung the bag over his shoulders, "I'm going to have to do something illegal."

A look of shock crossed her face as she said, "You what?"

Reaching out, he gripped her arms tightly before rubbing them up and down, "It's just a little breaking and entering. We're not steali-..." He paused, reconsidering, "I might steal one thing, but it would be to help you, and nothing more. I promise." He could see the hesitance in her eyes as he said, "Look..." His hand cupped her jaw as he explained, "If you don't want to do this, I understand, but I promise we won't get caught. You can remain in the dark about your supposed medicine, or you can find out the truth. The choice is yours, but I won't force you to do it if you don't want to."

Kirra could feel herself being ripped in two. On one side, she wanted to follow the rules and be a good kid; on the other, she wanted to discover the truth behind her medicine and what Devin knew about them.

With a groan of frustration, Kirra answered, "Alright, I'll come with you, but I'm not participating."

A smile brightened his face almost instantly before he leaned in to kiss her forehead. The action seemed to shock both of them before he cleared his throat, "You won't regret it, I promise." Stepping back, he pointed to her bag, "Leave that here, follow me, and don't make a sound."

With a look of confusion, she did as he asked and set her bag on his bed before following him out the door. Devin quickly looked around to ensure no one was arriving or exiting his apartment building before he led the way down the stairs. Reaching out, he took her hand and quietly started to lead the way through alleyways and streets on the Preserve. By now, the streets were getting dark, and most of everyone was either home or heading home.

The Preserve was set up much like a small town but much more compact, with very few streets. It functioned independently with a ship port for late arrivers looking to escape the war and its own businesses that functioned through trades. As Devin stopped behind a familiar building, she realized that was where she picked up her medication when she ran out. Giving a look of confusion towards Devin, she wondered what he was up to. It seemed she was going to have to be patient and find out.

Suddenly, she found herself being spun and pressed against the wall of the alley as his breath tickled her ear, "Put your arms around me."

Kirra was about to question him but remembered his earlier words. Deciding to question him later, she wrapped her arms around him, and he pressed closer, burying his face in the crook of her neck. The door they were next to opened with a creak, causing a blush to form on Kirra's cheeks before the feeling of fingers lightly digging into her sides caused her to giggle. Her squirming and laughter caused a throaty chuckle to come from Devin.

A sound of disgust was heard from the person who exited the building, followed quickly by retreating footsteps in the opposite direction. Before Kirra could react to the situation, she felt herself suddenly pulled easily with Devin before the sturdy metal door clunked shut behind them.

The moment they moved, she reared back to slap but quickly found herself pinned against the door with a hand covering her mouth. When she looked up at him, Devin's eyes were closed, and his face was a mask of concentration. When her eyes moved further up, she noticed a set of bat ears atop his head, lightly twitching as he listened to his surroundings carefully. The limited light from the street lamps shone in just enough for her to see this happening. The quiet was so loud that Kirra could hear her heart beating in her ears. Devin seemed to be listening for something she couldn't hear in the distance though.

Finally, he pulled away, raising his hands as he apologized in a soft whisper, "I was making sure they were out of earshot."

Getting her wits about her, Kirra smoothed a hand through her hair before starting to smack him with every word she whisper yelled, "You. Didn't. Have. To. Get. So..." Though she was hitting him, he was chuckling lightly the entire time.

While pausing to find the right word, he smirked at her, showing his little bat fangs, "Handsy?"

"Yes!" With a frustrated growl, she hit him one more time, causing him to laugh softly again.

He didn't appear sorry in the least bit as he stood there chuckling, "You liked it. Besides, I wanted to have a bit of fun."

Kirra huffed with frustration as she straightened her clothes and hair before hissing furiously at him even through the blush, "What are we doing here?!"

He waved his hand for her, "Come on." Before adding, "You didn't deny you liked it though." A cheeky smirk graced his face as he looked back at her.

As she followed him through a small row of shelves, Kirra made sure to comment, "You're a bad influence, you know that?" He merely chuckled at her response.

The room was littered with shelves containing pull-out drawers for each shelf labeled in Spiritoski. Kirra could barely read the labels, but it seemed Devin had no problem navigating the aisles in the dark. They looked to be in the back room of the pharmacy, where all the future orders and extra medicine were placed.

Stopping at a row of drawers, he started searching through them as it seemed they put the orders in bags to keep them separated for patients until they picked them up. He stopped in one of the drawers and pulled out one of the bags. Moving along the drawers, he searched through them, finding another bag, and pulled it out.

Motioning for her to follow him once more, he went to a counter further in the pharmacy. He placed both bags on the counter before pulling out the contents carefully, stating, "I might be a bad influence, but I'm the bad influence that might be saving your life…"

Slipping off his backpack, he pulled out a flashlight, turned it on, and handed it to her, saying, "Take a look."

Kirra read the names on both of the medication bottles. One had her name on it; the other had another name that she recognized but didn't know who it was, "Where have I heard the name Ripper Foster before?"

"He's the metal dragon that went nearly ballistic because one of the 'lower kin' insulted him." The sound of disapproval in his voice was thick as he continued, "He almost revealed what Spiritosk can **really** do to humans. He probably would have lost all the Spiritosk here their homes or worse, hundreds if not thousands of lives, not just here, but all over Earth."

Given that her Spiritoski was a little rusty, it took her some time to read through the medicine instructions. According to the label, the medicine inhibited the connection between spirit and soul. Covering a hand over her mouth, she realized what it did. From what she knew and read, the medicine essentially blocked the connection between a person and their spirit, rendering them basically human.

Opening the pill bottle, she spilled a few out on the table, causing her heart to sink. Her stomach twisted into knots at the sight of the same pills she had been taking almost her whole life. As her legs gave out, Devin caught her and lowered her slowly to the ground.

Kirra's chest tightened with the feeling of betrayal and hurt. The realization of everything hit her all at once. She had been lied to her entire life. The reason why she'd been bullied, why she felt so weak, why she probably didn't even have a spirit. All of it was due to those stupid little pills her parents had been feeding her her entire life.

Giving her time to process everything, Devin started returning everything to where it had been. Once he was finished, he started scrounging around the pharmacy for something. Eventually, he returned and sat down next to her, just staying with her. Despite his father being the Leader of the Bat Spiritosk, she could tell he cared and kept looking at her with empathy. He didn't try to start a conversation. He just sat there in the quiet with her until she was ready.

Finally breaking the silence, Kirra managed to speak despite her throat being clogged with emotion, "I just want to know why..."

Despite the room's darkness, she could tell Devin was looking at her with the same amount of empathy that came through in his voice, "I don't know." Letting out a sigh, he reached out and touched her shoulder gently, "What I do know is that we need to leave. You don't have to go home just yet, but we need to get out of here." Standing up, he offered his hand to her. Slowly, Kirra reached up and took the offered hand lightly, before clinging to it like he was a lifeline as he led the way out of the small business.

Barely paying attention, Devin led the way back to his apartment, taking his time on the walk home with her. It gave her time to think and meant that she could delay going home since she clearly wasn't ready to return any time soon. Kirra wasn't even sure what she was going to say to her parents after learning what she had learned that night. More than anything, she wanted to know why they had lied to her her entire life and caused her so much pain from the other spiritosk her age. All the years of bullying and constantly being segregated were her parents doing.

Once they arrived at Devin's, he settled her on his bed and covered her in a soft blanket, which she curled up with lightly. Kirra was chilled to the bone and hadn't even realized it until he pointed it out. Part of it could have been that she was in shock, which caused her not even to recognize that she was freezing. To help fight off the chill, he went to the small kitchenette to make some hot tea for her.

As he came back with a mug in hand, he explained, "I know it's not the fancy crap that you can get from Spiritoski, but it'll help calm your nerves and warm you."

For the first time since the pharmacy, she spoke, "I'm just trying to figure out why they've been feeding me these blockers. Why lie to me my whole life? Why...Why would they deny me the one thing that would make me accepted amongst everyone?"

Joining her on the bed, he leaned back against the wall, explaining, "There are a few reasons why, but not all of them are good. Sometimes, your spirit can hatch early."

Kirra gave him a questioning look, "Is that a bad thing?"

He attempted to explain it as best as possible, "It is if you turn out like Ripper. You take on a much more animalistic style of living; you're more prone to urges and drives than someone who is more mentally mature."

It seemed Kirra still had a lot more to learn, "I didn't know that."

Devin didn't pull the punches as he pointed out, "Your parents sheltered you from a lot of the bad. Some of us grew up with it. I was barely old enough to remember when my father started teaching me. He taught me about the blockers too. They use them on prisoners to keep their spirits docile. It's mostly for those who have power over the Major Eight. I don't know what's in them, but whatever it is, it blocks the flow of Ki from your spirit to you. The effect happens even if you're fully bonded with your spirit, and your mark is gone." He shrugged, "That's why I was surprised when I saw you taking them. You're past the age of when your spirit should have hatched."

"That's how you knew Ripper would have an active prescription." Kirra said solemnly before asking, "Why'd your father teach you about the blockers?"

A deep sigh came from him as he explained, "My father wanted to make sure I wouldn't get drugged when I came here alone. He wanted to make sure I was ready to defend myself. So, he taught me how to spot the effects of that particular poison, what it looks like, and how to battle it and reverse it. He even showed me the medicine that would battle its effects." There was a long pause before he looked at her and said with a sigh, "You should probably go home. Your parents might worry where you're at."

She'd lost track of time and how long they had been gone. Looking at a nearby clock, it was nearly 2300 hours. Reluctantly standing from the bed, she started to gather her bag before making her way sluggishly towards the door.

Devin was right behind her but stopped her at the door, "Here..." She felt him open her bag before he shoved something in it as he explained, "I nabbed these in the Pharmacy. They'll reverse the effects of the blockers you were taking." Opening the flap of her messenger bag, she saw a large plastic bag filled with pills. Before she looked up, he continued, "These are the same dosage as the blockers. To reverse the effect of the blockers, you take them at the same times you have been taking your blockers. You're going to hear a voice in your head.

It's not a hallucination, and you're not going crazy. It's just your spirit talking to you."

She paused as she situated her bag before softly asking, "How do you know all of this?"

Another long sigh escaped him, "Like I said, you're sheltered. This is all stuff that your parents should have told you when you were younger." Pulling out a flip-style phone, he handed it to her, "Give me your number." They had adapted to using human technology, but seeing him with a phone still surprised her. Each of the kids that went to the school had been given one a week after going to the school. It seemed to be an afterthought on the government's end.

Kirra looked at the phone as she adjusted the bag on her shoulder with a look of hesitation, asking, "Why?"

Devin seemed reluctant to explain, but eventually, he said, "It's for you more than me." Searching for the words, he finally explained, "The change that happens when your spirit hatches is extremely painful. I'm giving you my number so I can help you through it. If you happen to want to call me for another reason, that's fine too."

After he explained it to her that way, she entered her phone number in his and ensured she had his info. Once done, she lingered for a few moments before throwing her arms around his neck and hugging him tightly. Her voice was soft and trembled with the emotion that filled it, "Thank you. For everything."

It took a few moments, but his own arms wrapped around her and squeezed her gently as he was caught off guard by the sudden affection, "Yeah. No problem."

Managing to pull herself away from him, she wiped the tears that had formed in her eyes to stop them from streaming down her face and opened the door. Without another word, she left his apartment and started to make her way home.

4

THE BEAST WITHIN

The next few days were rather uneventful. Kirra had started throwing her medicine away in the toilet and had been replacing it with the ones that Devin had given her. She never did speak with her parents about the evident lie. She was afraid they might take away the pills Devin had given her, or worse, keep her locked away from the world. Then, one day, that deep, rumbling voice started speaking.

It never spoke to her directly. Instead, it spoke to her about her environment in a groggy deep voice, "*These humans. Do they not realize they are polluting their environment with their gas-powered death traps?*" Once, while she was in class, it commented in an almost amused tone, "*If only they knew that magic existed. That the gods and evolution go hand in hand.*" Another time, when she had been sitting at lunch, its voice sounded almost sad, "*A fallen. I wonder what they did to deserve such a sentence?*" That one had caused her to look all around her, but she spotted nothing unusual.

It was almost like living with a separate being inside of her that only she could hear, except it was saying the most random things. Sometimes it would wake her in the middle of the night, but it mostly spoke nonsense. The longer she was on that medicine, the more often it spoke, until it started to become unbearable. Then, one day, it started speaking to her directly, something it had never done before.

"Hey, kid... answer me." The spirit demanded before growling in annoyance, *"I will **NOT** be ignored kid..."* Kirra ignored the spirit until it let out a demanding thunderous roar, *"**ANSWER ME!!!**"* Almost instantly, she raised her hand and asked to be excused.

Kirra hurried to the bathroom as she started to feel a headache forming and thought it was because of the voice. She passed a teacher in the hall, showing them the pass before dodging into the girl's restroom, locking the door behind her, and making sure no one was in it before turning towards a mirror whisper yelling, "What!? What do you want?!"

Silence greeted her as she stared at herself in the mirror, waiting for a response. For a few passing moments, nothing happened, no voice, no headache, nothing. Then her head felt like it was being split open from the inside. Gasping in pain, she doubled over, gripping one of the white ceramic sinks hard. The pain floored her, causing her personal things to skitter across the floor as she cropped on the ground and curled up. She clawed at the floor desperately, wishing the pain would stop. Then remembered, she needed to call Devin.

Through eyes squinted with pain, Kirra saw the flip phone on the ground and started crawling towards it as she heard the voice speaking as though it was right next to her, *"Why did you push me away and force me to sleep?"*

As pain erupted through her skull at every word the voice rumbled out, she curled up and let out a tiny scream before finally grabbing her phone. Through tears, she opened her phone and scrolled through it in search of Devin's contact information and called him. The moment she heard his voice, she cried out in a shaky, quiet, and pain-filled voice, "H-help... m-mee."

In horror, she watched something writhing under the skin of her hand before sharp claws erupted from the tips of her fingers. Against her own will, her hand suddenly clenched, crushing the phone as though it were nothing but paper. The skin of her hand ripped and tore, giving way to a red sheen of what appeared to be scales underneath. Sticky, hot blood could be felt dripping down her face from her head as well as her back and ankles. It was almost like she was shedding out of her very own skin.

Finally, a full-blown blood-curdling scream ripped free of her throat as she had been trying her best to keep as quiet as possible. Kirra could hear and feel her bones crunching and shifting as things sprouted from her body. Her skin ripped painfully from her back as the sound of her clothes tearing could be heard before finally, she passed out from the pain of it all.

What could have been minutes or hours felt like only a few seconds as she woke to nothing but a black, inky void surrounding her. Kirra wondered to herself if she was dead as confusion flooded her mind. She wasn't in pain, but she didn't know where she was. Then, a warm breeze caressed her back, causing her to turn to a sight that made her green hues go wide.

Before her, stood a pure white dragon whose head alone was twice as tall as her own. A mane of white ran the length of its back, ending at the tip of its tail. Adorning its head was a set of large antler-like horns coated in white fuzz. The clear sign of a celestial dragon. It wasn't any celestial dragon that stood before her, but a pure white one.

Turning its head to the side, one large, glacial blue eye glared down at her before squinting. Kirra fell backward, staring up at the large, powerful beast that stood larger than life before her. Awed by its beauty and size, she was frozen in place as it slammed one large massive forepaw down over her, trapping her easily.

That familiar deep rumble reverberated through her as it spoke in her head, "*Tell me why. Why did you force me to sleep!?*"

Kirra stammered several times, trying to find the words to speak to the magnificent beast. Then the realization finally hit her, "Y-you're... You're my spirit..." Her words had been spoken with more astonishment and surprise than question as the realization hit her that she had the spirit of a white celestial dragon.

Carefully and slowly, the dragon spirit removed its forepaw from her "*Correct.*"

Her voice was thickly laced with confusion, "I'm a dragon?"

There was hesitation in his voice as though it was almost a question, "Yes?" Its eyes held a great amount of suspicion in them.

Kirra let out several panicked breaths before demanding, "How is that possible!?"

Sitting back on its haunches like a cat, the dragon tilted its head inquisitively, "*Did your parents not teach you basic reproduction?*" The sarcasm was thick in his voice, "*You were—*"

The void and dragon both disappeared suddenly as the familiar sound of a vehicle traveling down a road filled the air. Kirra faintly recognized that she had been in a dream-like state and had spoken to her dragon just moments ago. Blinking several times, she cleared the fog of her vision as she found herself staring up at the ceiling of a van as the sound of two voices speaking in low tones could be heard. Her body ached in places she didn't know she had, and her skin felt like it was on fire, like she had baked under the sun for far too long. The moment she attempted to sit up, she realized she was strapped down to some kind of gurney, and there was a mask over her mouth and nose that had been strapped to her face.

The moment she realized she was strapped down, Kirra started to struggle, flail and scream in fear, until her mother's face appeared above her, "Calm down Kirra. Calm down." Seeing and hearing her mother's voice stopped Kirra in her tracks as she pulled the mask from her face and asked towards the driver of the van, "How far away from that portal location are we?"

The sound of her father's voice calling out from the front of the vehicle caused Kirra's brow to furrow with confusion, "I'm not sure exactly. At least an hour. Justin reply back yet?"

At his question, her mother flicked her wrist, causing a holoscreen to float over her arm, making Kirra's eyes widen as Dayla answered, "He did. They just finished ransacking our house it seems." On the holoscreen were pictures of their small townhouse with items flipped over and torn apart before Dayla flicked her wrist causing the image to disappear. Turning back to Kirra she addressed her in a calm voice, "I know everything hurts right now, but we'll explain when we get you through the portal and far away from here."

It felt like the more she heard, the more questions she had. Without skipping a beat, Dayla started removing the restraints from her, allowing her to sit up slowly and stretch. Taking a moment to do that despite the pain, she was about to ask a question until she saw something move out of the corner of her eye. It made her jump, and her sudden start caused the appendage to bang against the side and top of the van, causing pain to reverberate through her. When she stilled, she slowly turned her head and realized that the thing she saw from the corner of her eyes was a wing. Kirra let out a startled gasp as she began inspecting her hands and noticed they were scaly and clawed. As she turned to look over her back, she saw a tail lightly thumping against the side of the van. All of her new body parts were coated in a fine flaking crust of brown which she assumed was her own dried blood.

Letting out a little cry of surprise, she jumped to her feet off of the gurney and almost fell as she realized that her feet had not only grown scaly and clawed, but had also become digitigrade in nature. Had it not been for her mother gripping her tightly, she would have fallen in the moving vehicle as Kirra asked in a shaky voice, "What's happening Mom?"

As Kirra looked to her mother for an explanation, Dayla sighed as she reached up and caressed her daughter's cheek gently, "You gained your spirit, and the war has finally reached us. We didn't want them to discover you were a dragon." Dayla sighed while looking at her in apology, "The Bat Colony forces have been ransacking other Preserves, capturing any kids your age with draconic spirits. It was only a matter of time before they came to our Preserve as well. They've been doing it quietly so as not to alert the local human governments, and the other Preserves have kept quiet about what has been happening."

As Kirra looked around with confusion, she heard her father call out from the front, "You popped early kiddo. Way too early. It's the sign of a powerful spirit that is well in tune with you. With the war going on, we didn't want them finding out."

A look of anger passed over Kirra's face, "Why not just tell me?!" She slapped her mother's hands away from her and stumbled as she caught herself on the gurney before growling out, "At least people wouldn't have looked at me like a freak!"

Words failed her mother, but her father called out, "It's a bit more complicated than tha—" Something suddenly collided with the side of the van, sending Kirra flying forward. Her mother had been quick to take her full form with a shroud of dark smoke as strong fur-covered arms and wings wrapped around her protectively. The sound of metal twisting and grinding, glass breaking, and her own screams were all she heard before everything went black.

The smell of smoke caused Kirra to wake as she felt her head throbbing and ears ringing. Something heavy, warm, and furry was lying atop her as Kirra struggled to free herself. Leveraging as much strength as she could, she faintly remembered her mother taking her full form and protecting her from the sudden collision. As she managed to roll the monstrous form off of her, Kirra started gently slapping its face to get her mother to wake, "Mom?... Mom, please wake up."

The sound of ripping and bending metal made Kirra look over her shoulder. From behind, a pair of soldiers were ripping the doors on the back of the van open. It didn't take her long to scan the outfits and realize they were Bat Colony soldiers.

Shaking Dayla violently, Kirra's voice cracked with desperation, "MOM! **MOM!!!**"

As the sound of metal groaning under duress stopped, Kirra felt arms start pulling her from the van, causing her to struggle and flail desperately for her life. All the while, Kirra was screaming for her parents to help her as she fought back. She was just too weak, and eventually, she was forced to sit with her legs out in front of her as one of the soldiers was securing her arms and wings. The other one in front of her pulled out a mask that looked like the one she had on before she woke, and she knew nothing good could come from it.

Waiting for the man with the mask to get closer, she jerked suddenly and clamped down on his wrist before using her foot claws to kick and claw at whatever she could. Suddenly, the man trying to put the mask on her was pulled away as a sickening crack could be heard in the distance. Kirra was suddenly shoved to the side by the soldier behind her as Kirra heard the familiar sound of a very angry-sounding Dayla in her full form, despite one of her wings bleeding and hanging oddly.

Kirra managed to sit herself upright as the soldier stepped away from her bound form. The soldier, dressed in all black with only a hint of red on the front, raised his gun. One of her mother's wings had moved suddenly and swiftly in an upward strike as a dark wave expelled outward from the appendage, cutting the weapon in two, as well as cutting a divot deep into the ground. Along the edges of her mother's dark wings were ebony metallic-like blades, something Kirra had never seen before. The soldier then charged at Dayla's larger monstrous form as his own form suddenly changed into a similar smaller bat creature in a sudden burst of black smoke. The fight didn't last long as the two crashed into each other before Dayla sent the other bat careening into the distance effortlessly. The sound of something heavy hitting branches and trees before the hard thud of ground caused Kirra to wince.

Dayla didn't instantly rush over to her daughter. Those bright green orbs surveyed their surroundings before moving towards the van lying on its side. Despite her clear injury, she easily scaled up the back and on the driver's side before reaching for the door. As the sound of the metal door being ripped from its hinges rang through the air, Kirra watched on, still trying to process what was going on. Her mother reached into the van and pulled Taro's large body out like he weighed nothing and laid him on the side of the van. Kirra couldn't make out what was going on, but she heard her father gasp awake as Dayla growled out animalistically, "Come on Love. Nap time's over."

Jumping off of the van, Dayla started turning back to her normal form before she cried out in pain as she looked over her shoulder at the limp and hanging wing. A growl of frustration came from her before she called out to Taro, "We're on foot my love. My wing is clipped." Walking over to Kirra, she checked her over for injuries, but all Kirra could do was sit there still in shock. The feeling of her Mother gripping her jaw and forcing her to look at her shook her out of it some as she asked, "You alright sweetie?"

Kirra's mind was still foggy. There was a word for the condition that she was suffering from at the moment, but she was struggling with the simplest thoughts at the moment. The first thing that came to her mind was her mother throwing those men, "Did you just kill those people?"

Writing off Kirra's words, her mother cut her free from whatever was binding her and helped her to her feet, saying carelessly, "They're probably okay." Kirra struggled to stay on her new digitigrade feet as she leaned heavily into her mother. Still attempting to process what her mother had just told her, she heard Dayla call out, "Get a move on it soldier. We've got to make tracks before they catch on to our location."

Looking over to her father, she saw Taro crawling out of the van with a bag that he was slinging on his back and a rifle hanging from his shoulder as he answered, "Yup..." As he moved over to join them, he clapped his wife on the shoulder, saying, "Send Justin the message."

Dayla and Taro switched positions. Kirra's father was now helping her to stay balanced while Dayla flicked her arm and moved away to pull up a holo-screen above her arm once more. She saw a separate holo-keyboard hovering just above Dayla's arm as she typed. Suddenly, the hand that had been typing flicked out to catch a blade that had come whirring from the forest's darkness. Kirra was the only one to let out a scream at the knife as she looked towards where her father was looking and saw a form in the distance about to raise a gun.

Only a moment had passed as Dayla had already twirled the knife so she was holding the bladed side before she tossed it back with deadly precision. The knife found itself buried deep in the man's skull causing Kirra to jump as she just stared wide-eyed towards where they had been standing. Kirra stood there dumbfounded, but her father gently began guiding her into the woods surrounding the road, following her mother's lead.

"That one... That one is definitely dead." Dayla kept walking and typing on the holo-keyboard over her arm before mumbling softly, "Bumbling idiot..."

Shock. Kirra was in shock. She'd finally figured out the biological symptoms she was facing at the moment as her father kept her steady and on the right path as she learned to walk on her two new feet. Her mind kept whirling around the recent events, trying to concentrate on what was happening in the present even as questions floated in her head. Where were they taking her? Why were there soldiers after her? What was going on? It felt like the questions she already had answers to only raised more questions.

Kirra needed to concentrate on the present. The feel of the mud between her new scaly toes, the breeze of the cool night that stung her sensitive new skin. She was going to concentrate on just learning how to walk until her shock wore off.

5

ON THE RUN

After the van wreck, Dayla and Taro were moving with a purpose while Kirra trudged along as best as she could. Everything hurt. It didn't help that she kept tripping on every fallen branch, rock, log, or anything slightly uneven. While Kirra struggled with just walking, her parents moved easily through the trees despite their injuries. The small group had stopped only temporarily to bind her mother's wing and the gash on her father's head. Kirra didn't know how they were able to move so easily despite their injuries and how much pain they were in. Every time Kirra scraped against a bush or a low-hanging branch with her wings; it was like a shock to her body, causing a small whimper. Her skin hurt, like an exposed raw nerve or severe sunburn.

Finally, Kirra mustered the courage to ask, "Where are we going?"

"Portal location. I was given an enchanted scroll to open one up. We're making our way to a spot that can support the portal long enough. After that, we're going deep into hiding. I still have a few contacts on Kanakka, and they might be able to help us out." Even with the explanation from her mother, Kirra was still confused.

The three of them continued on for a while, and Kirra felt like she was finally starting to get the hang of walking on her new feet. When she tripped, her father asked softly, "Are you following your mother using sight or sound, sweetheart?" The slightest hint of concern swept through his voice. Kirra was sandwiched between her parents, more than likely so her father could keep an eye on her in case she started to fall behind.

As Kirra went to respond, she tripped over another branch in her way before stating in a solemn tone, "Sight..." Her voice carried the slight frustration of attempting to learn how to walk for a second time in her life as she explained, "I'm still struggling to learn how to use these things... It's not exactly easy...."

"Don't worry, hun. You'll get the hang of it eventually. It just takes time. Everyone, even your brother, father, and me, struggled at first. When you master walking, I'll teach you how to fly." Her mother called out with a reassuring smile as she looked over her shoulder momentarily.

As Kirra was about to ask another question, her father shushed her before saying, "Dayla..."

They all stopped, and both of her parents met in the middle near Kirra. Dayla took a deep breath, closed her eyes, and let it out slowly as though she were trying to concentrate. After a brief moment, she opened her eyes and shook her head at Taro before stating, "Blind hounds..."

Kirra looked between them with a confused look on her face, asking, "What are Blind-hounds?"

Neither of her parents answered her. Just as Kirra was about to repeat her question, the forest around her grew quiet. As though a conductor had stopped conducting, the insects and small animals quieted near them in unison.

The familiar black fog overcame Dayla as she took her bat form and growled softly towards Kirra, "Run!" Kirra's heart leaped into her throat as she watched her mother suddenly launch into the forest's darkness around her. Her father shoved Kirra in a direction, causing her to stumble.

As she stumbled, Kirra felt something swoop past her head, causing a small shriek to come from her. Scrambling for her life, Kirra took off as the sound of fighting started to break out, and light beams zipped past. The sound was strangely reminiscent of electricity crackling as it moved through the air. Once Kirra stopped stumbling from her initial takeoff, she balanced out and sprinted through the trees, just concentrating on running for her life.

The sound of something growling behind her was motivation enough for her not to stop as she ran as fast as she could. Whatever was pursuing her wasn't something from Earth, given it sounded different from any normal animal she had ever heard there. Kirra's sprint for her life wasn't long-lived as she felt the creature tackle her to the ground. As they slid through the autumn leaf litter and mud, a soft whimper came from the young spiritosk, a snapping jaw near her head stopping her from moving.

Tears streaked Kirra's young face as she shook with fear of not knowing what would happen next. The creature had her pinned against the ground, and it wasn't moving from on top of her. The sounds of fighting could be heard for what felt like hours to Kirra, but eventually, it stopped completely. She lay quietly in the darkness until a voice called out in her native tongue.

As the voices called out, she couldn't discern what they were saying to each other. That was until a pair of voices started getting closer to where she was at. Fear started to claw its way up her throat once more as the creature atop her let out an unsettling howl that caused her very chest to vibrate from the sound. As the voices grew closer, the tears that had come to a stop at one point, started back up as scenarios started playing through her head.

Kirra didn't recognize either voice approaching, causing her fear to turn into the beginnings of panic. As the creature hopped off, she felt her arms and wings getting secured before they easily hefted her up and started guiding her back to where she had run from. With two soldiers securing her arms and a creature at her heels, there was no point in her struggling as they led her back to where her parents had been.

As they started getting closer to where the fighting had broken out, Kirra noticed damage to the trees and plants. Whole trees were toppled or broken off at thicker parts. The trees that were intact had severe claw marks and damage. Everything in the area was complete and total carnage. Several people were sitting on the ground or leaning against trees, addressing wounds of varying degrees. The sight of something made her halt in her path, causing her heart to stop and her breath to hitch.

Her legs gave out as she saw the unmoving bodies of her parents and the lifeless faces of both of them. Nearby, leaning against a tree, was a man who looked like Devin's older twin but had shorter smoothed back hair. As Devin's older clone saw Kirra, he started shouting orders at everyone present.

As though waking from a slumber, her spirit called out in her head, "*Rage. Fight. Do something...*" Kirra did nothing as the shock of her parents' deaths overtook her as she couldn't think of anything.

Their lifeless eyes staring off in the distance, blood surrounding their wounds, and their bodies carelessly tossed to the side. As she came back to her senses, it was too late.

Only the feeling of a sudden pinch caused her to snap out of the shock that held her captive. Someone was talking to her in a calm, soft voice as her eyes started to grow heavy, and a fog clouded her head. Kirra suddenly felt her body grow heavy, and everything went dark around her as she was drugged into a sleeping state.

6

BAT COLONY

S omething pungent and foul-smelling caused Kirra to jolt awake. Her mind was foggy and slow to come around as she watched a rather large man step away. As her vision cleared, Kirra took in her surroundings while trying to figure out what was happening and where she was.

The large man stepped away once he saw Kirra waking. She turned to watch him only to realize that her wrists and wings were secured by something attached to her waist. Wriggling some, Kirra tested the strength of her bonds before giving up and surveying the surrounding area.

Young dragon spiritosk, like herself, were chained up in varying conditions depending on the kind of dragon they were. All of them were sitting in a hallway made of metal that looked like the chute of some stadium where it sounded like some airships were beginning to take off. The other way appeared to open to the outside, but it was difficult for Kirra to tell as all she saw was light at the other end of the tunnel.

The feeling of being tugged to her feet caused Kirra to stumble as she heard orders getting called out and realized everyone was in a sort of chain gang. Looking around, she realized that the red dragon next to her was staring intently at her head, which caused her to try to step away. The chain prevented her from getting very far as she looked up at the mostly dragon-shaped head and saw purple hues glaring down at her as a growl rumbled from his muzzle.

Kirra quickly lowered her eyes, attempting to look small despite her being slightly taller than the young male. As she looked over at the soldiers surrounding them, she realized they all had similar black uniforms with red trimmings and the Bat Colony symbol on all of them. They were the same uniforms that had attacked her and her parents. The same people who were responsible for their deaths.

The familiar rumbling of her spirit could be heard attempting to rouse from his induced sleep. Without much time to orient herself, she heard another set of orders being given as a tear streaked down her face. Kirra was scared, confused, and very much alone. Her mind turned to escape as she started looking for a way out and tried finding weak points.

While Kirra started scanning for an exit, the chain she was attached to yanked to her left, causing her to stumble and nearly fall. Her muscles ached, she was tired, her bones hurt and her skin itched, burned, and felt as sensitive to everything still. As her tail dragged on the floor, the dragon behind her stepped on it, causing her to trip and nearly fall several times and yelp in pain.

Kirra had never felt such discomfort in her life. Her wings shook lightly against the chains with the urge to stretch, and her legs shook, trying to hold her weight; every little breeze, movement, or touch along her skin caused her pain as she moved along in the chain gang.

The familiar rumble of her spirit snorted tiredly, "*I finally get free from that slumber only to find out the child I am tethered to is an incompetent mess...*"

With a firm stomp of anger that resonated through the hallway, Kirra yelled, "I am **not** incompetent!" The drake in front of her tugged her along despite her momentary tantrum. Several of the other draconic teens leaned over, trying to see who was causing the ruckus.

Her spirit sneered, "*Maybe you are a dragon after all.*" Before he mocked, "*If you were competent, you would know that you do not have to speak out loud to communicate with me.*"

"What?" her soft response came with a note of confusion.

The red drake in front of her growled out threateningly. From the corner of Kirra's eye, she caught him looking at her over his shoulder as she quieted down. As she was swallowing past a lump in her throat, her spirit chuckled throatily, seemingly enjoying her suffering.

This didn't last long as the line abruptly stopped, causing her to nearly bump into the red drake. As Kirra attempted to figure out what was happening, she heard very obvious large booted feet heading towards her, causing her heart to race as she silently prayed they weren't coming for her. Closing her eyes tightly, she gripped the chain that connected everyone tightly and felt her heart instantly sink to her stomach as those booted feet stopped beside Kirra.

When Kirra finally opened her eyes and looked to her right, she saw the large man that had woke her staring directly at her. He stood almost a full head taller than Kirra and given she was about 6 feet tall with her new feet, that made him a very tall person.

Most of his face was shrouded in shaggy black hair, but Kirra noted he had tanned skin peeking out beneath. Paired with the two molten gold eyes and a set of bull-esque horns peeking behind his curtains of hair, the man had an unnerving appearance. He stood, taking in her appearance longer than she liked as she noticed a frown start to form.

The man abruptly grabbed hold of the chain that connected Kirra to the one that held all the other teens. Waving a card over the connecting link, it suddenly released as he gripped her chain and dragged her from the rest of the group. The other bound teens looked on with apprehension as Kirra attempted to dig her feet into the ground, only to slide along the metal flooring. Her heart raced while her mind started to whirl with thoughts of torture or death.

The golden-eyed man continued to drag her along until he stopped to briefly tell a pair of soldiers something in her native tongue. She recognized her language, but he spoke so rapidly that she didn't catch what was said. Shortly after, he began dragging her once more, causing her to start to struggle and fight in her restraints to no avail.

Kirra felt her chest growing tight, like a weight was pressing down on her and the world was getting smaller. Her breaths came out in wheezes and quick gasps as she felt herself getting dragged by the larger male. As he dragged her into what appeared to be a fully tiled room, her panic only grew. As the door closed behind her, the finality of her being possibly executed caused tears to well and spill down her face.

"This is it." She thought to herself. Her life was going to end. That singular line of thought caused her body to start shaking in fear. Her ears started to ring, and her stomach flipped uneasily. Images of her lifeless parents lying in the cold mud, abandoned, carelessly killed, drifted through her mind.

As the world around her began to spin, the feeling of rough skin gently forcing her to look up into golden hues steadied her. Then, the gentle baritone of a voice that didn't match the man's size calmly spoke softly, "Nothing bad is going to happen in this room." She looked up at him with wide eyes as one thumb smoothed over a tear-streaked cheek, "You're having a panic attack, understandably so. I'm a very large, intimidating person, but I'm not here to kill you."

His large, calloused hands left her face as tears streamed down her cheeks. The thing that shook her out of her panic more than anything was how his voice didn't seem to match the gentle and calm nature of the beast of the man before her. It caught her by surprise.

"Look around the room and tell me what you see." His words were a command, not a suggestion, and had only come once he noticed her calm slightly. For a moment, Kirra looked around her, about to argue. The mountain of a man spoke out before her lips hardly parted "Don't argue. Just do it..."

Not wanting to see how the man acted when upset, she warily turned her head before her eyes looked around her. At first, she took in the room, but quickly remembered he asked her to describe it. Her voice was shaky at the start but slowly grew steady. Wooden benches, one of which she was sitting on, were bolted to the ground. Much like the school she had gone to, metal lockers lined the walls here and there. Another tiled wall had an opening leading to some sinks with mirrors above them.

Metal slid over her skin, causing her to hiss as the chains that bound her dropped free. Kirra hadn't even heard him as describing the room had distracted her. As her wings relaxed free of the chains confinement, she looked at the male with surprise.

He slowly pulled back, like one would with a frightened animal, before he moved to lean against the wall near the door they had entered through. Nodding his head towards her he said in that same soft baritone, "Explore the room, stretch your legs and wings." Kirra's eyes flicked rapidly between the door and the man. One of his brows lifted as though saying, 'Try it and see what happens.'

Kirra wasn't brave enough to test her luck, so she did as he suggested. Her legs were sore, her wings were tired, and her whole body hurt for reasons she couldn't explain. Wandering the locker room made her realize that she wasn't in danger. It was just an ordinary locker room. Eventually, she found herself in front of a sink with a mirror above it and stopped in place with a look of pure shock.

Her once shiny black hair was now dull and matted to her face with mud and other things. The whole of her body was coated in a mixture of mud, leaves, and only the gods knew what. Her eyes were wide, like a scared animal, the greens barely visible. A large set of wings sat on her back, coated in what looked like mud and dried blood from when she changed. Her clothing lay in tatters about her skinny and sickly body. The most prominent piece of her was a set of antler-like horns that told everyone she was a celestial dragon.

The image that lay before her caused Kirra to stumble backward. Only the arms of the man who had taken her aside steadied her, making her jump at the touch. The man seemed to recognize her fragile state of mind at the moment and held his hands out as though he meant no harm.

That same soft voice reached out to her once more, "Easy. Clean up, and I'll explain things to you." He gestured to one of the two showers behind the brick wall that separated the room. He walked past her, giving her a wide berth as he set something down on one of the benches. Taking the same path, he moved back to the wall next to the door and posted up there with his arms crossed. Looking at the benches near the showers, she realized he had set down clothing and a towel for her to use.

Walking towards the benches, Kirra touched the fabric before looking at her image staring back at her and turned to look at the large man complaining, "Clean up?" She didn't think she needed to clarify, "With you in here?"

A snort of amusement came from him, "I'm not a pervert..." He clarified further for her, "I can't leave you unguarded Kirra. I'll stay behind this wall where I can't see you while you clean up and change."

Despite being nervous about having to change in the same room, she couldn't deny that she was in bad need of a shower and a change of clothes. Taking the large fluffy towel carefully and hanging it up, Kirra stood in front of the shower stripping. Stepping inside, she stared at the shower head and looked for a way to operate it.

Almost as though he knew she was struggling, the man instructed helpfully, "Silver frame inside of the shower. It'll light up once you touch it with a holo screen. The inputs to operate the shower are there. The technology here is much more advanced than what you are used to on Earth."

Kirra found the silver panel just like he had instructed her and found the shower was rather easy to operate. There were even separate dispensers for soap, shampoo, and conditioner in the shower that were easy to operate. A door slid up from below and fogged over so no one could see in. Before she knew it, Kirra found herself in the warm embrace of water despite the feeling of the droplets hitting her skin stinging.

Brown and red mixed together as it ran down her body washed away by a mixture of soap and water as she scrubbed herself thoroughly. The sight of blood and mud brought the memory of the previous day or days flying forward. The sight of her parents lying dead on the ground as a man she now seemed as an enemy standing over them as he wiped his blade clean of their blood.

The memory caused her to collapse to the floor of the shower as tears spilled down her face to mix with the blood and grime. Kirra started to sob and mourn the loss of her parents while the water washed the grime away from her. She tried to hide her tears initially given her company in the locker room, but eventually stopped. Sobbing out loud, she mourned the loss of her parents, uncaring of the prying ears nearby.

A list of questions began soaring through her mind. None of which she had the answers to, but still, she wondered. What happened to her brother? What was going to happen to her? Where was she? Why was she a white celestial dragon? Why were the bats kidnapping draconic children?

Eventually, she found herself standing once more in the shower as she scrubbed away the grime and horrors of the day. It was almost poetic. The water not only washed away the horrors of the days prior but also her emotions as she managed to at least mourn for a little while. She couldn't stay in that state, and she knew it, but that fact didn't make it any easier for her to move on from the past.

Kirra stepped out of the shower feeling like a new person. Her skin ached with what still felt like a light sunburn, but she pushed through the pain. Her muscles were sore as though worn from stretching and using new muscles she wasn't used to. Every little movement caused her to hiss in pain and soreness like she had been through a fresh workout.

Reaching out to fresh clothing laid out on the bench, she recognized the feel of the clothing. The fabric was enchanted. It would act almost like a second skin in a way as it would form around her extra body parts and transform with her own body as well. The style that the clothing was made in remained the same but formed to the wearer's body as needed as they changed shape. Putting on the clothing, she moved towards the mirror and addressed her appearance again.

Parts of her face shined iridescently as scales partially covered her face. Her eyes were the same green as always, but looking out were the eyes of what looked like a cat, the slit pupils of a predator staring back at her. The horns atop her head were fuzzy and the same antler style that signified a celestial dragon. Large wings stretched out from her back, almost comically large compared to her smaller, thinner body. Behind her, a large, thick tail slithered along the ground almost freely with a small white tuft of fur at the end. Last but not least, Kirra found small dagger-like fangs in place of her normal canines. Were she not so sickly thin, she would be quite the ferocious monstrosity to any humans who took note of her appearance.

Confusion still laced her expression as she was still stuck on the possibility of her even being a dragon in the first place. Both her parents were bats of black fur and energy types. She was considered an anomaly by all rights to her kin. It wasn't so strange for black bats to have a son who was a black wolf because Justin was still the energy alignment of black. To have a child that was neither the same animal type or energy alignment was just unheard of in their culture. It was a mystery she would have to solve another day. She couldn't keep staring at herself in the mirror all day.

Disposing of her ruined clothes in a nearby trashcan, she walked out from behind the brick wall, fiddling with her new clothing. It drew her attention to one of her clawed, partially draconic hands as she noticed there was no mark on the back of her hand.

The familiar soft baritone explained, "If you're looking for the mark, you won't see it as long as you take one of your forms." His voice caused her to tense and jump as she'd nearly forgotten he was there. Pushing off the wall, he moved to a bench in the locker room and patted the empty space next to him, "Please. Sit."

Despite the fact this man hadn't done her any wrong, she was still hesitant to sit down next to him. He explained in that same calm voice, "When you take on your half form or full form, your mark does not appear. Your spirit allows you to take these forms, so you are the physical representation of your spirit. You have three forms: normal form, your human-looking skin; half form, the form you are currently taking; and full form, where you take on the full form of the spirit itself. In your case, that would be a dragon."

Kirra's voice asked almost hesitantly while playing with her tail, "W-why are you explaining this to me?"

The man seemed to think of the best way to explain before starting with, "Because you were talking out loud to your spirit, which only newly hatched spiritosk do. That, paired with your torn clothes, blood-covered scales, inability to stay properly balanced on your draconic feet, and your looking for your hatchling mark, tells me you haven't been given the talk." The man looked at her as though he were thick and that all of these things were obvious.

In a bit of a panic, questions started to flood from her, "W-wh— W-who are you? W-where am I? Where is my brother? What happened to the Preserve?"

Holding out a hand, he answered her questions in that same calm, soft baritone, "You can call me Black Dragon. You are on Terra-468, better known as Spiritoski." Kirra's eyes went wide, but she stayed silent as he continued to explain, "More specifically, you're in Bat Colony about to be placed in a camp where you will be tested to see if you are the Prophecy that everyone is looking for." Kirra fainted and blacked out, leaving the man to gently lay her down with a long sigh, "This one is going to take a lot of work and patience."

7

THE LIST

A similar smell of something pungent and foul caused Kirra to claw out at the air as she woke up almost violently. The feel of meaty hands gripping her skinny and frail wrists made her pause for a brief moment. Black Dragon's soft voice pointed out calmly, "You're a bit on the skinny side for a dragon. Dayla and Taro kept you on those blockers for far too long. The other teens are going to eat you for breakfast."

His tone had been soft and calm, but the blunt harshness of the words caused Kirra to squirm and fight against the hold he had her in. There came the sound of gentle laughter from him, making her only angrier as he was clearly amused at her feeble attempts. The moment he let go of her, Kirra lashed out with claws, which caused him to pin her wrists and her body to the bench.

Almost tired of the child-like behavior, he growled out, "Stop..." Kirra was panting from her efforts as he told her in a softer, gentler tone, "Believe it or not, I'm here to help you."

With tears in her eyes, she shook her head, almost in denial of the entire thing, "I'm just a frickin' kid. I have nothing to do with this war..."

Before her rant of nervousness could get too far, Black Dragon snapped his fingers right in front of her eyes, "Knock it off." It caused her to concentrate hard on his next words as she looked at the serious expression etched on his face, "Listen, and you'll learn. If you don't learn, you'll die." Kirra had nothing to say to him and just nodded her head in understanding, "You are about to be put through challenges, trials, and forced to fight. Many of these kids have had the time to grow and get used to their forms. Many know how to take their normal form or show just parts of themselves. **You** are not granted that same chance. You **will** be targeted because of how you look, because they might think you're a threat, because you're a celestial dragon, and because you look like an easy mark."

Kirra's face contorted into a mask of confusion and fear, "I-I d-don't understand. Y-you c-can't force others t-t-to fight each other."

Finally, as she stopped struggling, the gold-eyed man released her, softly stating, "They have a way of making people do what they want." He sighed before staring at her with that serious note, "You are going to have to pick things up quickly. First and foremost, you can communicate with your spirit mentally. Listen to them. They speak with the prior wisdom of others who lived and died by their values. At times, you may find yourself at odds with your spirit, but they are there for your own good. Sometimes, they offer advice; other times, they take control. When both of you reach a certain stage in your relationship, you'll begin something called a bond. It will hurt, but it comes with benefits in the form of more easily accessing your spirit's strength, abilities, and faster transformation. The final form of the bond comes when you learn your spirit's true name."

Rolling up his sleeve, he showed the bare tan skin of his arm and the lack of a mark, "The mark will disappear, but your abilities will still be there." Kirra's eyes lingered on the numerous scars and signs of cybernetics on his arm before it disappeared from sight.

All of the books Kirra had read during her short life never mentioned anything about any of this, leaving her to ask in confusion, "Why am I just now learning about this?"

Looking at her calmly, "This talk is only had after your spirit hatches, a long-standing tradition that all young spiritosk have with their parental figures." He flicked his wrist, causing a holo screen to appear over it before it disappeared before he continued, "I don't have much more time with you. I'm going to do everything in my power to help you through this." His face softened, "I owe your mother as much. I'll do some talking and see about getting you some private training with me to get you up to speed. A lot of these kids were raised by traditional parents, which means most of them will have previous training."

Standing, Black Dragon let out a groan as though he was old before stating, "For now, just keep your nose clean and stay out of trouble. You don't want to know what happens when you anger the wrong people here."

Words seemed to fail her as Kirra found herself stumbling to speak, "T-training, I... A-all of this feels like a really bad nightmare..." She looked up at him as he helped her back to her feet and started guiding her toward the door back to the hallway they had come from. Kirra had so many questions, and not enough answers.

With a careful guiding hand pressing down on her shoulder from behind, his last words were, "All will be explained soon, but for now, we're out of time."

That same meaty hand guided her out of the room and down the path they had been heading originally. Still, Kirra found herself stumbling as she was pressed onward toward what had to have been the light of day. It was too bright for Kirra to tell exactly. The light of the outside reflected lightly off the metal panels of the floor and walls causing her to be lightly blinded. As they exited, Kirra found herself awestruck by the beauty surrounding her.

Perhaps it had been her new eyes and how they were taking in colors, but everything here seemed so much more vibrant than Earth's. The plants seemed healthier, greener, and thriving. The air smelled cleaner and like that of the woods. She stood there for a long while, taking in all the greenery, the trees, and the fact they were in a massive cave where light showed through holes in the top, allowing the underground forest to exist. Her admiration of the surrounding greenery didn't last long as she was shoved forward only to land face-first in the dirt.

Laughter bombarded her ears as she looked around to find several others had watched her fall. Just outside the hall was some kind of black pad with 3 circles in the middle, like a fighting ring. To her right was a set of bleachers where a few people were gathered and spread out from each other comfortably. To her left, Kirra saw a line of teens dressed in the same garb as her, making her move near them and line up at the urge of a soldier jabbing one of her wings. Looking down the line of people, she recognized them as the people she had originally been in line with, making her swallow a lump that had formed in her throat. She was in serious trouble.

The other teens in the line were staring at her, growling, or even calling slurs in spiritoski under their breath. Finding a spot on the ground, she concentrated hard on it before hearing whispers from the line, "That's him...", "That's The Bat Lord...", "He's the one who started the war..."

Looking towards the bleachers, Kirra's eyes instantly picked up the form of the person everyone was whispering about. The same exact person that looked like an older clone of Devin. Deep inside of her somewhere, a rumble from her spirit reverberated in anger, and with it, the memory of him standing over her dead parents. Walking just behind him was Devin himself. That rumble grew into a growl, and with it, the need for retribution at the deaths of her family. Her spirit's anger bled into her own, mixing together as she saw nothing but red. The longer she looked, the angrier she got.

The claws of her hands clenched and unclenched as the killer looked directly at her. Like his son, he had the same black hair and red eyes. Tanned skin peaked through the expensive-looking calf-length coat that split in two. He was all greys and blacks of varying shades. Unlike his son, his hair was shorter and slicked back neatly. His slanted eyes narrowed further on Kirra as he gave a gentle shake of his head as though to say, 'Don't do it.'

The overwhelming anger from her spirit took over, practically screaming at her, "*Kill him... Do it now...*" The earlier warnings of Black Dragon could be heard for her not to do anything stupid, but her spirit continued to egg her on, "*He killed your parents and took you from your brother, and you're just going to stand by and let him do it! Coward... Weakling... Wimp... You sorry excuse of a fledgling dragoness...*"

One moment, Kirra was standing at the edge of the pad with everyone else, and the next, she was hurling herself toward The Bat Lord.

Rage had overcome Kirra as she barreled toward the man, cocking a clawed hand back and slashing out at him once she was in range. It was the equivalent of trying to slash out at water. One moment, he was in front of her; the next, he had a grip on her wrist, and her momentum was used against her as she was thrown to the ground and pinned in an uncomfortable position.

Kirra could hear his deep sigh before he spoke to the group, "Let this be a lesson to the rest of you." Attempting to fight back against the hold, Kirra tried to wrench her arm free, only causing him to twist it and causing her to cry out in discomfort.

Left to do little more than writhe in pain at the hold he had on her arm that was twisted behind her back uncomfortably, she was forced to listen to him speak, "You cannot run, you cannot hide, and you cannot defeat me or any of the teachers here. If you try to run, escape, or do anything that endangers the people who call this cave home, you will feel my wrath." A sudden wrench of Kirra's arm caused her to cry out and claw at the ground before the pressure left.

The Bat Lord's speech continued, "If you are smart, you will learn to accept that you can do nothing to escape this place. Learn quickly, and you will live to see another day. I am harsh but fair. Put your very being into training and learning from your teachers, and you might live to see more than a month here..." Another wrench to Kirra's arm caused her to beat the ground with her fist several times with a cry.

Finally, her arm was released, and she curled the arm close to her chest as she rubbed her shoulder with her free arm as The Bat Lord continued, "Weakness can be overcome. This is why we have The List." Rolling to her side, she saw him gesture to a wall near the double-doored entrance they had come from with a list on a large projected holo screen. On it was a list of names with a number next to each. At the moment, particular names were highlighted. The last five names on the list were red, and one of those was highlighted as well. The word "Death" was spelled out in bright red letters as though it were an omen of what was to come.

He explained the rules behind their little system, "Once a week, you can challenge others. If you are challenged, you must answer your challenger in a fight. If you are the challenger and you win, you take the spot of the person you challenged. If you lost and were challenged, you drop in rank, causing everyone below you to drop in rank as well. You can challenge any person in any spot. If you are the challenger and lose, you retain your current position on the list."

Attempting to use the opportunity of his being busy giving the speech, Kirra attempted to get up and scramble away. She didn't get very far as the weight of a boot was felt pressing down on her back just between her wings as he continued, "You'll notice the bottom five names are in red. If you get in the red and stay in the red, you'll be put through a trial. A trial happens once a month. If you pass the trial, you live to see another month. If you fail…" His voice fell off momentarily before saying, "You'll see what happens when you fail…"

The boot pressing Kirra down on the pad lifted off her before a set of hands helped her rise to her feet. Next, she was pushed forward, causing her to stumble. She managed to stay upright with the assistance of her wings stretching out as she looked at the teens in the line before her. All of them looked muscular to some degree. The other thing they all had in common was staring at her with malice.

Her spirit's voice cut through her thoughts as she eyed the teens in front of her, "*I have my work cut out for me. Just don't die yet.*"

Kirra looked over her shoulder to the imposing figure of Devin's father as his voice called out, "Since Kirra was so kind to attempt an attack on me, she goes first. Which of you wish to challenge her?"

The red drake that had been in front of her in the chain originally stepped forward with a chuckle, "I'll challenge her." Now that she wasn't stuck in line behind him, she got a better view of him. His head was draconic shaped, and so were his tail, legs, and hands. As far as drakes went, he was about as far transformed as one of his kind could be. There weren't horns on his head; instead, there were several smaller spikes.

As the drake moved towards her, cracking the knuckles of his clawed hands, Kirra started to back away, looking around for some form of help from anyone. The one face that stuck out from her was Devin's as he held a look of concern before it fell under a mask of emotionlessness.

Turning back towards the drake, she called out to him, "You don't have to do this. You can choose to not fight."

The voice of her spirit hissed at her, "*What are you doing?!*"

Kirra's words gave the drake pause as he looked toward The Bat Lord, asking, "What happens if we refuse to fight?"

Gesturing to the bleachers where several other people were sitting, The Bat Lord explained, "One of them will make you." Kirra looked to the bleachers once more and realized there was a mix of people. Some were teens around the same age group; others looked older like they were there to observe the fighting. Kirra couldn't help but notice Black Dragon was among them with his chin propped on his knuckles while he lightly shook his head. Another of the teens caught her eye as one enthusiastically waved while smiling brightly, causing several teens in the bleachers to laugh.

Kirra's attention turned back to the sound of the drake walking toward her once more while she backed up from him, stumbling. The Bat Lord's words came next, "Begin."

The drake rushed her, clawed feet digging into the pad for easier purchase and leaving tiny scratches in the floor as he did so. Attempting to think quickly, she looked over every part of his body and decided she'd be better at evading since she didn't know how to fight. She somehow dodged his strike as he closed the gap but missed the follow-up. As the drake swept past her, sliding on the ground, his tail lashed out, sweeping her legs out from under her. The sound of her smacking against the training pad as she fell reverberated through the air, causing several people to draw in hisses.

Having had the wind knocked out of her, Kirra was slow to recover, but she started to rise slowly until she felt something grip her ankle. Her world was turned upside down as she flung over onto her back, and another loud smack rang out. Kirra's ears were ringing, her vision tunneled, and she saw something red flying towards her face before she knew it.

8

THE CAMP

The next memory she had was something very bright shining in one of her eyes before feeling a smack to the side of her face, "Wake up." The familiar face of Black Dragon filled her vision as she saw him hovering over her, "Take it slow. The kid throttled you quite harder than was necessary. I don't think he was aware you were already knocked out when he threw that punch."

Giving her a few moments to gather her wits, he kept a close eye on her, ensuring she would be okay. He asked her a series of questions she apparently answered correctly before deciding she was stable enough. As Black Dragon stood up, he held a hand out in an offer to help her up. Taking the hand, he pulled her up to her feet, and as she was about to thank him, she felt herself getting shoved backward.

Tripping over her tail she nearly knocked her head on the ground yet again. Anger consumed her expression as she sat up and was about to scream at him before he called out to her in that same calm demeanor, "Toughen up and do something about it. If you can't even stay on your own two feet, how do you plan on beating anyone in this camp." He held his hand out to her once more.

This time, Kirra didn't accept his help. Instead, she stood, glaring at him like a child who had been put in time-out. Once more, Black

Dragon shoved her, but she was ready for the incoming shove this time. What she wasn't ready for was his hands to instead pull her forward where all of her weight was going, making her stumble and fall on her stomach.

Letting out a huff of anger, she growled in frustration as she looked over at him, to which he responded, "You have to predict what your opponent is going to do. Don't watch my hands; watch my torso."

Despite the anger boiling under her skin, she gathered herself with a huff and pushed to her feet. Once more, he pushed and then pulled her, but she counterbalanced both times. A quick exclamation was released in celebration before her feet were swept out, causing her to cough as the wind was knocked out of her from her fall once again. Kirra caught a glimpse of a fading trail of dark fog disappearing as he tutored her, "Most importantly, you have to learn how to fall. Now I know where I need to start with you."

Kirra stayed on the ground this time, covering her face with her hands and screaming in frustration, "Why do you even care!?"

Kneeling down beside Kirra, Black Dragon explained, "I care because you're the daughter of an old friend whom I respected greatly." Kirra wiped the tears that had formed on her face as he added, "That and I made a very risky bet that by your second month, you would be in the top ten of the list. The rest of the trainers said I was crazy for making that bet but I see some potential in you."

Laughing at his last words, Kirra looked up at him as she sat back up and asked genuinely, "What happens if I'm still at the bottom?"

Black Dragon tilted his head as though he didn't care if that was what happened, "We'll discuss that when we get to that point. For now, concentrate on the tasks that I give you." He rose in front of her before looking towards someone in the distance and jerked his head to where they were, causing the male in the distance to start jogging toward them, "He is going to take you to your cabin and give you a tour of the entire camp." Holding his hand out, he offered her aid up to her feet once more.

For a moment, Kirra stared at the hand before taking it as he helped her to her feet. Not but seconds later, the teen he had called over approached. The boy was pale and tall and had a very mischievous look about him. His jaw was strong and rather well-built, but he had an awkward teenage lankiness about him. Atop his head was grey hair that had been cropped short but still long enough that it hid the partially twisted horns atop his head. Behind those twisted horns were grey, smaller spike-like horns as he stopped next to the pair.

Kirra eyed the boy with suspicion while Black Dragon introduced the boy with a wave of his hand, "This is Death…"

Recognizing the name from the list, she remembered he had been the one to enthusiastically wave at the new arrival of teens when they had been pointed out. Kirra eyed the young teen warily as he smiled towards her.

Letting out a bit of a laugh, the lilt of his accent came out almost instantly, "Oh, I don't blame you for the way yer lookin' at me. I didn' pick the name ta be fair. Parents thought it'd be bleedin' funny." Death let out a little cackle before turning to Black Dragon, "Oi BD. When ya gonna get me that invitation ta yer guild?"

A few chuckles escaped BD before he explained, "If I see you on the outside, perhaps I'll toss you an invitation. You'll have to finish schooling first. Idiots don't last long in my guild."

Kirra was looking very confused between the two, "Guild?"

Excitedly turning to her, Death was happy to explain, "An assassin guild. They train ya to kill powerful targets, work in war, and steal relics and artifacts. All sorts of jobs. Black Dragon happens to be in one." Kirra thought if Death had gotten more excited about the topic, he might implode right before her.

With a clear of his throat, BD got the pair back on topic, "Death is in the bottom five despite the fact that he doesn't belong there." He gave the boy a smirk before continuing, "He also happens to be one of the best fighters in the camp."

Sidling up next to Kirra, Death leaned over, mumbling, "What don' kill ya makes ya stronger right'?" He waggled his eyebrows playfully at Kirra before a playful slap on the back from BD caused him to settle his thoughts.

Giving the boy a firm squeeze on his shoulder, BD instructed, "Give her the rundown of the place and show her around." With a few pats, BD started moving off towards the woods.

With a clap of his hands, Death turned towards Kirra, stating proudly, "Alrigh' les get ya settled in then." The boy was already walking off, forcing Kirra to follow the excitable teen.

The cave was as beautiful as it was large. Nature seemed to be all over, and from what she could see, there were very few buildings in their location. Trees of green covered the place as far as the eye could see, and all of the paths were mostly natural though some were covered in gravel as they were more commonly traveled. Most of the buildings were made out of what seemed like all-natural materials that were in the area, like log cabins. Only a few of the buildings looked out of place as they were built out of bricks, besides the one structure that she had come from.

Death pointed back toward the building they had come from, "That is the Colosseum. It's where you come from when the trials are over. Large crowds an' all that. They sell tickets for others to watch the trials happen. I've heard that they even have people place bets on those who'll lose or win. It's also used to fly the newbies in. The bats use it for a few other things, but those are the ones I know of for sure." Pointing at a wall that nearly blended in with the rest of the nearby vegetation, "That's the Playground. That's where the trials happen. They have cameras all over that place that watch your every move. A large holo-projector displays everything happenin' in the Colosseum so the audience can watch in safety."

Tilting her head, Kirra could see a barrier over the wall of the Playground. It was a nearly invisible dome that, from the right angle, you could see distortions as to where it was located. The wall looked like ruins of something from the past that had just been reclaimed by nature and then repurposed. The wall was at least three or four stories tall with no discernable way to climb out besides the invisible dome barrier.

Continuing down the gravel path, she saw more log cabins come into view, but these were neatly organized in rows. A few of the draconic spiritosk teens were seen going in or out as they went on with their day. Death was rather helpful as he pointed out their particular cabin, "That's where we all sleep when we're not doing chores, working out, studying, cleaning, or just training."

As they passed a fancier, more updated building, he pointed out helpfully, "That's the Library. There are machines that can help you locate the books you're looking for, but the inventory is very limited. Mostly to do with fauna and flora."

As they passed the rows of cabins, the path started to bend a little further out. Kirra saw a fenced-off plot of land and what appeared to be a stable. Next to the stable were a couple of paddocks. The creatures inside the paddocks caused Kirra to pause as she stood in place on the large gravel path.

Wolves the size of horses with saddles on them were milling about in one of the paddocks or being ridden by a teen here and there. Teens inside the paddocks were either working on cleaning out the pens or inside the stable and moving about, working as farm hands. All of this happened under the guidance of a rather large woman covered in furs and leaves.

A soft elbow into her side was followed by Death's chuckle, "Yeah. Pretty much everyone has the same reaction to them."

Given the accent, she finally gave way to her curiosity, "What Preserve were you in?"

As Kirra turned to face him, she was met with furrowed brows as he stared down at her imposingly, "You askin' 'cause of the way that I talk?" He stepped up to her, causing her to shrink and back away before he said with a joking pat on her arm, "England. It's considered to be posh to talk like this, but to me, it's just how I speak." He laughed a few times, "You shoulda seen the look on yer face tho'. Right funny it was." A few more laughs came before he mentioned, "My parents and even my twin dope of a brother talk like this too. Well..." He paused momentarily, "Now it's just me an' my brother."

The look on Kirra's face caused Death to burst out, saying, "They're still alive. Just ya kno', we won't be goin' back ta them if we get out of here. Parents kinda just threw us straight inta a line of buses, in a manner of speaking." He laughed, "Anyways, my parents betta hope I neva see them again." He growled the last almost threateningly.

Motioning for her to follow, he escorted her around the corner of the stables, explaining, "Every group has a chore to do, whether it be laundry, cleanin' the pens, workin' the library, washing dishes, etcetera, etcetera." He motioned to a group of teens working in the gardens, which seemed to grow various vegetables. There were even some chickens with a coop that roamed in a small pen of their own. Pointing out the building next to it, "Kitchen and dining hall, we grow the food, and they cook it. At least some of the food. It helps to keep the balance a little bit. Chores also help keep your mind off the fact that we're prisoners in a way here."

As he continued down the path, he pointed out a few other buildings: mainly classrooms where they instructed them to learn to control their more bestial side and an armory where weapons could be checked out for those learning how to fight with weapons, though most of the trainers that taught weapons did so very privately.

Stopping at the end of the gravel path, before them lay a large pad similar to the one where Kirra had gotten her rear handed to her. On the side of the pad were workout machines, weights, boxing bags, and a few other things that even she didn't know what they were. Several teens were training with each other on the pad or using the weights at the moments before Death continued on.

Leading her back to the dining room, he got her some food for the night before returning to the cabins. Getting her set up with some sheets, pillows, extra clothes, and a few other amenities, he led her back to the cabin. While Kirra was putting together her bed and extra clothes, Death explained a few final things, one of which gave her some soft concern.

All the cabins were unisex, meaning they all slept in the open bunks together. Kirra had gathered this from the fact that the entire floor plan was open, with beds lining the cabin walls and a few tables and chairs on one side of the building, but everything was out in the open. Before she stressed about it, he clarified that the bathrooms were completely separate so that was where most changed. The idea of sleeping in the same room with a group of boys was less than thrilling for her to find out, but he said everyone got used to it after a while.

While the pair were talking, a voice similar to Death's pointed out unhelpfully, "We have the new girl at the bottom. Interesting." This version of the voice was pointed and precise. Every letter of his words was articulated.

At first, Kirra turned towards Death with a confused look. With a shake of his head, he pointed to a teen spiritosk of similar height, making her realize this had to be his twin brother. The only thing they seemed to share was their voice and height. Death's brother had green hair of different shades, olive-colored skin, less muscular definition, and horns that looked more like branches than actual horns, though his were less pronounced than Kirra's antlers.

Before Kirra could say anything, Death jumped in, stating, "Fortunate that. I get to help her if she's still in the red when trials come around. **And**..." He paused, sucking on his teeth before stating proudly, "Black Dragon is her personal trainer. All the other cabins turned her down, so I said why not bring her into the fold of misfits." Jerking his thumb towards his brother he added lastly, "This is my twin brother, Life."

Recognition at the play on names started to dawn on Kirra as Life asked, "Black Dragon is going to train her?" He paused as though considering his words before stating, "Odd that Black Dragon of all people would stick his neck out for a Celestial Dragon." Kirra's eyes narrowed at Life as a low rumble filled her head and a growl filled her throat, causing him to amend with, "No offense."

Looking between the two, she noticed that the pair were very much opposites of each other. Death was a chaotic ball of energy, pale, black hair, and seemed relaxed and improper. Life was cold and calculating; he even stood with a straight, upright back like he was uptight.

It caused her to ask curiously, "Did your parents pick your names because of the color differentiation between the two of you, or did they know what spirits you would have?"

The pair looked at each other before Death started with, "We're kind of a curse, or well, I am, at least. Some sort of divination about our birth or some crap. I'm a bone dragon. Supposedly, I'm supposed to be the living embodiment of death itself. At least, that is what I've been told from the day I was born."

With a clearing of his throat, Life was more than happy to change the topic, "I'm a life dragon, supposedly. I'm supposed to be able to bring plants and life back from the brink of death. Also, I can make plants grow from just a seed in some of the most hostile environments. I'm apparently destined to use Life magic at some point; at least, that is what was foretold for me."

An inquisitive look came over Kirra as she remembered that magic was a very rare occurrence in the realm of mortals. Crafting enchantments, potions, scrolls, and using abilities were one thing, but being gifted the ability to use magic overall was an entirely different affair.

Questioning his word usage, she asked, "Life magic? I thought only the Prophecy could use magic?"

The twins considered her question as they looked at her before Life explained, "It's a bit more complex than that. We're considered..." He seemed to be trying to figure out a word or how to continue.

Death was more than happy to cut in where his brother faltered, "We're Eternal Dragons. That's what the divinations say abou' us. Harder to kill, supposedly blessed with magic and abilities related to our spirits. But the truth is I've not seen us do anythin' particularly spectacular as this supposed divination says we're spose' to."

This is where Life continued, "Our parents are celestial dragons. Not just any celestial dragons. Gold Celestial dragons..." Death murmured something insulting under his breath, causing Life to reach out and pat his brother's arm, "Where I was praised for being the supposed Life Eternal Dragon..."

Death continued, "I was punished for being the supposed Death Eternal Dragon. One can't exist withou' tha other." Looking up at Kirra, he gave a shrug of his shoulders, "Anyway, when the soldiers came a knockin', my biological donors gladly threw me to them the second they appeared. Life didn' hafta go. He came outta hidin' after he saw what happened. So now I look out fer him."

Thinking about their words, she realized she could have had it worse. Despite how Death was treated by his parents, he still seemed to keep a positive outlook. Even though Life was treated like the next messiah or prophecy, he still joined his brother and turned his back on his parents. She realized then that BD had mentioned that Death didn't have to be in the bottom five. Death's statement that he looked out for him now made her question how exactly he managed to keep an eye on his brother.

Kirra decided to ask the question outright, "How do you look out for Life? I thought everyone has to fight here?"

More than happy to answer, Death said, "By manipulating the system. Basically, any newcomers that challenge my brother to knock him down into the red. I'll wait, challenge someone just above the red, and win. Then, Life challenges me, takes my spot, and I get knocked back down into the red after I let him win. Technically, we're still following the rules, but I did find that loophole ta keep him protected."

Life pointed out, "I'm not a great fighter, but Death is. Many of the others have picked up on what we have been doing, so they've mostly left me alone. I have been in a couple of trials with Death, but we have passed every one."

A giddy and girlish giggle came from Death, "I do love doing the trials. Righ' bit o' fun they are for me."

Life pointed out helpfully while changing the topic, "I saw her name wasn't on the chores roster yet."

With a snap of his fingers, Death declared, "Right! I almost forgot about tha'." He leaned toward the bed where Kirra had taken a seat, explaining, "Like I said, everyone has chores in the camp. Since you're new, you only get a choice of three." He thought of it and sucked in a breath, "They're all kinda shite just as a forewarning."

Kirra sighed, "Just tell me what they are..."

"Laundry, Gym Cleanup Crew, or Crap gathering."

For several moments, Kirra blinked at him as though she didn't hear him correctly, "I'm sorry, did you say crap gathering?"

While Death was snickering some, Life explained, "Most of every-thing here is done in a very old-school way to conserve as much energy as possible. The..." He cleared his throat, "Biological waste is turned into fertilizer for the garden as well as waste from the kitchen is fed to the hens and also turned to fertilizer."

With a shrug, Kirra stated, "Well, at least wolf poop can't be too much different from that of a pet dog from Earth." Death was giggle snorting at this point. Life just placed his head in one hand and began rubbing his forehead like he had a headache, "What?"

Life seemed to be trying to figure out how best to break the news to her before Death gracefully stated, "Oh, love. It ain't animal shite you'd be pickin' up."

Kirra's face turned to one of disgust at the realization, "Our crap!?" Death's snickers only confirmed her words as she asked, "What about for showers?"

More than happy to talk about something unrelated to feces, Life chirped up, "There are showers with heated water. It's one of the few amenities we're allowed. Shower water gets recycled for use towards laundry." The groan of complaint from Kirra made him add, "Don't worry, you'll get used to it soon enough."

Eventually, Kirra dejectedly stated, "Guess I'll wash everyone's stinky clothes."

With a grimace, Death stated, "Mmmm, right, you can't do that." Kirra looked at him, confused, as he explained, "If you have tutoring assistance from anyone, it means you'll have training in the morning, bright and early. Laundry gets washed in the morning, then hung to dry during the day. Which means you can't do laundry crew." Death gave a cheeky grin as though he was apologizing with his smile.

With a groan of frustration, Kirra stated, "Gym cleanup it is then."

Right at that moment, yet another stranger walked in, rubbing a towel through his wet hair, causing Kirra to blush and look anywhere **but** the boy. He had lightly tanned skin, slanted silver eyes, and silvery white hair that was short and swept back from his face. The boy was absolutely gorgeous in her eyes, and what didn't help matters was the fact that he was wearing nothing but black shorts and shower shoes as he trudged forward, stating in a soft, even tone, "So we got the last place girl in our cabin then?"

Despite his chuckle at Kirra's response to the half-naked boy, he responded, "Eh, I'm rootin' fer her." A soft cackle followed, "She took a swing at the almighty Zeke. It was great." Now she had a name to go along with the face of the person she hated.

Surprise tainted the teen's soft, even voice, "**You?** Took a swing at Zeke?" The boy's question caused her to look up and nod her head in response, causing a low whistle from him, "That's some ballsy stuff, especially as scrawny as you are." He seemed to dip down some as though trying to get her to look up at him, which worked as he held out his hand, "I'm Ky." Kirra took his hand tentatively as he gripped it strongly and gave it a shake before stating, "Well, I wouldn't expect that from you as shy as you are."

Kirra wanted to say something but instead remained quiet as Ky turned to the twins, stating firmly, "I'm turning lights out; keep it down the two of you. And Death..." He added as he pointed at him, "I'm going to race you tomorrow, so get ready to get your butt kicked."

As Ky turned to head to his bed, Death called out, "You bet it, but I'm gonna be doin' the butt kickin'." Death chased after Ky jumping on him as they play wrestled for a little bit.

Distracted at the scene of the two boys playfully wrestling, Kirra let out a soft laugh as Life came up and gently touched Kirra's shoulder, "Try and get some rest tonight." With that, he turned and left, heading to his own bed as Death and Ky separated and started to head to bed.

As the others started to settle down for the night, Kirra found it almost impossible to get the hang of trying to sleep with her newfound draconic limbs. Her wings uncomfortably sat pinned against her back if she lay on them. Her horns got caught in the sheets or against the bed frame. No one had ever told her about the struggles of getting used to the new body parts that she was starting to hate.

Eventually, Kirra found a comfortable position to sleep on her stomach as her wings draped on the floor along with her tail. Some tears came to her that night as the thoughts of her dead parents drifted through her mind, but eventually, she was able to get some rest. There still lay so many questions that she needed answered. Things about what her parents said before they were taken from her. It was complicated, and they'd explain everything once they got off the world. Now, she was left only to draw her own conclusions.

9

WHAT DOESN'T KILL YOU

A hand clapped over Kirra's mouth, causing her to wake instantly. She struggled and tried clawing out at the enemy before two brilliant golden eyes moved into view, whispering, "Quiet, or you'll wake the others." It was Black Dragon.

Releasing his hold on her, he raised a finger to his mouth for her to keep quiet while he moved to the front of the cabin and out the front door like some bulky predator. His every move was soundless, like a massive cat stalking prey at night. Kirra's exit was less than graceful as she followed behind with the sound of her clicking claws and the accidental bump of her nightstand. After her horns clipped the cabin entrance, she was finally free as BD stood there with his head in his hand, shaking his head at her less-than-graceful exit.

Figuring they were out of earshot enough, Kirra asked, "So you really are an assassin?"

The simple answer came, "Yes, and so was your mother. I even worked with her a few times. One of the best I ever trained." Kirra's face faltered at the confirmation her mother was an assassin, "And that look is why some of us choose not to have a family..."

Kirra spat vehemently, "What's that supposed to mean? You're a killer, she was a killer..."

Cutting her short, BD interrupted her, "So is a hungry dragon, an energy thief, or even you anytime you need to eat food. Soldiers kill so their families will live with the paycheck they get from their jobs. So why is an assassin any worse?" His gold eyes pierced her soul as he continued, "If I kill a dictator one day halfway across the multiverse, it'll save hundreds if not thousands of lives and stop countless battles from happening." With a sigh and shake of his head, he added solemnly, "You're still young. I do not expect you to understand this line of thinking for quite some time. It'll be decades possibly before you ever learn this lesson."

BD's words only angered Kirra more as she stated, "Justifying killing people? Yeah, that sounds great. Why don't you justify why my mother isn't here, or my father for that matter? Explain the good it did for my parents. You're no better than the rest of them in this war. The Bat Lord stole kids away from their homes when they were trying to escape the war, all for this stupid Prophecy. I can't believe any of you heretics." BD's face became a blank mask as she continued her rant, "You have to crack a few eggs to make an omelet right?" Squinting she shook her head, "That's really the line of thinking that all of you are going with? Steal children, to find the one special one? You're all horrible for even participating in it."

That same mask continued to eye her for a moment before BD shook his head and turned down the gravel path. Kirra was expecting a response, a possible lashback for her words and her calling him out. Instead, all she got was silence and him traveling down the path with her following behind like a lost little puppy. Some part of her thought what she said might have been a mistake, but she needed to defend her own viewpoints because that was all she had left.

Eventually, they wound up in the training yard. Slowly moving to the center of the pad that was slightly raised from the rest of the ground, BD just moved to the middle before coming to a stop. This training pad was different than the other as it was made out of a black tile of sorts. For a while, Kirra stood there looking at his back, waiting for something anything, but instead, he just stood there.

After minutes of this going on, Kirra finally asked, "So?"

His words came back in that same calm tone, "So what?"

Confused, Kirra asked pointedly, "I mean, you bring me out here and then just stand there in the middle of the pad doing nothing. I thought you were going to train me or something?"

Kirra was greeted with Black Dragon's chuckle, "I do not have to do anything. I **chose** to because I am an honorable person and I respected your mother a great deal. But you insulted me. So instead I'm teaching you a different lesson." Turning his head, he looked at her with one piercing gold eye, "Humility." Kirra was at a loss for words as BD turned to her showing just how serious he was, "So now this is going to be your lesson. Me, standing here, waiting for you to humble yourself."

A sarcastic laugh came from her before she demanded, "Insult? What insult?!" Kirra glared up at the larger man.

One side of his mouth lifted up in a soft smirk as he explained, "You said I was no better than the rest of the people in this war. I am not fighting in this war, nor do I need help learning how to fight. I am not stealing kids, but helping them. **You,** Kirra Smith, know nothing of me or my motives to accuse me of such things. Until you learn some humility, and realize that it is not I that needs you, but you that needs me... this will be my training."

One sleepy eye from her spirit opened as she heard it speak from deep within her, "*Perhaps setting our pride aside might be useful for the moment.*"

Kirra pursed her lips, stating firmly, "I stand by what I said..." She crossed her arms, determined to get her point across.

Those gold eyes seemed to be looking her over for every single detail of her pose to the look on her face. He seemed to be no stranger to hormonal teenagers and wasn't going to reiterate himself. Finding his voice, he finally stated, "Then you can leave..." Turning away from her he added, "Come and find me when you're done acting like a petulant child." Kirra's jaw dropped at the blunt insult thrown directly at her. Unable to come up with a comeback, she stormed off and found the cabin deciding to get some extra sleep instead.

Her sleep was interrupted once more as the sound of loud brass instruments played through the cabin. Battling to escape her sheets, she heard the running of footsteps out of the door as she saw Death running out of the cabin.

Pausing briefly in the door, he called out to Kirra, "You're gonna be late. You might want to hurry up." With a two-finger salute, he was off and running.

Panicking, Kirra raced to get out of bed nearly taking herself out on the doorframe with her horns a second time for the day before she scrambled out of the cabin. Seeing only a few of the teens racing away ahead of her, Kirra tried her best to sprint and catch up, but she was severely out of shape. She could see in the distance where they had all gone and slowly ran to the training pad where all the gym equipment was.

Once she arrived, Kirra spotted Death's tall form at the back of the assembly of teens. He held one hand out pointing at an open spot for her to line up next to him. All of the teens were lined up nice and neatly on the black tiles as Kirra ran over and took the hint. Not a single person was speaking or moving as they stood like statues causing Kirra to lean over and ask in a whisper, "What's going on?" His only response was a slow shake of his head causing her to ask again, "Death?"

The sudden sting of a cane hitting her right leg caused her to nearly double over and fall to the ground in pain. Wheeling around in her pained state, she lashed out from where the strike came.

As the world suddenly spun, Kirra found the arm she had used to lash out being used as a choke grip on herself as a feminine voice called out, "I see that **most** of the new arrivals have managed to catch on quickly..." Kirra felt like she was going to pass out while she tried to break the hold she was in as the voice gave her a hint, "The key here is to tap my arm three times and I will release you."

The spirit growled out inside of her, "*Tap out, girl. You are no match as you are.*"

Letting out a growl, Kirra ignored her spirit, fighting against the grip as she tried to free herself. Her vision started to tunnel. Her ears started to ring. She had no choice but to give in. Three quick successive taps set her free and sprawling onto the pad on all fours.

While Kirra was recovering, that same voice instructed, "For those of you who are new. I have only one rule: listen and pay attention. If you don't, you will get punished."

Catching her breath, Kirra tilted her head up to look at the person who had taken her to the ground. It wasn't a woman, but an effeminate man with long hair pulled back neatly into a bun. Their once dark hair was greying showing their age in wrinkles that barely etched their face. The extra detail that made matters worse, they were completely blind, as shown by their foggy eyes.

The instructor called out loudly to ensure they were heard, "Kykorronomo. You will pair off with the late arrival today. Clearly, she needs the most work." Kirra was already slowly rising to her feet, but she felt her face flame up as she was publicly humiliated, noted by several chuckles.

The laughter turned to pained cries and groans. With accuracy and haste, each person who had laughed quickly received thwacks from the cane of the instructor before tutting, "Thank you for being volunteers. Despite all of you being pitted against one another, you are in this together. While you are with me, you will not laugh at the mistakes of another. She did not choose not to be trained properly, nor did she pick her parents, or choose to be born." The groaning slowly stopped as they rose to their feet before instructing, "Those of you who are new pair off with those who are not. The rest of you know what to do." The cane tapped loudly on the ground as though to dismiss them.

From out in front, Ky came jogging over to her with a concerned look on his face, "I thought Death would have run you through all of this." Ky looked over to Death, who was watching the pair, and shook his head, "Or not..." Looking over at Kirra, he spoke plainly, "If **Death** thinks you need tough love, you did something wrong." Firmly crossing his arms, he demanded more than asked, "What happened?"

Unable to stop her own anger Kirra instantly commented, "He's a di--..." A small rock pelted the side of her arm, causing her to yelp while Ky masterfully stopped a laugh, "I thought you weren't supposed to laugh at other people's pain."

Ky had a smirk on his face, "Amusement is different from blatantly laughing at someone's misfortune." A snort came from Kirra as she glared at him before he added, "Miss Chetski hates foul language and belittling others, but she has a **great** sense of humor." Once more, he inquired, "Black Dragon?"

The question came almost immediately, "That's a she?"

With a long sigh, he explained, "That is what she prefers to be called, yes." Moving on from the subject as if it were old news, he asked again, "What happened with Black Dragon?"

Kirra stammered, not knowing where to start, "I don't know. I said something, and he took offense to it? I didn't think he was going to be a big baby about it." Ky looked at her as though she were crazy as she continued, "All I did was speak my mind and say how crap it was that they were stealing kids from their homes and families." Ky's eyebrows raised as he looked at her like she had a death wish.

After studying her briefly, he nodded before simply asking, "Can you fight?"

The answer should have been obvious, making Kirra state, "No..."

Before she could even question why he was asking, he continued, "Have you ever taken any classes on fighting at all?"

She started to get upset and gestured to her frail form, stating, "I spent most of my time trying to avoid people because all they did was try and pick fights with me for being a Soulless."

Driving his point home, Ky finally stated, "You know for a person who doesn't know how to fight, you've picked a lot of fights in the span of less than 30 hours." As Kirra looked like she was about to interrupt him, he raised a finger, driving the point further, "All of whom are far beyond your combat prowess..." He ticked their names off on his finger so she would understand the full gravity of her mistake, "Zeke, Black Dragon, and now Miss Chetski."

She stammered over her words, "I... look... I don't know what I'm even doing here. I'm not even good at anything. I can't fight, my mom is dead, my dad is dead, my brother could be dead..." The thought caused a tear to roll down her cheek.

Stopping her mid pity party, Ky stated bluntly, "Then you live for them. Because if you continue to anger people, you'll be left with no one but yourself and that is a lonely place to be. Trust me...." The look in his eyes made Kirra pause. It was filled with a pain that he seemed to know all too well. It felt as though Ky knew the type of situation that Kirra was in exactly and understood what she was going through.

Her spirit rumbled through her, "*You aren't the only person who has suffered. Stop throwing a tantrum and listen to someone.*"

She snapped back, "*Last time I listened to you, I wound up face-first in the dirt.*"

Her spirit huffed at her in response, "*My words were fueled by your overbearing anger, pride, and attitude. Even now, I am still waking and regaining strength.*"

If Kirra was going to survive more than a week there, she was going to have to try and let go of her anger and her pride and try not to let her hormonal teenage quirks get the better of her. With a defeated sigh, she looked over to Ky and genuinely asked, "What do I need to do?"

Ky shook his head before he explained, "Apologize to Black Dragon. He stepped up and stuck his neck out for you, and you spit in his face."

"Okay, Okay," Kirra said dejectedly.

His finger jabbed her in the chest hard as if to drive his point through her thick skull, "You have to mean it too..."

"Okay, okay. I get it. I'll apologize..." Ky stared at her as though making sure she would honor her word before letting the issue drop.

Moving on from that problem, he started by showing her some simple throwing maneuvers, advising her to concentrate on grapples and throws, given her inexperience and lack of strength. To Kirra, it felt like they had been training for hours on the same couple of takedowns and were getting nowhere. The sound of familiar loud clunking caused the entire place to fill with movement towards the gravel path as Ky motioned for her to follow him. Walking over, she realized quickly that the rest of her cabin members were gathering up while the others were wandering off down the gravel path.

Noticing their group was heading past the classrooms and towards somewhere else, Kirra inquired, "Why are we heading towards the playground?"

The answer came from a pleasant-sounding girl whom Kirra hadn't been introduced to yet, "Survival training..." The girl, who looked like she was a bodybuilder, moved up next to Kirra, stating excitedly, "We get to hang out with Black Dragon for a while, and he gets to teach us about wilderness and environmental hazards. His class is my favorite..."

The color instantly drained from Kirra's face as she tripped and almost ate dirt again. She would have to apologize to Black Dragon, and it had only been a few hours since they had their disagreement. The girl that had moved up next to her, caught her before she hit the ground.

Once Kirra was settled, the musclebound girl asked, "What's the matter? You look like you saw a demon." Holding her hand out in the form of an introduction, she finally said, "Oh, I'm Nicki, by the way..." Looking at the pleasant face that smiled over at her, Kirra couldn't help but instantly like Nicki. She was a pleasant person, and the voice attached to her overly muscular physique was quite the contradiction she would have never expected. Nicki looked like she could have fit in with the humans on earth, no problem. Dirty blonde hair, brown eyes, a nice smile, and an overall pleasant disposition. The only thing that stuck out was the black mark that trailed up her left arm. It looked like a drake shaped like it was made of boulders.

After gawking briefly, Kirra stated not so convincingly, "Hi, sorry, it's... uh... nothing. I'll be fine." Kirra didn't take the outstretched hand as they got to the entrance of The Playground, making her ask instead, "Death, I thought you said this is where the trials are done?"

With a snap of his fingers, Death quickly stated, "Oh, righ'! I forgot to tell you that they also do training here. Since the trial can go on for anywhere from a few hours to a couple days they like to give us survival experience." He paused as he tried to remember what else he was supposed to explain before continuing, "We go through training cycles. So, every day, we train with certain people during certain time slots. The schedule is on the board in the cabin." With a nervous laugh, he added, "I guess I forgot to explain that part." It earned a glare from Kirra before he cleared his throat, adding, "Anyway, if you get up early enough, you get breakfast. If you don't, well, you miss it, and you have to wait until lunch to eat."

The idea of missing a meal was less than exciting to Kirra, given the fact she was already so skinny. Given what they had been doing for the first few hours, she was burning energy that she didn't have in the tank to begin with. Letting out a sigh, she dropped the thoughts for the moment as the others had already started heading into the entrance of The Playground.

Almost instantly, she saw them looking around before Ky and Death moved towards the ground as though they had spotted something, causing Kirra to ask, "What are you guys—" The group unanimously shushed her as they all started looking around on the ground.

Frustration, confusion, and anger rolled over her all at once as Kirra demanded, "Don't shush me. Wha—"

The feel of a hand wrapping around her mouth caused her to squirm as Kirra attempted to use one of the grapples she had just been taught to throw Ky off of her, to no avail. Only when she had stopped struggling against him was she released. Despite her glare, Ky raised a finger to his lips for her to keep quiet as he finally explained, "Black Dragon does things differently, and we don't have the time to really explain it to you."

The sound of a bird called out, causing both Ky and Kirra to look over to Death as he waved everyone over. He pointed at a broken branch in the ground and a set of bootprints heading through trodden leaves.

As the group got closer, Ky hung his head, stating softly, "You're too good at this."

It was Death who started taking the lead and following the trail through the forest. Kirra wasn't as quiet or skilled as the others and was stuck at the back of the group. Her tail kept getting stepped on, horns and wings snagging on branches, and it was just overall a pain for her. Each important sign Death found, he pointed out to the others, Kirra included as she learned from them.

As the tracks led to a clearing, Death quietly ran over to a campfire that was still lightly smoking as he pointed out to the rest of the group. With an excited, quiet giggle, he whispered, "He was just here. The fire is still hot."

As the rest of the group rounded on Death, Black Dragon's voice filled the air just behind them, "You're getting very good at that Death..." While everyone else was turning towards the voice, Kirra screamed in surprise and fright before she doubled over, patting her chest from the little scare she got. It seemed the entire group had a bit of a laugh at Kirra's expense save for one person. As Kirra turned to look towards Black Dragon, he regarded her with a raised eyebrow and crossed arms.

As the laughter died down, Death stated firmly, "I told ya, I'm dead serious about becomin' an assassin."

Nicki's excited voice quickly chirped, "We're doing tracking today? Or is it something else instead?"

Before anyone else could question him, Black Dragon stared down at Kirra, stating, "I'm waiting for something first."

Given the stare that Black Dragon was giving Kirra, it didn't take long for the rest of the group to understand that he was waiting for her. Kirra could feel the stares of everyone like tiny little daggers at the back of her head. It was the stare from Ky and Death that made things more uncomfortable for her more than anything.

Finding the courage to speak, Kirra's voice came out with a shake that expressed just how anxious she was, "I-I'm sorry, okay? I-I just..." Kirra was trying to find the words to say to him, "I don't know what to say..." Black Dragon continued to stare her down, causing her to blurt out, "What? What do you want from me? I said I was sorry, okay. I just..." She paused before finally stating, "I-I don't want to die here." Wringing her hands, her eyes constantly flicked nervously to and from Black Dragon's face.

After a long, deep sigh, BD finally spoke, "Not good enough...." His words were like a knife to her heart, causing her to step back as fear clawed its way up her throat while he continued, "Until you're ready to actually apologize other than for selfish reasons, don't bother coming to my class."

Kirra turned to look at everyone in her cabin. Nicki and Life were staring at the ground intently to avoid any awkward eye contact. Death and Ky were looking at her with a note of disapproval on their faces as though she wasn't going to get their pity in this matter. She knew the looks all too well. It was the look that someone gave you if you didn't belong. A look she was all too familiar with from her entire childhood growing up.

It was almost as if her spirit could feel the discord of emotions roiling through her as he commented, *"If you're not going to be honest with yourself. You should be honest with those around you."*

As her spirit's words echoed through her, Kirra dropped to her knees, declaring, "I'm scared!" Tears started to spill down her cheeks as she continued, "I don't know what to do anymore. I'm all alone, and it's like nothing ever changed. I went from being a soulless without friends to a celestial dragon without friends. My parents are dead. My brother..." Her voice hitched at the thought of him being gone before moving on, "I don't know who to trust or listen to, and it's like everything just exploded in my face." She broke down into sobs, "I wasn't taught very much about our ways. I can't fight, I'm not strong, and I'm not fast. I'm not good at anything because no one ever prepared me for this world." As she continued to sob, she curled her arms around herself as she finally admitted, "I'm sorry because I'm scared and angry, and frustrated, and useless, and..." Her voice fell off as she was about to speak the last words and couldn't continue the list of confusing emotions that clogged her very being.

Her spirit finished it for her in her head as she continued to sob, "*Weak. That we can change, you can always become stronger, but it will take time... and help.*"

The others remained quiet. The only sounds being made were her sobs. A set of steady footsteps made its way to her, stopping just in front of her. Kirra's clawed hands covered her face as she sat there quietly sobbing, unable to hide from her own fears and the conflicted emotions of everything that had happened.

Black Dragon's voice came in a soft, understanding whisper directly before her, "Are you ready to fight back against your fears?" Kirra looked at him as tears streaked down her face, "I'm willing to forgive your slights against me and teach you to become stronger." He reached out and poked her chest, "But you have to push yourself through it. I cannot carry that burden for you."

With a shaky voice, Kirra finally stated, "I-I'll try to."

He poked her chest adamantly once more, "There is no try, there is just do. Forget it. All of it. All of your anger. Forget your worries and concerns and throw everything into learning and training. All you need to do is listen and learn. I'm not here to kidnap children from their beds at night or torture anyone. I'm here to help you prepare for the future, so you have the skills to survive." He gripped her jaw lightly, making her look at him. He stressed his last words, "I'm here for you and every other confused teen. Not for any political agenda. I'm here for **you**."

Nodding to him in understanding, BD let go of her face and let her calm before he walked her through an exercise to help her calm further. Despite her worries about delaying his instruction, he made sure to express that she was still one of his students and that if she wasn't there mentally prepared to learn, his lesson would be wasted. Once she was calm and centered, BD helped her to stand before joining the others by the fire.

As though nothing happened, Black Dragon jumped right into talking to the others, "Death, you are correct, the fire burnt out, but it's still warm. These coals are different than others. Does anyone know why that is?"

Everyone looked at each other, shrugging. It looked like a normal wood fire. Kirra leaned forward and smelled it, causing recognition of the smell to come to her. She remembered specifically that they had a pretend campout as her mother talked about her favorite type of wood to burn. She remembered the next morning that she showed her and her brother that the wood coals could be easily reignited with a little tender care.

As no one spoke up, Kirra said the answer in a soft undertone that practically no one heard, causing BD to speak up, "Kirra?"

Clearing her throat, she reiterated again, "It's Mesquite."

A smirk came to BD's face as he nodded, "To humans, it's called Mesquite, but most of us know it as Everburn Maple." Pulling out a few smaller pieces, he handed them to the others before giving Kirra a larger stick. He explained, "Smell it, feel its weight, how much it bends, how much it doesn't. Dried Everburn works better than wet, much like many woods." He turned to Kirra before motioning towards the fire while instructing softly, "Show them what makes this wood the superior." As Kirra used the stick to stir the ash and soot, she exposed the hot embers and coals of the fire before taking some tinder and placing it over. Blowing on it gently, the fire came to life, causing Black Dragon to comment to her, "I thought you said you were useless."

His words caused the smallest of smiles on her face as he looked towards her with a smirk before addressing the group, "This is some of the best kind of wood to have when you're in the wilderness and at a spot for a few days..." He nodded at the fire, "I started that fire last night and let it burn itself out..."

After teaching them about the properties of Mesquite, BD paired Kirra off with Death, who was ahead of the whole cabin regarding survival techniques. The very first thing he taught her was how to start a fire from scratch, which was important for several factors. Keeping warm, cooking food, signaling, and even using it to dry out wood. After finally starting her first fire without using already hot coals, Kirra was starting to feel not so useless.

After survival training, Kirra was separated from her cabin and off to a beginner classroom where they were teaching how to hide their spirits, or rather their animalistic body parts. It turned out that she wasn't alone when it came to hiding her form. A few other teens she had arrived with also had the same problem. Kirra was starting to learn that she wasn't the only one with problems, worries, and concerns, which set her at ease to some extent

As the days went on, she was beginning to get used to the early mornings and the long days. Both Black Dragon and Miss Chetski took extra time with Kirra to get her on track quickly. In the morning, she was training with BD, then it was mass training with everyone with Miss Chetski. After that came survival training and then some class-room time with a woman named Flower. Kirra thought the woman looked like the spiritosk equivalent of a human hippy, but she was nice.

Kirra was quickly gathering that the days there on Spiritoski were longer and it felt longer the more she trained. Some of the days during her first week with BD, he'd spend working on putting some muscle on her. Other days were spent training techniques for her to be more defensive than offensive.

The first few days were the roughest out of the entire week, but as the days went on, she found the soreness starting to wear down as her body grew used to the weights. Even Death volunteered to help Kirra during the one-on-ones since he had no extra classes. He had been there long enough that he only had the two major ones most of the week. She noticed that one of the days in the afternoon, he'd disappear for a while but come back looking exhausted.

As the week ended, Kirra felt she was ready to challenge someone. BD told her that it wasn't time yet, and she needed more time to learn, put more muscle on, and be better prepared overall. Instead, she took the time to sit on her number circle, watching the others fight. Her eyes occasionally wandered as she stared at the list with her name at the very bottom. For a moment, worry started to well up inside of her before she looked away. With an exhale, she concentrated on her trust in BD to help her through the camp so she could survive.

Her wandering eyes caught sight of Devin. He was staring at her as though waiting for her to challenge someone. She couldn't help but wonder if he actually cared about her or if everything he did on Earth had been a lie. Those thoughts of distrust and worry started to bubble up inside her before she averted her gaze and put it out of her mind.

Kirra had other things to worry about. She needed to concentrate fully on her training so that she could survive. She had a long way to go if she was going to stand a chance against any of the others there.

10

JUST SURVIVE

Two weeks of pure hell and hard work later, Kirra could feel the difference in her body from when she had arrived. All of the training and practice was paying off as she quickly put weight on. None of the weight was bad either. She was still skinny for her height, but everyone could notice that she was starting to tone up quite nicely and feel it in her punches as well. She was still quite awkward on her anthropomorphic feet, but now she wasn't stumbling clumsily with a tail and wings. It was clear to everyone who trained with or instructed her that she was putting everything into her training. It was challenge day once again, but she decided not to participate given she was at the bottom of the list.

Working a punching bag, a familiar voice graced her ears, "I'm surprised you didn't show up to challenges." Devin's familiar voice caused her to pause in front of the bag as he expressed concern, "This is the second week, and you haven't even challenged anyone. Why is that?"

Her spirit rumbled out to her, "*Don't let him get a rise out of you. Control your anger. It isn't worth it.*"

Punching the bag once very hard, she turned and faced him stating, "My trainers said I'm not ready to fight yet. So, instead of sitting down and just watching everyone else move up and down, I decided to work on my technique so that one day I might pay your father back for what he did to my parents." Even as Kirra stood in front of him angrily, Devin's face twitched with a smirk, "What's so funny?" The urge to punch him in the face was strong.

A soft laugh came from him while she balled her hands into fists and growled. Finally, his answer came, "You..."

Even as she growled, her spirit rumbled, *"Don't do it."*

Raising his hands, he explained, "I'm laughing at you, in a good way. In two short weeks, you went from this shy girl who was constantly bullied and sheltered to someone ready to stand up for themselves." He let out a laugh, "It's kind of hot actually." Devin reached for her.

Almost immediately, Kirra stepped back and pushed his hands away from her, stating, "I could possibly die in a couple of weeks, and you find it hot that I've grown a backbone?" Shaking her head, she turned back on the bag and started working it once more stating, "I bet it's a huge massive joke to all of your friends and your dad. The supposed future father-in-law of the soulless one, now her jailor." She turned back to face him once more as the smile had disappeared, "My parents are dead Devin. My brother is possibly dead too. And now..." She turned around and punched the bag once more before rounding on him, "I'm stuck here as a prisoner."

Devin's next words came out sincerely, "I had nothing to do with that, and I'm sorry your parents were killed. That was never part of..."

She interrupted him angrily, "You knew it was going to happen?!"

"I knew that they were coming for you, but your parents being killed was never part..."

Her anger was getting the better part of her as she growled out, "How many others died because of your father and this stupid war?!" Pressing him backward, she turned her anger on him, "Because he couldn't ignore some snide comments from other people and move on with his life like every other Bat?!"

Holding his hands out he tried to reason with her, "It's not that easy. It wasn't just snide comments Kirra. There's a whole lot more to this than just simple bullying. Trust me if I could, I would just run away from all of it, but I'm trapped in this just like you…"

She could feel her spirit squinting at Devin as he commented, "*He's hiding something…*"

"*How do you know?*"

"*It's hard to explain, but he is hiding something…*"

Kirra let out a frustrated snort while replying internally, "*Oh great, so you know he's hiding something but not **what** he's hiding and can't explain how you know? Because that's helpful.*"

A thunderous growl came from her spirit, "*Do not get snarky with me child. I am not the one your anger is directed toward.*"

With a shake of her head, she finally replied to Devin sarcastically, "Right because there's absolutely no civil way for change to be made. Oh, wait, I believe it's called talking." Pointing off in the distance, she added to him, "Why don't you leave me alone so I can train in peace. I have a lot of catching up to do since I might literally be fighting for my life."

"Don't blame her son." The booming voice came from the entrance of the training pad. The one and only Zeke made his way slowly across the pad towards the pair before finally adding, "She doesn't know any better." As Zeke moved next to Devin, the kinship between them was unmistakable as Devin looked like he could qualify as his younger brother. His hands were neatly clasped behind his back as Zeke tilted his head curiously towards Kirra, "So this is where you were? You didn't even deign to show up to the challenges today. That's rather bold given you're at the bottom of the list."

Anger boiled just below her skin at the very presence of Zeke causing her spirit to call out a warning to her, *"Don't let your anger get the better of you. It's only been two weeks, and you've followed his rules."*

Forcing herself to take a step back she countered, "I didn't see the point in showing up and spending hours watching people challenge each other. So I figured I'd get some training in."

Regarding her with a raised eyebrow, Zeke questioned, "So you figured you couldn't learn anything from just watching?"

Forced to defend her actions, she answered truthfully, "I watched last time. I saw people get put on the ground. I learn through doing, not watching." Her next remark came with a hint of her anger and hate towards him, "I need to get stronger more than I need to get my butt kicked."

Considering her words, Zeke rebutted, "You can learn quite a lot from failing in a fight. For instance, you can see how much punishment you can deal or take from an opponent." The snort that came from Kirra made him add, "You also learn to respect those that are either worse or better than you. Something you clearly lack."

Tired of others telling her how she should think, she practically spat, "In my personal opinion, respect is earned. I have no respect to give **you** for what you did to my parents. Even less so for starting a frickin' war because others think they're better because of some stupid abilities. It's not dragons' faults they're born with abilities and the majority of others aren't." Crossing her arms, Kirra stood proud and felt secure with her argument.

That feeling lasted all or one second before she saw an exchange of looks between Zeke and Devin. One second, the handsome young teen was standing there looking towards Zeke; the next, Devin was throwing a punch toward Kirra, making her have to backpedal to dodge and defend herself as she looked between the pair. Looking confused between the pair, Kirra questioned, "What the heck?!"

More than happy to explain, Zeke's voice cut through while Devin squared up to Kirra despite looking reluctant, "Rules change as others exploit loopholes. Everyone, no matter their position, must challenge someone."

Kirra started to contest Zeke's words, "He's not even on th—" Peering up at the board that was in that particular training pad caused her words to trail off. Devin's name was at the very top, and a quick glance showed that the majority of her cabin, including Ky, were near the bottom of the list. Kirra froze at the sight, "What the...." As yet another fist went flying by her from Devin, she pulled back, raising her hands up, declaring, "I surrender." Kirra wasn't just giving up, but she clearly remembered Devin talking about his training and she knew she didn't stand a chance.

Watching from the side, Zeke was quick to remind her, "Remember what I said your first day. You must answer your challenge, Kirra. Had you been there today, you would have been first in line to be challenged because Devin would have been at the bottom. He is now part of the list."

Not giving her another moment to breathe, Devin moved in now that all speaking was done. With a series of punches, Kirra could do nothing but dodge and block what she could. BD's training was working far better than expected as she surprised herself at what she had been learning. Even when he landed a punch or a kick, her training and muscle memory kicked in making her realize she was more capable than she thought. Not confident in her offensive abilities, she mostly just dodged and blocked until she got too bold.

As she attempted to throw her first punch, she took a hit to her face that set her off balance, which was quickly followed up. Devin took her to the ground as she attempted to guard herself, but her block got weaker, and his punches felt heavier. It was only a matter of time before it completely failed her. Blow after blow, Kirra soon felt her own fists in her guard start to hammer her own head before her arms fell away. A couple more hits, and she felt her head bounce off the black marble tile of the training pad.

The assault from Devin stopped, and she could feel something damp at the back of her head wetting her hair. She only closed her eyes for what felt like a moment before she opened them to find Zeke crouched next to her, whispering, "There is more to this war than simple insults and jealousy over abilities."

Everything went black, her body getting cold as she couldn't keep her eyes open. The first thing she remembered was something vibrating right on her chest. Something warm, fluffy, and large was sitting on top of her as it vibrated. Just as she started to come around, the feeling of something soft tapping her nose gently brought her around.

Kirra came around to that same void that she had found herself in the night she met her spirit face to face and hatched. She looked down to see what was on top of her. A very large tawny cat that looked to be more fur than body, was laying atop her chest contently. Sheer confusion came over Kirra as she watched the cat tilt its head and regard her with what appeared to be relief.

The real surprise came when the cat spoke without moving its mouth, "*I thought you were going to die there for a few moments.*" The feminine voice appeared to have come from the cat itself as its eyes flicked over Kirra's face making her look around with confusion.

The familiar sound of large feet softly thumping behind Kirra caused her to look behind her as she saw her dragon spirit walk up before laying down with its head on its feet. With a soft huff, his voice was filled with awe, "As I live and breathe, Cerinos..."

Confusion filled Kirra as she attempted to figure out what was going on. The thought crossed her head that perhaps she was dead before the serene voice called out with mild amusement, "*No dear child, you are very alive. This is how we gods commune with our children. This is the between. Limbo as we refer to it commonly.*" The cat looked over her with some soft concern, "*You did crack your head quite hard. I was certain you might be passing from this world before you even found out.*"

As Kirra's ability to think started to come back to her slowly, she began connecting the dots. Cerinos, the god of light, healing, guidance, and a slew of other things. It was one of two major gods that were commonly worshipped amongst spiritosk.

Kirra's spirit spoke out in awe of the cat, "Have you come to save her or heal her?"

An amused laugh came from the serene voice before she answered, "*Neither, mighty dragon spirit. What happens to her, happens to her. I am not permitted to interfere in the world of mortals...*" Her golden eyes sparkled with mischief as she cheekily said the last bit, *"...not at least directly."*

Still trying to figure everything out and overcome what was happening, Kirra asked finally, "I thought Cerinos was a Lion."

An annoyed sigh escaped the cat, *"Mortals do seem to always get the lore wrong, don't they? You see a glorious golden cat and think it would look better as a lion with a glorious mane."*

That one question finally entered her mind. Why was Cerinos there to see her? An intoxicating laugh came from the cat, *"You haven't figured it out yet?"* The cat leaned in and let out a laugh, *"You, my child, are more special than you could ever possibly know..."*

Cerinos reached up with one massive paw and brought it down upon her face, causing her to blink. The moment that her eyes opened, Kirra felt that same pressure on her chest, but everything hurt. Next to her bed was Black Dragon who was sitting with his head resting on his hands, lightly bouncing one leg. She could hear the voices of idle conversation in the background and the pacing of worried feet.

It felt like daggers were in her throat as Kirra hoarsely managed out, "It feels like a feels like a fat cat was sitting on my chest." BD's head shot up immediately as his golden eyes looked at her like it was some miracle, "I knew you were trying to kill me." A soft laugh came from her causing her to wince in the pain that shot through her chest.

The sound of several feet rushing or limping towards her bed was heard as BD quickly acted raising a cup to her lips. She trusted the man far more than she let on so she didn't second guess the liquid. It tasted foul and bitter. Kirra didn't like tea, but she would have drunk tea over whatever this was. On the other hand, a warm fuzzy sensation started to flow through her.

The feeling of her face being swollen like a peach wasn't as terrible. Her ribs and sides didn't feel like knives were stabbing her repeatedly. Then she remembered that BD was the survival trainer. He probably had a natural remedy for anything that he could find anywhere. She nodded her head to BD in thanks for the pain relief.

After a brief look over, BD helped her to sit up since she was getting antsy. Despite it hurting for her to do so, she propped up against the back wall of the cabin and saw that everyone was in finally. Death had a swollen jaw and bruising over his face in general. Nicki looked like she was completely bruised and was nursing one of her arms. Life had a bandage on the side of his head, which wasn't all that bad considering everything. Ky was nowhere to be found though.

After seeing the state of everyone, she finally asked in a slightly less hoarse voice, "Where's Ky?"

Everyone seemed unwilling to answer before Black Dragon finally voiced, "He's resting..." He pointed to a corner of the cabin before continuing, "You two seemed to get the worst of the punishment handed out. For that I am sorry."

Following BD's gaze, her lips parted in a soft sigh of surprise at the sight that lay in Ky's bed. The sound of wheezy and ragged breathing reached her ears causing a lump in her throat. Even with her face feeling like it was swollen and disfigured from bruising and punches, at least she could breathe, and she was at least awake.

With a soft tone, Black Dragon explained, "Between Life and Death abusing a loophole, the stagnant speed at which people were progressing, and the lack of movement in the list, Zeke brought his son in to mix things up and promote change. I should not have instructed you not to challenge anyone. That is my fault."

For once, Kirra spoke up and said, "Yeah, it was." BD looked at her as she had to take a breath, "But I was the idiot that decided to train instead, and that's on me."

Her dragon spirit rumbled in approval, "*Admitting one's mistakes is a step in the correct direction.*"

Kirra groaned internally, "*My head hurts. Would you please just shut up right now?*" The only response was a growl from her spirit before she addressed BD, "How did he get every one of us?"

After giving her a questioning look, he explained, "Devin was placed at the bottom of the list. I suppose he was going to challenge you, but you weren't there. Instead, he challenged Life. Death spoke out in defense of Life, so Zeke proposed the twins fight him together. They accepted but didn't account for Devin knowing Kidori..." The two sheepishly looked away at his words before BD continued, "After that, it was a free-for-all for the rest of whoever Devin wanted to challenge. Eventually he jumped to Nicki and beat her. In between Devin doing challenges, others caught on to what was happening and started issuing challenges to those already injured like Nicki and Death. It was only a matter of time before Devin reached Ky..."

The group collectively looked to where Ky was wheezing in his sleeping state as Black Dragon spoke, "After Devin defeated Ky, with him being injured, one by one, others started challenging him until he couldn't get back up." He blew out a breath, "I was beginning to think that no one would unseat him from his throne at the top of the list until today happened."

Death beat Kirra to the punch as he asked, "How long has Ky been at the top?"

It seemed as though Black Dragon was considering the question before he answered with a long breath, "A while. Ky is one of the first. He's been here the longest out of all of you, almost since the camp's creation. This has been going on for a little over two years. He's been through a lot..." As the news from Black Dragon reached their ears, the entire group went ghostly white. The thought of having to do this for a couple of years day in, day out.

The door to their cabin creaked open causing the group to look collectively. In the doorway stood Miss Chetski, scanning her environment with those large bat ears before she commented, "I heard what happened. I'm aiding those in my own cabin that fell prey as well."

Rising from his seat next to Kirra, BD stood up and turned to address the blind bat, "How bad off are they?"

"A few of them are very injured. Nothing they can't overcome, but, it will keep most of them from training for a while. I understand that the ones that were directly targeted were being punished? Tell me, what spurned on this sudden punishment when things have gone unattended for months on end?"

Miss Chetski walked forward, stopping short of Kirra's bed and approaching Black Dragon. The two started to converse rapidly in a language that Kirra was unfamiliar with. Even as the pair conversed in that strange language, the others present remained quiet. Finally, the two stopped speaking leaving a deafening silence to take over the cabin. Staring at the ground and rubbing his chin, Black Dragon seemed to be thinking long and hard. After what felt like an eternity, he finally spoke up, "Bring those of your cabin that are injured here, and I'll explain everything."

A snort came from Miss Chetski, "What could you possibl—"

"Bring them here, and I will aid them." Miss Chetski's face contorted into one of discontent causing BD to continue, "Or would you rather them stand no chance and have to face something in the trials while still nursing injuries." A sour look came over her before turning and leaving the cabin. Once she had left, Black Dragon turned addressing Death, "Death, I know you are hurting, but sneak into the Dining Hall and retrieve a few cups. Just grab a stack if you can."

Already grumbling, Death started to head out of the room grabbing a small black bag while complaining, "Why do I gotta do the borin' task? Break into the Dining room and grab some cups. Pick the lock Death. Why can't it ever be sneak into one of the cabins and stick snakes in people's beds?" Nicki had to cover her mouth in an attempt to hide her giggles.

"I'll teach you something cool if you manage to get back here in 5 minutes." An instant shift occurred in Death's demeanor at BD's words. Perking up, Death bolted out the door, causing everyone in the room to laugh.

Once the quiet of the room returned, Kirra found herself pondering a question that she was itching to get answered, "What is Kidori?"

Confusion filled the faces of everyone in the room save for BD, who offered the answer freely, "I keep forgetting your parents didn't teach you much about the real multiverse. In a way, it's an advanced form of martial arts. It's more about controlling the energy in your body and using it as a weapon. It's more easily explained with a demonstration..." Holding up a finger, he moved away from the others and found a lit candle.

As BD made his way back with the candle, he poured some of the wax onto the top of the far corner of Kirra's bed. Sticking the candle to the top of the post, he stepped back and held his hand out like a knife. A faint outline of dark energy encompassed his hand taking the shape of a knife around his hand like a fine blade. Sweeping his hand towards the candle, the top of it fell off in a nice even line like it had been sliced in two.

That dark coalescing energy just dissipated from his hand as he let out a breath, explaining, "You concentrate and focus your energy in your body to take physical form. Most use it to surround their fists and feet in combat, but taking a shape takes concentration and a lot of practice. Mastering it is a difficult feat. Even though I can form a blade I am barely considered an expert." He sucked in a breath and let it out, "I've also heard that one master cut a mountain in half."

The door to the cabin suddenly flew open, banging against a wall as Death proclaimed loudly, "Alright, how fast was I? And don't lie."

Black Dragon looked down at his arm as a timer came up which he stopped, "It's a wonder what you get done when you're properly motivated." Death still looked at him for a time as the only response he got was, "You beat the time limit."

"Oh come on!" Death complained and clearly wasn't going to get an answer. Despite his sulking, he still brought the cups over while BD moved the small nightstand from beside Kirra's bed and started setting out the cups from Death. Kirra was curious about what BD was up to exactly but learned that her patience would eventually pay off.

As the rest of the group settled down watching BD set things up, Kirra was left to her own thoughts. The dream she had before she woke came into her thoughts. Maybe it was just that. A dream.

A rolling rumble entered her head as her spirit said, "*It was real.*"

"*How do you know?*"

An irritated huff came, "*A visit from a god is considered an honor. Why they visited a loathsome brat like you? One can only wonder.*" Kirra let out an internal huff of disbelief. Her spirit was no help as usual, leaving her to sit in silent contemplation. Cerinos had said she was special. Perhaps there was a chance she was actually **the** Prophecy that everyone was looking for. It would make sense to some degree as to why she was a different color and beast type from her parents.

A scoff came from her spirit, "*I highly doubt you would be chosen for such.*"

"*My parents died protecting me. Maybe they were protecting the secret of who and what I was?*"

For a moment, her spirit remained quiet *before his response came, "It is a possibility but a stretch nonetheless. Whatever the reason, they still remain dead. Special purpose or not. Everyone who has someone close to them die wants to feel that they died for a reason or accomplished something in their life. Oftentimes, this is not the case. Do not dwell on their deaths, live in memory of them instead.*"

"*Easy for you to say.*" The only reasonable response she could come up with besides, 'whatever'. Thankfully, Kirra didn't have to pretend to ignore her spirit for much longer as Miss Chetski finally returned with her group. None of the faces from the cabin were ones she was familiar with.

BD didn't waste a second as he stared down the teens, "What I am about to do is for emergencies only. You are not to tell anyone I did this." After he spoke, he looked around the room to make sure everyone understood. No one expected what happened next.

Pulling a knife from his belt, he quickly sliced from the inside of his elbow to the wrist of his left arm. The cut was deep, but even then, he barely winced at the pain he inflicted on himself. Acting quickly, he held the sliced arm over the lined-up cups from earlier, and he started to fill them all with a small amount of blood from his wound. Once the cups were partially filled, he tipped his arm back gripping his arm tightly. Grabbing some bandages nearby, he wiped his arm before showing the pink flesh of a forming scar. It was as though his arm had healed in the span of a few weeks in mere moments.

Grabbing the cups, he started handing them out stating, "You all are going to drink this and keep your mouths shut. This never happened."

Several of the teens took the cups reluctantly while others held them at arm's length as though concerned about something happening. At the hesitancy of the teens who already had cups, he turned towards them saying, "You're supposed to drink it." Kirra was handed one from him as she looked at it and questioned it as well. She wondered if he was a vampire, had a disease, or had other malicious intent from him.

Just as the thought crossed her head, her spirit answered, "*It is safe. Drink it.*"

"*If he is a vampire won't it do something to me?*"

The next answer came almost tiredly, "*Are you going to continue to question me on everything?*" She didn't answer causing a deep sigh, "*He is a regenerative. It will speed up your healing. It will sap you of energy while speeding the healing up, but it will not be dangerous.*"

As others were still looking disgusted at the idea of drinking blood, Kirra saw Death raise his and tip it back like it was a shot glass. Letting out a sigh, Kirra followed suit as she raised the cup to her lips and drained it as quickly as possible. A few of the other teens looked at them as though they were crazy; BD just smiled as he passed through the group, letting out a chuckle.

A sharp pain started to run through Kirra, causing her to hold her breath as it felt like her ribs were shifting. The sound of cracking could be heard causing Kirra to groan out in pain. At the other end of the room, BD paused watching as Kirra arched in pain like her bones were shifting on their own. Eventually, the shifting stopped, causing her to lean back against the wall and sigh out deeply.

Kirra's face filled with surprise at the realization, the same one that her spirit came to with a chuckle, "*Yes you can breathe deeply. Your body responded differently. Usually, only someone with blood magic can make your blood and body react like that. Interesting that your body used it the second it entered you.*"

Once her twisting and writhing in place had stopped, BD turned back to Ky and began taking care of him. Kirra almost instantly began testing the movements of her body. Her ribs still hurt, but it felt more like they had been bruised than broken. She was uncomfortable, but not like she had been earlier. Looking towards Death, she'd find that his healing was going much more slowly than what happened with Kirra. The only difference in him was his face looked as though the swelling had gone down.

As the others noticed the change in Kirra and Death, they began tipping their cups back and drinking from them. Cuts started to close and look mildly better, bruises began to change color slightly, and swelling of faces and cuts began to go down. All of the healing done was marginal, but still an improvement as the teens began to heal.

Kirra was the only one who seemed to be massively affected by the blood.

A yell from the corner of the room drew the attention of everyone as Ky took a few swings in the air. With a steady hand from BD holding him in place, Ky slowly calmed. His breathing was noticeably better than the wheezing noises they had heard coming from him earlier. With a few soft words, BD helped the hurting Ky to sit up in the bed so he could relax back. He looked as though he'd been trampled close to death.

BD motioned to the rest of the others in the cabin to gather around, causing Kirra to follow suit and lean against one of the walls, wondering what this was about. When everyone was gathered, BD finally explained, "During an excursion, a small outfit of mercenaries working for Bat Colony came across a Dragon Colony Councilor. They captured him and brought him back here for interrogation and leverage. Several attempts were made to rescue him resulting in failures by all..." He let out a long sigh, "...Until last night."

"That's impossible. The security system here is practically un-im-penetrable." Miss Chetski blurted out.

"Not without blowing a huge hole in a wall or ceiling and fighting past several thousand trained soldiers, elite teams, and assassination squads. Yes... I thought so as well. There are ways to sneak into Bat Colony with its citizens for events at the Coliseum, but getting out without being detected is a whole other story." Raising his left arm, something raised from the top of it and projected a holo onto the wall right next to Kirra as he explained the layout of the cave and the reasons why it was so difficult to get out without raising too much suspicion.

"Wait, this is the Cave of the Fallen." BD looked towards Kirra as she spoke up about the cave and continued, "So that means the actual original entrance of the cave is marked with magic from angels, and it..."

"It breaks enchanted disguises when you enter the cave. This still stands. The impressive part about this particular break-in, is that it didn't happen by a portal or power that anyone has ever seen before. It happened from directly within the cave." He hit a few buttons on the keyboard above his arm causing a video to start playing from the holo screen.

The video showed an entrance to a building and a small amount of clearing as well as fighting going on in the distance. Suddenly, a girl appeared as though stepping through an invisible doorway. She looked confused, disoriented, and even scared as she frantically looked around. Flinching, the girl ran to the building the video was being taken from as she was seen going inside. The video continued, following her inside the building as she ducked in for safety.

Slamming the door behind her, something massive in the darkness of the large building caused her to become startled. The head of a massive white dragon lifted partially until it jolted to a halt. The creature could barely move, but it startled the girl. Something was strange about the girl as her image seemed to flutter and shift. It was as though she weren't truly there.

The dragon seemed to be saying something to the girl, but the girl looked hesitant. Looking from one direction to the next. They conversed before the girl moved towards the bound and chained dragon. The moment her hands touched the chains, they fell off causing the dragon to lift its head as it addressed her.

The video skipped to her riding on the dragon as it flew upwards toward one of the shielded holes in the cave ceiling. As they flew closer and closer, white swirling marks coalesced and spiraled towards the dragon's mouth. A ball of pure white energy formed in the mouth of the dragon before it shot a beam of light at the barrier. The barrier flickered and dispersed temporarily allowing them to slip through and escape before the barrier came back. They had escaped with only moments to spare before the barrier snapped back into place.

"In the name of Cerinos..." was uttered by a few kids, "That's magic..." and "Maybe she's the Prophecy..." a few others muttered.

"If she is the Prophecy why are we all still here?" Confusion and worry were etched into her face as Kirra asked the question. Her spirit was right about her wanting her parents to have died for a purpose. A satisfied huff from her spirit even followed the thought.

Black Dragon waited for them to quiet down as he explained, "There's no sign of magic use on the video. There's no trace of how she managed to teleport inside. Many people have analyzed the video and discovered this is something entirely different."

Several arguments began from the teens present. Part of the group was saying the girl was the Prophecy. The other part of the group was arguing against the girl not being the Prophecy. The arguments continued as Black Dragon explained the footage to Miss Chetski. The pair let it go on for a while, but BD and Miss Chetski eventually broke it up. The members of the other cabin left leaving only the members of Kirra's cabin behind to discuss things.

As the others talked about the video, Kirra returned to her bed. Her mind whirled with thoughts about everything that happened including her dream. Cerinos had appeared before her claiming Kirra was special, but there sat evidence of another girl about her age doing what looked like magic despite what BD said. Perhaps the Trickster god Trivitus was playing a prank on her. Part of her thought long and hard about all parts of the matter as she considered her parents' actions and reactions to everything. It was a lot to consider over the years of her growing up and the recent actions leading up to their deaths. With a sigh, she curled her legs close and ran her clawed hands over her face. She was tired of trying to work through the puzzle of her parents' deaths.

"You're being quiet. What's wrong?" Death's voice came from nearby causing her to jump at the sound.

After a few moments of calming down, she answered softly, "I just don't know what to make of this..." At the back of her mind, there was still that haunting glimpse of the supposed god cat sitting on her chest and speaking to her.

The spirit rumbled her thoughts at her deeply, "*You're afraid you might not be special after all...*"

Kirra groaned, tired of her spirit's harsh criticism, "Shut up..." Death looked confused and wondered where the hostility was suddenly coming from.

The spirit's deep voice rumbled, "*It's true, and you know it. Not admitting it chang—*"

"**Shut up**." Kirra's louder command was starting to garner the attention of the other cabin mates there.

"Kirra?" BD started to approach with concern on his features.

Her spirit's voice echoed her deepest fear, "*You're afraid that your parents died for nothin—*"

Kirra screamed out with a half growl, "**SHUT UP!**" The cabin became deadly silent around her, causing her to apologize to the others, "Sorry, my spirit is being annoying and won't leave me alone."

The spirit growled vehemently, "*You wish to be alone, then so be it...*"

A sudden cold rushed through Kirra, extending from her left hand to the rest of her body. It felt like a piece of her was just torn away. That wasn't the only problem. Her horns, clawed hands, and anthropomorphic feet just shrunk and became as she used to be. Her ears rang as the gravity of what had just happened sunk in.

The feeling of hands tightly gripping her shoulders and lightly shaking her brought her somewhat back to the present. BD was gripping her shoulders tightly and speaking, but with her ears ringing, she couldn't hear him. The sudden tight grip on her jaw as he forced her to meet her gaze broke her out of it as he questioned, "Kirra answer me! Can you still hear or even feel your spirit at all?"

The question confused her as she looked up pale in the face, "What?"

"Try and reach out to your spirit like you normally would. Close your eyes and concentrate hard. There's a chance your spirit moved away instead of fully detaching from you. If that's the case, you can still save your bond with it."

The others in the room were confused about what happened, but Ky watched on with a look of concern as well as BD.

Closing her eyes, she screamed internally, "*Dragon?! Please! Come back! I - I'm sorry. I didn't mean it okay. Just, a lot is going on at the moment.*"

The voice in her head sounded like someone shouting from the other side of a canyon, "*You wanted to be alone, so now, YOU ARE!*"

Frantically, Kirra began to explain, "I-I can hear him, but he's distant. He sounds like he's far away. L-like he'll be gone for good."

A sigh of relief went through BD before he rubbed her arms stating very clearly, "You could lose your spirit forever if you continue what you're doing. You need to be careful in the future with what you say and do **towards** your spirit..." The sound of an alarm started going off from his arm causing him to release Kirra, "I need to go. I've got work to do. For now, training with me is halted, though I encourage you to train on your own and work on your technique."

Turning to eye everyone very carefully, he spoke loudly enough so everyone could hear him, "From here on, all of you will have to take challenges seriously. Death, get out of the red. Life, concentrate on your evasive skills, use them to tire your opponent out, and then strike. Nicki, keep the boys in line and the men scared." A few of the teens laughed, "Look out for them, and help Kirra." Ky bowed his head from where he sat.

As he stepped out, everyone started to return to their beds after all the excitement. Kirra was too wound up to sleep, but she tried to force herself to get rest either way. Maybe the coming days would get better, or perhaps it would be a one-off. Kirra and the others could only hope and pray that would be the case.

II

THE PLANESWALKER

Girlish laughter haunted Kirra. Giggling echoed through the darkness of her dream as it tickled her ears. Before her, appeared a haunting image. A girl glowing in a light golden aura stood next to Kirra's dragon spirit. Reaching forward, the girl rubbed the head of Kirra's spirit before it slowly disappeared and became one with her. Kirra woke up with a scream and punched out at the air.

"Save that for later, you might need it." Ky had caught the punch from Kirra, which surprised her a bit. It was the first time Kirra had seen him out of bed since the night of those dreadful challenges. She'd been bringing meals to him before training, spending free time with him, and keeping him company. Despite Ky being bedridden, he helped her perfect her form, challenged her, and gave her exercises to help strengthen her body.

As the pair started to head toward the Dining Hall for breakfast, Kirra couldn't help but ask, "Why are you so chipper? I mean, this is the first day you're back up on your feet despite still being bruised. You're at the bottom of the list, and you have to work your way back up."

"Oh, I'm not at the bottom of the list..." He gave her a light elbow in the side, laughing, "When you're at the top, there's only one way to go. But when you're at the bottom, you can only go up."

Kirra didn't understand where his enthusiasm came from. She was starting to notice it as they had been spending a lot of time together, given the circumstances. The two had become fast friends and bonded quickly, given that it seemed Ky had gone through the familiar issue that Kirra was dealing with.

With Ky able to walk again, he began helping her with her offense. It had been time for her to pick up the pace in training, and she was more than ready for it. Every day, the pair worked on her endurance, running before the day started, doing strength exercises, and after the day was done, they worked on techniques. Kirra was getting better, faster, stronger, and more equipped for the fights ahead.

She had set aside her anger over everything and started concentrating on learning. Kirra put aside her knowledge of the old wars and the days of heroes. Her personal opinions no longer mattered, just her survival. She learned the hard way that this world wasn't like the humans back on Earth. Spiritosk were a headstrong people, especially dragons. You needed to be able to back up your words not only with intelligence but also strength or cunning.

Once breakfast was over, the pair raced over to the training pad. It was a new habit Kirra had picked up since she'd started getting better at fighting. Despite the injuries to Ky, he was still faster than Kirra and beat her to the pad every time. Running up next to him, she lightly punched his shoulder with a smile before she lined up next to him. The sound of a soft curse came from Death as he joined the group, lining up behind them.

As others finished joining the line, the sound of feet walking between the lines set Kirra on edge. The familiar sound of a stick lightly tapping on the ground every occasional step meant that Miss Chetski was on the prowl. Eventually, the steps stopped near Kirra, causing the hairs on the back of her neck to rise. The sense of something coming at her caused her hand to fly out as it caught the cane. Looking surprised, she looked over her shoulder towards Miss Chetski, who motioned for her to move to the side of the pad against a wall.

Following the instructions, Kirra moved to the wall, jumping off of the raised pad, as Miss Chetski made her way through the entire group there. It took some time, but so far, three of their group had made it. Kirra, Ky, and Nicki. A couple of others whose names she didn't know, joined them as well. This included the red drake that seemed to have it out for Kirra. She was certain it was because she was a celestial dragon.

Once all the students had been sorted through, Miss Chetski stepped off of the pad as a familiar face stepped into view out of the shadows. Zeke had moved up beside Miss Chetski. For a moment, the sight of him caused anger to bubble to the surface in Kirra before she closed her eyes and took a deep breath. She wouldn't win any fights against him anytime soon.

At her calming breath, Kirra heard a familiar welcoming rumble in her head, *"So you **are** learning..."* The sound of her spirit echoing in the distance of her mind was something she hadn't heard in a while, and her action at calming herself had clearly caused him to come closer to her.

Zeke started to type on a holo pad on top of the pedestal, causing Ky to suck in a breath. Kirra turned to eye him momentarily, realizing he knew something was up. She didn't have to wait long to find out as the entire training pad started to shift and move, forming what appeared to be the beginnings of an obstacle course. Once one length of the course was up, Miss Chetski called out, "Each of you five will run through the course at least once. You can run it as many times as you wish or until you get injured. It's just a matter of who is going first."

The red drake beat Kirra to the punch, "I'll go first. It'll save the wimps some face after missing the last challenges..." Kirra and Ky had been too injured to participate in the last set of challenges.

Despite his words causing a large portion of the teens to laugh, Ky seemed unconcerned. Death and Life stayed quiet, though Death had a smirk plastered on his face as though he was privy to some information the drake wasn't. Zeke even showed a slight displeasure at the words spoken by way of a small frown on his lips.

The drake looked at Kirra momentarily before letting his body shift to its normal form. Soon, the drake parts gave way to a stocky teenager with red spiked hair with a cocky smile. Suddenly turning, he cocked a fist back, feigning a punch right at Kirra's face. Many saw the lack of a twitch and flinch, causing several people to let out snickers as he drew back to move towards the platform.

As he stepped onto the platform, Miss Chetski's voice called, "Roc. The name of the game is to not fall off the platform. If you fall you start from the beginning. Mind the blades, they are **very** real."

"What happens if I fall?" Roc looked towards the course, thinking it would be easy.

Zeke stepped forward, merely saying, "If you fall, everyone has a good laugh at you. Karma, perhaps?" His face had a small smirk, causing Roc to glance back at Kirra, who just smirked at him.

Tapping the panel once, Zeke stepped back, and the whole course started to come to life. The first part was three large logs swinging back and forth across a narrow board that connected a second platform. The next obstacle was three clubs spinning in place, all in the same direction at varying heights. The final was the same as the second. Instead of clubs, blades spun at a faster speed than those of the clubs before it. The last obstacle seemed the most daunting task.

Roc seemed to be figuring out the timing of the logs and when to go. Rocking back and forth on the platform, he finally jumped. He timed his jump wrong. As he landed on the ground with a loud smack, the teens looking on winced, sucked in breath, or even laughed at the fail.

As he gasped for air and struggled to his feet, Miss Chetski asked flatly, "Do you concede to the device?"

Still recovering from the wind being knocked from him, he merely shook his head as he stumbled toward the starting platform. After taking a few moments to get his breathing back under control, he gave the obstacle another run. He made it to the second pillar only to fall again. It caused several more teens to laugh this time. Several times, this happened as he attempted the course, getting further along with every try.

Finally, Roc made it to the third and most challenging obstacle. As he looked over the spinning blades, he paused and attempted to figure out how to tackle this obstacle. The top of the next platform was much higher and farther than the last two platforms, begging the question of how to do it.

Several students started jeering at Roc, causing Zeke to call out, "Sometime this lifetime, Roc, or give up." Those words seemed to encourage him to move as he made a dash for the safety of the platform. Roc dodged the first blade pillar successfully as he rolled. When he rose from the roll, the blade of the second pillar caught his face making him cry out. He fell to the ground off of the course, holding the side of his face to stem the blood flow. The blade caught the corner of his mouth, slicing open part of his cheek.

A disappointed sigh escaped Zeke as medics ran to assist and treat Roc, "Who's going next?" Zeke was straight to business. He looked to the group that still had yet to do the course while the medics pulled Roc to the side and began treating his wound.

As Kirra looked towards the others, she found Ky shaking his head. Nicki was looking unsure, and the other boy, whose name she didn't know, didn't seem too sure about proceeding either. Letting out a long breath, Kirra decided to step forward as she moved towards the course. Normally, she never volunteered for anything because she was still learning. It earned her more than a few looks, as no one seemed to expect it, least of all from her.

"First time for everything, it seems." Miss Chetski's comment wasn't necessary, but she noticed Zeke tilting his head curiously as he watched her step up.

Watching Roc had been a blessing in disguise. She had learned where he had failed in the first section most of all. Stepping forward, she took her time between each swinging log. Patience was the key. The first part was the easiest, but the path was narrow, making it seem more daunting than it actually was. Once she stepped on the next platform, a few people applauded her as she looked over the next obstacle. Kirra was thankful BD had been putting her through the works with dodging and blocking because she would not have been ready to do this obstacle had he not. She recalled the amount of time he spent working on her rolling dives, dodging, and recovery. Since the path was a bit wider on this part of the course, Kirra knew the diving roll would be the best idea. Lowering her body, she rolled under the first, straightened, and jumped over the second and third as she dove and rolled to her feet on the next platform. She heard both jeers and cheers from the teen audience as she looked toward the hardest challenge yet.

Hesitating as she looked at the spinning blades, she watched them all very carefully and realized there was no safe path through the blades. It caused her to look over the course more carefully, which allowed her to spot the way through. Looking at the tops of the pillars, she noticed all of them were stationary compared to the spinning blades attached to the pillars.

She had her path through the blades, but she wondered how to end it. The platform sat much higher, just past a single horizontal bar hanging from rungs at the very end of the course. The bar wasn't attached to the rest of the course but resting on a set of rungs. The rungs ran parallel in sets between two poles, making her realize she was going to have to use the bar to jump up to each set of rungs to reach the top. She could see why Roc had paused, as he probably didn't see the path through the blades to the bar in the first place.

As people began to jeer at her, she took a few breaths and rubbed her hands together, hoping that she didn't fall. Taking a running leap, she jumped towards the top of the first pillar and kept her momentum going from one to the next until she jumped towards the bar. Catching it, she swung until she was hanging off of the bar and realized she lost momentum. Swinging her legs, she built up momentum and used it to help her climb up with the bar she was holding on. She moved from one slot to the next and made her way up the ladder.

The last one was the hardest, as she let out a cry and struggled to get the very last rungs. Kirra slipped twice before finally making it up and swung, jumping to the next platform. Several people cheered for her as she rubbed her hands, feeling the blisters start to form as she thought she had finished the course. Her face dropped as she saw another section start to rise out of the ground making her hang her head, "You've got to be kidding me."

Walls that were slanted slightly lay before her on both her right and left. They were conveniently spaced apart, so she couldn't go across on one side but instead had to jump from one side to the other to make her way across. As she approached the platform's edge, she checked over the side to see how high she was from the ground. It would hurt quite a bit if she fell from that height.

With a long breath, she knew this obstacle was clear-cut and just went for it, sprinting across the platform. Leaping to the first, she gripped the top of the wall and directed her body towards the next, finding it was easier than she had thought. Her hands were killing her, and her feet slipped, causing her to almost fall, but she still managed to make it to the very last wall. She jumped to the next platform, feeling her feet slip on the wall.

Reaching out desperately as she fell, her hands gripped the edge of the platform as she was left to dangle up above the ground. Looking up, she cried out with the effort she used to pull her body up high enough before she swung a leg over and pulled the rest of herself up. Once she was up far enough, she rolled onto her back, letting out a laugh of victory.

Laying on her back, Kirra took a moment to catch her breath. Her hands were already starting to become raw from not being used to gripping like she had been. With a groan, she forced herself to her feet and walked forward, looking at the next obstacle that lay before her.

Two rows of white tiles went straight toward the next platform. There was no indication of what she needed to do and she wasn't sure how she was supposed to continue. Kirra stepped back from the edge as her audience watched in complete silence. A familiar rumble rolled through her as she felt one icy blue eye watching her carefully. Running at full speed, she tried sprinting through rows of tiles.

The second tile she stepped on fell out from under her as well as the one she attempted to grab onto, making her flail helplessly. That was it. She was going to die from a stupid fall. Even though her training kicked in, it wouldn't do her any good from this height. As her back hit the ground, her head rebounded and cracked hard against the ground despite her trying to keep it tucked.

The one fortunate thing about being a spiritosk was they, as a people, were physically tougher for the harsh environment. Kirra forgot this fact as she lay on the ground, feeling as though her head was filled with cotton. As she opened her eyes and peered through the fog of her injury, she swore she saw her father standing over her. This caused a great deal of confusion as she watched him lean closer, inspecting her injury. Then her vision cleared as Zeke's face replaced her father's.

Kirra instantly tried to jerk out of his hands, causing him to hold her down tightly but carefully, "Don't move." He almost sounded concerned about her, though she had hit her head very hard. She knew better than to move anyway, given that everything was spinning, and any slight movement made it worse.

From nearby, she heard Roc's familiar voice call out, "You didn't check me over when I fell from the course. She falls once, smacks her head, and you rush over. Must be nice being a Celestial Dragon."

Zeke responded perfectly, "You want me fussing over that paper cut you have on your face?" He turned to address Roc, and the lack of response meant Roc realized he had overstepped, "That's what I thought. She cracked her skull three times in three weeks since being here. A fall like that one can still do some serious damage."

Kirra's head was shifted gently, and she soon realized something soft had been placed under it. It didn't take long for her to realize it was Zeke's own coat as she felt methodical hands run down the back of her neck and part of her back. As she watched him work over her carefully, he pulled back with a soft look on his face with a sigh. Was that a sigh of relief? Kirra couldn't believe he was relieved as he looked down at her before a smirk came across his face.

Zeke's next words came out softly, "You tucked your head at the last minute, but the momentum caused you to crack your head slightly. Just a mild concussion, luckily enough." Falling back into a sit with a groan next to her, he commented with a smirk, "Made it rather far for your first time too. Relax a moment and catch your breath." He turned towards the remaining three on the wall, asking loudly, "Who's next?"

It was Nicki who stepped up to the course. She was tall and clumsy. She was more fighter than agility, which showed heavily as she began. Fail after fail, a club to the face was what made her throw in the towel after not even making it past the second obstacle.

The other boy, Skink, went next. He was extremely agile and made it to the ladder bar but could only get halfway up. Unable to keep his grip, he slipped and fell to the ground. Skink had rolled when his feet hit the ground, resulting in him taking absolutely no damage. Despite the teens jeering at him for giving up after one attempt, he didn't seem to mind and went to sit on a wall where most teens were. Ky made the entire course look far too easy and breezed through it. Making short work of the entire course, he was methodical all the way. Kirra found out that there were only a couple more parts that she could have done easily if she had made it past the part where she failed. It turned out she was supposed to take her time testing the tiles before moving on. As he completed the last obstacle, he slid down a rope and gave a little bow, causing others to clap or groan. Once Ky finished, Miss Chetski started shooing everyone to their next class which meant it was free time for Kirra.

Wanting to get a start on her training again, she started to get up, but a hand kept her down as Zeke chided her, "It's not a good idea for you to move just yet. Just take it easy for a few." Once Kirra had been pressed back down, Zeke removed his hand from her but stared at her with a friendly smile.

She would have none of it, "I'm a big girl. I am perfectly capable of standing up now." This time, there wasn't a hand to stop her from getting up. Instead, she stopped herself as the world started spinning again. Closing her eyes with a groan, she realized he was right.

His sarcasm was almost playful, "Are you certain?" A glare was thrown towards him, causing him to chuckle, "I am not the enemy, Kirra. Nor am I an evil person."

"Tell that to my dead parents..." Zeke leaned forward, putting his arms on his legs as a long sigh left him. A look of sorrow and remorse etched the lines of his face.

Turning towards her, Kirra was surprised to see the empathy as he spoke, "What happened to your parents was unfortunate. I cannot even begin to express how upsetting their loss is." He looked down at the ground before speaking, "You know your parents hid you when you were young..." He looked over to her with a sincere expression, "They were dear friends of mine and were trying to keep you safe. When I found out about your existence there was outrage among other bat spiritosk. An extra mouth to feed, taking food from a people that had too many to feed already. My council wished to exile your family, which I refused. I instead decided to arrange a marriage between Devin and you to secure your place. Shortly after, they left, fleeing from the war, but promised to honor the arrangement when you came of age..."

A long sigh escaped as he continued, "Then I found out that your parents were doing everything in their power to keep Devin and you separated. The icing on top of all their lies, was finding out they were feeding you blockers." Zeke's face was a mask of seriousness as he asked, "Do you know what happens when you keep a spiritosk on blockers past the recommended age if they haven't spirit-bonded?" She shook her head, "It **kills** them." He picked up a stray rock and started rolling it between his fingers, explaining, "I was furious when I heard that my future daughter-in-law was deprived purposefully of the one thing that makes us special. My anger only worsened when I saw how frail and sick you looked."

Kirra was aware that the blockers were the reason behind her spirit not emerging, but not the reason behind her being so frail and weak. Examining one of her arms, she realized that though it had only been about 3 weeks, she had filled out quite a bit and even put on some healthy weight.

"I offered your parents a chance to bring you back willingly to be trained under the protection of Bat Colony without all of this..." He gestured around him, "But they refused to see reason and instead attempted to kill me."

"Why couldn't you just let us be?"

"If not sending Devin to Earth, you would have never known you were on blockers." He leaned towards her, explaining, "Think about it. Your parents were going to get you killed, and we were lucky to have saved you. They were willing to let you die protecting the secret of your spirit."

A tear ran down her face as she looked up at him with pain in her eyes, "B-but... did they have to die?"

This time, when Zeke spoke, his voice was thick with emotion, "I gave them every opportunity for a peaceful resolution. Your mother drew blades on me, willing to die protecting you regardless of any offer I made. She tried to kill me, and your father stood with her. We went so far as to restrain her, but she got free, and I was forced to defend myself."

"Why not just end this stupid war? People fighting each other for no reason..." Her voice trailed off as she couldn't even say out loud what she wanted to.

Zeke sat there quietly before realization hit him, "I think you should see something." Getting up with a groan, he turned towards her and extended a hand to help her up, "Get up slowly. Something tells me your parents kept you very far from the truths of this war and the real reasons behind it."

Kirra gave him a momentary hesitation as she looked towards the outstretched hand, but eventually, she took it. As he helped her to her feet, Zeke carefully watched her to ensure she could stand. She was still a little woozy, but moving didn't instill the need to puke. Taking one last look at her head, he gave her the okay and led her from the training pads toward the wolf pens.

She could feel the eyes of the other teens from the camp on her as she walked with Zeke. It caused her to tense as she looked towards them in passing and noticed them squinting angrily in her direction. Without giving so much a care to the stares or the teacher instructing, Zeke walked over to an already saddled wolf, gripped the reins, and motioned for Kirra to come closer. It felt as though everyone in the class was sneering at her as she moved towards Zeke and the wolf.

Without notice, he gripped her waist, hefted her up into the saddle, and turned to the teacher, explaining, "We'll be back shortly." before they could complain.

Without further explanation, Zeke hopped onto the wolf behind her and wrapped an arm around her tightly. Before Kirra could complain, the wolf took off, forcing her to grip the saddle's horn tightly. Given the size of the ancient wolf, it showed tremendous speed and grace through the forest as it weaved its way through. Looking over her shoulder, The Camp quickly disappeared from view, causing worry to bubble inside of Kirra.

"Don't worry. As long as you have an escort, you'll not get in trouble for leaving the camp perimeter." Zeke had clearly felt her worry.

Soon, they were bounding alongside a cliff that edged a deep valley. As it rose up, Kirra saw exactly how expansive the cave was as Zeke slowed the wolf and gave her a moment to take in the view. In the distance, she could see a large gathering of buildings closely smashed together. Most of the cave was filled with natural forestry, hills and valleys. Along the outskirts of the tight-knit city were mostly farmlands. It made Kirra ask one question regarding the restriction on population, given all the available land. She wasn't expecting the in-depth explanation that she received.

Most of the bat spiritosk were vegetarian or vegan at best because it was more optimal. On top of the fact that most of the trees were either nut or fruit-bearing, they provided a good amount of transfer of carbon dioxide to oxygen. It was a matter of energy consumption versus the ability of the planet to provide for their needs. Bats already had to import some things but were mostly self-reliant given the racism towards their race. They couldn't expand much further since they relied so heavily on the trees around them in the cave. He even compared Earth to Spiritoski and explained that a planet only had so many resources to expend. Humans on Earth were expending them far more quickly than what the planet could provide. The point was further made when he asked if she could smell a difference in the air quality. The answer was a profound yes, something she had noticed the moment she stepped foot on Spiritoski.

As the path began to narrow ahead, Zeke pulled the wolf to a stop as they arrived at their destination. Something flashed before Kirra's eyes, like a memory that wasn't hers. The sound of screaming, yelling, fighting, and the singing of sword-clashing roared in her ears. Spiritosk of all races were fighting against each other. Beings with wings clashed in the air before crashing into the ground, causing the very earth to shake beneath her feet. Before her on the path, a being with white wings stood before a pair of large ornate stone doors. A voice from within, behind the closing doors, begged for forgiveness.

The sound of feet landing on the ground brought her back to reality as she looked at Zeke. He had jumped off the wolf and offered her aid off the massive creature. After helping her off, he started towards the remnants of what appeared to be a cave. Wear and tear over the years must have worn the external doors away. She could picture exactly where they had been and saw evidence of where the doors had been initially. Seeing Zeke enter the cave, she started after him, hesitantly making her way in.

The cave was laden with bits of markings and hieroglyphics in another language. One of the walls had been carved in the image of a wolf with wings, the entire thing painted black and rimmed with gold. At the feet of the wolf sat several bat spiritosk miniature statues either kneeling or bowing to the wolf. At the farthest wall from her, Kirra noticed another set of doors that were completely broken and busted. What was beyond, she couldn't tell. On either side of the busted doors were two wolf statues with feathered wings and ornate crowns adorning their heads.

Already inside, Zeke was lighting the few existing candles as Kirra asked hesitantly, "What is this?"

"A temple. One to hide the greatest lie of all time..." The confusion on her face was clear even in the darkness as he explained, "A long time ago, a war known to us as The Great Fall happened. Not much is known about it other than that angels had turned their backs on the gods, deciding to lash out against them. Even a few Archangels followed as well." white-wingedThe image of the white winged being standing in front of the ornate doors flashed through her mind.

Kirra asked, "What does this have to do with the war between the bats and dragons now?"

Zeke raised a hand, asking for patience, "Because the bats helped the fallen angels fighting the war." Once more, the vision flashed through her mind as she realized that there were sides in the fighting she had seen while Zeke continued, "You see, in this temple, the bats idolized one of the fallen. An archangel who was helping to lead the revolution against the gods. The remains of the angel were placed here. Entombed and hidden away." He walked over to the pedestal and idly pushed over one of the miniature statues of a bat spiritosk with disdain as he explained, "You see, the bats helped the fallen in this war. So the fallen helped them in turn. The angels gave them technology and carved out the citadel, which housed most of the bats. They even molded the landscape so the cave could support bat spiritosk for millennia to come. The fallen created a true home for us and placed an enchanted threshold at the entrance."

Walking to one of the wolf statues, he lightly caressed it before adding, "Our ancestors fought next to the fallen in some of the bloodiest battles that the multiverse has ever seen. Several other spiritosk eventually came around, but the bats and wolves, despite them being split, were the first. Then, the gods blessed the multiverse with the dragon spiritosk. Dragon spiritosk never used to exist, you see. Then the war began. Kin against kin, species against species. Some of those who sided with the angels against the fallen became blessed. They became the first dragon spiritosk to walk the multiverse."

"That can't be true..." Kirra tried to call his bluff, "Dragons have always been around."

Zeke turned to her and approached with a smirk, "Please, prove me wrong. I urge you to do your research. Find any record of dragon spiritosk before The Great Fall." He smiled confidently.

"The library doesn't have anything about stuff like that."

"It's not meant to. But you will not be here forever." He turned towards a wall shrouded in darkness, tapping his arm, which caused a flashlight to pop free. As he shined the light along another wall, it revealed a mural that had been hiding in the shadows.

The mural showed dragons in various states of change, but all of them transforming from other animals, "This is the history they don't want you to know about. Had those people not stepped in, dragon spiritosk would have never existed in the first place. Those brave little idiots stepped forward and changed themselves forever. And thus the Dragon spiritosk were born and with it, the very first Prophecy."

The light shown over the image of something white before she realized what it was exactly. It was of a white elk, but the back half of its body had been changed into what looked like a fluffy-looking breed of dragon of some kind. Kirra started to reach up for the horns on her head but realized they were gone. Letting her hands drop back down, she asked her spirit hesitantly, "*Do you know if anything he is saying is the truth.*" Zeke must have known she was attempting to convene with her spirit as he waited patiently.

For a few moments, she thought he wouldn't respond before she heard that familiar rumble say, "*What he says is truth.*"

Afraid of her spirit leaving, she almost didn't want to ask the question, "*How do you know?*"

"*Do you trust me?*"

A question she often wondered herself, but slowly she realized, "*Yes...*"

"*Then my answer will have to suffice as I can only confirm to you what he is saying is true. I will tell you, I was quite proud of you when you stood your ground against that Roc, and for how you did in the obstacle course."* A soft bit of pride started to bubble inside of her at her spirit's words.

Kirra looked up at Zeke as she finally asked, "What does the current war have to do with the past?"

"I was waiting for you to come around to that." He widened the light to expose the rest of the wall so she could see the rest of the mural, "The bats were on the losing side of this war. So were any other races that are considered dark and evil in nature. Rumors got started, and soon, rumors became myths. Myths that said all bats are evil. Here in Bat Colony, people have jobs, lives, and families. In the multiverse, most do not like bats; they will not buy their goods or their products and are often treated as thieves. The racism goes further than just insults. It tracks back hundreds of thousands of years from this one moment that makes all bats look evil. It's not just bats, either. The wolves have mixed reputations as well. The same can be said with badgers, raccoons, and other small mammals. Any creature that is related to the dark or bad deeds in any way has had their names smeared across the history books."

Kirra eyed the mural that showed the two sides of the war he told her about, and she couldn't believe her eyes. She knew already that bats had been on the war's losing side in The Great Fall, but she didn't know about the rest of the spiritosk races.

"It has spread even to Earth where they did not even have Spiritosk. Black cats are bad luck, black dogs are seen as omens of death, cats are evil and attached with bad magic like sacrifices, rats are disgusting vermin, raccoons are masked bandits, foxes are sly, and snakes have silver tongues and are tricksters...." He listed off human examples, making her back up as he shut the light off on his arm. The candles, being the only lighting, gave an eerie feeling to the cave.

Kirra was quiet for a time before she looked at him with disbelief, "So you're saying that all of this is to change that? I don't get it; you have problems of prejudice, so you decide to change things by killing people?"

"You are young yet. I do not expect you to understand fully, but we have had diplomats get made 'examples' of. Those going to Dragon Colony and dragon allied cities were laughed at and chased out after attempts of diplomacy." Zeke heaved a long breath before continuing, "Trying to be nice gets tiring. You can only try to send the message the right way for so long before you want to make change happen yourself. The only way to do that is by sending a clear message with brute force if need be. Before the start of the war, our people were overpopulated with shortages of food, homes, and energy. Only the wolves wished to trade with our people, but they live long and far away from here. Now that Bat Colony has shown what it can do with its numbers, others from different universes have come seeking trade."

Kirra was quiet for a long time, thinking about everything he was telling her and trying to sift through the information. Her spirit already told her Zeke was speaking the truth, so she couldn't accuse him of lying. The thoughts whirled in her head from their earlier conversations about her parents and what had happened with her case in particular. She looked down at her arm, thinking of what to ask.

She finally came to one last question, "What does any of this have to do with the current Prophecy that everyone is looking for?"

Zeke smiled at her, "I'm glad you asked that." He walked over to the doors that had been busted open, "There is another temple just like this one. It contains something **very** important within it. The other temple, however, is protected with a very powerful barrier spell sealing it away. The only person capable of breaking that seal happens to be the Prophecy. My goal is to find them, help them learn to wield the magic they have control over, and break open the seal. That temple will reveal the lies that dragons have spread for eons."

Kirra was almost hesitant to ask, "What's in that temple that's so important?"

"The body of a powerful fallen angel."

His answer caused her eyes to widen before she slowly asked the next, "What was in this one?"

"Supposedly the soul of a fallen."

Curiosity got the better of Kirra, "What do you need the body for?"

Zeke leaned in, stating simply, "If you stick around long enough, perhaps you might find out." He paused to see if she would respond before continuing, "Mostly, I wish to free the individual that has been trapped inside the temple. They have been there for hundreds of thousands of years. It's time that they're freed."

Before thinking about the question and the consequences they could have, the words came flooding out, "What about the girl that freed the captive dragon? Couldn't she be the Prophecy?"

"Who told you this?" Zeke tilted his head as he moved forward, causing her to backpedal. He pressed her for information, "Where did you find this out, Kirra?"

Kirra began to stumble over her words as she found herself with nowhere to go against a cave wall, "I-I, I shouldn't have said any-thing..."

Just the tips of his fingers grazed the side of her face, slowly making their way up toward her temple in way of a threat. His voice was low and even, "Do not make me force you to tell me, Kirra. You have no idea how unpleasant it is to have someone force their way into your mind and dig around for information."

Her spirit responded quickly, his voice closer than it had been in days, *"Kirra, tell him! If he forces his way in, he'll see you communed with Cerinos and think you're the Prophecy!"*

Zeke loomed closer as she felt the beginnings of static energy pressing at her temple, causing her to scream, "It was Black Dragon!" The second she spoke, the feeling stopped, and she continued with a gasp, "He wanted to show the reason why we were all attacked. Said that it wasn't fair if we didn't know the reason behind the sudden violence towards our groups. So he showed us."

Taking a moment to judge if she was lying or not, Zeke gave her some breathing room, stating, "The attacks were punishment for rule breaks and loopholes. It was going to happen either way, but yes, that event did speed it up."

Closing her eyes, she managed to get her heart and breathing under control as she asked, "Isn't she the Prophecy?" Kirra's spirit rumbled, and she could swear she felt the touch of scales across her cheek and forehead to comfort her.

For a moment, she thought she wouldn't get an answer, but finally, he said, "No."

As she followed him out of the narrow cave, he waited by the wolf as Kirra asked, "What is she then?"

Zeke seemed to consider the question as they exited the cave and he arrived at the wolf. Finally, she got a response as he turned towards her, "To be honest, I am not certain. There were no normal signs of magic use. Everything that was done except for her sudden appearance was purely energy-based. But I suspect it could have been a Soulwalker who accidentally appeared."

"A Soulwalker?" She moved towards the wolf and reached lightly, rubbing its muzzle absent-mindedly.

Lifting her up on the wolf, he got behind her and started directing the wolf back down the path, "It's a person who can travel using their soul. The soul leaves the body behind, making them physically vulnerable. The soul can walk freely, even inhabit others or possess them if they're powerful enough."

Kirra looked over her shoulder, asking, "So are they a people, or a race or something? She looked to be human."

He answered, "It's an ability, an extremely rare one at that. Abilities are never relegated to particular races."

She finally decided to inquire about something she probably didn't want to know the answer to, "Is Black Dragon going to be punished for telling us about the girl?"

There was a bark of laughter, "No... No Black Dragon was curious, as is his nature. What happened would have been found out eventually. He is, however, correct that it spurned my actions since now we have to deal with someone who can evidently sneak in without even actually going through a physical barrier."

Letting out a sigh, she couldn't help but inquire further, "Soooo.... Is Black Dragon his real name?"

"No..." Zeke answered flatly.

"Sooooooo, what is his name?" Kirra asked

He let out a bark of laughter, "I'm not telling you."

Kirra sulked, "Rude."

Zeke let out a loud boisterous laugh, "I don't even know his name myself. Some assassins won't tell people their names outside of their normal work."

"Okay, so here's what I don't get. How is it that everyone knows he's an assassin? He openly admits he's an assassin, yet no one cares. I mean, wouldn't people be trying to kill him or something?" Kirra wondered out loud.

Zeke sucked in a breath as he said, "Being an assassin isn't a blasphemous thing. It's an honorable career field, to a point. It really depends on what guild you work out of, what kind of work you do, and everything in between. I know that one of the guilds has an elaborate application process. You have to do a walkabout through the multiverse and go to certain people or points. It's never the same for any one person. And then after that, there's a series of training, and you are in training for a very long time." He smirked down at her, "Honest question. Would you try to attack and kill someone just based on the fact that they claim to be an assassin?"

"Pfft no. I'm not stupid enough to try and kill someone who is a trained killer." Zeke looked at her like his point had been made, "Right... I see. That makes me feel stupid, given that I literally lost control of my anger and attempted to kill the leader of this Colony." A laugh came from Zeke at her realization.

12

CHALLENGES, WOLVES, AND DRAGONS OH MY!

A fter Zeke had taken Kirra back to the camp, things had gotten weird. People were starting to treat her differently, especially her cabin mates. It seemed the teens at the camp thought she was being given special privileges because of Zeke taking her out on a ride. During meal times, it was hard for her to get a few bites in before someone came and knocked her tray away.

The pranks were in full swing on her. Some days, she'd be tripped during training. Others, her clothing and personal belongings would be flipped and thrown everywhere. Sometimes, she'd get unlucky and have sticky or spikey seeds shoved in her clothes or even bugs stuffed under her sheets. All things that she could handle and was used to from years of previous bullying.

Challenge day finally came, the last one before trials, and Kirra was still in the red. She was currently sitting in the dining hall before anyone had even arrived. Her meal tray was empty, and her face held a blank expression as she folded her hands neatly in her lap. As if on schedule, Roc, her tormentor, finally arrived.

As usual, Roc took his normal path right past her so he could take his opportunity to bully her. This time, he would be left with only the disappointed clatter of an empty tray. Kirra turned and smirked at Roc as she saw the disappointed look on his face.

Still, she sat with her hands on her lap under the table as he leaned towards her menacingly, "You think you're so special now that you've become Zeke's favorite little pet..." The grin on Kirra's face didn't wave. The moment he turned his back, the crunch of an apple being bit into rang through the air, causing Roc to visibly stiffen.

When he turned, Kirra had an apple in one hand and a large chunk she was currently chewing. As he rounded on her, she swallowed the chunk she was chewing and stated confidently, "I think I'll be just fine Roc. It's you I'm concerned about."

Laughter came from her spirit like he was right in her ear, "*The balls on you, girl...*" Her spirit paused, thinking, "*I will make you a deal. You challenge **him**, and I will give you a second chance.*"

"*Deal.*" She wasn't going to pass up the chance to be reunited with her spirit. Roc gripped the front of her shirt like he was about to swing at her before she stated, "I am **not** afraid of you. You're just a kid with a complex who fears I might just be better because I went on a little field trip with Zeke. So now, everyone thinks I'm getting special treatment because of that, and you think you're justified in bullying me because of it." Kirra smiled maliciously at him as he growled in anger, "You've been praised since day one of getting here, but like a jealous child now that Zeke has shown favor to another, you're throwing a tantrum. See, while you haven't moved an inch on the list and have actually been trying to move up, I've been training and getting better." Standing, she looked at him in challenge, "You're scared, I might actually be better when you couldn't even make it through the obstacle course."

"You think you're better than me?" A bark of laughter escaped from Roc, "Those are some big words from a small dragon whose spirit abandoned them."

A malicious snarl formed on her face, "Oh, don't worry, I'll be backing them up with action soon enough." She could feel the intense energy of Roc's spirit pressing towards her and swore she could feel and hear it snapping its jaws. The white dragon of her own spirit stood over her protectively, letting out an aggressive roar as though to say he was backing up her words.

Roc suddenly stepped back with a shocked look. Kirra swore she could see the red outline of what looked like a drake cowering from her own spirit. Looking up at the line of white energy, she could make her spirit out clearly as it barely fit inside of the dining hall. The massive head of her spirit peered down at her with its icy blue gaze before snorting in approval. No one wanted to mess with her after that display. Satisfied with the effect she had, Kirra made a quick exit. Ky attempted to reach out and grab her arm, but she dodged the grab, flashing a glare his way as she continued on her way.

Kirra was still angry at the entire group for writing her off so quickly without asking any questions about what happened. It did, however, make her think that possibly, there was a chance the same thing had happened to Zeke as well given everything they had discussed that one fateful day. All anyone ever saw was just that one side of Zeke. The person responsible for a war that was razing through the entire multiverse. They saw a monster throwing a tantrum and uprooting homes, whereas Kirra now saw a man putting the betterment of his community before the sake of his own reputation. She didn't know who was right or wrong anymore.

As she arrived at the challenge pad, she put all of it at the back of her head and moved to her spot. Knowing she was still worked up from the earlier confrontation, she sat and worked on calming her mind. If she was going to take this seriously, she had to let go of all her anger. As others began to arrive, she stood and stretched her limbs. Kirra could see Ky staring at her as he crossed the pad to his own spot, but still, she said nothing to him.

Out of everyone in her cabin, it was Death who seemed to have an actual death wish. He ignored the glare she was throwing at him and instead walked over to her, leaning down to whisper, "Keep him at a distance and wear him out. Keep low to the ground and use your speed to your advantage. He's stronger than you, but you're faster. Use that to your advantage." He pulled back with a wink, patting her arm before jogging over to his spot next to Ky.

The last to arrive were Zeke and Devin. Devin jogged over to his spot, taking his place as his father moved to the set of risers that sat in front of the lined-up teens. Looking up, Kirra spotted Black Dragon in the risers for the first time in a long while. He seemed to be looking at her intently.

Zeke's voice rang out, drawing Kirra's attention back to him, "Who's first?"

Before anyone could say anything, Kirra chimed, "I challenge Roc!" As Kirra announced this, there were various reactions from the risers filled with teachers. She heard a few cackles, a couple of people voicing interest in that fight, and even some of the teens were cackling at want of seeing the two face off.

Kirra started stepping onto the pad as Zeke asked, "You are certain this is who you wish to challenge?" A thermos was in his hand as he regarded her with a raised eyebrow.

"Yes."

Taking a sip from his thermos, he nodded in approval and waved to the pad, "Take your positions." Roc started moving onto the pad, regarding her with a bit of nervousness from their previous interaction.

Her spirit's voice rumbled through her head, *"I might be able to deter his spirit with my power, but you are still weak compared to him. You are more than likely going to lose. Are you prepared for that?"*

Her voice echoed in answer, *"I'm sick and tired of being bullied. Even if I lose, at least I lost sticking up for myself."* The dragon rumbled back at her, satisfied with the answer she gave. The rumble turned into a growl, causing Kirra to bristle confidently as she saw Roc's nervous gestures.

Watching the pair step onto the pad opposite each other, Zeke took one last sip from his thermos before waving lazily, "Begin..."

Roc came swinging towards Kirra the second the cue was given. The height difference between them meant that he had a slightly longer strike range than she did. But she was fast and had been practicing her defense. Roc was gaining some confidence as he watched her dodge and cockily threw a wild punch. It was sloppy and predictable. Ducking, she let out a couple of quick jabs to his rib and a hook to his face. It caused him to stumble as she sidestepped to gain her balance. There were a couple of surprised laughs from the onlookers as no one expected her to even land a hit.

After the little spurt of attacks, she stepped back out of range following Death's advice and kept her distance. Given Kirra actually landed a hit, the mood had changed from laughing and giggling to everyone suddenly paying apt attention. Even Black Dragon leaned over the railing as he watched her with a smirk on his face.

Roc looked surprised as he wiped a bit of blood from his lip before angrily stating, "You're dead meat..." As he moved towards her, throwing more punches, Kirra dodged and blocked what she could throwing jabs where she could. As he stumbled again, a growl of frustration left him. He turned to see onlookers cheering for her, which did wonders for her confidence.

Kirra was like water, dodging his punches as though it was easy. She was getting overconfident and wound a punch back to go on the offensive for once. The mistake was realized instantly as the bottom of his boot made contact with her chest and sent her sliding backward across the pad. The wind got knocked out of her, causing her to cough and gasp as the sound of laughter hit her ears. Roc turned to those watching and raised his fists in the air, letting out a cry of victory until the crowd got quiet. He turned just in time to see Kirra slowly rising to her feet. She wasn't ready to call it quits yet.

"You lose Kirra. Just surrender..." He attempted to coerce her, but Kirra shook her head as she raised her fists and began approaching. Sighing out, Roc readied himself for her once more. Going on the offensive, she managed a few punches toward him before one powerful one from him sent her sprawling to the ground once more.

This time, Roc remained facing her, waiting to see if she would rise once more. Refusing to quit, yet again, Kirra stumbled to her feet, spitting blood on the pad, before stumbling towards him. Roc wanted her to stop as he called out, almost begging her, "Come on, just give up already." Wiping blood from her mouth she shook her head in response.

Roc was at least being honorable as he waited until her fists were raised. The entirety of the pad got quiet as she moved toward him once more, deciding to play it safe. She was barely standing on her feet and needed to be careful. As soon as he came within range, she dodged a few of his punches, spotting an opening.

Throwing a hook, the arm was quickly grabbed and locked in place as he maneuvered her into a harsh choke hold. As he locked in the hold, she tried to break it but was already weak. As he applied pressure on the hold, she continued to fight even as she felt her vision start to tunnel. Refusing to tap out, she passed out as everything went black.

The first thing she woke to was the familiar deep rumble of her spirit, "*I will say this much for you kid. You have guts. Even if it is matched only by your stupidity. I'll help you to get to where you need to be.*" It took a moment for Kirra to realize she had come back around. The sound of something scraping against metal made her pause as she reached up and felt the familiar white and fuzzy horns atop her head.

Confusion filled her voice as she didn't think she'd earned the right for her spirit to come back to her, "*I lost though…*"

The throaty chuckle came, "*It wasn't about winning or losing. It was about gaining the respect of others and showing you have what it takes.*" Looking around, Kirra realized she was on the bleachers before her spirit drew her attention back, "*Dragons respect strength, and that strength takes many forms. Strength of heart, Strength of Mind, Strength of Will, and so on. You have spades of the three that I mentioned.*"

177

Kirra looked over towards Roc as she considered his words. That was when Roc spotted her looking at him and nodded at her with a smirk on his lips as she concluded, *"It wasn't about you or what happened with Zeke... They thought I was weak and was still being favored."*

Her spirit rumbled softly, *"If you can take that much damage and keep getting up to fight with no spirit, they can only imagine what you'll be capable of with the help of a spirit. You'll be a menace if you could manage that after only a month of training."*

Once Kirra started to feel a bit steadier, she sat up and tested moving around to see if she'd get woozy or sick. Touching her antlers once more to make sure they were still there, she noticed Black Dragon smirking at her as he tipped his head in approval. Sitting up fully on one of the bleachers, she decided it was time she slip back down onto the pad and back to her spot.

On the way past a few people, a few faces that were familiar murmured things like, "Good try," "Nice job," and "Almost got him," and a variety of other encouraging words. The one person who took the cake though was Death, who, as she passed, gave her two thumbs up before slapping her on the back, which almost knocked her off her feet. Gods was he strong for his age.

Taking her spot, Kirra looked at the list, noticing some things had changed. Ky was back in the top ten as he finished his fight with a full knockout. Nicki was in the top ten, but just barely. Death was a long way from the bottom, but it seemed he stuck to right in the middle. Life was barely out of the red, but he was no longer in the bottom five. Then, finally, her name. She was at the very bottom of the list and debating if she wanted to try for a second challenge.

Not wanting to risk an actual injury in testing her luck with a second challenge, she accepted that she was going to a trial with no one she knew. Her stomach was doing flips at the thought as she sat down. Her mind whirled with thoughts of what she would have to do for the trial as she had never done one before. Not realizing everyone had left, she heard a set of feet moving toward her causing her to look up. With a hand outstretched toward her, the unlikely face smiled down at her, taking her by surprise.

"What you did today took some serious guts…" Accepting Roc's offered hand, he helped her up and shook hers before he included, "For a spoiled brat."

Reacting to the insult, Kirra took hold of the arm attached to the hand and suddenly flipped him over her shoulder. It ended with him getting slammed down onto the pad and leaving a small series of cracks under Roc's splayed-out body on the pad. The same ghostly white that she had seen of her spirit earlier overlayed her hands. This time, she noticed they looked like draconic claws before they faded away. Surprised, she looked between her hands and Roc before exclaiming, "Holy crap, I didn't mean to throw you that hard!"

Roc lay on the ground coughing and laughing simultaneously, "No one explained this to you?" As he got up from the ground Kirra answered him with a shake of her head before he explained, "The same thing happened earlier. We're bonding with our spirits. It's gonna happen. Eventually, you get control over how strong you are, but in the beginning, sometimes it just comes out. The other spiritosk are like that as well, but usually, dragons and drakes are adept at pretty much everything." He nodded down to the crater, "You can take harder hits too, which I'm surprised you were able to keep on your feet without your spirit with you earlier." He looked at the list and then toward her, "When you make it back from the trial, we should be sparing partners."

Kirra was confused about why someone bullying her wanted to spar with her now, "Wait, why do you want to spar? Also, I don'—"

"You've got instinct. You'll be fine. All you gotta do is trust it. And... I can learn from you, and you can learn from me. That's all... Nothing more."

Considering his proposal, she finally answered, "Yeah, okay. We can spar if I get through this."

"Not if, When!" He was already jogging off, "Gotta have a winning attitude! Think positive!" Kirra was baffled by the change invoked in him, which made her shake her head.

Since the rest of the day was hers, she decided to go and get some food since she had no idea what to expect for the following day. The moment she plopped down at a table, Death was right next to her, jabbing her with his elbow despite the glare she threw at him. His smile and goofy personality were intoxicating, causing her to let out a few giggles as she elbowed him in return.

Once Kirra seemed to be in a better mood, he questioned the reason why she came back laughing the day she had gone with Zeke. The others started to move near her, and she realized that was the real reason why they were upset over anything else. She made sure to fill them in with the events of what happened. Almost instantly, Death wheeled around and punched Ky in the shoulder, stating, "I told ya ya twat. Shoulda just feckin' asked her 'stead of assuming."

Kirra didn't take anything that happened to heart, and after the group made up, the twins got to work explaining the rules of the trials to her. It was a simple game of cat and mouse mixed in with a few extra tidbits. Five people would be placed in the playground with a monster of some sort. Depending on the difficulty of the monster type they were placed against, they could face just one or many. There were three ways to win: Eliminate the monster, be the last standing, or survive for the allotted time given. The higher the class of monster or beast, the shorter the time required to survive.

"So you're telling me you can knock other people out of the trial to end it?" A concern that Kirra felt she needed to express.

Death held great confidence as he explained, "That's correc'. The other fecks dun have ta do much either. Jus' lure a couple beasties toward the other bloke they wanna mess over an' itsa dun deal. The key par' is in gatherin' yer info on everythin' before the whole thing starts."

It was Life who finally told her, "You are going to get a hint before the challenge even starts. They give you time to research, but it mostly seems random as to when they come and nab you." He paused, thinking for a moment, and included, "There will also be kits lying around in the playground, but you have to look for them."

Death continued on, "Right, there'll be caches, and some will be trapped. You've been a pro in our training sessions at seeing trips, traps, snares, pits, and the like during our survival training, so that should be a breeze for you." He paused before stating his major concern, "It's your competition I'm worried about."

"Okay so who's my competition because I don't recognize any of their names, at least not yet." Kirra looked between them for a few moments.

The twins looked at each other as if wondering where to start before they both looked back as Death spoke up, "Tera. She's an earth dragon. She's not that strong, but she's really quick-witted and knows beasts really well. She's good at hiding, but I'd bet she'd be the first to figure out what it is and how to kill it."

"She's a possible ally, more than likely one you might want to try to make." Life added, "Yamesh, on the other hand, is experienced and deadly. He's also a bit of a loner. More than likely, he'll stick to the trees and stay out of reach. He has great accuracy with spears. He's not much of a fighter but he's been here almost as long as Death and I."

"The other two... we don't know anything about. They have never once been in the drink." Kirra looked at Death with confusion.

Life simplified it for her, "They've never been in a trial before."

"Right, so I've got two possible allies. When do I get my clue?" Kirra looked between them.

The twins shrugged before taking turns speaking as Death started with, "The clues come in different forms, sometimes it'll be a flicker in the list."

"A drop of a letter left somewhere."

"Sometimes there's one."

"Sometimes there's multiples."

They both looked at each other after taking turns speaking before they spoke as one, "It's completely random."

Kirra dropped her head on the table and let out a complaining groan, "I'm so screwed."

Death attempted to cheer her up, "Nah, we'll help you when the clue drops. That's the little we can do for you."

"Well, you might have led with that in the first place." Her response caused death and Life to snicker.

Death looked like he was about to speak, but whatever it was fell short as he eyed someone who just entered. Their walk was graceful, elegant, and, most importantly, accentuated with the tapping of a staff that seemed to resonate throughout the entire hall. The room started to break out in whispers as Kirra heard Death ask, "Is that an elf?"

"I think so. I have only read up on them, but I think he is a high elf. They're more of bookworms than anything..." Life paused before continuing, "I've heard that the more gifted elves can do magic. He is the meditative trainer that helps us connect to our spirits and use Kidori." The constant tap of wood against tile continued to resonate as the brilliant white wood of the ornate staff thumped with each step. The staff was decorated with a unique dragon wrapped around an obsidian crystal that seemed to float in the center.

As Kirra turned to watch the figure cloaked in white, they stopped at the front of the dining hall and turned to face the crowd of young faces that stared. Reaching up, they pulled back the hood of the cloak, revealing pale blonde hair that framed a sharp, angular face. Their brows were high and arched above two large golden eyes that swirled like miniature suns without pupils. Knife-like ears cut through the pin-straight hair as the elf stared toward the gathered teens. The lack of two digits on their hands only made the elf seem more alien to Kirra.

A thick blanket of silence weighed heavily as the elf took in the young teenagers. It felt as though all present were afraid to breathe with the androgynous creature's eyes boring through the teens. Finally, the silky and deep baritone of the elf droned out in an almost bored-sounding tone,

"Sometimes two, sometimes three

Sometimes four, sometimes more

Never one. Never alone.

Sometimes strong, sometimes weak

Sometimes wrong, sometimes reek

Those who are good hate us

Those who are evil use us

Fear is our weakness, but also our strength

Numbers are our strength, but also our weakness."

Without another word, the elf left the room with the same grace with which he appeared. It wasn't until the door clicked shut behind him that a roar of chattering teens took over the room.

Life suddenly gripped Kirra's arm tightly, causing her to look at him, "We need to go to the library and start doing some research."

Almost in unison, Kirra and her cabin began gathering their trays up and disposing of their food. Together they hurried over to the library as Kirra realized, this would be the first time she set foot inside of the place. The size of the place made her pause as she took it in.

The building was set up like a U, with two levels that were accessed through a double spiral staircase. The walls were lined with rows of books, and a row of tables and benches broke up the room in half so that you could sit and gather as a group. Floating kiosks with blue screens were intermittently set up throughout the library so others could look up books and their locations.

Leaving the others to start the search, Kirra moved to sit down at a table with Ky as they wrote down the hint to attempt to narrow things down. The group was piled closely at the back as they began flipping through pages together. Death chuckled, "There's a monster that takes the form of a flower. It waits for its prey to enter its trap, springs closed, and slowly digests its meal. Gods, what a way to go. Slowly being digested. It's actually called Sweet Death because of how sweet smelling and beautiful it looks."

"We're not looking for flora, Death." Life glared at his brother, "Stick to fauna."

"I mean, we could be. It could be absolutely deadly if there was a field of them."

Nicki spoke up, "What about a Blind Hound..." She paused, thinking she might have nailed it, "They hunt in packs. People usually use them to track someone down when they can't see their foe."

Kirra immediately shot her down, "Yeah, but Blind Hounds aren't hated by good people. Usually, you only need one. This specifically said they never hunt alone."

Kirra sighed, rubbing her face and flipping to another page of a book. Flesh Render. A beast that was mostly exposed muscles with claws that would rip through its flesh. Their acidic blood burns anything it touches except its own bones and flesh which was why it couldn't grow skin. "'Flesh Render – The Flesh Render gnaws the bones of its enemies into spikes before piercing its flesh with the sharpened newly made spikes and storing them in its body as ammo. When it is threatened, it shoots the bone spikes out. The act coats the bone spike in its acidic blood, causing it to become lubricated in acid as a deadly weapon.' If the gods made these creatures, they have some seriously messed up ideas."

"Sounds like a fun pet to take care of." Death commented with a chuckle as he flipped through another page and continued going on. "Oh look, a tree of Life... Oi Life... you think that might be you eventually?"

Life threw yet another glare toward his brother, "Death... Out of the floras... We're looking for a pack beast of some kind."

"Hey, I'm just trying to think outside of the box. Maybe there's some tree dog that runs on six legs and loves company." Life gave him a dirty look, causing Death to get up and put the book back, "Alright, alright... I'm puttin' your bleedin' personal journal back. Keep your dirty plant secrets to yourself." Almost all of the group snickered.

Life pinched the bridge of his nose while shaking his head, "If I didn't know you were, for a fact, born from our mother, I'd think you were a demon sent to torment me..."

"What did you say?" Kirra stared at Life intently

Death poked his head out from around the corner, "He called me a bloody demon. That's quite ruuu - Oh, we are looking in the wrong place completely..."

"That's what I've be—" Life started.

Death cut him off, "NO! That's not what I'm talking about." He turned to Kirra and pointed at her, "Kirra, you might be onto something, love. Hang on..." Death was seen dodging in and out of aisles. The group didn't see the path of destruction but rather heard it as several other teens angrily whispered or even yelled at Death in some cases. A few chuckles came from the group as Life placed his head in his hands at the realization that he would have to clean up his brother's path of destruction.

Finally, Death returned with a stack of books that went over his head before spilling them out on the table. Kirra read the one that slid in front of her, "Minor Demon Summoning. This is... some dark stuff..."

"Nah, demons are just misunderstood for what they are." Death picked up one book and began to thumb through it, "They're usually used by evil people, but that doesn't mean they're evil."

A sigh came from Kirra, "It's organized alphabetically. We're gonna be here all night." She read the first one out loud, "Air Fiend. It enters the lungs of your enemies and **literally** chokes them to death from the inside out. Most victims will look as though they imploded. Air Fiends will leave no trace. Great for assassinations." Looking towards Death her voice was filled with sarcasm, "Totally innocent... right..."

"I'd be angry too if I was forced to do someone's bidding." Death stuck his tongue out at Kirra, "But it proves the point of the good hate us, and the evil use us."

Losing track of time, the group sat there flipping through pages of books containing information on demons. The sound of a throat clear made them turn to see a mousey-haired girl looking intently at their group. In a small voice, she looked towards Kirra curiously, "Have you, um, figured anything out yet or um... teamed up with anyone?"

Kirra had never noticed the girl before and didn't recognize her. She realized that she seriously needed to pay more attention to the other teens in the camp and start figuring out who to watch out for. She took in the small girl's appearance carefully as she decided it was a new habit she was going to start.

The girl's clothing fit loosely around her thin body, and the only indication she was a dragon at all was the small horns in two rows that gradually got smaller on top of her head. Her hair was a normal brown color that was loosely braided. One of her sleeves hung past her fingers and the other was rolled up as though to prevent that very thing.

Kirra turned back to the book shaking her head, "Uh, no not really. We've been more concerned about trying to figure out what I'm going to be up against that I haven't even considered looking to team up with someone yet." Without thinking about it, Kirra went back to flicking through the pages as she skimmed over the information before her.

The girl stood there for a moment swaying before announcing shyly, "Right... I guess... I'll um... be on my way... Have my uh... own research to do too... I guess."

"Oi! You Clara?" Death called out as he caught Kirra's missed opportunity. Several people shushed or groaned at his blatant loudness.

"I am... yes." Rubbing one of her arms lightly, she turned, clearly embarrassed by Death's sudden burst out.

"Why don't you team up with Kirra?" Almost instantly, Kirra flicked her head towards him in surprise. She didn't know anything about this girl or if she'd try and screw her over.

After a moment of glaring at death, she turned back towards the girl, "Yeah. I guess we can figure this out together." With a soft giggle, the girl moved to scoot in right next to Kirra. As she did so, a tingle went up Kirra's spine like she was in danger.

"*Something isn't right about that girl.*" The familiar rumble from her spirit confirmed all she needed.

"*I thought so too. Something feels off. She could have sat anywhere, but instead, she decided to sit next to me.*"

A deep chuckle of amusement rumbled out, "*You should feel honored.*"

Hours had passed, and still, the group hadn't managed to narrow it down past it, **possibly** being a demon of some kind. By this point, Kirra had her head on one hand as she lazily flipped through pages. Kirra idly said the names of demon spawn out loud to the rest of the group as they listened.

"Shadow wolf summon. They're made of shadows from the plane of shadows, and you control them using fear. Those who fear them will feel their bite. More often than not, they're summoned in a pack."

"No…" Death said in between, bouncing his head on the table.

"Hounds of Doom. Serve as omens of death for those who are about to die. Once they have the scent of the prey, they won't stop until they kill their mark or they die."

"No…" Life spoke up

"Plague walker, it holds a nest of insects in it…"

Almost everyone at the table responded instantly, "Nooooo…"

Kirra let her head fall in the book as she whimpered, "Why are there so many of these things? The more I read, the more I feel like the gods just **want** us to die. Like on the hounds alone, there are hundreds."

"There's a lot of planets in the multiverse. Every creature serves a purpose." Life said the same line he had probably said hundreds of times that day alone.

Kirra argued, "Yeah, to decimate the population, it seems. Every single creature here is literally documented for the purpose of killing, wreaking havoc, or just to cause pain." She flipped to another page, shaking her head.

Death lifted his head momentarily from his book pillow, "Why don't you ask the Ancient Wolves… They're supposed to be ancient descendants from the heavens or some stupid rubbish." Right as he was done speaking, he flopped back down on the book.

"You might be onto something there, brother." Life's head perked up instantly over the book his nose was buried in.

"Wha'?"

Life explained, "If they brought something here, the wolves would definitely smell it. They might be able to identify it just by scent alone." The majority of the group all turned and looked at Kirra, Clara included.

"Why are you all looking at me like that?" Kirra leaned back in her chair, uncomfortable from the sudden attention.

Life helpfully offered, "You're the only one in our group that's ridden one. Maybe you could ask them?"

"Ohhhhh no... No, no, no, no... I was just a passenger on that ride. There is no way I could possibly even actually ride on one of those things. They are **far** too scary." Kirra shook her head several times.

"Why am I here?" Kirra whispered to herself repeatedly. The others watched from the side of the paddock, where Kirra was entering with apprehension. As she closed the gate, the loud clang caused her to tense. She turned to see glowing sets of eyes staring at her. The wolves had been all gathered in a massive cuddle puddle until they heard the gate close. Like a deer in headlights, she stood there, afraid to move, and slowly, the wolves yawned and settled back down after nothing of further interest happened.

Waiting briefly, she cautiously started moving towards the cuddle puddle. Inch by inch, she got closer until she was only a little ways away. Slowly reaching her hand out towards one of their heads, her heart raced a million miles a minute. The second it got within a few inches, the wolf she was closest to started showing its teeth. It made her retract her hand and curse inwardly, much to her spirit's amusement.

"What do you think you are doing?" The booming voice demanded. It had caused her to jump away from the wolves as she grabbed her chest.

Approaching from behind the gathered teens was a large woman covered in furs and leaves who looked furious. It was the Beastmaster. Kirra hadn't gotten a good look at her until just then. Large horns like that of an elk decorated the top of her head, followed by a halo of curly red hair that cascaded down her shoulders. Parts of it were woven and braided, while others were dreads mixed in with the normal loose strands of her hair. She looked like she had just lived off the land for the last few decades.

"Nothing, nothing, nothing. I was just uh... trying to... uh—"

The Beastmaster interrupted to make a point, "Trying to get your throat ripped out. They're not pets, they're intelligent beings. Treat them with respect, and they'll treat you with respect back." She paused, looking around at the gathered group before addressing Kirra again, "I'll ask again. What are you trying to do?"

Kirra stood there unsure and tried to think of an excuse, "I'm..." She decided the truth was the course, "I'm trying to see if they can tell me if they smelled a demon recently and identify it." The Beastmaster hopped over the fence and started to approach her with a squint in her eyes. Clearly, she was trying to see if Kirra was lying.

Moving past, the Beastmaster gave a kick to the rear end of one of the wolves lightly as it let out a growl and showed some fang. That didn't seem to deter her as she gave another light kick to one of them, "Come on, ya grumpy lot. Get up and get movin' ta yer beds." Kirra realized it wasn't a threatening growl or warning but really was just the wolf being grumpy. A chain reaction happened as the whole group moved into the stables without further guidance. Walking over, she closed them in the stalls and returned to address Kirra, "Usually most jump when they hear tha one givin' me attitude. You didn' tho'." Her accent was odd and almost sounded like Death's but different. The Beastmaster shrugged her shoulders and said, "Yer nae ready. But I tell ya wha'. Ya try to bond wit tha wolf I be pickin' then ya can try an ask yer questions."

Barely able to follow her accent, Kirra understood mostly what she was saying and shrugged her shoulders, "Alright, agreed."

A devilish cackle came from the woman as she motioned for Kirra to stay put. Looking over at the others, Kirra shrugged her shoulders, questioning her life choices now as they all just gave her the thumbs up or mouthed 'You got this' at her. Kirra only got more nervous as she watched the Beastmaster disappear through the stables, ensuring all doors were closed. It started to make Kirra question her life's decisions. That was when she heard the low warning growls of an agitated wolf.

Tensing up, Kirra turned towards the sound with wide eyes as she soon saw a massive white wolf getting pressed backward and into the pen she was currently standing in. The thing pushing the wolf towards her was a set of wall shields covered in spikes, continuously moving despite the snapping, angry wolf. Once the wolf was past the set of doors that closed the stable off, they were slammed shut, trapping the wolf in the paddock... **With her!**

Slowly, the wolf turned and faced Kirra after giving a few sniffs. For just the briefest of moments, as it turned towards Kirra, she couldn't help but admire the creature's beauty. It was not only flawlessly white, but it stood with a sense of pride and moved with a grace an animal that large shouldn't have. That image fell away as it showed its fangs and lunged with one great leap toward her, closing the gap between them almost instantly. The screams of her friends rang out as she was tackled to the ground.

One moment, Kirra was falling to the ground with the fangs of the wolf wrapped around her throat; the next, she was standing in that familiar void-like space. The white wolf circling her was the only thing that held any color besides herself. The wolf wasn't threatening her but appeared to be more cautious than anything. Circling around to her front, it came closer, staring right at her as though seeing straight to her soul.

Its voice came out masculine, gravelly, and domineering as he demanded, "Have you no sense, *girl? Are you not afraid*?" While he spoke, his jaws snapped out as a gravelly-sounding growl erupted forth from the wolf simultaneously.

Her answer surprised even her, "No... I'm not..." There was a long pause before she said, "It's not that you're not terrifying..." She was unsure as to how to put it into words, "I was more awestruck by you." The wolf had been slowly creeping closer, seemingly curious of her.

"*Awestruck...*" The wolf's words came out as it breathed heavily on her face, "*I could get used to that. So tell me...*" He snapped his teeth right next to her face, "*Why are you standing here?*"

"I need help or rather information. It would be about something that would have been brought here recently." She figured honesty was the key.

That same gravelly laughter came once more, *"Information? Not here to brag about how you deserve me as a partner or all the feats you have accomplished in your short life at the behest of entertaining some human bats."*

Kirra was honest, "I don't. I don't think I deserve you as a partner." Her instantons answer made the wolf draw back and sit on its haunches, "I'm not the strongest, or the fastest, or the smartest, or the best. I'm just average. I probably don't deserve you. There are plenty of other people here who are better than me. I'm just here for information. I'm not great at fighting, but I'm training and practicing. I'm not smart like Life, but I'm learning." The wolf continued to watch her with intelligent blue eyes as he listened to her speak, "I'm actually genuinely afraid. I'm afraid of a lot of things, and I'm sure that there are others here that are way more worthy of you."

The quiet bore on for a while before the wolf spoke with the wisdom that came from their kind, *"The worth of a person does not come from what you are in a single moment or the strength of one's physical or mental prowess. It comes from the kind of heart a person has."* The wolf leaned forward without malice and pressed its nose to her forehead, his hot breath spilling across her face.

She wasn't afraid or terrified of the creature. The gasp left her throat as a rush of emotions and memories flooded her mind. Her father's voice whispered words of encouragement or joked with her. Her mother looked at her with love whenever she thought she wouldn't notice. The surge of sadness burst through her like a dam breaking. It crashed through Kirra so violently that she dropped to her knees and sobbed.

Something heavy and soft laid across her lap. Instinctively, Kirra wrapped her arms around it and hugged it close to her head. The wolf had laid its head in her lap, and as she sobbed tears into its perfect white fur, Kirra let her weight fall across the top of his head as she clung to him desperately. When she calmed, his voice pushed through her sadness, "*You have had the strength of heart to hold back your sadness and mourning while your life has been in danger. You have found joy, knowledge, and friendship and pushed on despite the pain you hold in your heart. You are stronger than you know, Kirra, and I, Snow of the Mountain Peaks, would be honored to be your partner.*"

A sudden rush of warmth filled Kirra as the wolf started to glow. The next she knew, the light of the wolf in its entirety seemed to be absorbed into Kirra as the dream melted away. Inky blackness turned into the reality of her falling on her back with the wolf at her neck.

The screams of her friends slowly came back. The crash of a gate filled the air as the Beastmaster came rushing to Kirra's aid. Instead, what everyone saw happening next caused them all to pause.

The feeling of a wet tongue sliding the length of her neck, where it was bruised from the bite of the wolf, caused Kirra to giggle. Snow's licking was making her ticklish and caused her to laugh, squirm, and bat him away.

Pulling back with one last slurp, *Snow chuckled softly, "Come now, little one. I was merely apologizing for the bite."* Kirra sat up in surprise as she realized she could hear his voice in her head.

Wiping the slobber off, she just decided to accept what was happening, saying, "Well, I could do without the tongue bath that you just gave me. Especially since I don't know how much time I have before the trial."

The Beastmaster stood by, watching with awe, "He bonded with you..." Then, shouted out incredulously, "**He actually bonded with you!?**" She paused, looking between the two with surprise, "He was supposed to just chase you around like all the others. I didn't actually think...." Kirra went to stand up and found assistance in the form of Snow, letting her use his neck to help pull her up.

Looking down at her hands and then at him, she saw him shaking out his fur in some slight annoyance, "You will learn to get used to it, *but by the gods, you have no filter or block in your head. It is like annoying little flies buzzing in my head.*" He continued to shake his head before pawing at his ears.

The Beastmaster approached Kirra, instructing, "It's called mental static. Ancient beasts are severely susceptible. It's not common, but it means your mind constantly buzzes with thoughts." Gripping Kirra by her shoulders she explained, "You need to focus. Imagine a wall between you and him. Build it up. Allow his voice into your head, allow his eyes to see through yours."

Kirra looked confused, "I don't even know how to..." Watching Snow back up, whimpering as though in pain, she closed her eyes and slammed a wall up in place. The moment it slammed in place, a yelp came from him, causing her to jump. Quickly thinking, she imagined an open door on the wall with him in view. As Snow relaxed, huffing out on the ground, that seemed to fix the issue.

Growling in annoyance, he stood and walked towards her, *"You shut me out like that again, and I will make sure you regret it!"* His jaws snapped out towards her in irritation.

"Okay, okay, sorry. This is all new to me..." She gave a few apologetic pats to him before addressing the Beastmaster, "It's done. I don't know how long I can keep it up, though."

The trainer didn't seem too concerned, "Usually, once it's up, most forget it's even there. The first few times will take practice. I'll tell them you're ready to learn how to ride." Kirra looked at her in question before she continued, "It's not a common class for everyone. There are a few that take to it, but most don't. It's rare that an Ancient beast lets anyone ride them, and rarer still to find a partner with one." The Beastmaster planted her hands on her hips with a smirk, stating, "Well, if you return from the trials, you'll not be doin' whatever chores ya had afore. You'll be muckin' his stall and feedin' and takin' care of 'im instead."

"*When.*" Snow corrected the woman despite the fact she couldn't hear him.

Death blatantly called out to put Kirra back on task, "Well, that's great and all, but has he said anythin' about smellin' any demonic entities or summons he might recognize?"

Kirra gasped, "Crap, I nearly forgot!" Dropping the hand absently scratching Snow, she questioned, "Snow? Do you know what they brought into the playground? What creature or monster I'll be up against?" As Snow looked at her, the surmounting seriousness of her issue flooded through.

13

FIRST TRIAL

K irra wasn't sure if she was hearing him correctly or not, "I'm sorry, could you repeat that? I don't think your voice came through our bond clearly enough."

"I said, Hell Hounds. Quite a few of them from the severity of the stench." Snow's nose wrinkled a bit just at the thought before he sneezed.

"Okay, so how do you kill them?" Kirra frowned some as she inquired.

"Technically speaking, you do not. You just send them back to where they came from. These were summoned in. The real ones are much harder to kill, and most mortal kin do not bother going on that side of the multiverse. All you need do is cut off their heads, and they will disappear."

"Well, that's just perfect..."

All of the others started asking questions causing her to hold a hand to shush them so that Snow could continue, *"Calm yourself, pup. They have a very good disadvantage against themselves. They instill fear, yes, but Hell Hounds in this large a number are more likely to fight one another. Your greatest defense is to group up with whoever else is in these silly trials and kill them when they attempt to squabble over who gets first pick."*

"Anything else?" Kirra asked, looking a bit concerned.

"They are clumsy. They have hooves on their hind legs, making them liable to slip on hard surfaces. Their paws on the front have claws that do not retract, which means they can get stuck in objects more easily."

The Beastmaster cleared her throat, starting to corral Snow back towards the stables, "Alright, come on you, back to the pen, ya beasty. You two can speak on the morrow if'n the lass is quick of foot an' mind."

Snow gave a bit of a snarl but complied as he reached out to Kirra mentally one last time, *"We are always connected, Kirra, but the bond will grow over time. Eventually, we can speak to each other over greater distances... but... new... hear... as... further."* As he got further away, his voice fluttered in and out before she finally couldn't hear him. The warmth his presence brought in her mind seemed to vanish as well. The effect wasn't as harsh as when her spirit had almost pulled away completely.

Returning to the group, The Beastmaster explained to Kirra that she could visit as often as she wanted when she didn't have classes. Shooing the group away from the pens, they decided to head back to the library and get the information directly from a book now that Kirra knew exactly what they were up against. As Kirra found the book, her stomach dropped as someone had torn the page regarding the demons in the trial out.

Groaning out in annoyance, Kirra declared, "I guess that means someone else knows what we're up against."

"What is it?" Clara asked meekly as a finger wrapped around a length of hair that fell free from her braid.

"Hell Hounds." The afterthought hit Kirra, "I forgot you guys couldn't hear what Snow was saying."

Death burst out into laughter, causing others to look at him like he was crazy as he shrugged, "What? It's funny. Something that large is coming down on you with all fangs and claws. I mean, come on. 'Sic' em, Snow!' Don' induce fear and horror exactly. Why not name him Fluffy Butt The 3rd." Kirra's glare only made him snicker more, "What?!"

"I didn't name him..."

"Well, how was I supposed to know tha'?" He looked around as the others shook their heads.

"I will suggest that you get a nap in before the trial. At least some rest or try to. Both of you..." Life looked between the two in the trial, "It could potentially run all night or day and you might as well get the rest while you can."

Agreeing with Life, Kirra nodded, "I'm going to do just that. Clara, I'll try and find you in the playground. I would say we should probably try and find the others, too, but I don't know where they are right now."

Before leaving, Kirra shared the information that Snow provided. Clara seemed insistent on looking the information up herself and remained in the Library despite Kirra's information. Most of the others decided to call it a night as well. As they left the library, they went their separate paths to either do chores, last-minute training or clean up before bed.

Stopping in the middle of one of the paths, she moved to lie down in some grass, and stared up through one of the holes in the top of the cave, smiling. Stars. Something she hadn't actually seen or taken the time to watch in a long time. These ones were different. She wondered how far away Spiritoski was from Earth. Kirra considered her question, recalling her lessons since arriving at Bat Colony.

According to their integration teacher, everyone existed in a multiverse containing several universes. Each universe usually only had one planet with the ability to sustain life. There were exceptions to this rule but it was rare nonetheless. In each planet in that universe, places of power where the energy was stronger naturally connected the multiple universes together. These universes were placed on a dimensional spherical map of sorts. Using these places of power, portals could be created permanently or temporarily. Their locations were shared, mapped out, and used to move through the multiverse. Using a single travel portal, time continued to move and flow naturally, as it was a natural way of traveling from one universe to the next using the dimensional map. As more planets and universes discovered this portal travel, the need for moving and transporting goods en masse became highly desired. Thus came the invention of warp portal travel.

It was a mix of enchantment and science. Large cargo ships, like the one Kirra arrived on, would bend space, allowing for interdimensional travel on a mass scale. The only problem with this method of travel was the cost. Time. Time was the one constant throughout all of the universes connected in the multiverse. Despite quite literally bending the fabric of space to travel to another alternate universe, the price paid was time. It wouldn't be time spent by those making the jump, but rather time that had passed during their travel because of them literally bending space to their will. The price would fluctuate depending on how far the dimensional warp on the map was.

The familiar rumble of her spirit entered her mind, "*It is beautiful, isn't it.*"

"*It's amazing to think that the gods created something so complex and still managed a way to weave everything together.*" Her mind turned to the trial ahead, "*You think I made a mistake by not setting up a meeting spot with Clara?*"

The rumble of her spirit called out, "*I think you'll be fine in the trial. You won't be alone either. I'll be with you every step of the way.*"

For the first time in a long while, Kirra felt some semblance of peace drip through her as she lay back and watched the sky from her spot in the grass. A soft smile graced her lips as she thought about all she accomplished that day. Someday, she'd become the person that Snow said she was. His words gave her confidence.

Sure things started off miserable, but she got her friends back, her dragon spirit back, and an ancient wolf as a partner as well. All in all, it was actually a good day, even with the trial looming over her head. The ghostly white of her spirit became visible for a mere moment. His head settled down atop her chest while he curled around her with a protective rumble before disappearing. With a sigh, she closed her eyes and drifted off to sleep. Amidst all the chaos, she found some peace for once.

"Sssssuch a precious little one you are." The snake-like voice hissed out.

Once more, Kirra found herself in that void of darkness as an unfamiliar voice rang out in the dark. It echoed all around her, even inside her own skull. The feeling of something warm, growing hotter with every second, shot through her left arm. Crying out, she gripped her left arm, trying to stamp out whatever was burning her in a panic.

After the pressure didn't work, Kirra went to claw at her arm, but a sudden streak of black dashed out from the inky void surrounding her. As the creature tackled her, pinning her to the ground, she cried out while trying to break the pin.

"Ohhhhh, poor Kirra..." It mocked her while cackling madly.

Her eyes caught sight of her left arm and watched lines being burnt and branded into her skin. As it moved up her forearm, she let out another scream of pain. It felt as though hot metal was being pressed onto her skin and held there to cool against her flesh. The mark only traveled up to her elbow, but it looked like it was still emerging from the egg on her hand.

As the burning started to subside, she slumped back against the ground, no longer fighting the creature that had her pinned. Her left forearm throbbed like a fresh burn as the creature jumped away. Slowly sitting up, her eyes blinked through the tears of her pain and watched the strange creature circle as though it were hunting her.

It had the frame of a very large dog. Barrel chested with a skinny and sleek waist. The head looked to be a mix of a dog and a drake, where black skin met scale. Atop its head sat a set of ears that rotated like a dog's, but its tips were squared off instead of pointed. Where paws should have been, the clawed feet of a drake sat, allowing for easier catching during a hunt. Its long, slender tail wagged and flicked behind it like an irritated cat, the fluff of fur at the end, the only hair on it. The body was a mix of skin and scale, like a large hairless dog with plate-like scales.

Two yellowed eyes stared and cackled at her as she demanded, "Who or what are you?" She reached out to her spirit, *"Dragon... Where are you?"*

"Oh, I wouldn't bother if I were you..." The voice echoed around her once more as she realized the creature disappeared, "Your spirit is in a deep slumber." Kirra looked for the voice and paused as it came from directly behind her, "The spirit bond can be rather taxing." Turning instantly, she lashed out with an arm cocked and ready to punch but instead found herself in trouble.

A hand caught her around her throat and lifted her as though she were nothing. The voice that belonged to the hand cackled out, "You mortals never seem to learn." Kirra struggled, clawing at the arm helplessly until she was dropped back to the ground.

When she recovered and looked around, she found that the man was gone as she demanded, "What did you do to me?!"

The voice cackled from the darkness, "Call it... A favor..." The face of the creature appeared from the darkness as she looked towards it. Rising to her feet, Kirra prepared for the incoming leap that tackled her to the ground.

Flailing out, Kirra realized the world around her was suddenly different. It was another dream. As she looked around, she realized she wasn't next to the path in the camp anymore. Just as she was about to question where she was, the feeling of something crawling on her caused her to jump and bat any bugs off. She shuttered at the thought of bugs crawling over her. The second realization she had was that she had a jacket on. Something she didn't have on her person when she drifted off to sleep. Realization finally came over her.

She was in the Playground...

Considering her training, Kirra remembered the first thing she needed to do was inventory everything she had on her person. Several times, she attempted calling out to her spirit but got no response. Pulling back the sleeve of her jacket, plain as day lay the irritated skin and mark that now ran up her forearm. What she experienced in her dream had actually happened.

Pulling the sleeve back down with a sigh, "I guess I'm on my own for right now." She mumbled to herself, "What happened in the dream happened here too." Her arm still throbbed painfully, causing her to rub it despite it not doing anything to alleviate the pain.

"*You're not alone, kid...*" A loud, grumpy yawn echoed, "*Trivitus forced us to spirit bond. First Cerinos, and now Trivitus. Being visited by both gods cannot be a good thing.*"

Kirra was still coming around herself, "*What do you think it means?*"

"*Cerinos is usually an omen of good. Things that you do will have a pleasant outcome for others. Trivitus, however, is an omen of evil. Usually, he appears if you are meant to do very bad things for the multiverse...*"

"So what does that mean for me?"

"I'm not sure to be honest."

Now that she'd contacted her spirit, Kirra started to take inventory of what was on her. She had a braided cord bracelet on her wrist, a box with two matches, and a fixed-blade knife attached to the belt on her waist. She smirked softly, *"Well, that's something at least."*

"Yes, if this goes for too long, that will prove useful." The dragon commented.

Kirra knew the knife was mostly used as a tool but at least she had something to use as a weapon if need be. Learning survival skills from Black Dragon was a blessing. The other great part was running all over the playground helped her learn the lay of the land. Given that she didn't know exactly where she was, Kirra knew she would have to search for somewhere high to better establish where she was.

Securing the items, Kirra started off at a clipped pace, looking for any familiar landmarks along the way. She commented to herself, *"I'm going to start becoming more aware of my surroundings and the others here when I get out of this. I should have memorized the landscape more and paid attention to my competition."*

Her spirit chuckled at her, *"That would be wise to do, yes."* Letting her concentrate on the task at hand, her spirit remained quiet and let her keep her eyes on her environment. Kirra wasn't the best at tracking, but she still attempted to look for signs of creatures and people alike. She didn't know how long she had been walking for. It felt like time was dragging while surrounded by the quiet of the forest. She stopped occasionally for a small break here and there, but the sound of a branch snapping drew her attention instantly.

Kirra immediately ducked behind a tree, pressing as close as physically possible. This was the exact moment she realized her horns were missing.

"*Spirit bonding. Since the process has begun, you can much more easily hide the parts you do not wish visible.*" Her spirit helpfully provided.

Finally, a feminine voice broke through not far away, "So an hour in and still no sign of the others. Think that might mean I'm in the clear, for now." Silence came after she spoke.

As the same voice spoke again, Kirra realized the girl was talking to her spirit aloud, "No, I don't think I trust either of them. Kirra is up in the air. I know I can't kill these things by myself, but I don't know how useful she'll be either."

"*Well, that's just offensive.*" Kirra's spirit scoffed, "*They don't even know you.*" Hearing the footsteps lightly shift in place, she wondered what to do as her spirit continued, "*I would say it is safe that this might be your friend Clara.*"

"*It doesn't sound like her. Clara has a different voice. It's one of the others. They might be willing to work as a team, though.*"

Taking the risk, Kirra slowly stepped out from behind the tree. The girl she saw had short, spikey hair with curved horns like a ram. She was wearing the exact same outfit as every other teen there. The bag slung over her shoulders made her look even thinner, but that could have just been the jacket. She couldn't tell exactly how tall she was from this distance.

Since the girl hadn't spotted her, Kirra began to ask, "Where'd yo—"

An axe sent flying at her head cut her off. Pure instinct took over as her hand reached out and closed around the haft without her so much as blinking. The girl's jaw dropped after seeing the display.

Shaking out of her own stupor, the girl commented, "Uh, well, I guess that answers one question. Kinda..."

The girl had her body turned side-faced to Kirra, giving the impression that she was still armed. Kirra dropped the axe she'd caught and kicked it away while keeping her hands raised and finished asking, "Where'd you get that bag?" She paused momentarily, looking at her, and decided on an introduction. Slowly reaching out a hand in the form of an introduction, "Hi, I'm Kirra..."

"We need to work on your social skills." The rumbling chuckle came.

"I grew up sheltered with a family of liars, surrounded by bullies, and am now in a concentration camp that forces kids to fight. I think my social skills are just fine given the circumstances." Her answer only caused another deep chuckle from her spirit.

Moving towards Kirra, she picked up the thrown axe and took hold of the offered hand, announcing pleasantly, "Tera." She pointed to the bag on her back, "Supply cache. Handy if you know where to look or rather how to identify them." Both of them relaxed as they let the handshake drop. She pointed to Kirra's left arm and asked, "You find out your power yet?" Confusion entered Kirra's face, causing her to say, "Ahhh. I forgot you've only been here a month. You probably **just** spirit-bonded. Or it's a rash from a poisonous plant..." She looked down at her own hand that had shaken Kirra's, "Please tell me it's not a poisonous plant..."

"And I thought you were the socially awkward one." She barely started to think what she was asking before she got the answer from

her spirit, *"She's talking about your bond and your ability. It can exist before you become bonded, and your ability can emerge. Now that we are bonded, your ability may come out on its own with emotion. Most do not discover their ability until they become spirit bonded."*

"How did she know I was bonded?"

He said softly, *"When you raised your arms in the air, she must have seen your mark."*

Tera suddenly blurted out, "Shut up! I just don't make friends with a lot of people, okay..." As Tera rolled her eyes, Kirra started watching as the girl was being really loud, "Whatever... I prefer plants, okay. They're a lot nicer than people are...."

Realizing she could have been seen as rude, Tera finally turned to Kirra, "Sorry, we do that a lot. It's like a love-hate relationship, but she completes me in that way." After laughing awkwardly, she motioned for Kirra to follow her up the hill. Kirra did as she was told, with no choice but to follow and let her do all the talking, "Okay, so I just saw Yamesh take off somewhere down there." She pointed at the bottom of the cliff, "I think he might have found a cache and was looking for something to kill the hell hounds with." Tera turned to Kirra, stating matter-of-factly, "Oh, they're hell hounds, by the way. I'll tell you some more things about them in a second."

For once, Kirra got the chance to speak and stated, "I know." Tera turned and looked at her with confusion, "I know they're hell hounds, and in order to kill them, you have to cut their heads off."

Tera nodded in approval before leading the way back where they came, explaining, "You're not actually killing them, by the way. Summons aren't actually here, not these summons, at least. It's kinda sad being a summon, I suppose. Constantly being forced to do menial tasks at the whim of a stranger..."

"Aren't they Demons?" She told her spirit, "*I think she thinks I'm an idiot and is over-explaining everything.*" The sound of deep, rumbling laughter filled her head.

Tera commented softly, "Well, yes, but they still feel, have emotions, and even if they're not sentient, I mean... it still sucks being at the beck and call of someone."

"*Shouldn't you two be keeping quiet? She is especially loud. And is easily excited, it seems.*"

Before it got too quiet for Tera to spout off again, Kirra asked, "Should we be talking like this?"

"They're not over in this part of the forest yet. You'll smell em' before you see em'." She considered her words before adding, "I can also sense most anything that is alive. Which is weird that I didn't sense you..." She gave that some thought.

"Okay, what about Yamesh, Clara, and the other?" Kirra asked.

"Yamesh is good peeps. He knows he needs at least me to kill the demons off, and he's not good enough to try and eliminate four other kids. Clara and Slash. I don't know about them, but the plants will tell me if someone is nearby." She considered being unable to sense Kirra once more, "You, on the other hand. You're like the up-and-coming Ky. Everyone's noticed how good you're getting. You'd have to be stupid to try something on you after the beating you took from Roc."

Kirra retorted back to Tera, "I'm not that good. Even after challenging someone, I'm still at the bottom of the list. Not to mention, I'm weak."

Tera smirked, "If I listed every single thing that I wasn't good at, it'd be a really, really long list."

"What are you saying?"

"I'm saying that you concentrate too much on the bad. So what if you haven't beaten anyone? So what that you're weak? You looked like you barely weighed more than a sack of flour when you got here, if that at all. Since then, you've put on weight and actually look healthy. You've toned out some and gone from knowing nothing to actually being able to hold your own somewhat. Not to mention taking a punch like a champ because if I faced off against Roc like that, there would be **no** way I'd be able to take that kind of beating." She laughed before looking to Kirra, "You're stronger than you think you are, but you're still just starting out and you're not going to get there quickly. This isn't some story where you're the hero and you instantly pick up on everything. This is real life, not a fairy tale. You're going to fail. You're going to be really, really, really bad. But here's the fun part... You'll get better."

With a pat on her shoulder, Tera let out a little laugh and started leading the way down. Kirra was certain she was trying to get to where Yamesh had been. Soon enough, Kirra had her answer as she realized the trail they were following wasn't a trail at all. She saw the signs of someone having passed through. Tera was right that she had improved greatly over the course of a month. Despite missing out on the challenges due to training or injury, Kirra had improved.

Despite Tera giving them the okay to speak openly, they mostly walked in silence. The pair carefully followed the trail and tracks as the forest sounds filled the air around them. As the tracks swerved unnaturally, Kirra reached out and yanked Tera back.

As she was about to turn and yell at her, Kirra explained in a calm and hushed voice, "Trap..." Pointing to the pile of underbrush and leaves that had been moved around, "The leaves have been moved." It was obvious to Kirra as she noticed the bad leaves that had been shed off were in the path and a bit raised as opposed to the others that littered the area.

Tera looked around for it but noticed the trail, "Whoa.... Thanks...."

Taking the lead because of the trap, Kirra walked around and continued following the tracks. Spotting something, she halted in her tracks, causing Tera to nearly bump into her. Ahead of her on the outcropping of a cliff lay a blue marking that lightly glowed. It was the Spiritoski symbol for "cache". Pointing to the symbol, Kirra asked, "That one of the hidden caches?"

"That certainly is, but it looks like Yamesh has already been to it. He probably cleared it out." Tera pointed out the stamped-down leaves on the ground as she started moving toward it. "Keep a lookout; I'll just double-check in case." Moving towards the wall, she pulled out the container from the wall and started rifling through it. Tera started commenting softly to herself about various items that had been left there while Kirra looked around, moving slightly away from her. Mostly, it was so she could hear without the sound of items being moved around in the small wooden chest.

Staying quiet, Kirra felt a shiver run through her like something malevolent was nearby. That feeling only grew stronger as she wandered closer to a hole in the side of the cliff, a small cave-like den. Soon, the feeling was accompanied by the strong smell of mold, as a chill ran up her spine. The sound of crunching could be heard further in the cave as it echoed off the walls and rang through the air. Hissing softly, Kirra tried to get Tera's attention, but to no avail.

Tera seemed too busy, and the noise of her rooting through the cache didn't allow her to be heard. Backing up from the small cave and moving closer to Tera, Kirra tried hissing to her again, "Tera..." A low growl was heard. This time, Kirra felt a wave of fear run through her.

"That fear isn't from you. It is from the demon. Ground yourself." Kirra closed her eyes at the instructions and let her body relax. She took a deep breath and let it out slowly, *"Concentrate on me. Picture us as one."*

The smell of something rotten entered the air, causing Kirra to gag and retch. At this point, Tera covered her own face and pulled away from the cache she had been sorting through. That fear left Tera frozen in place as her eyes widened at the sight that lay before them.

A small portion of a skull-like face poked out from the shadows. Rotting flesh, patchy needle-like fur, and cloven hooves on back legs greeted the pair. It was only the one, which meant there would be more based on the recited poem and the information she'd learned.

The Hell Hound. It smelled of death, mold, and decay. The creature looked like a large breed dog, save for the cloven hooves that made up its back legs. Instead of actual eyes, there were only two sockets with glowing red orbs. Along its body, the flesh was missing in places, ripped and dangling as it slowly stalked forward. Claws that stuck through from the knuckles of the creature scratched and scraped on the cave's stone surface as it padded ever closer toward Kirra.

"Concentrate, kid!"

Kirra concentrated on the warmth of her dragon spirit deep within her. It was like a wealth of knowledge suddenly flowed into her. Without thinking, Kirra felt her hand reach back toward Tera and pull an axe from her belt. The throw wasn't perfect, but it hit home in the creature's chest just as it had leaped towards the pair. Despite the axe landing deep in the demon's chest, the hound stumbled back to its feet, whimpering out pathetically.

With the creature injured, Kirra glanced back toward Tera, who seemed to be still under the effects of the creature's fear. She didn't have any time to waste as two more started to move in from the darkness of the cave caused by the commotion. Out of the corner of Kirra's eye, she spotted a sword leaning against the wall near where the cache was. It was long, curved ever so slightly, and within arm's reach. Gripping the blade, Kirra could feel the glow of blue eyes looking out from hers as her movements were directed. There was no time to try and snap Tera out of her shock.

In one single movement, Kirra drew the blade free of the sheath, taking a stance unfamiliar to her as the pair of hell hounds came out snapping towards her. Kirra positioned herself between them and Tera so she would be the harder target. Then something unexpected happened.

The pair of hounds turned on their third injured member. Growling while backing up, the injured one started snapping out in warning towards the two hounds that had turned on it. As Kirra moved forward, the moves came almost instantly to her as she performed them. It was as though her spirit was making her move as his knowledge flowed through her.

Running forward to close the distance just as one of the hounds lunged at the injured one, Kirra brought her sword down in a swift, easy movement. Its head drifted away from its body before disintegrating into ash like it had never been there. Following the movement, she angled the sword up in one flawless move, taking the head of the other. The last one lunged at her, making her sidestep as she took the remaining injured hound down in one swift movement.

As the last one disappeared into nothingness, out of more habit than anything, the blade flicked off to the side as her spirit's words sprang forth from her lips, "Still got it..."

The connection faded, causing Kirra to feel drained and making her drop to one knee while panting like she'd just run a marathon. Tera moved up, looking surprised and impressed all at the same time, "I didn't know you'd gone through weapons training yet..." She still looked shaken as the effects of demons' fear still gripped her.

Standing with no small amount of effort, Kirra stated, "I haven't..."

"*That would be the link. A shame... I thought you might be able to hold it for longer. I shall give it more time then.*" Her spirit rumbled thoughtfully through her. For a moment, she swore she saw a ghostly apparition of a man dressed in traditional garb from another era with white hair in a top knot before it disappeared. She didn't get a good view of it before he disappeared.

Looking towards Tera, she started to hand the sword to her, to which she stepped back, shaking her head, "No, no, no. That's yours now." Tera walked over, grabbed the sheathe, and handed it to Kirra with a look of astonishment still on her face, "That's some natural talent you have."

Sheathing the sword, Kirra fixed it to her belt before saying, "It wasn't natural talent. I think my spirit took control of me for a few moments." Tera's eyes went wide, "What?"

Giving her a nervous laugh, "If you and your spirit are linked like that already, you're way stronger than you think you are." Kirra seemed confused by that comment. She still felt shaky from whatever burned through her, guessing it was the link between her and her spirit as Tera said, "Sorry about freezing like that. Their fear effect hit harder than I thought. I'm just trying to figure out what they were doing hanging around here."

"I heard them crunching on something further in the cave. Might have been too busy enjoying their meal to notice us at first." Kirra wondered softly, "Does that mean the trial is done since I killed them?"

"Don't let it go to your head." A soft masculine voice called out from behind the two girls.

The guy was skinny, tall, and very lanky. A row of spines went straight down the middle of his head, gradually getting bigger and smaller again beside the other set of horns that curled back around forward like an odd bull. Eyes that were sunken slightly in his face were blood red, and the pupils were slit but went horizontally, making him look like quite the sight. The oddest part about him was that he was covered head to toe in mud and leaves.

He clarified for the girls, "There's still six more left. Someone left these ones a present and it caught me off guard. I killed the one keeping guard but heard the others and decided to move on."

He held his hand out to Tera and motioned, 'Hand it over' several times. Tera sighed and started pulling out several spade-shaped objects. Taking hold of one, he clicked something on it and it made a shaft extend from the bottom. Kirra realized those were spears and figured out who the teenager was now.

Always pointing out the obvious, "So you're Yamesh." There was a curt nod from the male, covered head to toe in mud and leaves, "Sorry, I don't know either of you."

Yamesh didn't seem to be much of a talker as he merely replied, "You're with the right group…"

Without much more, he just started taking the lead down a path, leading the little group of them. It gave her a chance to get a better view of him or, rather, size him up. It was then she realized he wasn't covered in mud and leaves; instead, it was a suit that allowed him to blend in. The second thing she noticed was that he didn't leave tracks unless he stepped in mud. When that happened, it left behind an imprint of a large cat's paw, which might explain why Kirra didn't hear him as they tromped through the woods.

After a little while, Yamesh seemed to be attempting to formulate a plan, "Since there's three of us now, we should be able to take on the last six ourselves before the other dickheads decide to find us and try to take us out."

Kirra figured it might be best not to ask too many questions about him as he led the way through the forest. Given that the three of them had managed to meet up, it might have meant that the other two met up as well or were eliminated. She was lucky to have the other two since she was certain they had done this before. Her spirit taking over her earlier also earned her the bonus of not being completely dead weight.

Given their aversion to the other two, Kirra finally asked softly, "What do you two have against Clara and Slash? I get the feeling that neither of you thinks too highly of them?"

Yamesh actually turned and faced Kirra as he stopped in the path, "They're Shivers." The word meant nothing to Kirra, causing her to shrug at him cluelessly, "It's just what they do. They can't be trusted. Shivers are the equivalent of sidiotts."

Kirra and Tera asked at the same time, "A what?"

Turning to continue down the path once more, he explained, "A sidiott. It's a type of demon that can blend in with their environment. There's a whole plethora of them, but they're rare, like Shivers. Shivers are drakes, though. It's just what they were named given the motion they make when their scales change color to blend in with their environment. They can change shape in their normal form, too."

"Yeah, but they can't fool me..." Tera practically beamed softly before her face fell, "Which begs the question of why I couldn't sense the demons."

Almost certain she knew the answer, Kirra piped up, "Because they're not actually here..." As they continued to walk, Tera looked at her with a furrow of her brow, "Okay, so you said they're summons, right, but they're not technically here, or at least their bodies? So that would mean you can't sense them if they're not actually here."

Tera commented, "Well, we're not exactly sure how the summons work, but it's more like they're here and not here at the same time..."

"Demon summons are technically **physically** here but aren't simultaneously. When a summon gets summoned, they are drawn from whatever plane or universe they were on to the one they were summoned to." Yamesh explained before commenting, "That isn't the reason why, though." Both Kirra and Tera looked at him before he explained, "Hell hounds are summoned from the plane of the dead." Tera and Kirra shrugged their shoulders at him, "They're not technically alive."

Tera pursed her lips at the thought, "Well crap… That means I'm useless in regards to that."

"Which means both of you should shut up." Yamesh gave the pair a stern look before walking down the trail again.

"Do you know about planes and how summons work?" Her spirit inquired.

"Apparently not."

"Planes exist throughout the multiverse on the planets that we live on. It is like air. You cannot see it, but you know it is there. The plane we exist on is that of the Physical Plane. When they are summoned from a plane, they cannot die. They can only be returned to the plane they were summoned from. To kill them, you would have to go to their plane and kill them there. That can be quite dangerous."

Kirra's brow furrowed in thought, *"How is it that you suddenly know all of this?"*

"Fun part about being a spirit… The more you experience, the more memories that are triggered. Facing off against that hell hound brought forth some of my memories."

Yamesh paused in the middle of a small clearing. The familiar stench of rot, mold, and rotting meat smacked into the group like a hammer. Kirra reached up to cover her face with her arm, looking for the location of where the stench was coming from. It was completely useless as the stench surrounded them from all sides. That near-crippling fear smashed into the group of teens like a wave trying to drag them out to sea. All three managed to steady themselves and overcome that wave of fear and the need to run. With it drove back the smell of festering rotting flesh.

"I thought they were on the other side of the forest..." Tera spoke through gritted teeth as her eyes scanned the tree line.

"Something must have led them here." Yamesh pointed out as he scanned the tree line as well. The sound of soft, taunting cackles gave way to the ambush that had been laid by their competition.

Kirra had half hoped that Yamesh hadn't been correct and wanted to think the best of that mousey-haired girl with the braid, but it seemed all of it had been a lie. Kirra saw Tera pull an axe from the corner of her eye as she closed her eyes and realized what she was doing. Reaching out, she snatched her wrist before she could loose an axe, "Save it for the hell hounds. We'll worry about them later."

The sound of a spear extending as she heard the crunch of leaves beside her drew Kirra's attention. Yamesh had just moved away from Tera and Kirra, causing a soft curse to come from their mouths.

Tera called out, "Yamesh! Get close to us!"

"I need room to throw and can't do that if we're right next to each other." Already, Kirra could hear the familiar sound of growling and almost hyena-like cackles as they started to close in on Yamesh efficiently from the tree line.

Tera tossed an axe into the tree line as it disappeared behind a row of bushes while a hound jumped out with a partner, and the pair pressed between Yamesh and the two girls. From behind, the others started to come out from the trees, causing Yamesh to swing wide with the spear to keep them at a distance. Kirra called out, instructing him, "We only need to injure one! They'll turn on it instead of us."

Without much of a thought for her own safety, Kirra drew the blade on her hip and swung it down at the pair in front of her. It did what she wanted, which was to create a gap as she yelled out, "Yamesh on us!"

As Yamesh took the chance and rolled through the gap right after it was created, all three put their backs against each other. Soon, the group was surrounded on all sides as the demons started to circle around them. Kirra instructed, "They go for the weakest target. I injured one and the two turned on it instead of us."

With a fully extended spear, Yamesh stabbed at a hound that got a little too brave. He caught it from above, so it sliced through its back, making it yelp and pull back as it squealed in pain. While it was trying to recover and pulled back from the circle of death, two other hounds turned on it and started to loom toward its injured pack member. It didn't take long for the other hounds to notice an easier prey to terrorize. All five hounds eventually peeled off from the three and took the injured demon to the ground, ripping it to shreds while it was still alive.

Yamesh wasted no time. Moving forward away from the three, he threw his spear into one of the demons. The throw was hard enough to pin the poor thing to the ground as it tried to break free. Moving up with a short sword, he cut the head free of the beast, causing it to dissipate. Tera moved in right after Yamesh. She pulled an axe out and brought it down on the creature's head with a scream, causing it to scream and dissipate into the air as well. Kirra stepped up with an unpracticed swing; she was the last to attempt an attack but missed as the demons were no longer surprised.

The moment the demon dodged the sword, Kirra was tackled to the ground, causing her to cry out. At the last moment, Kirra wedged the sword into the creature's snapping jaws as it attempted to go for her throat. As it clawed at her, she cried out as those sharp claws ripped into her shoulders. With a scream of adrenaline, she rolled the creature onto its back and pressed with all the strength she had, driving the sword through its mouth almost severing it from its body. Kirra was left panting and shaking as she stayed on all fours. Seeing a pair of cat-like paws standing in front of her caused her to look up. They must have dispatched the last of the demons.

Holding his hand out to help her up, she took it as he asked, "I believe that is the end of the trial."

"What happens no—" As soon as the words left her mouth, a pressure took over her like she had just been dunked deep in the ocean without getting wet. It was as though gravity all around her had suddenly started changing and was encompassing her entire being. Suddenly, everything around her started to swirl and ebb, as if the surrounding area was changing. When everything finally stopped, she was no longer in the Playground.

Her feet landed on solid dirt, and her stomach twisted and flipped violently. The dirt around her feet was lightly singed black with markings and symbols that were unfamiliar to her. As sound started to rush back in, the sound of a stadium full of people greeted her ears. The lurch in her stomach drew her eyes to a nearby bin, causing her to drop to her knees and double over. Almost immediately after, she violently vomited into the bin, hugging it close as she gasped between bouts of puking.

As Kirra began to recover, she saw movement from the side, drawing her attention. From the corner of her eye, she saw a hand offering a washcloth, which she took as she slowly stood, afraid if she moved too quickly, her stomach might lurch again. Looking around, she noticed she wasn't the only one who had succumbed to whatever it was that caused her to puke. Feeling a hand on her shoulder, she hissed in pain and was about to retaliate until she saw who it was. Black Dragon.

While checking over her injuries, he explained, "You're in the Coliseum. Bat Colony uses these trials as a way to make money from those of you who go through them. They bet on who is going to make it and who isn't. Ultimately, the person who did the best is declared the 'winner'." He gave her a careful pat on the shoulder while helping to keep her steady.

Kirra took this time to look around only to realize there were more trainers speaking with the others in the trial. Beastmaster was speaking with Yamesh, Flower with Tera, and one she'd never seen before was speaking with the two Shivers. She'd never seen the trainer speaking with the shivers before.

All grey and black clothes covered their body and seemed to fit around them loosely. A couple of cat-like digitigrade feet stuck out from below the calf-length pants tied at just the bottom. Dark hair shrouded their face, not grey but not black either. As though sensing she was looking at them, they turned their face towards Kirra and gave her a very thin, creepy smile. As it grew wider, the smile revealed thin, needle-like teeth on a mouth that spread wider than what should have been natural. Kirra was instantly unnerved as the individual stood to their full height and continued to smile at her.

A squeeze on her arm drew her attention back to BD, who pointed to the massive floating holo screen that seemed visible from every angle possible. It showed highlights of each endeavor the teens had faced during the trial. As Kirra's highlights started to come up, she heard a roar from the crowd as it showed her cutting down the three demons in one go. She didn't realize how skilled and talented she looked, but she did, in fact, see her eyes glowing blue while her spirit possessed her.

An announcer talked over each shot during the entire time the highlights were being shown. Not long after, their voice called out, "And the winner of this trial is..." A drum roll started over the loudspeakers before Kirra's picture popped up on the screen, "Kirra Smith! Let's give her a hand, ladies and gentlemen." Most of the crowd erupted into a mass of boos. She realized it might have come on because most had probably betted against her given her lack of time in the camp.

The hand pressing her forward didn't let up as she was guided into a hallway that looked rather familiar to her. As she was led down the hallway, Kirra was pressed into a room that she realized was even more familiar. This was where she had first met BD.

Walking into the room, she sighed softly, "Guess the crowd didn't like me too much."

BD chuckled, "They're just upset because you passed with flying colors for the first time despite your fumble near the end. The odds were stacked against you heavily. Most were betting on Yamesh to take the win." He smirked as she turned towards him, "Either way when you leave this place finally, you'll have a good amount of money set aside for a new start." Kirra looked confused, "I bet a large sum on you to win. That money is yours minus what I put in on the bet."

"You bet on me to win?" Kirra looked astounded.

A bark of laughter came from him at her surprise, "Of course! If anyone should have faith in you, it should at least be your teacher. You have a keen instinct, and when you follow it, you're rather good." He nodded to the back of the locker room, "Take a shower and get changed, we have some things that need to be discussed." Kirra wanted to stay and talk, but one sniff of her clothing caused her to retch as the familiar stank of rot filled her nose. On the wings of laughter from BD, Kirra practically ran to the shower as he stayed behind just like the first time she'd met him.

14

THE PROBLEM

The shower was a welcome reprieve after spending all day trudging through muddy and leaf-trodden trails. It also helped to clean the stink of the demons away, as well as the stress on her shoulders. Running fingers lightly over the wounds under the water, she realized the wounds weren't as deep as she thought they had been. She could have sworn they almost cleaved through her shoulders to the bone, but as she looked at them, they looked more like shallow cuts than anything.

Changing into fresh clothes, she felt them move and flow around her like they were made of water, but at the same time, they were still the same fabric. Examining herself in a mirror, she noticed she had filled out and looked quite different from when she had got there. Kirra looked healthy. She was still skinny, sure, but she had also put on weight and muscle. Doing a few jabs, she tested the flexibility of the new clothes.

"Are you done playing around?"

Kirra stepped out from behind the wall separating the two areas and fixed the clothes some, "Yeah... I hadn't realized how much I'd changed in a month..." She curled an arm and pushed on the muscle of her bicep, causing BD to chuckle, "What's with the new clothes? It feels almost alien." He merely pointed at the dragon mark on her arm.

As she examined the mark, she swore the chest was moving as though it were alive and breathing. Kirra hadn't had a chance to really examine the mark fully. The more she looked, the stranger it looked. It felt almost as though she were being watched through the mark itself. The dragon was only partially outside of the egg despite it crawling up the length of her arm. Eventually, looking at the head of the dragon, she leaned in a bit further before the eye opened, making her draw back with surprise, "That's weird."

"They do that a lot while you're learning, like to keep an eye on you. When you get older, they mostly sleep, but early on, it can be a struggle as they wind up biting you through the mark. Usually, they don't do damage, but the stronger the connection, the more painful and visual their actions are."

Black Dragon gave her time to look over the mark before speaking, "As I said earlier. The money I won from your victory will be going into an account so you can access it later. You'll get the details at a later date and you can use it for whatever your heart desires. You won't always be here and it's the one thing I can provide to help you out for when you do finally leave." A snort came from Kirra which he ignored, "You'll be starting training with swords."

"I thought you were the Survival Training Expert?"

With a bored sigh, he corrected, "Survival Training Master, but I am also an expert in swordsmanship." Kirra nodded as he continued, "You'll have some of the same classes with the rest of your cabin, but given everything that happened today, you have some new classes for specialty training. You'll be taking riding lessons, swords training with me, energy control, and one more which is difficult to explain. Your new schedule will be listed in the cabin."

She seemed almost hesitant to ask, "Does that mean that I'll have to..." she paused, not wanting to think about it, "...move to another cabin?"

Black Dragon took in a long breath, "No, but honestly do you really care?" he pointed out to her. It felt as though he was testing her somehow, "They thought you were under special treatment by Zeke because of one incident. The second you stood up for yourself, they changed their minds."

Kirra didn't know how to respond so she just spoke how she felt about it all, "Yes and no. I was upset at first, but we're all kids, and we're all going to make mistakes. I think the only one that didn't care was Death, to be honest, but he never really spoke up about it."

Black Dragon was quick to explain, "Death didn't care. I spoke to him about it when I saw what was happening and he was the one that explained what was going on. Something about trying to explain to the others not to judge a book by its cover, but they ignored him. Ky has his own problems as he's being targeted like Death. Death figured it better that you either learn to float or sink. You floated with style. I was in agreement with his reasoning not to aid you. I'm glad you finally stuck up for yourself." Kirra seemed a bit relieved that she was right about both Death and Ky given their particular situations regarding the list.

After getting a measure of her response to his words, he finally answered her question, "No, in fact, you'll be in training with my other apprentice, but you'll be in separate sessions. There's only two of you, after all." He smirked before saying, "You'll also be given a new chore."

"Wait, what? I don't have to clean the training pad anymore?" Kirra started to get excited as she pumped her fist at not having mop floors anymore, "Woooo! I got sick and tired of cleaning up spit, sweat, and blood off those tiles."

"Kirra…" She stopped doing a little victory dance and looked at him, "Your work from here on out will only get harder. You have to maintain a balance of what you have already learned and practice what you are currently learning." She nodded to him in understanding, "The rest of the day is yours to do with what you want. I would recommend getting some rest, but it is up to you."

"I thought this place looked familiar. When Death told me there was a coliseum, I didn't think he meant a literal colosseum."

"A little slow on the pick-up, but yes, this is the same locker room I brought you to day one. The others had been taken to separate, larger locker rooms for girls and boys. Given your lack of knowledge, I pulled you to the side… That and you were in desperate need of a shower. I got verbally scolded for doing it, but Zeke also seemed to have a soft spot for your parents." Stepping off to the side, he waved towards the door, "Go on. Get some rest. You deserve it, as you've had a busy day."

Kirra moved past him and paused with her hand on the door. Looking over her shoulder at BD, she finally said sincerely, "Thank you for… uh, not making this awkward. You know, being in here while I change and all that. There are some really creepy-looking people who are trainers, like the Shivers' trainer. They gave me a very creepy look."

Letting out a bark of laughter, he looked at her, shaking his head, "Kirra, I am going to make this abundantly clear for you. Children do not interest me. In fact, not much really does interest me nowadays. Some of the people here are stuck in their ways and habits. Well, I am an extremely honorable person. That's why I work for an honor guild. I do not kill children or mothers with babies. I have been with this guild for a very long time, and most of those that are here, are experts in what they are teaching, if not masters. Zeke might not be doing things in the most ethically correct way, but he did find people who are in good standing with a moral compass that would make most jealous. I might work for an assassin guild, but that does not make me or anyone else in this line of work corrupted, twisted, or otherwise."

He paused briefly before saying solemnly, "I am only in my guild because someone said yes to me when everyone else said no. For that, I will always remain loyal to our guild leader and his decisions. Even if Zeke does things in a way that could be deemed corruptive and toxic, he did bring in stragglers like Ms. Chetski and myself." Kirra opened her mouth, looking like she wanted to ask a question, as Black Dragon encouraged her, "Ask your question, Kirra."

She paused again, unsure how to word her question, but finally found the wording, "What do you mean stragglers like yourself and Ms. Chetski?"

Taking a deep breath, he pushed off the wall and waved for her to follow him. Kirra was unsure where he was taking her, but she trusted BD, maybe even with her life. He led her down the hallway and eventually out of the colosseum down a path that wasn't well-worn. Every once in a while, Kirra had to jog just to keep pace with his longer strides. Eventually, he stopped in front of a tree with an almost comically small treehouse. Around the trunk were makeshift steps that spiraled up to a door where the house sat. As though he did this daily, BD jogged up the steps with ease.

Kirra took her time and carefully hugged the tree, afraid of tumbling over the edge at any moment. There were no railings to keep from falling, so she stepped carefully while mentioning, "I guess this would be a lot worse if I were afraid of heights."

A few chuckles came from his soft, baritone voice, "A dragon afraid of heights. Never heard of a thing like that before." He was thankfully pausing every other step or so as if to make sure she wouldn't fall before adding, "They're wedged in rather well. You shouldn't fall off unless you miss a step."

"Oh yeah. Thanks, I **really** appreciate the heads up now." Her sarcastic tone came through, making him laugh a bit louder.

Once at the top of the house, he opened the door to what looked like a kid's cabin. Even Kirra had to carefully bend not to hit her head on the door as she slipped in, but she was surprised at what she found inside.

The room was larger on the inside than what she thought awaited her. It was almost as though the space had been warped and changed so that something larger could fit someplace smaller. There was equipment lying neatly about, like a personal gym of sorts, as well as a training mat. Most of the equipment she recognized, but some she didn't. The entire room was a pristine white, as though the light was coming from the floor, walls, and ceiling. Black Dragon had to push Kirra to the side as he moved past her. She was awestruck and standing right in the way.

The door disappeared as if it had never been there the moment Black Dragon stepped inside. Not even a seam where the door had been remained. The parts of the room that didn't have training equipment were ornately decorated like they were being used as a living space. There were a couple of tables, some dark-colored, over-stuffed couches that looked comfy, a full kitchen, and a singular large bed adorned with gold and black linens. It wasn't something one would expect from a survival master.

Black Dragon seemed right at home as he walked over to the kitchen while tossing aside the black knee-length wool coat, "Find yourself a seat. Would you like some tea?"

Still in awe, Kirra moved to one of the couches and sat down but didn't fully get comfortable. It had been a long time since she sat on something out of comfort. Sitting on the edge of the couch, her back was straight, and it appeared as though she was almost afraid to relax as she replied, "Um, no, thank you. That was more of my parents than me."

Despite her saying no, he brought over a set of cups and set it down in front of her, stating, "Try it anyway. You might find it to be to your taste." Taking a place in a chair that seemed to be formed to his body from the many years of use, he leaned back, taking a sip from his own cup, sighing as he relaxed. It was something Kirra had never seen him do before.

Watching BD relax, she reached for the cup hesitantly and eyed the liquid within. Kirra's eyes flicked to the form of BD as he sat in his chair, relaxing back and seeming to enjoy the quiet and the flavors of the tea. Leaning in, she took a hesitant sip of the honey-colored liquid and was surprised at the flavors that assaulted her taste buds. A mix of florals and fruits took over her senses reminding her of home. When she looked up, two golden eyes peered at her curiously, stating softly, "That was your mother's favorite as well."

The comment surprised Kirra, making her pause as she set the cup down, asking, "Why are we here? Or rather, where are we?"

"We're in a portable home. To explain it more easily, let's say it's the equivalent of a pocket dimension. It's incredibly expensive to set them up, but when you use them, it's hard not to want to use them. Basically, it's a miniature portal to another part of the multiverse. You usually have someone else build it and set them up for you. Most don't use them for homes, but I decided to because I didn't want to be disturbed. You didn't see it, but before you got to the top, I put in the access code to open it up." He put down his tea and leaned forward, saying, "As to why we are here..." He pulled out a device from his coat where it hung and set it down on the table. A holo screen opened up between them before he held his arm out, pulled another screen up over his arm, and seemed to search for something on the one over his arm.

Tapping on the holo screen over his arm, a few news articles and reels popped up on the screen between them. Moving pictures of a black dragon spewing fire over a town and several articles titled "Terror of the Skies," "Golden-Eyed Terrorist Returns," and "The Black Death Looms" popped up with brief descriptions or writings of the articles. BD watched her face and asked, "What do you think when you see these?"

Scanning the articles, Kirra spoke truly to him, "I would say that the person who did these things is a terrorist and needs to be dealt with."

"Those pictures were taken during times of catastrophe in larger towns. There are some from smaller towns throughout the multiverse as well. The biggest problem was that I was saving people, but that was not the picture that was illustrated to the masses. The people I was able to save knew what I had done, but others thought I was the one that caused them. At one point I had a few bounties put out on my head. Black dragons like myself have a very bad stigma around us as we're associated with Trivitus, the god of chaos, darkness, violence, and several other dark deeds."

A long sigh came from him before he continued, "I've been around for a very long time, but I have never done anything menacing or with malicious intent toward the common public. It's always been painted that way though. When you see someone like myself, you don't see someone who is kind, decent, or honorable." He let it sink in momentarily before saying, "Kirra. The Justice Guild sent one of their best after me, chasing a bounty. They had me dead to rights and could have easily killed me, but they didn't. They saw past all those lies and instead invited me to the guild, given the chase I put them through. I rose in the ranks quickly because of my years of experience and eventually became the trainer for the Survival class. Your mother went through my class and was one of the brightest students I ever had. She led her class to success and later used those skills to save several people who would have died without the knowledge I taught her. What I teach and train here can mean the difference between life and death."

After some time and a sip of tea, she asked, "Was my mom a good person?"

"She was the best. She did something most wouldn't do in our line of work. Retire and have children of her own." Black Dragon smiled, "Not many retire from this lifestyle. Usually, the only way most get out is by dying, and that is just because of how dangerous our jobs can be."

"What about Miss Chetski? You said she was a straggler, too."

He took a few moments to figure out how to word what he wanted to say, "Miss Chetski is a one-of-a-kind individual. She was a child of a notable family. Her parents were the descendants of a long line of leaders of Bat Colony. She was supposed to be next in line, but given her conditions, she decided not to, and her younger brother took over instead. Eventually, Zeke stepped up after her younger brother started to botch things. The population got out of control, there was not enough food, not enough supplies, and people started to fight. Zeke saw where he could make a change and did so."

Setting his mug down, he looked at her, "He turned this Colony around. He started making trade deals with companies outside of this planet. Set up the army so the people had a proper military to help control things should they get out of control again. Started to fund research and development and put the council into play like the dragons so that each head ran a specific area with qualified people."

Running a hand over his jaw stubble, he thought over his words carefully, "Before any of that, Chetski was thrown out of her home. When Zeke rediscovered her existence, she was living successfully on her own and running caravans across the planet through the wilds. It turned out she had a very rare genetic disorder. She was raised as a girl; her parents thought she was a girl, but realistically, she was a he, and she didn't find this out until the idea of her being female was embedded in her head. That's why she got tossed out. It turned out that the genetic disorder she had also caused her to be born blind."

The real reason why she was thrown out is much darker than just some genetic disorder. Chetski discovered the reason behind her disorder. She was going to leak it to the rest of Bat Colony, but her family banished her for life and told all of their houseguards that she had dishonored them with some gambling debt. Her name was dragged through the mud, and her reputation was destroyed. Despite that, Zeke went out of his way to ensure he found her and brought her back to her home. Now she is here."

Kirra couldn't believe what she was hearing from him. As she sat there in contemplation, Black Dragon gave her a hard look before she said, "You're lying to me."

"I am not."

She stammered over her words, "That can't be right. Zeke started an entire war and caused a lot of people to die. He killed my parents."

"Do not get me wrong when I say this. Zeke is going about things in a way that could be viewed by most as morally wrong. He has tried to change the views of others towards bats, other supposed lesser kin, and wrongfully looked upon spiritosk, but stubbornness and wrongful thinking have led the masses astray. My example lies in yourself right now. You are predisposed to believe that Zeke is a terrible person with horrible motives because he killed your parents." Black Dragon was clearly trying to make a point about something as he stared her down.

"And say that he hadn't killed my parents?"

"Let's say your people were being turned into slaves. People that you had known your entire life were being tortured and abused, but you could do something about it. The person responsible for all that pain and problems, and you knew their schedule. If you could end it all with one kill, would you?" He proposed the theoretical question.

Kirra didn't even have to think of an answer as she spoke up almost instantly, "Yes. One hundred percent. I would if it stopped the persecution of my people."

"Say that when you finished the job, their three children walked out and saw you. Do you think they would ever see you as anything but a monster? You took away the one thing in their life they knew, just like that. Do you believe that they would eventually ever see you as doing something that was justified?"

Kirra didn't know how to respond to him. There was no good answer because then she would be siding with him if she admitted it out loud, so she said nothing. After waiting for her response, Black Dragon finally pointed his finger at her, "And that is exactly the problem. You're too stubborn to even admit out loud that he might somehow be justified in his actions." He leaned back, taking a sip of his tea before setting the mug down once more. Lifting his arm, the holo screen above it appeared and he typed in something on it as the door to the outside appeared, "I'm not siding with or against him, but rather trying to get you to think for yourself instead of based off your prejudice because of what happened to your parents. Think on this tonight when you go to bed. Everything isn't as black and white as you think it is, and the dragons aren't the white knights that history makes them out to be."

Taking one last sip of tea, she set down the cup, gave a light bow of her head in thanks for his company and advice, and took her leave. Returning to the cabin, she noticed that her clothes had all been replaced with new ones. They were neatly laid out on her bed and folded. Taking a small amount of time to mark her name in the new clothes, she refolded them and put them away. Eventually, she found exhaustion starting to take its toll, and crawled into bed with questions whirling in her mind:

Who were the **real** bad guys in this war?

Were the Dragons as terrible as everyone made them out to be?

Was Zeke the bad guy? Or were the Dragons making him out to be like that?

Why hadn't her powers come out and shown themselves yet?

Where was her brother? Was he even alive?

There were too many questions for which she had no answers. She had seen the prejudice of being something other than a dragon, but she had also seen that prejudice being thrown back at the dragons as well. She hoped for once she could have a dreamless sleep without gods or nightmares clogging it up. She didn't want to think about the war and that Zeke might actually be the good guy or that the dragons could be the bad guys. It was just simpler for her to train and concentrate on her survival. Sleep came, and with it came the reprieve from the complex questions congesting her mind.

15
NEW RECRUITS

The presence of someone near her woke her, causing her to jolt upright. Looking around with sleep-ridden eyes, the figure that had moved near her bed started to clear some. A hand was outstretched near her as though meant to wake her before withdrawing and motioning her to stay quiet and to follow them outside. With a sleepy groan of annoyance, Kirra got fully dressed and went outside while rubbing her eyes. The realization of who had woken her caused her to snap awake as though ice water had been thrown on her.

An amused tone overtook his voice as Zeke commented softly, "I thought we were on better terms than that, Kirra." Stepping off of the porch, he started walking down the path.

Sighing out, Kirra begrudgingly followed, "More surprised. Usually, it's Black Dragon creepily waking me from sleep in the early morn. Not you." An amused chuckle came from him, "Why **are** you waking me up?"

"I like the fact that you ask questions. It means you're smart." He climbed the stairs towards the dining hall and held the door open for her, "I believe in the 'seeing is believing method.'" He looked down at her as if waiting for her reaction.

For a split second, Kirra swore she saw the blurry outline of something around Zeke. It was only a moment, but it caused her to pause. A black spirit surrounding a smaller gray one. The two were fuzzy, and perhaps the shadows were just playing tricks on her. Rubbing her eyes, she ignored the visual momentarily before moving through the door as he gave a polite bow to her.

It took a moment for her eyes to adjust to the light of the dining hall as she entered. The first thing she noticed was that each of the people present was from different cabins and on different spots in the list. Before them lay a buffet of breakfast foods before the teens, which they were all already partaking. The only person she really recognized from the rest of the cabins at the moment was Roc. Seeing her enter, he gave a soft wave to her and flagged her to sit down with him. Despite their differences at the start, Roc had taken a liking to Kirra after the beating she put up with from him.

A little hesitant to join him, she sat near Roc, grabbed a plate, and took a small amount of food. She was used to eating light because of her rigorous workouts and often snuck into the dining hall for a snack between classes or free time between training. After a few moments of awkwardness, Kirra eventually started opening up to him. They mostly talked about the new classes she'd be in and the special bond with Snow.

Allowing the teens their excited chatter momentarily, Zeke finally addressed the group, "Some of you know what you're here for, and some of you don't. Each cabin has a representative picked for the selection day. This is the day we get new arrivals, and it's your job to make it as hard as possible for them to make it high on the list.

"Each of you is a placeholder in the list. Most of you are new to the camp, so I will explain this once. As you all know, your rankings will be shown to the new group. The new ones can challenge others in their group or your lot. They will be angry, hateful, and downright unwilling. You lot are here because you have all held your positions for quite some time, even after improving from having almost no experience." His eyes stopped temporarily on Kirra before continuing, "For now, eat your fill. You have earned a good little meal as you might be called to fight multiple times." Zeke's eyes stared down at Kirra at his last statement before sitting down and joining the teens in their meal. A few of the others started to take the opportunity to ask questions in hopes of answers from Zeke.

Feeling the tension of the day, Kirra picked at her food. She knew she might be forced to participate in quite a few fights because she was low on the list. Several of the teens asked questions in regards to the extra classes, like what Kirra was in. She'd forgotten that the schedules were open for others to see.

More than happy to answer the questions, Zeke politely explained, "Kirra showed a higher skill set that needed to be addressed, mostly with spirit training, given what happened in the trial. Some get them, but most don't. Ky has been here for a long time and only has two extra classes. We attempted to get him in mount training as well, but he didn't take to it." It quieted down after that one answer, but it didn't take long for others to continue asking questions.

There was one question Kirra wanted to ask, but she was hesitant to speak it out loud. It was practically burning a hole in the back of her head. Given the noise of everyone else bothering him, she remained quiet and decided against it. She wasn't even sure if she wanted to know the answer. Instead, she returned to the food on her plate and toyed with it using her fork.

Deciding to remain quiet, she watched the other teens chatter excitedly about the upcoming fights. Roc leaned over and commented, "I remember only a few days ago, I would have been more than excited to just bully the crap out of someone. Now I get absolutely no joy out of doing it."

A look of curiosity crossed her face, "What changed that?"

"You. I realized it takes much more than strength to be a dragon. It takes some serious balls and a whole lotta crazy." His answer caused her to laugh before he elbowed her lightly, "Why you so quiet?"

"I have a question, but I'm afraid to ask it, to be honest. Don't want to come off as too confrontational." Roc looked at her curiously before she explained softly, "I want to know what happened to my brother. If he's alive or what's going on." She looked over her shoulder where Zeke was engaging with another teen before she mentioned, "My parents were messaging him the night that –"

"Kirra?" Zeke peered over the other teens and asked, "You said you had a question."

"I uh—" The feeling of everyone's eyes on her made her pause before she finally asked, "I was curious about what happened to my brother. Wondering if he's still alive mainly."

Zeke took a long breath before saying, "He's alive and well. Perhaps we might be able to arrange a visit in the future."

Kirra perked up, asking almost immediately, "Is he being held captive? How soon could I see hi—"

"No, no. He has offered to join up with Bat Colony's Army. He is in training at the moment but is progressing quickly. Dayla and Taro did an excellent job in training him."

Sobering some, she asked, "When can I see him?"

Considering her question, he explained, "It will be a little while, but not too long. A month or two, perhaps, but I cannot say for sure as I don't want to lie to you and promise you a date without knowing exactly when. This is the best I can do at the moment." His answer seemed genuine, and it felt like he was trying to work with her but not mislead or misinform her simultaneously, "Will this suffice as an answer?"

Nodding to him, Kirra was attempting not to get her hopes up too much. Knowing how close he was, she couldn't help but get a little excited. Instead of focusing on the fact that he was in the army, she returned to her food. Nervousness about the upcoming fights gnawed at her insides, making it hard for her to stomach anything. On the other side, she had more reason to fight harder, given the knowledge that her brother was right within reach of her.

As everyone finished their food, Kirra watched Zeke stand. At first, she assumed he would address everyone once more, but instead, he waved his hand as though dismissing something. Mid gesture, she saw him stare down at his hand as a frown formed on his face. Looking up at him, she saw disappointment etching the lines of his face before he clapped his hands to get everyone's attention. Almost immediately after, he started ushering everyone out of the dining hall and towards the challenge pad.

"*I recognize those movements.*"

She inquired, "*What was he trying to do?*"

245

Her spirit seemed to pause with a deep rumble, considering his words before finally giving her an answer, *"He was trying to use magic..."* Kirra let out a mental snort, *"I'm serious. That's a very common spell movement. The way he moved his hand and made a sign with his fingers. He was trying to use magic..."*

"Bats can't use magic. Maybe you're mistaken."

"Perhaps..."

As the group traveled towards the challenge pad, Kirra could already hear orders being yelled out in the distance similar to what she heard when she'd arrived. Once they got to the pad, the group started heading toward the numbers out of sheer habit, but all of them were redirected to the bleachers. As the lot of them filed into the bleachers in neat little rows, Zeke found a spot off on his own. He helpfully pointed out, "You can spread out. You do not have to crowd each other."

Several sighs of relief were heard as most of everyone started to spread out. Kirra and Roc stayed exactly where they were, content sitting beside each other. Not long after they had settled, some of the teachers started filtering into the stands and mixing with the teens. The one that moved next to them was the same trainer that creeped Kirra out as they moved behind the two young spiritosk.

Their voice commented softly from behind, directly addressing Kirra, "You know you knocked my two apprentices off the list, riiii-iiight?" Something about the teacher felt off like they weren't mortal.

The hair on the back of Kirra's neck stood on end as she replied evenly, "They did it themselves. All I did was participate in the trial."

The creature leaned back with a cackle, speaking in that same eerie whisper, "Oh, I'm not angry, just disappointed in the pair of them. You, however, will start training with me soon." So this was her mystery trainer named Ryse, "That is if you don't have some sort of accident today."

Her spirit let out a growl inside of her, causing her to turn and spit at the creature, "Is that a threat?"

Ryse sat there with that creepy needle-toothed smile before chuckling, "No threats, but I know how dangerous it can be fighting against others when they are experiencing unbridled rage." Even Kirra had to admit that there was truth being spoken there. Ryse's attention quickly diverted to another's presence, "Aelbryst! Nice of you to join us for such an occasion." The alien-like elf that had given the hint for the trial joined Ryse, "I thought you might be withering away in your library using your corruptive magic."

Aelbryst was as elegantly dressed as the day he'd given the hint. He was apparently the trainer who would be teaching her energy control. This not only applied to the use of Kidori but also to abilities.

Aelbryst replied pointedly, "It is called enchanting, and it does not corrupt, *demon.*"

Kirra realized that the feeling she got from Ryse was the same as those hell hounds. It made sense now that Aelbryst had called Ryse for what they were. The idea of being trained by a demon made Kirra nervous. She sat quietly, watching the pair interact just as Roc did.

Aelbryst's voice was as elegant as he was alien, "I am here because there is a celestial dragon in this group, and there is a high possibility that they are, in fact, the Prophecy that Zeke is so desperately looking for."

Another cackle came from Ryse, "If there is a celestial dragon here today, the **only** reason they survive is because they are, in fact, the prophecy, or someone takes mercy on their soul and decides to help them." The demon paused and looked towards Kirra, "Though this one faired alright."

Given that Ryse was so close, Kirra had a better view of the demon in loose grey clothing. A slender, agile tail with a spade-like tip flicked almost lazily behind. Elongated sharp nails protruded from dexterous fingers, sharp and long enough to do damage without being bothersome. It was too difficult to see what kind of frame was hidden under the dark grey clothing. Despite the hood over their head, she still had a view of the angular jaw that held a bit of masculinity to it. Even the dark curtains of hair surrounding his face couldn't hide the details of his face. Tufts of fur behind the curtains of hair poked out and spoke of something more animalistic.

Ryse's voice called attention to her staring, "Take a screenshot. I can't pose for you all day." The red cat-like eyes glinted with some minor amusement toward Kirra.

It was Aelbryst who spoke in her defense, "Don't tease the girl, Ryse. She's probably never seen a Sidion. Let alone even heard of them before today."

Aelbryst's face swiveled towards the tunnel as the whole of the bleachers went quiet. A pair of soldiers preceded a row of confused-looking kids. Whatever response Ryse was about to belt out, halted as he leaned forward with his arms braced on his knees. He squinted at the teens with his head propped on his fists. Aelbryst straightened up as well, his hands folded neatly in his lap, seemingly analyzing the group as they came out.

Looking over at the group as well, Kirra squinted, trying to see what all breeds of dragons were in the group. That was when she noticed someone from Earth with whom she had gone to school. The celestial dragon that they were speaking of was the one and same that had bullied her through high school on Earth.

Ryse leaned back in the bleachers, huffing out, "Nuthin'. Not a single blip of any kind."

Aelbryst commented softly, "The group seems to contain mostly common energy types, and all are weak and untrained." He sighed, "Only one energy is that of a lighter source, and that is coming from the celestial dragon. The last group had more potential."

"What is it with these children? The majority of them are all underpowered, and all have common energy types. It's almost as though there's been a shift in power through the multiverse." Kirra listened inquisitively as the pair spoke. Their words were soft as Zeke gave his speech, "Lucky the demons are content to live where they are currently. They'd be running amuck if they found out about these changes."

Aelbryst commented, "That is a good point. It seems the balance is being pushed heavily in a different direction. I've noticed the same pattern among elven kind as well. The skill for enchantment and summoning is not what it used to be." Kirra was watching the celestial dragon as she stumbled forward in line with the other teens. For the life of her, Kirra couldn't recall the scared girl's name.

As Zeke finished his speech, the list dulled and showed only those currently present, "Now, who do you choose to fight?" Kirra hoped that no one would instantly challenge the celestial.

A boy who was a black dragon stated firmly and confidently, "I pick the weakling at the end..."

Kirra sighed as she was about to stand since she assumed he was talking about her, "... the celestial dragon with the pretty hair." Double crap. Kirra looked to the girl with golden blonde hair and watched her about have a panic attack.

Zeke looked behind him to the bleachers and called out lowly enough for them to hear but not the others out on the pad, "You can choose to take her in your cabin and take her place in the fight or let the fight play out." Several of the kids commented that the girl was going to be ground meat when that kid was done with her. Kirra didn't want to vouch for her, but she knew the girl might actually die, given the size difference of her opponent, if somebody didn't do something.

Standing up, Kirra called out to Zeke, "I'll take her place."

Zeke seemed slightly surprised as he looked back at her, "Are you certain? You can't go back after this?"

Kirra confirmed her choice, "Unfortunately, yes. I'm certain."

Making her way towards the pair, Kirra felt her breath hitch in her throat as nervousness of the coming fight started wracking her nerves. Shaking out her arms, she could hear the boy yelling threats towards the celestial dragon girl. He kept commenting on how he would make her wish she had never been born.

Forcing herself to calm down, BD's voice from a previous lesson echoed through her head, *"I know that being in a fight will bring your body to a level of intensity you aren't used to, but you need to control it. Find your center, remember your goal, and keep a level head."* Taking her Master's advice, she centered herself and stepped between the dragons.

As she stepped just in front of the celestial dragoness, Kirra advised her softly, "You're going to want to step back."

The sound of feet shuffling backward from her made Kirra raise her gaze toward the male with a look of pure malice. Raising her fists and taking a stance, she narrowed her eyes on the boy, still jeering at the girl. Kirra didn't pay much attention to his threats. She listened for the one thing that would allow her to shut him up.

Finally, the command from Zeke came, "Begin..."

The boy recklessly charged at her. His stance was untrained; he didn't know how to throw a punch properly, and everything was completely wrong about his posture. He was nothing but a bully.

He tossed one wildly thrown punch with as much power that could be mustered. It was easily dodged. Kirra's punch, however, was far more dangerous as a left hook took him straight to the ground like a sack of potatoes. "*One punch. That's all it takes. Your head goes too far in one direction, and that's it. The fight is over.*" Black Dragon's voice echoed in her head from a previous lesson.

The boy barely managed to get back to his feet. It seemed he wasn't down for the count just yet. As he started to stumble towards her with dazed eyes, he took another wild swing at her, clearly furious she had put him on the ground. She dodged easily and struck out with a kick to put him back on the ground again. He didn't get up this time. As her adrenaline faded, she could hear her environment tune back in as laughter rang out from the bleachers.

As the laughter calmed, Zeke spoke up, "Nyte loses. Kirra moves up in ranking. Alyssa sits at the bottom now." Kirra started moving back towards the bleachers as Zeke smiled at her, "Stay on the pad and keep your muscles warmed up. I have a feeling you'll have to fight again."

Kirra nodded her head as she felt a soft pat from Zeke. She moved back to her place and kept her body moving lightly so as not to get stiff. She wasn't making a show of it, just loosening her arms and legs up. As a few medical personnel checked on Nyte, they helped him up to the side but saw no major injuries. He escaped the fight with only a split brow. Once he was moved to the side, Zeke started to stare down the group of new arrivals.

"You either pick who you wish to fight, or one by one, you will fight Kirra. Pick who you wish to fight, or I'll call you by name to fight her."

At that prompt, one of the other females called out to fight someone from the new group. Kirra decided to move to where Alyssa was, given there was another fight going on and settled in front of her. Alyssa was having a mini panic attack at the entirety of what was going on as she curled up on the ground, lightly rocking in place. The feeling of familiarity rolled over her from Alyssa, like a strange attraction.

"*Why does that keep happening?*"

"*I am not sure...*" Her spirit answered, "*She gives off the feeling of kinship. Perhaps it is because she is also a celestial.*"

Shaking the feeling off, Kirra squatted in front of Alyssa as the sounds of fighting erupted behind her. Snapping her fingers in front of Alyssa, she tried to shake her out of the state she was in, "Hey, remember me?"

It took Alyssa a few moments, but the spark of recognition finally lit up her eyes. She stammered, "K-Kirra?"

"Yeah. Turns out I'm a filthy dragon, just like you. Because of how we are, there's a chance any one of us could be the prophecy." She took a deep breath and finished with, "Yeah, there's a lot more to it than that, but you'll be bunking with my group. That was kind of the price of not letting that jerk wad beat the crap out of you just because he could."

Alyssa was clearly surprised as she stammered, "W-Why? I - I was terrible to you in school, and... and I—"

Kirra stopped her with, "I don't like bullies. I've been picked on my whole life. By other bats, by other races, by adults and kids. I just don't like bullies." She struggled with the words to explain as one fight finished and another started. Finally, she continued, "I was like you when I arrived. I got picked out because I'm a celestial dragon, and they knocked me around. But then I learned and got stronger." She lightly tapped Alyssa's shoulder, "Don't worry though. You'll get there too. We have some of the best fighters in our cabin, so they'll help you if you ask." Kirra gave her the briefest of smiles.

Alyssa looked at Kirra like she didn't know what to do, "I - I don't have anywhere to go. I - I don't know how to fight."

Kirra shrugged, "You'll learn, or you won't." Kirra thought helping Alyssa might change how she acted and her attitude somewhat.

"Half-blood." The comment was snorted from her spirit.

Kirra squinted at Alyssa questioningly, *"Who? She is?"*

The deep throaty chuckle filled her head, *"Mmmm... I remember sleepily calling it out while I was starting to wake from that eternal slumber."*

"Do you remember anything before the slumber?"

"No... Only the sleep."

Kirra stayed near Alyssa, watching the fights happen one after another. Finally, she saw one of the new arrivals walk forward on the pad and look directly at her. It seemed that she was being called to challenge. Sighing, Kirra stood and walked out onto the pad, taking a stance as she waited for the word to start. From what she had seen, the guy had some experience fighting. She didn't know if the fight would

253

turn out the same as Nyte, but she didn't feel so bad about herself anymore with at least one victory under her belt. It did wonders for her confidence going into the next fight.

Unfortunately for the boy, Kirra made quick work of them. They were predictable and sloppy, as if they hadn't been training for long. Wildly thrown punches mixed with a lack of confidence and balance made for a poor opponent against her. As the fight concluded, Kirra looked over to Zeke. He smirked as he applauded, and she got the feeling he was about to do something she wanted no part of. That was the last fight from the new group of arrivals.

16

THE DARKNESS WITHIN

"**R**oc, step onto the pad." It wasn't a question; it was an order from Zeke.

Kirra looked uncomfortable as she looked between the approaching form of Roc and Zeke's confident posture as he stood off to the side of the fighting pad. He wanted her to fight Roc, but Kirra wasn't sure she was ready for that fight yet. She scanned the bleachers for her Master and found him giving her a head nod. Looking at Roc, he looked as reluctant as she was in this endeavor as the pair looked toward the formidable Bat Lord.

His voice rang out with authority, "You two have been matched before. Kirra still has room for improvement, but you, Roc, have stayed at the same ranking since you arrived. Let's see if the last few days of trial and rest have done some good for you, Kirra."

Kirra countered, "It's only been a couple of days..."

"A lot can happen in those days, or would you rather fight my son again." His voice came across in challenge as though daring her to refuse.

Her spirit growled out to her, *"Stick up for yourself..."* The voice of her spirit sounded slightly different. He radiated rage, anger, and violence. Something was wrong.

"What am I supposed to do?"

There was nothing but malice in her spirit's voice, *"Fight his kid. Don't be a coward. Make. Him. Suffer."* This wasn't like her spirit. He growled out with nothing but pure viciousness and murderous intent.

"Kirra?" Zeke's question came with a raised brow as he saw her hesitate.

"Do it!" Her spirit insisted

"No!" Disappointment was clear on Zeke's face as she attempted to reason, "Something is off about all of this. It's not even been two days." The rolling thunder of chaotic laughter filled her head.

Zeke sighed, shaking his head, "Kirra..." he was clearly disappointed in her. Kirra looked for help from her own Master, but he was shaking his own head in disappointment.

Devin leaped up from the bleachers and approached the pad as his father looked at him. Roc almost immediately backed out of the way while looking concerned about Kirra. Cracking his knuckles, Devin gave one last look to Zeke as though seeing if his father would change his mind. One simple nod from Zeke and Devin started to round on Kirra.

Her spirit's voice echoed with a satisfied cackle that sounded very familiar to her. As she listened more closely, she realized it was filled with the undertone of a voice from her dream. Trivitus.

Panic clawed at her throat as her heart pounded like a drum. As Devin rounded on her, she dodged as a familiar warmth filled her. The next punch from him, she caught his arm in a grapple and easily tossed him over her shoulder as he was slammed down onto the floor. The sound of stone cracking echoed through the air as several people were heard gasping at the intensity of which she had just thrown him.

Devin was left gasping for air on the ground as a cackle came from Kirra's throat. It wasn't one of her own doing. Kirra was trapped in her own body, unable to stop the train wreck of carnage that she was unleashing. Several times, Kirra tried to break her spirit's hold over her, to no avail.

Her own hand twisted Devin's arm, making him cry out as she cackled out teasingly, "What'sssss the matter, Zeke? Your threatssss don't work on ussss anymore. What are you going to do now?" Kirra was screaming internally at her spirit for him to release her body. She tried to fight back for control but to no avail.

"She has no control right now, does she?" He stepped onto the pad, holding his hands out while speaking with caution, "Why don't you let go of that boy's arm and face me instead? After all, I am the one you are after."

There was a clear moment of consideration before Kirra released the arm she held and slowly walked toward Zeke. Her hands became claws as maniacal laughter rang out from her, "Kill." The thing controlling her rushed at Zeke while Kirra internally struggled to force the control of her spirit from her body.

"How long can you force control over the girl before you push her body to the point of death." Dodging the claws effectively, he commanded, "Release control of the girl..."

It was like being trapped in a fleshy prison of her own accord. She could hear her voice, see her actions, and feel her environment, but Kirra could do nothing to stop what was happening. Only mad laughter rang out in response as her claws swiped out in a flurry of blows towards Zeke. It looked as though Zeke was struggling to keep up with her, but he seemed reluctant to damage her while she was in this state.

The set of arms gripping her from behind told a different story. Zeke had been buying time. Kirra's legs kicked out and flailed in an attempt to break the grapple she was in while Zeke moved in from the front. Eventually, the pair wrestled her to the ground on her knees as Kirra stared up at Zeke with an unnatural, cruel smile.

The voice growled out to the body's owner as it came out in Kirra's voice, "Unworthy runt!"

Zeke's hands gripped her head firmly, but not hard, as he stared into Kirra's eyes with empathy, "Brace yourself; this is going to hurt a lot, Kirra."

Searing hot pain ripped through her entire being as claw marks appeared along her arms. It was as if whatever gripped her was trying to cling on desperately while being ripped out. Kirra didn't just feel the pain on a physical level but on an internal level as well. It felt as though she was having her very soul ripped from her body as she screamed in agony. The feeling of claws ripping up the length of her arms and sides as though the force that had a hold on her was desperately clinging to her still. Next, her head felt as though it was going to explode as she tried to fight against the pain. All at once, the pain stopped, and everything went black around her. No pain, no feeling. Just the feeling of her floating.

The sudden sting of a smack caused Kirra to stir. Zeke was standing over her, holding the back of her neck gently while trying to call out to her. She didn't hear anything right away because the ringing in her ears was too loud until the sound started to filter back in. His voice echoed, sounding like he was off in the distance despite his being right next to her, "Say Something. Come back. Can you hear me?"

Kirra's body was cold. Everything was sore and hurt like a parade of ancient wolves had just run over her. The feeling of a hand gripping her wrist as she tried to make sense of things caused her to look around in a confused state.

Black Dragon's voice said, "Her heart rate is extremely slow."

"Her spirit burned through more energy than she could actually give. She'll be out of it for a few days at least."

Aelbryst's voice next, "I've never seen such a strong spirit bond before."

The familiar cackle of Ryse rang out, "More like she was taken for a drive, and the owner was bound, gagged, and thrown in the cargo hold."

Zeke gave the order, "Take her to the Hospital and let them look at her to make sure she will at least live." Her body was hefted up by Black Dragon as he continued to give orders, "Tell the staff to notify me when she is coherent. I need to have a discussion with her."

The feeling of wind whipping past her as the sound of large wings flapping drew her to look around. She was certain she was dreaming now. She kept falling in and out of consciousness while being carried. One moment, she was floating through the air; the next, she was on a soft bed while others worried over her. She remembered someone coming in and checking over her as the earlier rush quieted.

The sound of a machine lightly beeping roused Kirra from her sleep. She felt tired, sluggish, and like hell itself had run her over, but she was alive. Looking around the room, she gathered it was full dark and she wasn't alone. A nurse was in the room reading a book.

Not even glancing up from the book, she called out in a bored tone, "Good morning." The words came from the nurse as she yawned, "I always like to give my patients a few moments to realize they are awake before saying something."

Kirra seemed confused as she asked, "How did—"

"Your heart changed pace." It was said like she had said it one too many times before she asked, "Can you tell me where we are?"

Kirra couldn't believe she was being asked that question, "How would I know? I was practically dying on the way here. I'm going to take a wild guess and say Bat Colony."

"Oh no, you definitely died..." Kirra was in the middle of sitting up and paused, staring at the woman, "Actually, you died twice. Luckily it seems stubbornness bleeds into you being special."

The woman had a few wrinkles on her face and was on the thicker side. She wore purple scrubs with little cartoon bats careening across the fabric's surface. Her look was completed by brown eyes and dark brown hair placed in a messy bun that suggested she'd had a long shift. Dark circles hid just underneath the half-moon spectacles that hung down her nose.

Rubbing her face, Kirra tried to wake faster, "What's that mean?"

Setting the book down, she pulled off her half-moon spectacles, causing them to swing from the chain around her neck. She spoke as though talking to a child, "You're long-lived. You'll get to live forever unless someone kills you. You'll stop aging at a certain point. We call your kind regeneratives." As Kirra took in this new information, the nurse walked over and explained, "You'll find out it's not all that bad. Actually, it's kind of great. Faster healing, you stop aging, you're more difficult to kill..."

Zeke suddenly rounded the hallway and paused before jabbing his thumb towards the door, commanding, "Get out." Not wanting to argue, the nurse left instantly. Closing the door behind her, Zeke approached with caution as he let out a long, slow sigh, "You have a very long and rough road ahead of you, Kirra."

Kirra could feel the hairs on her arms raising as he paused before turning to face her. It was clear from the look on her face that she started to panic, as the full brunt of what she had felt would come back. As he got closer, Kirra looked away, clenching her jaw as he explained, "I wish it could have been done another way, but your spirit was determined to kill you. Something chaotic took hold of your spirit. I was forced to separate the two of you, which is extremely painful." His lips thinned into a line as Kirra still refused to look at him, "You died today."

Kirra finally looked at him with a bit of confusion, "How am I not dead? How am I still alive? Did someone bring me back?"

"No, you brought yourself back. The sheer willpower you had not to die out there is almost inspiring." He sucked in a breath and let it out slowly, "You're alive because your body wanted to live..." Zeke paused as he tried to grasp words to use, "Your spirit is stubborn, and your connection is strong."

"I know..." Kirra admitted with resentment before explaining, "We've been at odds from the start, and he took over my body once already to take out those hell hounds, but it was more shared that time.

This time was completely different." Kirra sucked in a shaky breath before explaining, "I couldn't do anything. I screamed, I tried so hard to move and stop what was happening. Even before it happened... I don't know. Something was—" She couldn't figure out how to word it.

Zeke finished for her, "Something was off..." There was a pause before Zeke continued, "Black Dragon told me you had a keen instinct. He thought it was odd when you denied the fight as well." Zeke was quiet for a while before he said, "I'm sorry that happened to you, Kirra. No one could have predicted such an outcome. We saw you and your spirit connect in the trial as well. I stupidly thought I could bring it out of you so you could realize the potential your spirit offers you. It's always scary the first couple of times it happens."

Kirra looked up at him with concern, "You mean it could happen again?"

Zeke shrugged, "It could, but you have to remember, your emotions are amplified through them. When he takes over, he still feels what you do, only more strongly. You're still angry at what happened, and I don't blame you for your anger." Kirra looked away as Zeke laughed, "I expect it from all of you. I am not going to say I am a good or bad person, but rather a leader trying to bring my kind out of the dark ages and out into the light. Sometimes tough decisions have to be made."

Kirra frowned momentarily before saying, "Like making yourself the bad guy because you're trying to make things better for your people." Zeke looked at her with a tilt of his head as she explained, "Black Dragon had a sort of an ethical-based discussion with me. Offered a question about if I had the chance to make a difference if I would or not by killing a bad guy. I said yes. And then he modified the question, asking what if the kids of the supposed bad guy that I killed saw me do it? That I would be viewed in their eyes as a monster." She took a long breath and let it out slowly, "It painted a picture for me to better understand."

Ruby eyes stared at her sparkling with wisdom, "Black Dragon is an intelligent man. He likes forcing people to think critically. It seems odd if you think about it from the perspective of knowing what he does."

"What do you mean?"

Arching an eyebrow at her he said very bluntly, "He's a Master Survivalist. Which in and of itself doesn't mean a lot to most people, but when you think about it in a harsher scope and broaden the picture, it means something completely different." He paused before following up, "Sometimes, when the worst-case scenario happens, you have to do things that you would not usually do. Morally, ethically, or otherwise, just so that you or the greater amount of your group can survive. Sometimes hard choices have to be made."

It was quiet in the room for a while before she said, "Black Dragon wants me to think from a place that is more based on logic and facts rather than from my emotions."

Zeke winked at Kirra and clicked his tongue at her, "You got it, kiddo. He wants you to make your own choices. Not choices based on emotions of a certain singular moment in time or rather that of someone else's opinions and ideals, but on your own intellect and thoughts. The biggest reason I decided to hunt down the Prophecy with such harshness is that I don't want them to become brainwashed with the ideals that Dragon Colony likes to instill in young minds. Especially those that perpetuate that of racism towards those considered to be a 'lesser' race."

Kirra looked up at him from where she lay in the hospital bed and asked, "So what's the point of selling tickets and advertising our misery and suffering for other's entertainment."

Letting out a long sigh, Zeke replied, "Necessary profit to help sustain the lot of you that are staying here while I search for the Prophecy."

"Say you do find the Prophecy. What happens to the rest of the dragons here?" Kirra couldn't help but ask the question that had been bothering her.

"They will continue to stay here, and I will ransom the Dragon Colony for their release. If they care enough, they will agree to the terms. If they disagree, I will offer the kids two choices when they come of age. They can choose to join and serve in Bat Colony, and the people will welcome them with open arms, or they will be offered one free portal ride off the planet to a different sector that is accessible. After that, their lives are their own." He shrugged his shoulders, "That is, of course, only once they come of age and Dragon Colony decides they wish to ignore the ransom."

"What's going to happen to the Prophecy when they're discovered?"

His reply was instant, "They will continue to be trained so they can amply protect themselves, and a teacher will be found to train them. Realistically, the best teacher would be an angel, as they have a natural affinity for magic, but I will do the best I can to provide what is needed."

Something nagged Kirra in the back of her head. Part of her wanted to tell Zeke about her dreams and who was behind the torment that had occurred. Kirra just wanted the other teens' suffering to end more than anything. As she opened her mouth to speak, her spirit's voice roared through her head, *"**Don't tell him about the gods!**"*

She paused, considering it for a moment before asking, *"Why not?"*

"If I said later, would you listen to me?"

Not sure if she should trust her spirit after what happened, she asked, "Are you going to use them to help you win the war?" Only to hiss at her spirit angrily, *"You nearly killed me."*

There was a chuckle, "You and everyone else are so ready to misjudge what I have planned for the Prophecy. No... I do not plan to force them into the war." He shook his head and looked down at his arm, "I have time for one more question, then I need to head back to my office to handle some business." He looked back up, waiting for a few moments.

"How long am I going to be in here?" Kirra asked, "And how do you have so much time to spend on us when you're running an entire colony."

"That is two questions. You'll be here for a couple of days since your dragon drained you of energy completely, and you're running on fumes. A couple of days on an energy drip will make you whole again." He sucked in a breath, "And because you amuse me somewhat, I'll answer your second question. I have others that do the grunt work for me. I trust them to handle certain matters and have heads of certain sectors, and I only need to check up on things here and there. I largely make the big decisions but leave my subject matter experts in charge of running other areas and bringing concerns to me, which I deal with in appointment-based meetings. I'm a leader first and foremost, but that doesn't mean that I am an expert in everything, so I leave it to those who are."

He looked down at his arm again, which showed a digital time clock over his wrist, before he looked back to her, "If I can establish a rapport with those that have been lied to about the supposed opposition, then it means I am impacting how the future of other races will be raised. Fewer people will be oppressed because of their race and gender. It's how actual change is made. Though this, by and large, will be my last attempt to change the thoughts of others. I've begun to give up on the idea that change can be made throughout the multiverse." There was a solemn look on his face, one that held ages of oppression on it.

Once more, Kirra saw that large blurring of spectral-like black energy surrounding and encasing the grey aura that surrounded Zeke. Like it was being held prisoner. She didn't mention it as she tried to get a clearer picture of what it was without letting on that she even saw it. Just like that, the aura faded just as quickly as it showed itself.

Her spirit grumbled softly, *"So you do see it..."*

After a few moments of standing in silence, Zeke bid her farewell and left the room. Kirra stared blankly at the wall for a few moments before she saw a very clear form made of almost pure white. It was almost ethereal, the same form she had seen back in the playground as she watched it float up from her side before leaning against a wall and looking toward her. Like before, their hair was up in a traditional style top knot. The man's face was angular, with scarring down the left side that looked like it had healed poorly. There was no color to his eyes, but they were slanted. The crooked nose only added to the battle-hardened look he gave off. She didn't recognize the style of clothing, but she knew it was some kind of cinched robe with decorative swirling patterns over it. With him came the feeling of familiarity as Kirra realized this was her spirit.

Finally, she questioned, "Why did you almost kill me?"

Despite her being able to see him propped against the wall, his voice still floated through her head in a soft, sad tone, *"I do not know what overcame me. It was as though rage was flowing through me. I have never felt such a grave need for violence in my life before."* Kirra let him speak as she silently watched, *"My loss of control nearly got you killed, and that is a grave sin that I may never recover from."* Suddenly, that scarred face turned to face her before he bowed from the waist deeply, "I do not deserve your forgiveness, *Kirra, but I will still ask for it and apologize for almost getting you killed."*

"I forgive you. Just fight back against that impulse, or whatever it was, next time." Kirra thought for a moment and remembered how she spoke when it happened and how he was speaking now, "It sounded like Trivitus." The dragon spirit rose with what looked like watery eyes as she asked, *"Why can I see you now?"*

"It is an ability. We call it spirit sight. You can see spirits or the essence of such. More likely, it is better explained as energy-based anomalies. Your eyes shift or rather adapt to see things in a different view. The important thing to note about this is that it is your second passive ability. This isn't normal for any other dragon. I remember most dragons having at minimum control of one of the major eight. There was a rare chance at possessing a passive like being regenerative or the ability to invoke powerful emotions with your voice, but never more than one passive ability."

Kirra looked around making sure no one was around before she said the next in her head, *"So what, I don't have any actual abilities like any other dragons. No telekinesis or fire control or anything like that?"*

"So far, it seems that is the case. The ability to wield magic like angels is another passive, which is why the prophecy can be any dragon, though usually white or gold dragons are the ones that wind up receiving the gift."

"Okay, so what can the prophecy do?"

His form moved to sit on the bed next to her, *"Mostly, it is the ability to use spells itself. But your magic will be wildly attached to your emotions. When you are in severe distress or danger, they will save your life and act of their own will or rather your thoughts in moments of dire stress, but it is in no way a miracle worker."*

"How do you know any of this?" Kirra asked.

There was a pause as if he was unwilling to share the response he finally gave, *"I was a prophecy in my time, among one of the first. The memories of such started returning to me after the first meeting with Cerinos. I was reluctant to share with you since you already distrusted me."*

Kirra decided she would finally ask, *"So since you seem to know more about this, any hints on controlling this weird ability of spirit sight."* Kirra continued, *"There's this weird thing with Zeke. It looks like there are two spirits, and one of them is trapping the other one."* Kirra mentioned.

"There could be something to that, but I have also heard of two-toned spirits that take up different types of energy, though it is rare." There was a long breath before his form disappeared from next to her, and his voice echoed loudly in her head, *"An ability of that kind will take time*

and patience to learn how to use. Either you find someone who already knows how to use it, or you learn to use it yourself the hard way. Trial and Error. Personally, I had no passive abilities of any kind."

"How come other people's spirits come through as blurry, but I can see you perfectly fine?" She had been curious about the question for a while.

He answered almost instantly, *"You are inexperienced with using the ability and it has bubbled up of its own accord. You can see me clearly because we are connected, and you can use the Spirit Bond to help with that."* There was a pause before he continued, *"With other people, you are going to have to learn to see them. You are going to have to learn to focus in on them and see their spirits. Perhaps with time, you might be able to, but only through practice and training will you eventually master it and be able to use it."* There was a long pause before he spoke again, *"These are things that should not exist in your thoughts for the moment. Try and get some rest."* The voice almost rumbled out affectionately.

Kirra thought about his words for a time. Eventually, her gaze wandered over to the tube in her arm with a viscous-looking white liquid that glowed softly. Part of her wondered how one couldn't see energy normally, but here she could as she was having it slowly drained into her. Her spirit piped up as if he was reading her thoughts, *"Since your mind won't let it slip. Know that every living thing has energy and a type. Yours is that of white. This is refined from others of white energy. Essentially, blood has been refined to the state you see now. There are two ways to get it back: slowly allowing you to regain it from eating and resting or absorbing it from something else. It is said you can do it from one person to another, but it requires practice. Now go to sleep."*

Kirra held a smile as she listened to him speak while following the tube to the glass that seemed to hold raw energy. It was half empty. Eventually, she managed to settle her mind and lay back down in bed. Exhaustion started to kick in as she caught herself staring at the ceiling.

17

PAIN IN THE TAIL

Kirra was more than happy to be out of the hospital a few days later. She had been getting pent up, being unable to stretch her legs or move around much. Since the discharge took so long, she missed the first class of the day with Miss Chetski, but the next one with BD, she was going to make. As she entered the playground and started following tracks from the group, she smirked as she spotted them all huddled around some plants as Black Dragon taught from a tree higher up. As the group of them seemed preoccupied with getting to know the plant they were inspecting, BD suddenly disappeared. Her spirit helped point out to her that the shadows were moving. Watching the shadows carefully, she saw Black Dragon reform right next to her.

The conversation was short, but he pitched an amusing idea, making her almost cackle out loud. Despite not being a deft climber, at the behest of Black Dragon, she made her way up into the trees as quietly as she could and perched on a branch behind the group. Armed with a handful of pebbles, she started to tactically throw them at the group gathered around the mushrooms, attempting to figure out which ones were edible and which ones weren't.

As the Kirra picked Life as her primary target, she watched as one pebble after the next began to irritate the cool-headed brother slowly. Life seemed certain Death was messing with him, resulting in the twins squabbling with each other. The next thing Kirra knew, the pair were rolling around on the ground, playfully wrestling with each other. Ky and Nicki were laughing at the two, and Alyssa looked tired while trying to get the brothers to stop since she was struggling and needed help. Eventually, Kirra hopped down and landed next to the group while laughing at the ridiculousness of it all.

The sound of her laughter caused the squabbling pair to stop and stare at her in disbelief immediately. Death ran over and lifted her off the ground while swirling her around in his arms out of sheer joy. A pat on the back seemed to suffice for the others as they greeted her. Once everyone was finished welcoming her back, Kirra explained what had happened the day she almost died. After the excitement of her coming back died down, BD got them back on track before their time ran out. With her new schedule in effect, Kirra's next class was mount training.

Riding Snow was one of the single most freeing experiences in her life. It was like her mind connected with him and she could feel the dirt and rocks under her toughened paws. The only problem was that she was stuck doing circles in a pen learning how to ride him as a partner properly. There were a few others in the class, but not many. It seemed like most of the people she had originally seen with the wolves were just ones who wanted to be near or around them and not actual riders. As the class concluded, the soreness of being in a saddle for so long started to set in, but it could have been worse had she not been training all the time.

During the night, she got to spend extra time with Snow and cleaned out his stable before going off to the library and studying independently. Since she had new classes and none of them had to do with books, Kirra took time to brush up on her reading. The number of books they had there for them to learn from was insane, but most of them concentrated on species and flora from the multiverse, as Life had explained to her. Despite wanting to learn history, she instead took to reading about demons given that the last trial haunted her still.

Her spirit explained that there would be time for it later. History was extremely important to spiritosk. To fully bond with their spirit, they needed to find out who their spirit was in their former life. This was why it was so important to become known or know the history of one's family in case you wound up with a prior relative, which seemed to be a common occurrence. It was why being born as a different race of spiritosk from the rest of your family was deemed so dishonorable. It was just easier to track lineages of others who were from the same family, given the knowledge was passed on by word of mouth unless they were someone of note. Kirra's spirit had been a previous prophecy, so there was a higher chance of her finding something, but she didn't know where to begin looking for information.

Her new training with Black Dragon was rigorous and strict. There was no more room for playing around. She wasn't his only student in swords, but he preferred individualized training so he could concentrate on them solely. He wouldn't tell her who his other student was, but she swore she saw Ky walking to meet with him at one point or another.

Having a spirit and a spirit bond apparently were two different training schedules. Some stayed with your group, such as the fighting and survival training. However, having a spirit bond was extremely serious, and she needed to be trained quickly, given that she had access to her dragon's strength, speed, and prior skills. If control wasn't learned over the newfound strength, speed, and skills, it could mean Kirra could wind up accidentally squeezing someone to death.

Black Dragon took the new training very seriously. It seemed like every day Kirra woke up with new or different marks. The blades they trained with were made out of real metal. Even though the blades were dulled, it still hurt to get tapped by one in a mistake. They were also heavier than she thought, so her arms hurt from holding the blade up and out. This added to the fact that after she was done with BD, she went to hand-to-hand combat training with Miss Chetski. At least she got a break with her meditation training here and there. She was supposed to be meditating to help her "connect" better with her spirit, but usually, she found herself falling asleep from exhaustion.

The weird part was that when she fell asleep, her spirit visited her, and the two had deep conversations. Mostly they took the time to get to know each other, where their faults lie with each other, and spoke about the things he could remember. Aelbryst was mostly a boring and dull man, so she didn't ever see herself liking his training.

Kirra didn't know what to expect when she was instructed to go to the coliseum for one of her trainers. Excitement coursed through her as others told her it should help her learn her ability, but no one told her what to expect. Traveling down the hall, she looked at the numbers on the doors until stopping in front of a pair of double doors. Confusion caused her brow to furrow as she saw the room's name under the number.

107

C.A.S.E.

As she pushed the door open, an expansive room made of pure metal lay before her. It made Kirra feel like she had just entered a torture chamber of some sort minus the torture equipment. Every surface seemed to be made of the same metallic material on a grid. Then she heard the voice, causing her to turn and look as they spoke, "You'll not need your mortal mask here, little dragon." Ryse absently waved at her, "Take your half-form child." That same creepy smile greeted her from him, but this time, he was absent a hood on his head. Two pointed fur-covered ears sat at angles on his head. They almost looked like a horse's ears but she couldn't tell from the distance she was at.

"I actually like this form best... demon." Venom laced the end of her sentence with clear distaste.

Kirra had barely blinked and he disappeared only for his voice to come from directly behind her, "I won't ask a second time." Instinctively, Kirra threw an elbow.

Almost immediately, Kirra realized she had messed up as she found herself on the floor with her arm twisted in a position she'd been in more times than she'd like to admit. Letting out a strained groan of pain, she arched her back trying to relieve the pressure. Ryse obliged her by rolling her onto her side while still maintaining a grip on her wrist as he stepped in front of her.

With a giggle, he leaned down as she realized that his tail was, in fact, the thing that had the grip on her wrist, "You're spicy...." Crouching down near her, he smiled creepily at her, "I like spicy. Means I won't be bored." Stepping back, the tail relinquished its hold.

Almost immediately afterward, Kirra swiped at him from the ground as he danced just out of range, still cackling like a madman. He was goading her into attacking, and the worst part was that it was working. The floor beneath Ryse started to shift as a pull-up bar formed just above him, which his tail took hold of. Flipping upside down, his feet pressed against the bar. He smiled infuriatingly at her while she rose to her feet.

"You're kind of cute, like a helpless little kitten. Don't have much in the way of claws though." Kirra's brow twitched angrily as another giggle escaped, "Welcome to CASE. The Closed Adaptive Survival Environment. I prefer to call this session the Gauntlet as I will put you through your paces. I heard that you made it farther than anyone on the first try of the obstacle course. It means you think on your feet. That'll come in handy during your training here."

Flipping off of the bar, he approached with mild amusement, "Most dragons aren't known for their stealth, but you can be resourceful." Reaching out with the tip of his tail, he tapped her hands and feet explaining, "Hands can become claws and feet into paws with the ability to grasp. If you were lucky to be blessed with a more powerful spirit, a nice strong tail, a set of wings, some horns, and possibly even the voice or breath of a dragon as well."

Kirra looked at her hands as she slowly released her human form, and some of her draconic features started to appear. Her horns, claws, paws, and tail were the features she chose. As Kirra's horns grew, she swore they felt larger since the last time she'd had them out. It took a little while for her to adjust to the form as she stumbled lightly before recovering.

He clicked his tongue in disapproval, "No, no, no, no, no. What is this, a dragon losing their balance? You act as though you were just hatched yesterday." She felt something lifting and dropping her tail making it thump on the ground before she whipped it away and let it settle again. "You can't even keep your tail up in the air and it is so long that it drags on the ground..." Tisking once more, he pouted at her, "You're getting your cute little white floof at the end dirty. And where are your wings? I was told you had wings..."

Kirra snorted out, "My wings get in the way. Of everything..."

Planting his hands on his hips, he mocked her, "Well then, learn to keep them out of the way, and that won't be a problem." He exaggerated Kirra's grumpiness almost comically. Suddenly, he poofed away with a cloud of smoke that disappeared rather quickly before reappearing in the same manner. In his hand, he held a broom made of wood and straw and held it out to her like a child proudly displaying something they found amusing.

Reaching for the broom with her hand, the handle suddenly smacked the back of her hand, causing her to hiss in pain as he chided, "No, no, no, no, no, no... with your tail..." Ryse urged her, "Go on..."

Kirra had to concentrate on moving her tail as it slowly wrapped around the handle as he instructed, "Now sweep. You do know how to do that right?" Shooting an angry glare at him, she struggled to right the broom with her tail. When she finally managed to make the bristles touch the floor, she attempted to make the motion of sweeping before a snap echoed through the air. The two pieces clattered to the floor as a growl of frustration came from her.

"Ooooo... strong tail. Don't worry, there's more..." He poofed away before the sound of wood clattering on metal right next to her, accompanied by his incessant giggling, "Lots more..." When she looked, a pile of brooms haphazardly lay next to her.

A look of frustration and anger crossed Kirra's face, "I thought there was going to be fighting or some crap. This isn't a frickin gauntlet, I'm just doing chores."

"It's called the gauntlet because I'm going to put you through a gauntlet of things that you are going to hate." A cackle came from him once more, "Starting with the simplest crap that even a child could handle." He teleported next to her in a poof of that black smoke and got right in her face, "You are not a child, so do not act like one and perform the tasks I give you." The playfulness in his voice was gone. He was outright threatening her. It caused her to curl her lips as she growled lightly.

Her spirit echoed his dislike, "*This demon is starting to get on my nerves. Back in my time, I would have shown him where to shove those brooms.*"

"*Oh, I plan on it.*" Kirra didn't give a warning as she picked a broom up and tried to sweep Ryse's legs out from under him. He didn't teleport away like he had been. Instead, the bastard just dodged with a cheeky little flip as his tail whipped at her hands, making her drop the broom.

Standing just out of reach, he cackled before lowering onto all fours like some demented being and tilted his head sideways. Kirra was starting to understand how not human Ryse truly was. Those feline eyes glowed with ferocity as the smile on his face only grew. The entire display was unsettling. Kirra had to remind herself that this thing wasn't human or probably even mortal. It was a demon. The foulest of the foul.

Kirra chased him down with a yell and missed every punch, kick, and every attempt to damage him in every way. All the while, he just cackled while evading every blow like he was made of water. Eventually, he stood up straight again with that cocky smile in place. Letting loose a growl of frustration and anger, she charged at him. Once more he evaded, but this time, the feeling of something clamping in place around her neck with a click caused her to stop.

"Did he just put a collar on me!?" She reached up and started to tug at the thing before a jolt of electricity caused her to yelp.

Dropping to her knees, she let go of the collar as the shock caused her wings to spring free, and the last piece of her half-form came out. Ryse practically danced around her humming happily, "You know what your problem is? You're weak." A scream of rage erupted from her as she reached out to grab him, but he dodged easily once more moving behind her. The feeling of a tug on her tail caused her to gasp before she was thrown across the empty room as she rolled to a stop. While Kirra was groaning and slowly recovering, his teasing continued, "Now I don't mean you're weak in the physical sense or lacking in willpower because I will admit..." He cackled lightly, "I have seen some angry people in my time, but you, my girl, have some serious repressed rage."

"I'm not angry." Once more she rushed at him with a growl, and once more, she felt her tail getting used against her as she was thrown. Rolling across the ground, she struggled to get up as her wings got caught under her during the roll.

"No? Then why are you so easily frustrated at my **almost** calling you a child? Hmm?" Ryse was suddenly next to her as foot pushed her down while claws threatened to dig in if she struggled, "You have no experience when it comes to using your actual animalistic side, but the ferocity is there. The things that make you special and superior are nothing but a weakness to you."

He stepped off of her, backing away as she stumbled to her feet, "I haven't had them for more than a month." Once she was finally stable, she glared, "You think that I'm going to have it mastered after that long."

"No... but I would expect you to be able to pick up a broom without snapping it like a twig." He eyed her before leaning an inch away from her face, "You spent so much time trying to hide how powerful you could be that you never actually got the chance to use or experience how powerful you would be if you learned how to use what has been gifted to you."

Kirra didn't respond. She knew he was right. She'd been so worried about trying to hide her draconic side as much as possible because her wings were always in the way, and her tail only served as a balance for her lower limbs that she never actually learned how to use them. A defeated sigh came from her, "Okay, I get it..."

"Good. Now... pick up the broom without breaking it and sweep." There was no smile on his face as he rose to his full height and moved away. Walking over to the pile of discarded brooms, Kirra groaned as she leaned over to grasp one with her hand before stopping. Old habits were hard to break. Instead, she stood up and reached with her tail, concentrating on wrapping around one of the handles and pulling a broom out gently. As her tail wrapped carefully around it, she attempted to sweep.

Kirra trained with Ryse for most of the day. Since she had missed the previous training because of her near-death experience, she got special treatment. So far, she hated the training with all of her body. Her time with him was spent mostly working on balance and how to walk and use her tail and keep it lifted off the ground. Using her wings for balance and trying to keep them closed tight against her body despite their size. By the end of the day, Kirra was hurting and it showed.

Ryse delivered one last gut punch to her causing the shock in her voice, "What did you just say!?" Kirra had just been forced to do the most mundane tasks for hours as she had toiled and his news was devastating.

The cackle showed his amusement in her reaction, "I said that collar is staying in place around your neck to ensure you continue to learn how to work with your more primal parts."

Kirra tried to argue, "They're going to drag me down in the competition during the fight this week. My wings are a huge disadvantage!"

Ryse spoke almost disdainfully of Kirra's pleading, "Then I guess that means you will have to learn to work with your more primal side and use it against your opponents. Toodaloo." He blinked out in a puff of black smoke leaving Kirra standing in the room with a look of defeat on her face.

Letting out a huff of smoke from her nostrils, she trudged back through the camp to her cabin. Several passersby snickered behind her back, made idle comments, or showed awe at how draconic she looked. As she made her way back into the cabin, her cabin mates showed concern, interest, and even surprise at the sudden change of her taking her half-form. Sliding into bed, her wings hung sorely around her like an all-white tent as though to block others from seeing her humility.

Alyssa was the first to comment with a bit of awe and nervousness, "Wow... Kirra, you have... almost a full draconic look." She couldn't help but to ask, "Why... Why are you showing everything off?" This caused a few of the others to glance at her curiously.

Ky's voice floated over to her from where he was sitting with concern, "You know the others are going to openly challenge you, right?"

As comments of telling her to transform back started to ring through the room, she explained, "Ryse put a collar on me. It's forcing me to stay this way."

Death piped up, "Oi that's pretty much sabotage." He thought better of his words, "On the other hand, technically you could probably do better in the fights. That's if you learn how to use this form."

It was Alyssa who questioned Death's suggestion, "Do you see how massive her wings are? How is that going to help her?" Several agreements were made, but Kirra just pulled a pillow over her head as best she could, just wanting them to stop. She wanted all of it just to end because she knew it was going to be hell on earth for the next month for her.

The next day was worse than what she had thought. She could barely sleep so she woke early and went to the cafeteria for food. She could still hear the chuckles and giggles of the other teens making jokes about how she was too weak to hide her actual form. Ryse's words floated through her head once more with that stupid smile on his face, *"I prefer to call this session the Gauntlet as I will put you through your paces."* He had never specified that it would be included in carrying over the next week.

Just when she didn't think it could get any worse, it did. At the group training session with Miss Chetski, she kept losing her balance, tripping on her wings, tail, and feet, or having her tail used as a weapon against her. Even her wings were used as a weak spot that was exploited. Everything seemed to be weighed against her.

Survival training was no better. Her wings kept getting caught in branches, her tail catching on bushes and anything that was sticking out. All of her draconic parts kept getting snagged or in general, in the way. Originally, she had learned to hide her wings early because of their size. Now, she was having to deal with her lack of training with them and the consequences it brought. There was also the fact that she stood a bit taller with her draconic feet. At almost six feet even, she was hitting her head on almost everything. Given how she had been handling just walking around in the forest, Black Dragon decided that it would be best that her sword training be halted temporarily.

The final blow came from her newfound partner, Snow. Originally he showed concerns before she had even gotten on him for the first time riding, but allowed it anyway. That was until he felt her wings open up against the wind, causing her to fall off and almost injure herself. Given the risk, he refused to let her ride him claiming it was a danger to herself and others.

For the first time in over a month, Kirra broke down. She had gone to a corner of the camp where no one could find her and sobbed at the struggles she was dealing with. The training was going horribly. Snow wouldn't let her ride him, and even Black Dragon refused to train her on the fact that she needed to 'work on herself'. All of it finally piled on top of each other making her break down.

She didn't sleep much that night and found herself dragging the whole next day. It went about as terrible as the previous day. The lack of sleep was only making matters worse. Since half of her training schedule had been canceled due to her new form, she sulked off somewhere else to just try and get some rest. It seemed impossible given the circumstances but she needed the sleep to prepare for the next day since Challenges would be happening.

Her nervousness and tension were almost palpable. Kirra was an easy target and the others knew it. All it had taken was one person to challenge her, and the others followed suit knocking her back down the list. She hadn't been at the top, but this challenge was supposed to be hers to move up and stay off the bottom. With her wings and tail added in as extra grip points and weaknesses, she was an easy mark. Defeat after defeat, she was slowly pushed back near the bottom. Only a few newer faces didn't challenge her.

Kirra lay on the ground, beaten, defeated, but conscious as the others started to leave. They had all been ordered to leave her be as she lay there bloodied and struggling to get up. It seemed someone had made a plan for her as a set of cat paws came into view. Picking her head up, she managed to see Ryse's face before collapsing and passing out.

When Kirra woke, she found herself propped up against a wall. The second that she moved, a soft whimper of soreness sprouted forth. It was a familiar feeling after having been beaten several times before. Her eyes adjusted to the darkness, and the feeling of cold metal against her skin gave her a clue as to where she was. Room 107, C.A.S.E. Ryse was going to put her through the gauntlet. Kirra struggled to her feet, wings stretching to help work the soreness out before settling again.

Ryse's voice cackled above her, "Oh good, you're alive. I was certain I was going to have to perform chest compressions on you. Possibly all of CPR..."

Looking up, Kirra saw him making a kissy face only to earn him a glare from her. It was only afterward that she noticed he was sitting on what looked like a cable as though it were easy. Tossing a ball to himself, he only stopped as he looked down at Kirra commenting, "I hope you don't mind, but I called in a favor for some extra help with you since you failed your test so horribly."

Kirra's retort came quickly, "What I need is a few years' practice of getting used to body parts I don't know how to use." The sound of animal-like clicking echoing through the chamber caused her to look around. The clicking resonated through the chamber, sounding like it held a rhythm, but Ryse remained unconcerned about the noise.

The landscape of the entire chamber was changed to look like a metallic city. Small buildings of varying heights were around her as she tried to find where the clicking was coming from. Some buildings looked like one-level stores, while others were several floors tall. Cables extended from one building to the next like power lines that possibly held no power.

Ryse's voice drew her attention back to him, "Naaaah... You just need a crash course with a friend who knows what you're suffering through. He's a big boy at that." Ryse cackled, "Oh this friend of mine is another demon. Don't worry, though; his bite is definitely worse than his bark." He stood up on the wire partially speaking to himself out loud, "Oh wait. I'm supposed to be reassuring you, aren't I?" Ryse seemed rather amused at his own teasing.

That clicking continued to rattle on in that methodical way. Kirra was certain she wasn't crazy now, but couldn't locate where it was coming from. It sounded as though it were getting closer. Looking around her, she continued searching for the sound's source.

Ryse's voice cut through the clicking, "Either way, you're going to spend the next week with him in here. But don't worry, I told him to take it easy on you. You'll still get your meals too, if that was a concern. That is if you live through the training." Without explaining further, he disappeared in a poof of black smoke.

Kirra's eyes searched the surrounding empty buildings, looking all over for the clicking sound. Occasionally, it stopped but then continued once more. She finally decided to look for the door out of the room and started to steadily make her way to a wall and work around the edge to look for the exit. As she steadily walked and kept herself on point, she was certain now that the clicking was following her and getting closer.

A bit of fear started to crawl up her throat at the sound following her. At her spirit's behest, she closed her eyes and concentrated on breathing to calm herself. Ignoring the clicking, the soreness, and racing heart, she felt her body calm. The hairs on the back of her neck raised causing a shiver to run through her. The clicking was no longer happening. Turning to see what had caused her hair to stand on edge, she found no threat. Slowly, she backed up and scanned her surroundings but couldn't see anything until a familiar flaw caught her eye. Pure fear froze her in place and wracked her entire being as the cloaked creature standing before her shed its invisibility in front of her eyes.

As the creature's cloak fell away one scale at a time, Kirra found herself staring up at a beast that had to be at least 8 feet tall. The head was angular like that of a snake, with slit nostrils flaring as it took in air. Jagged and serrated teeth lined its jaw from what she could see. Large pointed ears that sat back against its head sat atop like that of a wolf. Between them sat a small set of pointed horns jutting back along its head. The creature's head sat on a strong neck that led to a large chest, which suggested strong lungs and heart for running. Upon the chest sat two large plates pulsing in time with whooshes of air with its breathing.

What had felt like minutes was only a matter of seconds as she took in the creature's appearance as its camouflage fell from its head to its toes. The creature that stood before her had what appeared to be fur covering its entire body in a pattern of scales that shook as its cloak dropped.

Large talons sat on both hands and toes of the creature that looked razor sharp. The shape of its legs hinted the creature was quadrupedal despite it standing on its hind legs. The last part revealed was a long and thick tail at the rear that waved and flicked like a cat's. Flashes of a pointed tip at the end suggested one more dangerous weapon to be used. Kirra's eyes fell back to its face after her quick scan of its body as two large piercing eyes with needle-like pupils that fluctuated from round to slit as though trying to zero in on its prey.

Frozen in fear, goosebumps ran up along what skin she had left in her half-form as her tail curled around her feet instinctively. It was almost as though the thing leaked fear, causing her to be frozen. Even the hell hounds had never evoked such a response in her, not as strong as this. Cold sweat ran down her face and scales as she stared up with wide eyes. She watched in horror as the demon slowly pulled back its arm. Crackling could be heard as a wave went through the creature's fur turning its fur to hardened scales. Next, the sound of ripping flesh drew her focus to that drawn-back arm as something sharp and dangerous ripped through the flesh and slits of its scales.

A bone blade of black covered in its blood, and it was bringing it down upon her. Even as the thought registered in her head that she should move, her body couldn't because of the fear.

Her spirit roared through her head, and the shock of fear, "***RUN GIRL!***"

Muscle memory and instinct kicked in as she dodge-rolled forward toward the creature instead of away. Narrowly dodging that wicked curved bone blade, she rolled into a jump clumsily as the tail whipped out attempting to knock her back. The prickling on the back of her neck caused her to dodge once more as the sound of metal being ripped rang through the air. A glimpse through the roll offered the sight of the demon's tail piercing through the metal as it narrowly missed her with the needle-like point.

Rolling back to her feet and taking off at a clumsy sprint, she glanced back at the sound of crackling behind her once more as she noticed its scaly body returned to fur. To her horror, two large appendages on its back flipped open revealing large leathery wings. As a loud, terrifying screech rang out from its jaws, Kirra concentrated on running for her life once more as fear pulsed through her. With it having wings, Kirra knew she stood a better chance dodging into a building and hoped its larger size would slow it down through the entrances.

Dipping into one of the fake metal buildings, Kirra ran up the stairs as the sound of metal being ripped outside made her realize that its tail had ripped out of the floor and it was now pursuing her. Dropping to all fours, Kirra rushed up the stairs like an animal as fast as she could, only to stop after she had made it a few floors up. Looking down the center of the stairwell, she thought she had lost the creature for the moment. Then it came into view.

It had moved from two legs to four and back again as it started to lift its snout taking in large rushes of breath. Whooshes of air sounded like a miniature jet engine as it rapidly expelled air from its chest. The demon's fuzzy ears rotated forward on its head, flicking attentively for a few moments before its black-furred head jerked to look right up at her. To her horror, with a deft quickness she didn't expect from something that large, it started to climb up the banisters of the stairs.

With a little scream, Kirra started towards the stairs and changed her mind as she saw a building within jumping distance from a window. She rushed towards it and jumped through the hole to the next building over. Barely making the jump, she caught the window's ledge and struggled to pull herself up. Her spirit reminded her of her clawed feet to which she growled out, dug them into the metal, and climbed over the ledge more easily. The shriek just behind told her there was no time for a break causing her to start running through the building down to the street of the cityscape.

Ryse's familiar voice teased her over a loudspeaker, "Oooooo, he almost got you on the first go." A few obnoxious giggles escaped, "And you said you needed years of training. It's funny what a person can do when the correct stress is applied." His laughter only infuriated her, driving some of her initial fear away.

Staying just out of the demon's sightline, Kirra jumped through a window of a building and ducked below the surface of the window. Making herself as small as she could, her wings wrapped tight around her form and obscured as much of her as possible. Reaching up, she cupped a hand over her mouth and held her breath as quiet took over. She initially didn't hear the demon lean over the window until she heard the familiar sound of whooshing as it tried scenting for her.

As the whooshes let out rhythmically from stuttering inhales, she could hear it directly above her as the shadow of it passed over her wings. Kirra remained still as a rock, holding her mouth tightly as the clicks could be heard from directly overhead. Another screech from directly overhead was let out. It was multitone and inhuman sounding as she stayed still, even as a fresh wave of fear washed over her.

"*It still doesn't see you. Don't move.*" Only sheer willpower and her spirit's advice kept her from moving. Finally, the creature moved on, followed by a series of clicks. The grating sound of metal on metal could be heard as though a door was being opened and closed, could be heard. Releasing the breath she was holding, she could feel her heart start to pound in her chest as the wave of fear started to teeter off.

Even with the possibility of that demon no longer being there, she remained still as a leaf, her wings wedged firmly around her in her hiding spot. Then, the sound of agile footsteps could be heard. Another smaller shadow loomed over her as she held her breath once more so as not to give away any sounds.

The sound of Ryse's voice keyed her in that she had been found, "Camouflage... That's very cool but kind of odd for one of your type to have." Unfurling her wings, she looked up with confusion and saw the outside of her wings shimmer as her movement destroyed the invisibility effect that they had on them. Her wings had been mimicking her surroundings and hid her clothing from view.

Hopping over the window next to her, the demon reached down with a hand to help her up, saying, "Gotta say, though, you looked rather smooth as you ran from him."

The urge to smash his face into the side of the building was strong, but her spirit reminded her that he could take her easily. Slowly she reached out and took the hand as he helped her to stand as she angrily questioned, "So all of that was just to show me that I could do something?"

Ryse's smirk only grew, "Why, of course, girly. The best runners work best under stressful situations. It's hard to feel the soreness in your bones and muscles if you have adrenaline pumping through your veins. Now..." He clapped his hands together, "You'll be with me the rest of the week. The other kiddos know what they are doing, but you have no such training, knowledge, or preparations. We're going to have so much fun. By the time I'm done with you, you'll never want to make yourself look human ever again." He practically giggled once he finished speaking.

"I'm not allowed to leave here?"

Ryse shook his head in response.

She inquired, "But you're training me for a whole week, I thought you were split up between several others?"

Ryse decided to clarify for her sake, "The others don't need special attention like you do. They got a chance to grow into their half-form; you were shown how to hide it and never learned how to use it properly. Now its a weakness. We want them to be a strength, now don't we?"

"I don't have much of a choice, do I?" His only response was a smirk.

18

THE PRIMAL SIDE

K irra was put through a ringer of trials. Every single one left her sore, exhausted, and just overall broken. Occasionally, that demon would be sent to chase her when she least expected it, but she always managed to stay just out of reach. The only thing that kept her sane was the communication between her and her spirit while in that place.

She'd eventually learned to adapt to the harsh environment she was in. With no way to track time, she turned to concentrating on learning to use her half-form as best as she could. Gliding was something she had picked up on, even managing to fly with little jumps at a time. Her wings grew stronger, her feet more dexterous, and she'd found balance more easily with her tail off the ground instead of sliding behind her. Finally, the sound of a door opened, and the cityscape disappeared around her. She was finally allowed to leave.

It was dark when she returned to the cabin, and not a sound was made during her entry. Making her way to her bed, she lay on her back and stared at the ceiling. Despite the comfort of the mattress, sleep didn't find her. The sound of that grating door had woken her from her from her slumber. Since she wasn't tired, Kirra instead made her way to the dining hall.

The sound of familiar footsteps entered while she ate her meal. Before they could say anything, she called out in a soft voice from her usual spot, "Hey, Roc." It half startled the boy to death. She hadn't even looked in his direction when he entered, so he was obviously confused.

Her call out to him not only confused him but frightened him, given how honed her senses were just at the sound of his boots. When he inquired how she knew it was him, she mentioned the sound of his boots and size and how it sounded like he was stomping around in them. Slowly, the hall started to fill with more teens as they woke. A few threw concerned looks toward her at her form, but the rest of her cabin seemed excited just to see her returned. She was free of the collar from Ryse but, he instructed her to remain in her form. She'd spend another week in the Gauntlet if she didn't do her Challenge in her half-form. That included his demon friend chasing her for yet another week.

Kirra would be ready for Challenges that day. She'd learned to keep her tail off of the ground, her wings tight against her back, how to walk with and without her claws clicking on the ground, how to grasp with her feet, how to use her tail, how to use her wings as an advantage, and had no problem with keeping balance anymore.

Even as the newer group came into the hall making snide and rude comments, she kept a calm and steady demeanor. They'd grown cocky from her easy defeat in the last set of Challenges. It made them easy prey. Eventually, she stood, made her way to the challenge pad much earlier than needed, and stood on her number, waiting for others to arrive.

Seeing Alyssa walk onto the pad brightened Kirra's face instantly. She leaped over using her wings before landing in front of her with a large smile showing those fangs of hers, "Ready for the day?"

The show of fangs caused Alyssa to stiffen. It seemed even amongst their own kin, the sight of them made them nervous, causing Kirra to clear her throat as she smiled without showing teeth, trying once more, "Ready for today?"

"Yes, I think I am... Just... concerned about you. We all thought that perhaps you had been pulled out or worse. But Ky pointed out that your name would have been pulled from the list, which it wasn't." Alyssa's smile returned, "Are you ready? You didn't do all that good last time, and you're still in your half-form." Alyssa paused, "Are you going to be okay?"

Kirra's tone was even as she recalled the last week, "I'll be fine. I've been being chased for the better part of the last week by some crazy-looking demon that Ryse has been siccing on me. I'll be okay though."

Alyssa looked around her before speaking in a low tone, "I heard them speaking about how if this continued on, you'd probably be removed from the program. You need to win today, or else they might... you know..." She made choking noises and mocked being choked as Kirra just stood there with a neutral look.

With a sigh, Kirra quipped, "I'm going to go and stretch. Good luck to you though." With a shake of her head, Kirra padded softly over to her number, commenting softly, *"What a weird girl. I'm starting to think I made a mistake bringing her into our cabin."* Sitting down at her spot, she meditated and concentrated on her spirit.

Opening her eyes after a time, he was sitting in front of her, mirroring her pose as two icy blue eyes peered at her, *"It is a possibility that you made a mistake, but you only wanted to save her from the same pain that you went through."* A smirk came to his face, causing the scar to twist, *"You're ready for today. If you could make it through that week of hell, you can do this."* Her eyes shifted momentarily at the sound of other teens arriving, *"Ignore them. They are in for a treat today."* Nodding to him with a small smirk, he dissipated.

As more of the teens started to appear, she could see the newer of the group looking at her like it was a feeding frenzy for sharks. Slowly, their trainers started to arrive, and eventually, so did Zeke. He didn't take to the bleachers but instead stood closer down next to the pad and asked in his usual way who was challenging first.

Three distinct voices called out her name at the same time. As Kirra looked towards the kids who challenged her. All of them were the same ones she had beaten their first day there. Given what happened during the last set of Challenges, they thought her to be an easy mark.

Ignoring their challenges, Zeke offered instead, "Kirra, is there anyone you would like to challenge." Given the three that challenged her, she seemed to be given a choice.

"I wanna challenge Roc." The three that challenged her were below her. There was no reason for her to entertain fighting them.

A smirk came from Zeke, "Kirra vs. Roc." As the pair made their way to the circles on the pad itself, complaints rang out, but were quickly silenced with a glare from Zeke. Roc seemed hesitant, if not downright reluctant. His eyes kept scanning over her half-form with concern etched deeply on his face. Kirra gave nothing away, just that same placid calm plastered on her face. Her tail, however, twitched ever so slightly in annoyance at his concern which was clearly for her.

When the command was given, Kirra leaped from where she was and came down at Roc from above. Moving to block what he thought would have been a punch, Roc's arms suffered slash marks from her claws as they swiped down. He yelped in pain, firing back with a punch, which was dodged with Kirra's movement of going to all fours. In the same movement, her tail wrapped around one of his ankles and flicked hard as she leaped forward. The movement was flawless as he smacked hard on the ground and landed on his face.

Onlookers went silent as the fight went on. Anyone who had been cheering for Roc went quiet, and those who had yelled insults at Kirra stopped. Roc rose to his feet, holding a bleeding gash on his head, turning to face Kirra. A look of rage boiled on his face just beneath the surface as he looked at her.

This wasn't the same girl that had been gone for a week. Before she had left, she had been stumbling about, bumping into everything, and was easy prey. The girl who stood before them was a predator. Something the new group was finding out quickly about.

Still, on all fours, Kirra bared her draconic fangs as a very animalistic hiss escaped her maw, followed by a snort of smoke. At the sound of that challenge, Roc answered in kind as he took his own half-form in a shimmer of red. Raising claws in a threat display, let out an animalistic challenge roar before charging at her.

They met halfway in a slap of flesh. Claws met claws, fangs snapped, and tried to tear each other into pieces. Kirra's wings kicked up dust as they neared one of the edges of the pad during their tumble. As the cloud continued to fog the display of animalistic fighting, it grew louder as yelps of pain cried out from certain hits. It was hard to determine who the yelps were from though.

Things took a quick turn, but none of the trainers reacted. The sickening sound of bones snapping and crunching resonated through the air. A cry of pain and rage accompanied the bones, causing a few of the teens to look around in panic. Their minds went to the worst of possible situations, thinking either Roc or Kirra were dead. Then the sound stopped. A deathly silence took over the area save for the sounds of something large huffing in exertion.

As the dust began to settle, a set of large brilliant wings that shined in the sun with a fresh sheen of blood poked out from the top. They were spread out wide, and the sight caused several teens to release gasps of awe. As the rest of the dust settled, an awkward-looking dragon stood on the pad. Its paws and wings were too large for the rest of its body, tufts of black hair came out in the form of a mane along its neck, and its antler horns looked red given its most recent transformation. The slightly elongated neck looked too weak to hold the prize that it was holding in its mouth.

A red drake lay motionless in the jaws of the white dragon. The only hint of it still alive was the heavy panting as the smaller drake dangled from the dragon's maw. The scene was delicate, and it seemed all the trainers were very aware, given the slow movement toward the too-skinny dragon. A growl emanated from its throat at the general movement toward its direction, causing the drake to let out a strangled cry. As green eyes fixated on the movement in the bleachers, a dark blur of velvety wings darted towards the dragoness, causing her to release Roc and face the thing that was attacking her.

The moment he was released, Roc darted to a corner, shaking like a dog as he pressed against a wall out of fear Kirra might target him again. The blur of darkness that had been seen was a grey bat fighting with the dragoness as it put up a hell of a fight from the ground despite trying to reach into the sky and bite it. It didn't last long as the bat wrapped a hold around the dragon's throat and squeezed, causing it to collapse and stop moving save for its chest rising and falling in hard breaths.

With a mist of grey exploding around the bat, it shrunk down, revealing Zeke as he moved towards Roc while adjusting the dark knee-length coat he always seemed to have. BD moved towards Kirra, still in her dragon form, and touched his hand to her head, which caused her form to turn back to her normal form slowly. Leaving Kirra for the moment, BD and Zeke moved to meet each other in the middle and spoke in soft tones. After briefly exchanging hushed words, the pair moved to the bleachers and discussed the situation with the other trainers. After a few heated moments, BD returned to Kirra, picked her up before sprouting large, feathered black wings, and flew off with her. Beastmaster walked over to Roc and convinced him to return to his normal form before they also left the pad together.

Kirra woke hours later with a start as steady hands pressed her shoulders down calmly but firmly. As questions started to bubble forth from her, Black Dragon calmly explained the situation, given how upset she was. He informed her that it was a natural reaction for a first-time full-blown dragon transformation and continued explaining that spiritosk were very much primal-based creatures. He stressed that what she experienced was completely natural. He continued explaining how the tests and constant fighting were meant to stress them so that their abilities and transformations would be forced to emerge.

Given her still confused state, he continued to explain the stigma behind their half and full forms. Most other races in the Multiverse associated them with being monsters or mindless beasts, despite it not being true. She learned that sometimes their bestial sides could become unhinged, like what happened to her, and further explained that their emotions could trigger such changes. Given that wild dragons were very territorial, this also explained why it happened to draconic spiritosk.

"I can't believe I almost crushed his throat..." Her face was buried in her hands, "If Zeke hadn't stopped me..." She didn't want to think what would have happened.

BD tried to console her, "Dragons have always had lower numbers with their populace because of territorialism. It's usually only a problem at younger ages. He's a strong young male. I'm sure he'll be fine."

"Still, I just wanna – I wanna tell him sorry to his face so he knows." She sighed a long, deep sigh, "I just want him to know that that wasn't the real me."

The silence drew on before BD sighed, "Roc has been removed from the program."

Her face shot up out of her hands, "What?!"

"He's been removed." Kirra swallowed loudly after he gave her the news.

Voice rough with emotion, she inquired, "What... What is going to happen to him? Wait... Does that mean I am getting removed as well?" The last was said with hope for her to be free. She remembered the words from Zeke, though, and quickly realized she would still be trapped there until she was a certain age. Then, there was the matter of her brother joining their military as well.

"No…" Just that one word felt like an arrow to her heart. She didn't even hear what he was saying after that. Her eyes started to water some.

"Why? Why am I still here and he isn't? I got my dragon form and my power…" She could feel tears start to form, but she blinked them away, trying not to get too emotional.

Black Dragon attempted to reason with her, "Your form and power have nothing to do with it, Kirra."

Confusion filled her young face, "What do you mean!?"

"Your powers…" He paused, thinking about how to continue, "A lot of things do not add up. It's unheard of that a celestial dragon like yourself can cloak."

Kirra insisted, "But shivers do!"

"You're not listening to me…" Giving Kirra a few moments to calm herself, she realized she was overly emotional and nodded as she looked to him when she was ready for him to continue, "Shivers cloak, and completely mask their body from view. You didn't just cloak and mask your body. You hid your scent completely." The surprise in her eyes showed it was the first time she had heard this news, "Ryse didn't share that part with you because he didn't want to alarm you by telling you he didn't know what your power was. No one has seen anything like what you can do." He pulled out what looked to be a personal journal of sorts and opened it to a page before handing it to her.

She took the journal and looked at the page, "Nightshade Sid-Sid-iott?"

"Sid-ee-aht…" He corrected her

"Nightshade Sidiott. Class S Demon — The Demon is considered highly dangerous and a hyper-nocturnal predator. Demon releases pheromones that induce fear (ability depends on the age of demon). Ability to cloak and mask themselves almost seamlessly with their environments. Impenetrable scale-like fur, razor-sharp claws, teeth, and tail point. Infects and changes others via parasite in tail (Avoid tail at all costs). Able to smell and track efficiently using either hearing or scent. Bone weapons explode from their limbs in different areas (proficiency of weapons use depends on demon age). Demon is to be considered highly dangerous, mobile, and efficient. Can also grow wings, making it one of the single most dangerous sentient demons in existence." She flipped the page to a rough sketch of exactly what had been tormenting her for the better part of a week. "That... is the exact demon that chased me for a week."

Black Dragon sucked in a breath and explained, "That 'demon' is a flawless tracker and can find anyone with just the smallest trace of a scent. He tracked you down with your scent but then lost it like you disappeared." He paused to let her absorb that information, "I promise, you were never in any true danger. The sidiott that was chasing you is a friend."

Her eyebrows would have shot off her face if they weren't attached, "You're friends with that thing?!"

"Yes, and believe it or not, they are a lovely individual."

Kirra persisted with, "Lovely individual! It straight up was trying to kill me!"

"If he wanted you dead, Kirra, you would be very dead. Trust me." Kirra wasn't having any of it as she crossed her arms and shook her head. Despite her childish behavior, he continued, "I know it is hard to believe, but that was how he was told to treat you."

"You're not going to convince me otherwise. Both that thing and Ryse are absolutely horrible monsters." Kirra seemed to be an immovable rock on this subject.

Letting out a sigh, he seemed to be used to this kind of idea about demons and just said, "Have a good rest of your day, Kirra. Get some rest. I'll see you on the morrow for sword training." With that, he got up and started to leave just as Ky walked in.

Once Black Dragon was gone, Ky leaned on the wall, looking at Kirra before finally asking, "You okay?"

"No..."

"I know it can be rough, you know, but you'll be okay. Eventually." Ky spoke in a soft voice as though she were some delicate thing.

"What would you know about it?! I just almost..." She had to pause to get her thoughts together before she continued in a solemn voice, "I just almost killed someone. And I wasn't even in control. Just some violent beast."

Sucking in a breath, Ky spoke in that same soft voice, "Because I did exactly what you did." Kirra looked at him with shock and sobered some as he continued, "It was early on, and I went ballistic in my form. Everyone thinks that my dragon abandoned me. That's why I don't show any traits. For a few months, that did happen, but then he came back. I don't show any dragon traits because I'd rather not be treated differently."

Kirra couldn't help but ask, "What do you mean?"

"I knocked out four others in one foul swoop. They were so badly injured that all of the other dragons in the camp feared me for a really long time. Eventually, the others just stopped talking about it having happened, and now anyone that remembers what happened is gone." He sucked in a breath and let it out, "The only reason I'm still here at the moment is because my power hasn't revealed itself." He looked around before continuing, "They're trying to force the prophecy to show themselves by putting us through life-and-death scenarios. The danger is very real, and if you're put in a situation where your life is in peril, the powers are supposed to take over."

Kirra looked a little confused, "Wait, wait, wait, how exactly do you know all of this?"

"I've been here for over a year, Kirra. I've found out more from just listening and being quiet than I would like to have found out." There was some noise from the outside as a few others started coming up the porch stairs, causing Ky to raise his voice slightly, "Don't let it get you down, okay? I know it was rough for you, having what happened, but it'll be fine." He bumped his fist lightly against her shoulder, making her laugh and nod at him.

As the rest of their cabin showed up, the first through the door was Alyssa, who froze upon seeing Kirra. Nicki bumped into her at the sudden stop because she wasn't watching where she was going, which made Alyssa topple over. Helping her up, Nicki started to ask something but stopped and smiled toward Ky and Kirra, "Heeeeey, how's it going tough stuff? That was some show you put on."

Kirra looked confused, but it was Alyssa who asked the question, "You're not afraid of her? Or what she did?"

"What'd she do, Celestial?" Nicki started to glare down at Alyssa for a few moments.

Alyssa pointed out the obvious, which still stung, "She almost killed that boy." Kirra winced as the words came out.

"Roc..." Nicki corrected.

"Roc, whatever. She almost killed him, and now he's kicked out." Alyssa stopped and glared at Nicki, "And you're just okay with that?"

It was Death that spoke up this time as the twins walked into the cabin, "I hate to be the bearer of bad news, Celestial, but uh, it's kinda in our nature to try and kill others."

Life commented, "I am... sadly in agreeance with my brother for once."

Alyssa looked at the whole group like they were all nuts, "You guys are crazy." She stormed out of the cabin and screamed, "I'm going to see if I can get assigned to a new cabin because you all are out of your minds!"

Death's very sarcastic reply came as he stared at his nails like they were interesting, "No. Wait. Stop. Please. Come back." It caused a few choked-back snickers from everyone but Ky.

Pursuing after Alyssa, Ky punched Death on the shoulder in passing while calling out, "I'll go and talk to her." He disappeared from view as he chased after the emotional Alyssa.

Death looked at the group, completely baffled, "What?! She's being a—" Life cleared his throat to stop Death's curse, so he changed it to, "...Terdling." A few more chuckles were had.

As silence took over, and the three others joined her at her bed, Kirra asked, "You guys... Aren't afraid of me?"

Death burst out into laughter, shaking his head, "Are you bloody out of your mind?" He laughed a bit more, "No offense, Kirra, but you're not exactly scary in your dragon form. Kind of scrawny, actually."

Nicki let out a snicker behind her hand before she said in kind, "You spirit shifted for the first time. Given the size of your wings and how massive your paws were; you'll be a long way off before you're considered a terror of the skies. Besides..." She got up in her face and growled the next part, "I revel in a good challenge."

Kirra could feel a growl start to bubble in her throat. Life pulled Nicki back and let out a nervous laugh, "Okay, Nicki, calm down, she's a fresh turn. Better not to aggravate her just yet."

As soon as Nicki was pulled from her face Kirra shook her head and looked at them with surprise. Death waved his hand like he was swatting the issue away, "Oh, don't worry about that bit. You get used to it as time goes on."

Kirra couldn't help but ask, "How do you guys know all this and just accept it?"

Nicki shrugged, "My parents explained everything upfront. I was kind of ready for all of it. They've been training me since I was like five."

Life said, "I read... A lot."

"I just straight up asked way too many questions, and our despicable parents told me." Death said with a shrug, "Now that I think about it. Maybe that's why they hated my guts. I was kind of a little shite." Life cleared his throat, which made him change his word usage, "I was a right little terdling." This made Kirra laugh and Life groan.

Nicki asked Kirra curiously, "Your parents didn't explain any of this to you?"

With a shake of her head, she replied, "No... Now that I keep seeing more and more things, I'm starting to think that they didn't want me prepared at all. The blockers I was fed, their jobs prior to Earth, and how they sent my brother to watch me in my classes. It feels like they were working against me. I mean, at least all of you got warnings about what would happen. I literally got nothing. Just a bunch of books about things I can't use."

Life questioned her, "What did they give you to read about?"

Kirra listed off a few of the things she learned, "Stupid crap like people from history. Facts about angels and the ancient families. Texts about the gods, Mostly Cerinos and Trivitus, and how we were supposedly created, Ascension trials... Most of it all is just mythos and legends. None of it really matters here." The group traded looks with each other as Kirra buried her face in her hands. Next, she looked up, and she couldn't help but ask, "What?"

Life shook his head, and he held out his hands, meaning no offense. "Nothing, just I've not heard anything like that before. I mostly studied plants and the like. I want to go to university and become a healer."

Death elbowed Life, "He's the weird one, I was just taught the basics of being a spiritosk. You know, what age it happens, important history crap, like prophecies and keeping the balance, the dragons of Light and Dark." Nicki nodded her head as Death spoke.

Kirra spoke solemnly, "I didn't learn any of that." She placed her arms around her knees and leaned against the wall, "I learned some about the bats. Mostly, I experienced it. Most of them are associated with being bad or evil."

Nicki was the one to state the obvious, "They did start this war."

Kirra's retort came quickly, "No. It was before this war, like really, really long ago. The book referred to it as the Great Fall. There isn't a lot of reading on it. I asked my parents, and they knew nothing about it, and my mother knew a lot of history, especially about wars, which makes sense now that I know what she used to do. The point is that she said it was only referenced in texts. Either way, the bats were on the wrong side of the Great Fall, and they're still paying for it today. Everyone always believes that they're out to do harm. I mean, it was bad enough getting treated like crap by every bat, but when you watched how other races treated bats as well, you can kind of understand where their anger comes from, especially with this war going on with those who aren't even involved. It's a vicious cycle and wheel that no one is breaking. Except for Zeke..."

Nicki couldn't believe Kirra's words, "Oh come on... you can't actually believe the musings of a madman like him. Talking about making changes for the good of the people."

"Yeah, I actually can because I grew up as one of those people. Even segregated from the war, I had to deal with that constant prejudice that I was a no-good, rotten child of a bat. And now... I'm a no good rotten child of a bat, who is a white celestial dragon..."

Nicki regarded her with a closed posture as she crossed her arms, "I can't believe you."

"All I can say is that I – I kind of understand where Zeke is coming from. He tried to make a change with the route of least resistance, and nobody listened. So he used force."

"Yeah, and it's us paying for it in the end. We're the end result product here, Kirra." Death explained to her, "You can't just throw a tantrum and make a war because you don't get your way."

Kirra sighed, "You're – you're right, but it doesn't change how others treat them just based on their spirit."

Their arguments continued for a little longer before they meandered towards the dining hall for dinner. They could have sat there debating the entire topic for a long while, given that they all had different ideas of the war. Either way they cut it, they were all stuck there.

19
SPIDER'S LIES AND ITS FLIES

A lyssa didn't come back that night. She refused to come back after the others accepted Kirra openly after what happened. The group didn't seem that upset about the entire affair as Alyssa rubbed them all the wrong way. Ky didn't say what group had decided to take her in, but there was a tenseness anytime their cabin crossed paths with her. It was a disappointment for all of them to see someone from their own group turn so sour, so quickly. More so than that, Alyssa had turned into what she had always been. A bully.

Even though Kirra had stuck up for her during her initial day there, Alyssa started resorting to picking fights with Kirra. Mostly, it seemed she did it to impress her newfound cabin mates more than anything. It was odd to think that despite the fact that Alyssa was actually quite terrible at fighting, she somehow managed to think that she was better and above Kirra's entire cabin group. The funnier part was when she attempted to pick at Ky and couldn't come up with anything because Ky just didn't seem to care. She also didn't have anything on Ky, but no one really did when it came to him because of how long he had been there.

Kirra continued to get better and more capable, but it seemed her transformation into a dragon was a one-off event. She couldn't force it out a second time. Ryse's once-a-week training was still a hellscape for her. He had moved on from making a demon chase her to what seemed like potentially trying to kill her. Whatever he had been up to, they were still trying to force something out of her, but it seemed like nothing was working. It was almost like he was either trying to anger her or kill her, and she could never tell which it was.

She was starting to get really good but still had no control of her full form at will. Despite being unable to figure out what her ability was, she kept her head up. Aelbryst, however, had taught her a new trick, which she seemed somewhat adept at. It wasn't magic per se, but it wasn't exactly Kidori either. It was a method to coalesce energy in the form of her spirit's dragon paw to swipe at the air. He warned her against using it given that on the first attempt, she managed to produce a result that made her pass out.

She was taught many practical things that she never knew about. Energy was essentially a part of every living thing. Some people had a lot when they were born, others not so much. Aelbryst explained it to her like the core was something he could see. He described it as a vault of all the energy a person had. It was the equivalent to that of a battery and how much energy one could put out. The best example she could come up with was battery sizes. You couldn't use a double-A battery to power a car. Aelbryst told her she had the equivalent of a double-A battery at the moment, which felt insulting to her. The good news was that she could train it with time, practice, and patience. It wasn't that she couldn't do impressive things, it was that she didn't have the energy in her to do them. He also told her that if she used too much energy, she could die like she almost did. Apparently if she used too much energy, it could sap the strength from her body physically.

It was weird thinking that she would come to like the class she thought she would hate, and hate the class she thought she would like. With Aelbryst, it had gone from meditation to channeling her energy and finding out what she could do with it. Kirra struggled with it, but it had turned into a challenge she accepted and was determined to figure out. Despite her shortcomings, Aelbryst was an amazing teacher and extremely patient.

Days turned into weeks, and before they knew it, the next trial was on them, but there weren't any hints dropped out in the open. Everyone knew it was the day of the trial, but it seemed whatever hint was given, was done in secret. It seemed the people who were having to deal with the trial had kept the hints to their selves.

It wasn't a problem for their group, as Kirra, Death, Ky, and Nicki were all in the top ten. Life was quite a bit lower, but he still wasn't in the red. Even one of the newer kids had challenged him and found out Life wasn't going to make things easy. Given that no one in their cabin was in the red, they threw a small impromptu party to celebrate. When they wore themselves out, the lot of them passed out late into the night.

"Kirra, wake up!" A blow connected to her side, making her groan and roll over onto her stomach with a cough. The chill of a fresh morning in a temperate forest hit her bones, and it made her shiver, but it didn't last for long. Bolting to an upright position, Nicki grabbed her shoulders, "We're in the playground!"

A mixture of confusion, surprise, and fear filled Kirra, "What!?"

"We're in the frickin' playground!" She pointed to a cowering Alyssa as an angry Ky and Death stood over her. They were already trying to get answers from her and figure out what happened. Over and over again, she continued to repeat that she didn't know, and it wasn't supposed to be like this.

Kirra walked over to Alyssa and grabbed her jacket, growling angrily, "WHAT DID YOU DO!?" Alyssa's answer was the same regardless as she started to cry out of sheer fear from the group. It took a few moments before she calmed, and Kirra tried asking the less hysterical Alyssa when the bouts of sobbing had finally stopped, "What challenge were you issued?"

"I wasn't issued a challenge; it was just a piece of parchment with the words Friends and Enemies on it... a-and four lines under both." Alyssa answered with a panicked voice, "T-Trust me, this is a mm-m-mistake... I-I didn't put any of your names under f-f-Friends." Almost as a unit, the group of them growled out before moving away, except for Death.

Death just moved towards her, causing a scream to erupt from her in fear. All he did was grab a hold of the pack on Alyssa's back as she continued to scream out. It sounded as though he was torturing her, but everyone else knew he was just getting the bag. She was the only person out of the entire group with one. The second he freed the bag from her, she ran off in the distance as Death stood there and murmured softly, "I wouldn't do that..."

While Alyssa continued to run off, Death started rooting through the bag, pulling things out to do an inventory. A singular yelp followed by a thud caused everyone except Death to look as he murmured, "Dumb cunt." Kirra sometimes forgot that despite Death being a gigantic goofball, she respected him because he was highly intelligent like his brother and caught on to things quickly. He spoke in a soft tone so everyone could hear except for Alyssa, "Dumb celestial zero, trial one. She marked how far we can spread out, so don't go further than that, which means no scouting, and that sucks."

Ky asked, "Dealt with this one before Death?"

Death answered almost immediately, "Only once, back when my brother and I were chosen as a team, but it was only the one time." Starting to close the bag, he commented, "Looks like the usual crap. I'll carry the bag for now."

Spotting something he didn't, Kirra called out, "Wait..." Before he closed it, she reached into the bag and pulled out a sheet of silk parchment causing her brows to furrow in confusion. One side was blank, but the other had their names and the names of others in the four lines under Friends and Enemies. Slowly, a smile spread on her face, "It's an ambigram..."

"Bless you..." Death looked at her with a smirk, causing Ky to groan and Nicki and Kirra to snicker.

After laughing, she showed him the paper, "It means it can be read upright and upside down."

She flipped it to show that the words could be turned into each other. Friends read as Enemies, and enemies read as Friends. Despite knowing he was supposed to keep quiet, a bark of laughter escaped from Death before his hands clapped over his mouth. As their group started to snicker quietly, Alyssa recovered from her shock treatment and returned to the group hesitantly. When she realized what they were all laughing about, her face went ghostly white hissing, "This is bull crap!" Death was still struggling to hide his laughter at the situation and failing miserably as Alyssa rounded on him, hissing, "This isn't funny."

Eventually, the group's choked laughter ended as Death motioned for them to follow him. Not a single member of their group questioned him leading the way. Despite Ky having been there the longest, it was Death who was the experienced member of the party when it came to trials. Alyssa refused to follow for a while, but another round of her getting shocked caused her to trail behind the others. Now that everyone was on board, the group silently made their way through the forest.

As the group trudged through the forest, they quietly debated the hint. To them, the silk parchment and the ambigram didn't provide enough of a hint. Even Alyssa had grown relatively quiet with her being placed with a group of people she disliked greatly. The trick the parchment had played on her was still rubbing her wrong.

Slowly, their quiet discussions stopped as the group concentrated on keeping their eyes out for anything, whether it was an enemy or a friend. Death kept them moving, and Ky kept an eye on the back. Since Alyssa was the weakest of all of them, she was sandwiched in the middle between the two pairs of teens.

Picking up the discussion again, Ky and Kirra began theorizing about what they were up against. They concluded that the silk and the ambigram were definitely linked, but as to what it could mean, there was no definite connection. While discussing the possibility of creatures or monsters it could be, a girlish scream caused Ky and Kirra to tense and look for a possible threat. Their tenseness was quickly alleviated as they saw Death dancing around and swatting at his head.

He was muttering and cursing something about webs and hating spiders as he seemed to run headlong into a spider's web.

With a shake of their head, Ky moved forward to go and check out the cache Death had started to aim for, as Kirra moved up to Death, speaking softly, "Nice job, bonehead. Let the whole forest know we're here." Death glared at her and let out a growl as she patted his back, "Let me see the hint again." Death didn't question her as he turned around to let her dig through the pack. Finding the hint, she pulled it out and looked at it closely.

The more she looked at the silk sheet, the more she realized that it wasn't silk at all. Near one of the edges, she started to pull at the woven fabric, and a familiar feeling could be felt. The ambigram made much more sense as she recalled a tale her mother recited to scare her and her brother into behaving.

As Death turned around and saw the look on her face, he questioned, "What is it?"

"I figured out what we're up against. At least I'm 90 percent sure I know what it is." Kirra's comment caught the attention of everyone else, making Nicki and Ky come over as well. Putting her hands on her hips, she commented, "There's this poem, sonnet, or whatever. I remember my mother used to recite it to me at night. I didn't think of it until Death ran into those webs. The parchment isn't silk; it's made from spider's web." Kirra sighed and recited the verse:

"It slinks, it walks on its massive stalks.

With its eyes, it spies the little flies

The flies don't know the lies that will fly

When it spins its tale of woes

It spins and winds its words to the flies

Its story enraptures the little winged pests

And soon, it's too late for the little flies

As they've been caught in the spider's web of lies.

Spindly stalks, webs of lies, it makes a quick meal of the flies.

Even the flies that think they've escaped get caught in the web of lies.

For the bite of the spider is the deadliest bite for even those that escape.

Not one fly survived past the 30 hour, that spider's web of lies."

Kirra paused briefly before finally mentioning, "It's a warning about Energy Thieves. There's more to the poem, but the parchment, the ambigram, and the web of lies are all references to an Energy Thief." Kirra crossed her arms and rubbed them from the goose bumps that had risen at the thought of what they were up against.

The positive response came from Nicki, "Alright, so we know what we're up against at least." She was trying to think positively, but everyone just stared at her as she sighed, "What? Knowing is half the battle, so how do we kill the little buggers?"

Kirra spoke softly, "Killing it isn't the problem. It's the not getting bitten. If you get bitten by an energy thief, it slowly kills you. It's like it takes a piece of your soul or something until it drains your energy. The only way to save yourself is to kill the spider." Kirra looked at everyone around her after she explained it to them. She didn't know much about energy thieves, but her mother told her about their more dangerous aspects. She'd wished she'd paid better attention.

Death instantly commented, "Got it, don't get bit by the little buggers."

"They're not exactly small."

"Alright, so don't get bit by the cat-sized spider," Death attempted to correct himself. Kirra shook her head at him as he inquired, "Dog-sized?" Another shake, "Bloody hell... How big are these things?"

"Try like the size of a small dragon." The second Kirra spoke about the potential size of the spider in question; she saw Death's jaw drop as Nicki and Ky looked at each other. Meanwhile, Alyssa started to pace back and forth, panicking and rambling about how they were all going to die.

Death eventually reached out, grabbed Alyssa, and covered her mouth with his hand. He could very easily bully anyone there, and he knew he was not only the strongest but probably the best fighter in their group. He calmly started trying to organize them, "We need to get the jump on it before it gets the jump on us. Kirra do you know where it might possibly be er, nested, or denned up?"

Alyssa clearly wasn't happy at the bullying as she tried to free herself from Death. Ignoring Alyssa's clear complaints, Kirra answered, "Probably a cave large enough to hold it, but that's only a theory."

"Got it, I think I know of one cave around. We'll post up near it and gather what we can on the way."

Ky pointed out, "Alright seems we have a plan." Ky handed a sheathed sword to Kirra as he and Nicki had finished going through the cache. He had a sword as well and gave Death a few daggers. Finally, Ky said with a wink, "Lead the way, Death."

Letting go of a complaining Alyssa, Death started off, seeming to know exactly where he was going. It felt like it had been hours of walking through the trees as they approached a familiar ravine that Kirra recognized. It was the spot where she had met Tera, but she never realized a cave was under the cliff. Along the way, they managed to find one more cache, which Nicki seemed extremely excited about. It contained another sword but in a different style than the one Kirra and Ky used. Nicki's hand and a half sword made Kirra's weapon look like a knife.

Getting to a good spot to monitor the cave, the group settled in and took turns taking watch. Alyssa was the exception because they didn't trust her. Most of the group was posted up in the trees or against them as they took naps and swapped keeping watch every couple hours. As hours of nothing happening passed, eventually, it became Kirra's turn. She sat in her tree, a leg dangling off the side while munching on one of the rations from the bag. What she wasn't expecting was to become hunted.

A little scream came from her mouth as a shot of webbing came from the creature that had taken a higher route up and decided to jump on her unsuspecting form. The creature was fast and accurate with its shot of webbing as Kirra became lodged against the tree she was in. Pinned and panicking, she tried to get herself to transform at least into half-form to fight it but couldn't.

The little scream had been enough for her team to get a bit of an advanced warning as she heard the sounds of fighting below, though it didn't sound like it lasted long. This was it. This was how she was going to die. She was spider bait.

She felt the tree shake as the Energy Thief moved back toward her squirming body as she attempted to free herself, then, she felt the pinching fangs bite into her side. Almost immediately, she let out a scream and desperately tried to free a limb to fight back. There was nothing she could do; the toxins from the bite were sinking in, making her completely immobile. Soon after, her body was pulled free from the tree, and she was wrapped in a cocoon of webbing. Slowly, she passed out, the effects of the toxin taking full effect.

"*WAKE UP!*" The familiar deep voice of her spirit called to her. She remembered where she was and what had happened and started to fight back in the cocoon as she came to. Kirra could hear the creature's footfalls in the cave as it moved around, checking the cocoons and placing them as needed.

Remembering the poem, she realized her life was in imminent danger. The clock was ticking, and she didn't know how much time passed while she was knocked out. Her heart sped up, her breathing and even her limbs started to gain feeling as fight or flight kicked into overdrive. She let out a breath-shattering scream in her cocoon, and with one sudden fell swoop, Kirra started to transform.

Light burst out from her human body, surrounding her as a dragon soon erupted from the cocoon, a very angry one at that. An inhuman screech reached her ears, causing her to look at the spider leaping towards her. The second Kirra spotted the spider, she felt power surge through her very being. Parting her jaws, a sudden white ball of energy formed in her maw. Inside the ball was a little flame that was contained within. It was hurled towards the spider.

The spider exploded into bits, spreading its guts, limbs, and blood all over the cave. The small explosive ball that had been shot out caught part of the spider's webbing on fire, causing some of it to melt and fall to the floor like liquid napalm. Exhaustion smacked into Kirra, causing her to collapse to the ground with a loud thud.

She was safe, her friends were safe, and that was all that mattered as far as she was concerned. Whatever she had done, had drained her of all of her energy.

The next thing she remembered was a familiar voice screaming at her as one green eye opened to peer at the person, "Stand up and fly away. Now!" Black Dragon was desperately trying to get her on her feet.

The first question she had was why Black Dragon was in the Playground. As the realization kicked in that she was still in the Playground, she looked at him, asking in a soft rumble from her full form, "W-what? What is going on?" She started to rise, shaking her scales out, trying to shake off her groggy state.

"Look at me!" As she looked down at him, he explained urgently, "Run as fast as you can and fly hard and fast. You need to leave. Now!"

"I-I don't know how to fly."

He desperately willed her to leave once more, "It's instinctual, just run and flap your wings. Now **GO**!" He physically tried to push her out of the cave.

Kirra didn't understand anything that was going on. Her confusion was understandable, given the mix of the toxin, the grogginess of waking from energy exhaustion, and just, in general, her overall confusion about the situation. She trusted Black Dragon, though, and did as he said as she started to stumble out of the cave. A few more body shakes came from the sleepy dragoness as a large yawn escaped. Her yawn was rudely interrupted as something pinged off her scales, making her look around. On the ridge of the cliff, she saw several people with guns as a few more shots pinged off of her scaly hide, making her release a roar of pure anger.

Kirra started to run almost clumsily, spreading her wings and flapping them. The clearing just outside the cave was large enough for her to get a few good jumps in before her wings caught the air, and she started to climb into the sky for the first time. There was so much joy in her at getting in the sky with the first attempt at flight. A cry of pure joy came from her draconic form. At first, Kirra thought she might slam into the barrier over the playground, but as she flew over the wall, nothing happened. Looking up overhead, she noticed the barriers over the holes in the ceiling of the cave were gone.

Determination filled her as she realized Black Dragon was helping her to escape! Narrowing her eyes, she started flying up toward a hole as hard and fast as possible. Despite the soreness in her wings, she pressed on, making a mad dash to escape. Kirra didn't know how long she could stay airborne to get out of there, but she was going to try with everything she had.

As she flew through the hole in the cave, she was surprised that she had made it with little to no interference. Kirra was finally free! Letting out a little celebratory call in the air, her eyes squinted, looking at the mountainous region surrounding her. It was an expansive mountain range with trees coating it as far as the eye could see. Kirra only got but a momentary glance at the view before something flew in front of her making let out an alarmed sound as she was forced into a hover.

It was a very large, full-formed bat. Like most bat spiritosk, this one's arms were free of its wings as it held out a hand and tried speaking. Zeke's voice came from the dark-gray muzzle as it spoke, "We do not have to do this, Kirra. Come back peacefully, and it will be favorable for you."

Looking around, Kirra found herself surrounded. She was barely above the trees and hadn't gotten very far into the air as she looked at the forces on the ground. Turning green eyes back at Zeke, she said in a soft rumble, "Favorable to me how? That you won't hurt me if I come peacefully? That I'll be allowed to travel freely? In which way will it be favorable for me?" She questioned him with narrowed eyes.

The usually quick-witted Zeke was slow to respond, "I do not wish harm to come to you, Kirra. I need your help. Once you're done, you can go free on your own and do whatever your heart desires."

A derisive snort came from her, "And be a puppet to you?" Kirra shook her head, saying, "No thanks, not a chance in this life or the next." Before he could actually respond, she changed direction and began to fly around him.

"I am sorry for what comes next then." Zeke spoke too softly for Kirra to hear.

She heard something akin to a cannon being fired, followed by a whistling sound, but paid no attention to the sound. Something collided with her body, tangling one of her wings around herself while the other flailed in an attempt to keep her airborne. One moment, she was in the air; the next, she was crashing through trees and smacking into large branches. The crash into the ground caused something to snap as pain shot through her free wing. An animalistic cry of pain came from her as she flailed on the ground, partially trapped in a powerful net of some kind. As soldiers started to surround her, she snapped out at them. Grasping one unlucky soldier by the arm, she tossed them aside until ropes were hooked around her head, pulling her flush against the ground. As something was stuck between two scaly plates, the fight went out of her, causing everything to go dark.

20

CHOICE

Excruciating pain vibrated through her wing as Kirra woke still in her dragon form. Her wing was clearly broken and the pain caused her to start thrashing in the chains that kept her still. Through her pain, voices argued whether they could knock her out again. With her being chained, Kirra started to squirm what little she could as she tried to fight back even panicking from what was happening to her. An alarmed and pained sound came from her as a hand settled gently on top of her head causing her to focus on whoever the hand belonged to.

The second her emerald green hues glanced at the red sapphires of Zeke's eyes, it felt as though she was falling into a pool of blood. The next moment, she blinked, and she was standing in an ocean of wildflowers and grass that never seemed to end. The rolling hills out before her rolled with the soft wind, causing waves through the endless field. Giggling soon tickled her ears as she turned to see two children about the same age, a boy and a girl, playing and running through the grass and flowers.

The kids couldn't have been more than six years of age. At this distance, she could catch vague details. The boy had dark tresses that curled ever so lightly and dark clothing to match. The girl, however, wore a white lightly frilled dress with white silky smooth hair. The pair looked almost ethereal in nature. Afraid of scaring the children, she stayed where she was.

"You can't scare them. It's a memory." Startled by Zeke's voice, she swung at him, but the punch phased through him like he wasn't there, "You also can't hurt me here. I'm not physically here."

She paused and eyed him with scrutiny, "What is this?"

His voice, still as soft as ever, replied with, "I told you. It's a memory."

Another pause came from Kirra as she continued to question him, "Why?"

"Because you have fought off your sleep more than once. I did not want to have them dose you again because you require a lot in your full form and they could inevitably wind up killing you by accident."

Kirra practically growled at him, "So you are just sitting here playing with my head." There was another long pause, "Why?!"

"So you do not feel the pain." There was a long pause before he commented in a solemn voice, "I miss the simpler days." The boy started to cry catching Kirra's attention. He was surrounded by a perfect circle of dead flowers as the girl with the long white hair moved forward and consoled the boy. Zeke commented softly, "It wasn't complicated with all the politics that envelop the multiverse now." The boy stopped crying as new life in the circle of dead plants started to sprout and grow as the girl whispered softly in the boy's ear.

Her voice came in a much less hostile tone, "How are you doing this? I thought only dragons had powers of the Major Eight."

He continued in that soft tone, watching the boy and girl, "Having control over the Major Eight was something that had been considered special. Those that were turned into dragons, were all people with powers over the Major Eight. Now... It is seen as special if you aren't a dragon, but you are still regarded with less respect than that of a dragon."

There was a long silence before Kirra asked softly, "Are you the boy?"

"Yes." The simple answer came softly.

Another long pause before she asked, "Who is she?"

His voice was soft, almost delicate, "A girl I loved very dearly. One who I wanted to become mated to but couldn't as she was promised to another." There was a long pause before he finally spoke, "Kirra, I only need you to do one task for me and that is all. Doing that task will help me change the multiverse for the better. In exchange, you will have the best training you could ever ask for."

Confusion filled her voice, "What are you talking about?"

"You used a spell. Kirra, you are the prophecy. All I need from you is one small spell, but in exchange, you will get all the training you could ever want in your life. You would see things that only others could possibly dream of. Just say yes and follow the training and the multiverse will be at your every whim."

Kirra didn't even think about it, "No." A look of determination fell over her face.

Taking a deep breath in and releasing it, the real world around her came back into view as Zeke stepped back. Back in that larger hospital room, her wing had just been set and pinned in place. With the fogginess of the dream wearing off, the pain that she was in started to come back causing her to pull at her chains in irritation.

Zeke looked down at her like a disappointed parent, "You are leaving me little choice, Kirra." He knelt down right next to one of her eyes and warned, "You have until your wing is healed to make your decision. After that, there is no going back." Not waiting for a response, he took his leave from the room.

Another lesson was learned by her that day. Kirra would be stuck in her dragon form until her wing healed. The older spiritosk could work through the pain and take their human form, or even half-form, but when you were younger, that kind of pain usually caused them to lose concentration, which meant being able to slip from one form to the next. Reaching out for her spirit for some measure of comfort, she received no response back. She was alone.

Days passed and Kirra began to wonder if this was what animals in a zoo felt like. She had been released from her prison of chains, but she was still trapped in the room as she either paced the room or slept the day away. Being trapped in her dragon form allowed her time to get more familiar with it as she practiced using her tail and doing small pounces on rocks. At one point, Kirra was certain her bones had shifted in her wing as it healed. It felt like it was healing faster than it should have been.

Finally, after a week, Kirra felt the last little pop as a sigh of relief shot through her. Deep inside her, she knew her wing was fully healed, and she was about to test that theory. Changing back into her human form with a flash of light, the emptied wraps fell to the floor as Kirra crawled out of them. The unfortunate part was that Kirra did this right when someone walked in to check on her condition.

As the nurse entered with another right behind, there was a sudden gasp as they saw Kirra in her mortal form. It caught both by surprise, to the point they left the door open and Kirra instantly took advantage. As she pushed her way past the two males, one of them grabbed a hold of her in a grip she knew quite well which made her laugh. They'd been training her for the past few months on counter grips, throws, and punches.

All it took was one small slip and a twist of the waist, and Kirra merely reversed the hold and tossed the nurse into the other, causing them to be knocked back into the large room. While the pair of nurses were trying to recover, she ran over and grabbed their badges. Closing the doors on them, she started running down the halls frantically looking for a way out. Her thoughts were running wild as she panicked about what to do.

"*Calm yourself. You must think clearly at the moment.*" It was curious that he wanted to speak to her now.

"Oh so now you're speaking." Whispering angrily, she found a supply closet and ducked inside it while trying to figure out what was going on.

"*I can't talk to you while you're transformed **as** me. You cannot communicate with me when we are one as we were.*"

"Good to know for the future I suppose. So now what? What should I do?" Kirra looked around in the closet and just slipped against the back of the wall.

He pointed out helpfully, "*Well, you're in a closet; perhaps start by getting out of it before they use surveillance to track you down and fill me in on what happened.*"

Kirra explained to him that they had figured out that she was, in fact, the Prophecy they had been looking for. A deep sigh emanated from him as she cracked the door open and looked down the hallway both ways. Peaking around one corner two soldiers rounded a corner, causing her eyes to widen as they turned straight toward her. One of them pointed and yelled as the other reached for some sort of rifle causing her to bolt down the hall. Her escape was short-lived as she dashed around a corner.

Smacking face-first into a man who felt like he was made out of solid metal, she stumbled backward before catching herself. Looking up at him, one red eyebrow raised as Kirra attempted to kick the man in the groin which she instantly regretted. His hand shot out and caught her leg before he smiled widely showing off large canine teeth, "Mine now." Twisting her leg, Kirra spun her body so her leg didn't break and she wouldn't fall on the ground before a swift punch was delivered straight to her hamstring. The pain leveled her to the ground before he took to a pressure point grip, causing her to cry out any time she struggled, and he applied pressure.

Not long after, the soldiers arrived, putting her in restraints before she was pulled back to her feet. The group of men started to escort her down the hall, but if she stopped or struggled, the large red-headed man applied pressure on her wrist making her compliant with a cry of pain. He increased the pressure every time, starting to slowly get worse until she stopped trying at all, given she didn't want to have a broken wrist.

As she was pressed out of the hospital towards what looked like a helicopter pad of some kind, she was shoved into a flying vehicle. It had two sets of rotating blades on either side, like nothing she had ever seen before.

Finally, Kirra asked, "Where are you taking me?"

The large man who had been bullying her replied, "The Black Citadel…" Her eyes scanned over him, trying to size the man up before she caught his eye, making him smirk, "Go ahead and ask. Fates already blessed you with terrible timing."

The man's red eyes were filled with a mischievous twinkle. It was almost as if his personality matched the short mop of fiery red hair on his head that was spiked in all directions. A sleeve of tattoos wound up his left arm and his right arm had some crazy enhancements and cybernetics. His entire right hand had been replaced with a shiny gold etched with colorful swirling patterns. Across his face, jagged scars ran along in various angles, suggesting a rough patch job and years of experience fighting. Then there was the matter of his gear. The man was armed to the teeth with sets of daggers, a couple of pistols of some kind, and what looked like various other sets of gear she couldn't identify.

"Are you an assassin?"

A boisterous laugh came from the man, "One of the 12 wishes they had me as an assassin. I'm a Mercenary. Competition is a little fiercer in my line of work." He smiled wide, showing those large fangs again, making her uneasy. He wasn't a spiritosk, but Kirra didn't know what he was.

As a set of soldiers moved to sit on either side of her, she wriggled a bit uneasily testing the cuffs some as she asked, "What'd you mean the fates blessed me with terrible timing?"

"I'm here to train you, darling. I only came here because I wanted to see exactly what I was dealing with." A smile played across his lips as he toyed with a knife, "You should count your lucky stars you got me to train you." His accent was similar to that of Death's but different at the same time. She couldn't identify what it was exactly.

Watching the man spin a knife in his fingers with ease, she countered, "Good luck with that. I already told him I wasn't going to participate in whatever he has planned."

"He has a way of convincing people to do things for him. I mean, he could mentally force you to, but then you'd be nothing more than a puppet. I don't think he wants to do that though." While he spoke, his knife movement didn't stop once.

Kirra looked away momentarily with a pause, "Yeah, I don't doubt that."

He laughed, "You're too easy to read, you know that? So angry, it's how I knew you would throw that cheap shot. I was told you were better than that."

Kirra commented with a shrug, "It was a simple choice, you're bigger, stronger, and obviously more skilled. I'd be an idiot just to try and punch you in the nose."

With a large smirk, he playfully pointed the knife at her, "I like you, kid. You could go far in this world one day." Putting the blade up he let out another laugh.

With a snort, Kirra leaned back, bracing as the blades of the machine started to spin up to speed, and the four-bladed copter took off with relative ease. Surprisingly, the flying machine was rather quiet as it took flight. Leaning back, Kirra sighed as she closed her eyes, wondering what she was going to do. Even her spirit didn't know what to say as he knew she wasn't strong enough or skilled enough to fight these people.

Once they landed, her arms were grabbed and she was escorted off of the copter. She'd already learned that fighting back against him would get her nowhere. When she was pressed in front, she was surprised to feel him stop her and remove the cuffs from her wrists. Instant relief shot through her as she rubbed the soreness out.

The man stated, "You run here, and you'll get far worse than what I was doing earlier." Nodding in understanding, she walked with the armed escort and paused momentarily in awe.

Before her, stood a castle carved straight out of the side of the mountain of the cave they were in. It was at the very back of the cave and the most protected area. It didn't look as ominous as it sounded with the rows of different types of flora that complimented every little path with trees that were groomed and well-kept. At the same time, it looked as though it had been there for thousands of years and would be for thousands more with the care that was put into it. Kirra could see other bat spiritosk coming out of holes in the Citadel's walls and realized it wasn't just a castle, but other people's homes and places of work. The place was buzzing with movement as she was escorted up the grand stairs, getting distracted from all of the people who lived there.

All around her were smaller buildings that looked like they were carved out of the same stone but shaped like someone had done it with the ability to move earth. She remembered Zeke telling her that the fallen had helped them carve out homes and realized that it literally meant they had made their homes out of the natural stone around them. There was so much confusion to be had by Kirra as she walked past the rows of homes and shops that were all smashed together as she was pressed forward through the cramped city. Residents either flew with their wings from one place to the next or walked and ran on the ground. Her eyes got carried away with watching it all.

Kirra started to realize that this was the heart of the city. Even a few kids were running around giggling and laughing as they played on the steps. Wasn't Zeke a tyrant though? Shouldn't these kids be looking sullen and angry or starving? Kirra wasn't sure what to make of all the happy faces as she was pressed forward. Her dark hair and green eyes made her blend in with everyone there as she was led up the stairs into the main lobby.

The more she looked around, the more it looked like a place of business. All fancy suits and people wearing badges getting access to certain doors and the likes. As she was pressed forward to a desk, the secretary was going through holo screens and typing on a floating keyboard. Without looking up, she asked, "Who are you here to see today?"

The Mercenary instantly replied, "Lord Zeke."

The girl took in a long, deep breath, letting it out before stating with a bored voice, "What's the purpose of your visit?"

Kirra felt a hand clap on the back of her neck as he squeezed making her grimace at the pressure. He stated firmly, "Bringing him his almost escaped twice Prophecy..." He paused for a moment, "What's your name girl?"

Kirra and her spirit growled in unison as he applied more pressure. Unable to help herself, she attempted to counter his grip on her. It was a mistake on her part once more, but there had been no need for his harshness. Before she could even blink, her face was suddenly pressed against the counter, and her arm twisted behind her back in an uncomfortable manner. She swore she could feel her arm about to break as she slapped a hand on the counter several times in the form of a tap out as she cried out in pain.

He merely laughed, "Oh, ain't no tapping out here, darling. Now tell the nice lady your name."

Kirra cried out a few times before calling out in a panicked voice, "It's Kirra. My name is Kirra." Tears had formed in her eyes from the pain. A moment after she spoke, her arm was released. Kirra instantly withdrew her arm and cradled it with a few whimpers as she stayed on the counter.

"There you go, now see that wasn't so hard." A hard pat on her back was paired with a chuckle, "And **we** are here to see Zeke."

The secretary didn't know what to make of the interaction or, rather, the sudden violence before finally touching her ear and mumbling a few words. After a moment she looked up and replied, "He's not expecting her to be out of recovery for another couple of weeks. She was very injured."

The mercenary got close and growled, "Listen here cupcake, I'm not leaving until I make sure she makes it to where she is supposed to be. So, here's what we're going to do. You'll hop on your little com, call him, and tell him that she almost escaped from that hospital wing. And while I was going to observe her, she tried to escape, but I stopped her."

The young woman behind the desk looked over the man before sighing and tapping her ear once more, "Sorry to bother you again, sir, but the vampire is saying the Prophecy almost escaped, and he stopped her." There was a long pause as she listened, "Yes sir." Kirra slowly managed to stand as she rubbed her wrist and arm as her eyes flicked about. While he was watching the secretary, she took one very slow step to the side. A hand suddenly gripped the back of her neck once more and squeezed making her let out a little cry as she squirmed.

The woman didn't even spare Kirra a glance, "He's refusing to leave sir." There was suddenly a large smile on the man's face as the secretary let out a long, drawn-out breath, "I will inform him to do so." Touching her ear once more she crossed her arms and looked at the mercenary gripping Kirra tightly, "He's in his office straight—"

"I heard the man." Kirra felt the grip on the back of her neck tighten as the man pressed her onward, causing her to stumble some. There weren't even any soldiers stationed outside of the door as they arrived. "Wait out here." The mercenary barked at the two soldiers that were with him. As they flanked the doors, the mercenary pushed them open, throwing Kirra forward. She stumbled to the floor on all fours from the harshness of the shove. As she attempted to stand, a boot found her back shoving her down, "Something tells me you brought me here to teach this one a little bit of respect." A cry of frustration came from her before she looked over her shoulder at him with a growl.

The room was ornate, but not opulently so. Most of the decorations seemed to be what most would be considered artifacts or art. Some of it seemed to be functional. Zeke was sitting behind a large wooden desk that looked stained naturally. His office had a view of the mountain range behind him as the entire back wall seemed to either be a barrier of some kind or a window.

Zeke had been sitting at his desk as he stood up, speaking, "Kirra, I do believe you continue to get stranger and stranger." Rounding the desk, he moved to stand in front of her, "First you resist and wake early from the spider's toxin, then you resist and wake up early from the drugs that were given to you while they were trying to set your wing, and now you heal much more quickly than a bone break should have healed. Rather impressive actually." Zeke crouched down speaking softly, "I know none of this means anything to you or the rest of the world, but it does to me."

He stood up and moved back towards the front of his desk, "It pains me to do such a thing to a majestic creature such as yourself but you are giving me little choice in the matter. If you do not agree to cooperate, I will be forced to do something I very much do not want to do." He looked back at her with somber eyes and asked her again, "Will you do as I ask?"

Kirra looked up at that somber expression and those red eyes and snarled vehemently, "Screw. You."

Zeke studied her for a few moments before turning his back, pulling out a device, and started doing something with it. It looked like a sort of small controller of sorts. The silence was almost deafening as Kirra waited for whatever punishment or trick was coming her way. Before long, he turned around and leaned on his desk, saying, "Let her stand."

The boot lifted from her back and Kirra slowly moved to her feet. Her eyes scanned the room as if looking for an escape, knowing her chances were slim. Eventually, she tried to reason with him, "Just let me go okay." A snort came from the Mercenary, "I'm not going to do what you want, and you aren't going to kill me, so there's no point in me even being here."

Zeke remained motionless as he watched her remaining silent. His posture, the way he crossed his arms, and how he was standing told her he had all the confidence in the world. He was acting as though he held all the cards.

"Kirra..." Her spirit tried to get her attention.

The silence continued on from him as he stood there staring her down. Unable to take the silence, she tried to appeal to his honorable side, "Zeke, listen to me. I've seen how kind and reasonable you **can** be. I'll spread that word if you just let me go. Let the others go too. Let them find their way home. I'm sure if you release all of us, Dragon Colony might relent their attacks and you could end this senseless war. Show them how kind you can be."

The Mercenary laughed, "Girlie, why in hells would he want that? He's currently winning the war against the dragons, and it's caused more to side with him."

"Kirra..." Her spirit called out softly one more time.

Finally, Zeke spoke, "There is a saying that I live by. The needs of the many outweigh the needs of the few. My entire life, I have lived under the privilege of others. Serving them and doing their bidding. Not just the dragons. I was loyal and kind and did everything that was asked of me. And still, despite all I have done, I was painted as the villain. But I have learned in my lifetime that sometimes you have to be the villain."

"Kirra... He has your brother..."

The realization made her go white as laughter could be heard just outside the door. All at once, she looked back to the doors as she knew whose laughter that was. Kirra turned to look at Zeke one last time. His face was a mask as she shook her head in disbelief. Turning back to the doors as they opened, her eyes widened as fear rushed through her. It was her brother.

Time slowed as Kirra locked eyes with Justin and started screaming at him. Justin turned to throw an elbow at Devin as he seemed to understand what would happen. The two other soldiers that were with the mercenary rounded on Justin from behind and quickly got control of him. Even as Kirra used her spirit bond, she fought with the mercenary, countering a few of his grapples before he put her in a lock with both of her arms locked back and his hands on the back of her neck. She screamed out for a few moments, cursing Zeke, Devin, and the mercenary before she locked eyes with her brother.

As the two stared at each other, Justin shook his head at Kirra. She knew what that small communication was, but she shook her head in turn with somber eyes. He wanted her to fight back no matter what, but she couldn't do it. He was all she had left.

Zeke finally pushed off of his desk and stood between the two siblings as he asked, "You know what I hate more than liars?" He walked over to Justin and gripped his jaw making him grunt out in pain before finishing his sentence with a growl, "Traitors." For just a moment, Kirra saw the outlines of his spirit once more. A grey mess of fuzziness wrapped in darkness.

He let go of Justin's jaw, pacing between the two of them before stopping to say, "I have to admit. I admire your devotion and loyalty to your parents in trying to save your sister. Trying to carry out their orders even after they've been long gone from this plane." Justin let out a scream of anger and rage as she could see he was attempting to turn into a wolf before he stopped, "She doesn't know... Does she..."

Justin screamed, **"SHUT UP!"**

Zeke pulled out a knife as he brutally gripped Justin's head by his hair and yanked it back exposing the line of his throat. As the knife was pressed to it, Kirra let out a soft whimper as she struggled with a bit of a scream before crying. Zeke's voice spoke softly to the boy, "You still couldn't protect her." He turned to Kirra addressing her even as the knife still pressed to Justin's throat, "Now. I'm going to ask you one more time. Are you going to do what I ask?"

Staring at the familiar green hues of Justin's eyes, they were wild with rage and loyalty as he managed past clenched teeth, "Don't do it Kirra. Don't agree to anything!"

Once more Kirra called on her spirit's strength as she screamed out and struggled in the arms of the vampire who had a hold on her. His grip gave some and there was a grunt of effort that came from him, but she eventually relented. Kirra finally went limp and sobbed as she knew she was too weak to fight back. Her head lolled forward as the fight left her as the mercenary was the only thing keeping her standing. She couldn't watch her brother die, *"I'm so sorry spirit. I can't... I-I just can't..."*

"I know Kirra... Do what you must..."

Eventually, Zeke called out to her softly "Kirra?" Her face was tear-streaked as she looked up at his own solemn face, "Are you going to do what I ask?" There was no teasing in his voice. Zeke got no pleasure out of doing this it seemed.

Kirra looked at Justin's face, which was filled with nothing but rage and anger, then at Zeke's once more as he waited for her answer. Finally, she relented as she lowered her head in shame, sobbing, "I'll do what you want. P-Please, don't kill him."

The mercenary holding her loosed her from his grip with a laugh, "Ah, like music to my ears, mah friend." He looked towards Zeke propping his hands on his hips proudly, "That's a power move if I ever seen one."

Crumpling to the floor as she was released, Kirra sobbed while the rush of footsteps started escorting her brother away. She could hear his screams down the hallway as she remained on the floor, a crumpled heap of tears and shame. Behind her, the mercenary seemed to make light of the situation as she cried while the vengeful screams of her brother died out.

As the door clicked closed softly, she could hear Zeke moving towards the mercenary and Kirra. The smirk on the mercenary's face was washed away with one sudden grasp. Zeke was in his full form and had him by the throat, lifted in the air as anger and malice tainted his bestial voice, "I do not take pleasure in making children cry and weep mercenary, and I will not accept you doing such either. Have I made myself clear?"

The mercenary didn't bother trying to struggle or fight back as his words came out strangled, "Cry-stal." He was dropped on the ground, gasping for air right behind Kirra.

The violence going on behind her didn't seem to affect Kirra. She stayed where she was on the ground staring where her brother had once been. Her mind kept running through the scenario as she tried to find an alternative. Even her spirit couldn't find a course of action that would have resulted in a good outcome. Instead, the dragon spirit spread warmth through her while rumbling lowly in an attempt to comfort her.

Kirra saw Zeke's bestial feet move in front of her before they dissolved into boots once more as he crouched down. Gently gripping her jaw, he made her look at him. His face held a look of pain on it, as he explained in a pained tone, "Know that I do not do this lightly, Kirra. I like your spirit, and I do not like seeing it broken. But I **need** your magic. Else, I wouldn't have resorted to such cruelty."

Despite the softness of her voice, it overflowed with malice, "I. **Hate.** You…"

An amused snort came from him, "That I believe."

Gently releasing Kirra, Zeke stood and addressed the mercenary threateningly, "You are only here to help train her because I cannot. If I find out you do anything to torture, humiliate, or abuse her, you will see the real reason why all those rumors exist about me." The mercenary nodded his head lacking the smile he once held. Dismissing him with a wave, Zeke turned to Devin, speaking in a caring, fatherly voice, "Show her to her room, then go and get checked out by medical."

Kirra had slowly managed to work to her feet even if her face was an emotionless mask. Her eyes flicked towards Devin, who was holding his nose as blood dripped from it steadily. He replied, "I'm fine, though." All it took was one look from Zeke, and his response turned into, "Yes, Father."

Even as she was led down the halls of the Citadel, everything was a blur. She didn't pay attention as she was doing everything in her power from breaking down and crying. Even when they arrived and he showed her the room and explained things, she didn't hear him. The walls of her mind were doing everything to hold back the storm of emotions she was going through. Eventually, she was left alone. Left to her thoughts. One thought stuck out in particular.

She was a prisoner.

21

TRAINING

Kirra wasn't sure how long she had been in the room for. It had taken her a long time to sleep after Devin had left. She must have cried for a few hours at least before exhaustion took over and swept her off to sleep. The day had been exhausting for her mentally and physically.

When she finally did wake, she lay in her bed, unsure of what to do. Her spirit rumbled at her, attempting to comfort her in her troubled time while she stared at the ceiling, but she didn't respond to him. She was numb and full of loss at the moment. She felt like a caged animal. A week, she had been trapped in a hospital room with nothing but white walls and herself. And now she stared at the black marbled contours of ceilings and walls with no natural light.

The knock at the door broke her from her trance, "Kirra, are you awake?" It was Zeke.

A debate raged in her head as she questioned, answering him before a somber "Yes..." finally came from her.

"Are you decent?" The next question came.

Her reply was quicker, but still somber, "Yes."

The door opened, and in he stepped as he looked around the dark room with an almost questioning gaze. He walked through the darkness to a very blank stone wall before light was suddenly being let in. Kirra lifted her head and perked up, as did her spirit as she took the view in. Before her, lay the iconic landscape she had glimpsed as half of the wall had disappeared and gave way to a window on the upper half of the entire wall. Moving towards it, she seemed fascinated by the display that lay before her. She saw no glass for a window, and it looked more like just a half-wall.

"The others forget you were not raised here and are not used to all the amenities that are offered." He stepped away from the window and watched as she moved to perch on that side of the room taking in the view, "That and spiritosk prefer nature."

She was hesitant to ask the question, "Is this an actual window?" Her voice was hoarse from the previous day's breakdown.

He responded to her calmly and earnestly, "It is. There is a magical barrier that was put in place eons ago. It lets in the natural woodsy scents and the warmth of the sun but none of the stormy weather like rain, snow, or otherwise." Zeke watched Kirra press her face directly against the barrier as she closed her eyes and just took in the moment. After a few beats, he finally asked, "How are you?"

Kirra pulled away from the window at his question and stiffened. Her dragon rumbled somewhere deep inside of her trying to keep her calm. The silence was long and thick with a lot of unsaid things before she finally declared, "Fine."

"Be honest."

Kirra didn't know how to truly answer him in that moment so she just said, "Numb... Hurt.... Hopeless. I don't know how to feel." Kirra didn't want to state the full of her emotions.

Almost like a chiding father, he called out to her, "Kirra..." He was waiting for her to look at him. When she finally did, he asked with an empathetic look on his face, "How are you?"

Her spirit warned, *"Kirra... Don't show this weakness to him. He'll use it against you."*

Unable to stop the floodgates of emotion, Kirra broke down once more, "I'm not okay. I'm scared out of my mind. I'm afraid that my only remaining family is going to be killed because I screw up... Or-or if I don't do well enough or learn fast enough that he'll be used against me." She could hear her spirit sigh as he rumbled and just tried to comfort her with that warmth spreading through her again. There was nothing he could do about an emotional teenager and he wasn't going to hold it against her. Kirra found herself on her knees once more sobbing in fear as she said, "I'm trying to keep strong, I am, I promise, I just... I'm just a kid. And... And I don't know what to do, but I can't lose him."

Zeke crouched down in front of her, speaking seriously, "Kirra, on my soul, I promise that no harm will come to your brother from myself, any of the people under my command, or anyone in my employ while you are in training. And if anyone ... I mean **anyone,** touches him, they will feel the full of my wrath." She looked up at him managing to stop her crying for a moment as he said with complete conviction, "You will be trained. You are going to make mistakes. Those mistakes are not going to be held against you or your brother. And they will not be used as a source of punishment. You will learn to use magic and your ability with time. The faster you learn, the faster you can bring down that barrier. The faster that happens, the faster you can get to the real world, but only once you learn to use magic will that happen." He gave her a moment to process this information before asking, "Understand?"

Kirra seemed to calm in strides, "Yes."

"Do you feel better?" Zeke seemed like he actually cared, which confused Kirra.

It took her a moment to answer but she finally responded with, "A little."

He nodded his head at her, "Good." There was a brief pause before he rose and gave her a once over asking, "You think you can eat anything?"

She knew that she was hungry. It felt like she hadn't eaten in days but she didn't know if she could stomach anything at that moment, "Do I have a choice?"

Letting out a bark of laughter, he responded, "Kirra, you have a choice in everything. You could have chosen to not care about your brother's life. You still have that choice, and you always will. I only ask because you have been asleep for a few days. Stress has a different effect on everyone." Kirra's eyes went wide as he said, "Yes it's been two days. I've taken time out of the days to stop by occasionally and check on you." This news surprised Kirra and her spirit. The thought crossed both of them... Why did he care?

Instead of asking that question, she settled with, "How did you know I was asleep?" Zeke merely pointed to his ears, "Right... bat hearing."

Giving her a moment to think, he asked again, "Do you think you could try to eat some food?"

Rubbing her face, she finally decided, "Yes."

Zeke rose from his squat, "I'll wait for you to get cleaned up outside then."

As he left the room, there was a confused look on her face until she leaned over and smelled her armpit causing her to gag a little. Kirra had been in the same set of clothes for over a week and just slept in them for the last couple of days. Taking a shower was a godsend. Despite knowing Zeke was sitting right outside her door, she broke down again from the situation she was put in. With everything going on in her life, not even her spirit blamed her for the reaction. He'd also thought it was better for her to let out the emotions when she was somewhat alone so it wouldn't give way to the anger attached to it. Something that seemed to be ever-present in the back of her mind. He mentioned it was also understandable given all the changes with her body. Being that she was a teenager, it only made sense that despite everything she was dealing with, her changes in hormones were not aiding her in keeping calm.

When Kirra finally stepped out of the shower, she felt more like a person. Even more so when she put on a fresh change of clothes. Stopping in front of the mirror, she couldn't help but examine herself and think about how much she had changed. At the moment her eyes were bloodshot and her skin a sickly pale, but her whole body had changed. She'd grown an inch in height, her hair was longer, and she'd even gained weight, but it had definitely been muscle. It was the first time since her last trial, her first month there, that she'd really looked at herself. She almost looked like a person, except for her sickly skin.

As she stepped out of the room, she found Zeke leaning against one of the stone walls, messing with a strange device. It looked like a sort of controller with a holo screen between the two parts that were held as he typed on it. As he spotted her, he collapsed the thing together and pocketed it, saying, "You look marginally better."

She bundled her hair and tied it back, mentioning, "I feel more like a person." There was a pause before she finally asked, "What was that device you were on?"

Humoring her, Zeke showed her the device and explained that it was the equivalent of a human's cellphone. He was patient in explaining the differences between the technology she'd grown up with on Earth and the technology on Spiritoski. Spiritoski's TVs were called Screens, and the shows watched on them were called screen shows. Screenshots were pictures, screen time was when you video-called someone, and screen calls were just voice-to-voice. The most commonly used device for personal communication was a Kondorak, named after its inventor.

That first day, she attempted to eat but couldn't stomach much. Zeke was more concerned with giving her time to adjust and regain her strength for training. He promised that she'd get to see her brother at some point, but not until she'd shown some improvement in her training. She'd had no reason not to believe him just yet as he'd never lied to her, yet. Something told her that he probably never would. The other positive that made her feel much better was the privilege of riding Snow. Because of her responsibilities, she'd ride with him a minimum of once a week, but usually more than that. The Citadel was stifling, and riding with Snow gave her a reprieve and an excuse to look for possible exits and routes.

It gave Kirra an excuse to train harder. Originally, it was something she had been forced into, but Kirra found a reason to get stronger and better. She would take every moment possible training hard and working towards the goal of escaping Bat Colony with her brother. She'd need all the experience and practice she could get. When she wasn't out riding with Snow, she was memorizing the halls and watching for where the prison was. When she wasn't learning the maze that was the Citadel, she was studying about the creatures that lived on Spiritoski, mainly the different types of Energy Thieves.

When she wasn't working with Cash, the vampire who had stopped her from escaping, she was with Aelbryst, who was teaching her energy control. At first, it came in the form of small, simple abilities that she could momentarily hold like her dragon claws. Then he moved on to things like creating shapes with pure energy, something she was struggling with. He mentioned that angels had no problem manipulating such simple Kidori forms. It was his polite way of stating that she had a long way to go in her training.

It was strange that she was getting into the beginnings of learning energy control, the first step for learning magic, but still had no idea about her ability. She could cloak, hide her smell, and heal rapidly. Cash even commented that her healing was almost as fast as that of a vampire's, but didn't comment further.

During the weeks of training, she spent every other second learning more about the planet's history, as well as the current politics going on with Bat Colony and its territory. The world had found out that she was the Prophecy, causing the attacks against Bat Colony to get harsher. It seemed that the cave wasn't the only territory that Bat Colony held, but rather their main capital. Several other settlements were being attacked and they were making their way towards the cave and its citizens.

The worst of it was that she had learned that the kids that were in the camp were, in fact, being held as ransom to Dragon Colony, as Zeke had said. She'd found out one of the teachers had gone AWOL. Kirra guessed it was Black Dragon since he'd attempted to help her escape. Another person had sabotaged the barriers and tried to incite a full-blown escape from the camp, but most believed it to be a trick, so no one had taken advantage of it.

Months went by, and Kirra could feel that she was losing hope. She'd made little progress in her energy control training and was starting to get frustrated. They still hadn't allowed her to visit her brother either, on top of her starting to lose hope of escaping at all. The first problem was that she would need access to disable the barrier temporarily. Next, she would either have to fly him out or escape on foot, and flying wasn't an option. She hadn't even tried to take her dragon form since the time she had been stuck in it. Then, there was the matter of figuring out where her brother was being kept.

Since she hadn't been allowed to see him, she'd been doing her best to figure out where he was, but where he was more than likely located, she didn't have access to. All Kirra could do was train endlessly. Her normal routine was getting up, going to her trainer for the day, eating her meals, taking her shower, reading and studying, going on her rides, and wandering where she had access.

Kirra woke up like she always did and headed to breakfast like normal. She usually dined with both her mentors, Devin, Zeke, and whoever Zeke spoke with that morning. Today was different as she walked out to breakfast and took her place. Falling back into her chair, she noticed the person seated near Zeke today didn't wear any normal sigils or representation. He wasn't from any of the Colonies or territories on Spiritoski. He was older with short white hair. The man had no scars that she could see, and his eyes were a deep blue that seemed almost inhuman. She'd never seen anyone like them before, and she was certain he wasn't a Spiritosk. He was dressed in loose clothing and had an almost pure white robe that lay overtop black clothing that was hidden by the loose robe.

The tension at the table was thick enough that a knife could cut it. Despite the clear tension, Kirra still worked on getting a plate of food. While starting to eat, her eyes wandered over the man and his associates that were with him. The pair were dressed in pure black, looking like mercenaries. The only problem was these people didn't show their faces. Two masks with different intricate patterns that were colored differently stared towards the conversation until one of them turned to look at her.

The mask was unsettling to look at as it had no holes to see out of, though they were clearly looking at her. Two little horns poked up at the top, looking like a demon. The entirety of the mask was blue except for the markings, a vibrant onyx black. As the masked associate turned to follow the conversation again, a breath left her as she didn't realize she'd been holding it.

It seemed Kirra had stepped in mid-conversation as Zeke spoke out, "I thought it would be a simple matter of respect and capability for your assassins to do their jobs as they are told to Kain. Black Dragon's task was simple. All he had to do was train the recruits brought here. Nothing more."

The older man in white, who was apparently Kain, responded simply, "Did my assassin not train your 'recruits' to your standard? Did they not provide the knowledge you sought to train them with?"

Zeke stood up as he addressed the man more firmly, "It is not that he did **not** train them, it is that he sabotaged our security system and almost allowed the one thing everyone is after to escape. **Your** assassin did that, which was not part of the contract."

"You should have been clearer in your contract then. You **are** dealing with the Justice Guild, after all. Did you think he would idly stand by while dragons were being caged and kept prisoner? Children nonetheless. He did not break the contract and trained the children as you requested until the Prophecy revealed herself. As I see now..." He gestured towards Kirra, "You still have her as your 'ward' at the moment."

Zeke's eyes narrowed as his tone became dangerous, "I will remember this, Kain of the Wilds."

Kain straightened up in the chair and tensed at the title that Zeke had just used. His face contorted in a mixture of confusion at the use. Slowly, he stood, firmly stating, "The assassin did exactly as he was instructed to do. It is on you for not being specific and looking through the contract to ensure no loopholes." The moment that Kain stood, his two assassin bodyguards stood with him as they left. A silence followed, blanketing the room heavily.

It was Kirra who finally broke it, asking, "You called him Kain of the Wilds. What does that mean?"

Zeke seemed to be happy at the momentary distraction from his poor mood, and he happily answered, "An old term used for a race that lives in the wilds of another planet in another universe. Humans refer to them as werewolves, but they are much more than that. They take on the form of a monstrous-looking wolf. Something feral that doesn't think with intellect but rather with instinct. Instead of turning on a full moon like humans' fairytales speak of, they are born as feral monsters." Zeke sounded as though he despised their kind, despite how amicable Kain seemed to come off as.

"You mean that person is a Vulfadin?" Aelbryst commented with surprise.

"No, he **was** a Vulfadin." Not elaborating, Zeke changed topics, "You'll be training with me today, Kirra."

The comment made Kirra pause as silence took over the room. She stammered nervously over her words, "I... I've been training as hard as I can, Zeke."

His reply came quickly, "I wish to test your progress. Nothing more than that."

Zeke's reply only made her more nervous and anxious, even as she now found herself lacking an appetite. After his statement, she'd only eaten a little of the food she had dished out. As the lot of them traveled to the training room, her stomach knotted and twisted with her anxiety. Once they arrived, Zeke was quick and methodical; taking off the knee-length coat that almost always adorned his shoulders. He folded it up neatly and set it off to the side. Moving to the center of the mat, he turned towards Kirra, causing her to freeze.

Eventually, Kirra made her way towards Zeke as anxiety wracked her body, causing her to shake with nervousness as he asked, "Why are you nervous?"

"I... I don't want to screw up my chances of getting to see my brother."

Sighing, he calmly said, "Treat this as any other match. I've seen your progress, but Aelbryst says you are struggling. I'm going to help you get over that hump. Now, come at me as hard as you can." Kirra's eyes flicked over to Aelbryst, who stood with his arms crossed and a frown set firmly on his lips. Did he look... Nervous?

Letting the thought go, she faced Zeke, who looked completely relaxed. Calming herself, she concentrated, raising her hand and screaming, "DRAGO—" As she brought her hand down in a swipe, a large glowing white dragon paw of pure energy encompassed her hand and slashed through the air. At least it would have if Zeke hadn't stepped forward and clapped a hand over her mouth, which made the paw suddenly dissipate.

He flipped her on her back with relative ease before looking down at her after he pinned her, "You're not in some cartoon. You don't need to say it out loud. If you need to speak, say it quickly, and don't scream out what you're visualizing." He lifted his hand from her mouth, helping her to her feet, "You only need one thing to do this kind of energy control, and that's your mind. How ridiculous would you look if you had to scream every move out every time you did it?"

Kirra looked between Zeke and Aelbryst and caught sight of the elf holding his chin tentatively between two digits. She was certain he was nervous now. Zeke instructed her to try the Dragon Claw without screaming out, but she couldn't manage it. Seeing her frustration, he moved over, deciding to guide her through the steps as he asked, "Where does energy come from?"

Kirra looked confused, thinking it was a trick question, "Inside of me?"

"From where?" When she didn't answer him, he continued, "Every being has an energy core in their body. It is not a physical thing you can see in its natural state. We can pull out the next best thing through transfusions, but energy in its essence is life itself. It is like the wind.

We know it exists, that it powers everything, and can feel it when it is chaotic or even gentle, but we miss it when it is gone. For us, it is, at our core, the life-giver." He poked the center of her chest, "Here... You're not making magic, not yet..." Kirra calmed down as he explained and watched him move as he taught her, "You're harnessing control over your own energy and exerting it as a force to push, move, slice, and impact the environment around you." She was surprised to find he was an excellent teacher, far better than even that of Aelbryst.

He waved around him and stomped on the ground a bit, showing her physically, "These are all just limits that we place in our minds. When you realize that these limits can be broken, anything is possible with energy, and I mean anything. I've watched a person who used to have wings imagine ethereal wings and use their pure energy alone to fly and slice through the air. I've seen someone jump higher into the sky than I have ever seen anyone do because she put a burst of energy down into the ground that forced herself upward. Another person using a string of pure energy, wrapping an enemy up and turning them into a helpless crying baby in their Kidori web." He moved back over to Kirra and gripped her shoulders tightly to grab her attention, "But you can't just force it to happen. You need to draw it from your core and push it to where you want it to go and where you need it to travel."

Stepping away, he took a stance before suddenly punching down into the ground as a crater about four feet in diameter appeared as his fist touched the ground. The punch seemed to centralize at one point and compress outward, making a miniature crater, "You are your only limit." He stood up, facing her once more, "Take your time, and try it yourself."

As Kirra started to work up to the idea of doing it, Zeke threw a challenge to her, "Tell you what. I will allow you to see your brother if you can summon a dragon paw without words. You have my word." Pausing, Kirra looked at him with surprise as he placed a hand over his heart and bowed his head. She knew it was true because Zeke never lied about anything. As she started to get in a stance, he guided her one last time, "Be calm, control your breathing, and take your time."

Kirra hadn't been able to do it without words yet. It felt like she was taking a really long time to control her breathing and calm down. Her spirit also seemed to want to help, *"Breathe slowly; don't think about what is at stake. Just picture a giant dragon stepping on top of Zeke. Squishing him."*

The laugh that bubbled through her had seemed to calm her enough. After a moment, she let out a long, deep breath and could feel the ebb and flow of energy through her. The thought came to her then that her spirit was that energy. It was no different when she called on his strength and speed, and the two worked together. With more confidence than she'd ever had before, she brought her fist down towards the ground. With complete and total ease, the paw appeared at the last second as it slashed down onto the ground. It didn't make as deep of a dent as what Zeke's fist made, but it was clear as day she'd done it. As the white energy-induced paw petered out of existence, Kirra could feel a sudden drain on her as she fell backward.

Zeke rushed towards her and caught her before she fell to the ground. Slowly lowering her into a sit, he patted her shoulder and commented, "Amazing what happens when you're actually being taught how to do something the correct way."

Zeke slowly looked up towards Aelbryst with clear accusation in his eyes. The soldiers that were present in the room for her training session started to move off of the walls towards the elf. None of that mattered, it seemed. Aelbryst mumbled something under his breath in a different language quickly, and with a loud snap, he was gone. In his place was a piece of paper with symbols written in a circle that were lightly singed. A few other markings were dotting the paper as one of the soldiers grabbed it and brought it over to Zeke.

Examining the paper, Zeke sighed as he handed it back to the soldier, "Burn it. I don't want him using it to get back in. Make sure his room is scanned to see if he also placed any markings in there as well." He looked down at Kirra and explained, "We found messages that he was purposely slowing your training directed towards the Justice Guild. We've been watching him since Black Dragon's betrayal and participation in your first escape attempt."

Kirra inquired softly, "They knew each other?"

Zeke nodded, "Yes, all of them. Kain, Black Dragon, and Aelbryst." Standing up, he helped Kirra to her feet before moving to retrieve his coat.

He didn't bother turning towards Cash as he gestured at the vampire, "The day is yours, sir." Cash pushed off the wall, giving a two-finger salute, not questioning him. He walked over to Devin patting him on the back before jerking his head for the two of them to leave.

While Cash was ushering Devin out, Zeke turned to speak with Kirra, "Are you sure you want to see your brother?" She nodded fervently.

Sighing out, Zeke led the way to where her brother was being kept. After badging through one set of doors, he led the way down a maze of hallways she'd never seen. Kirra attempted to keep track of the turns, curves, stairs, and badge points, but it was nearly impossible for her to remember. As they continued, one thing became evident. They had arrived at what was, more than likely, their dungeon for prisoners. Most of those inhabiting the cells appeared to be dragon spiritosk, but some species were different. One of which called out to her.

The familiar cackle greeted her ears, making her pause as soon as she heard them, "Succeeding in your training, little dragon?"

22

The Plan

R yse. He had some sort of collar around his neck, very similar to the one he had given her. He sat on the floor of his cell like he owned the space, lazed out like a giant cat with no care in the world. Reaching towards a nearby wall, he scratched a little X in what appeared to be a game of tic-tac-toe. She thought he was playing the game by himself until she saw the shadow move, making a little O in the same game.

Even she seemed a little unsure as she questioned, "R-Ryse?"

He gave a two-fingered salute before turning a wide-toothed smile towards her, "In the flesh... or shadows... or fur even!" He nodded several times while cackling wildly, then suddenly jumped to the barred window of his cell with a loud bang, "Are you here to free me, little dragon?"

The sudden movement startled her, making her step back as she said softly, "I uh... no..." He pouted, running a finger down the side of his face in a mock teardrop. Jumping back, causing the door to rattle, he returned to his game. Curiously, Kirra moved a little closer to peek into the cell and found it was bare. Only a set of grey tattered bottoms covered him so the mix of fur and dark flesh became much more apparent. The demon was completely ripped, every muscle on display twitching with the slightest of movements. It explained how he could do what he did during the times she trained with him. The demon seemed more animal than man.

The feeling of a hand on her shoulder brought her back to the present, "He was aligned with Black Dragon." Pressing her forward from Ryse's cell, Zeke explained, "He was the one who set up the toys that interfered with the barrier."

A silence drew out between them momentarily before Kirra stated, "You knew I was the prophecy... didn't you..." It wasn't a question. Kirra realized that he had others following her movements and watching over the trainers who spoke with her. How else would they have known that Ryse sabotaged the barrier that allowed her to fly through? Then there was his interest in her, and Devin being sent to the Preserve to protect her and his knowledge of the medicine she was taking.

"I had my suspicions. Yes."

Stopping, she turned to face him asking, "How? I didn't even know."

"Your parents did. When Devin discovered you were the proper age, but your parents kept you on blockers, that was the largest indicator. Then, they continued to keep you as far from Devin as possible. Protective parenting. I could give them that. So, I didn't think too much about it." He paused, "But your brother was watching you, making sure you took your blockers so your spirit wouldn't hatch. Then, when he came to the Military Training Academy, we found the messages on his Kondorak that your parents had sent him. He had attempted to hide them by deleting them, but it showed some rather incriminating evidence. With all of that evidence piling up, we knew he only joined the army to stay close to you and honor his oath to protect you no matter what."

A shuttering breath escaped Kirra at all of this information, "When you took me to the ground my first day...?

"I knew you could be the Prophecy."

"What about sending Devin after me?" The answer was the same as she added, "And the obstacle course?"

His voice came out in a flat, unamused tone at what she was implying, "If you are thinking that I gave you special treatment because I thought you were the prophecy, you are incorrect. You bashed your head several times in only a few weeks' time and the medics were stitching up Roc. I don't believe in causing undue harm to children." He suddenly gripped her arm and made sure she was looking at him as he spoke the next, "What happened with your parents... It hurt for me to do. They were good people, trying to do their best to protect their daughter. The pair refused to give you up without a fight though."

Kirra looked somber but nodded as she said, "It was just a... strategic move. Was my mom really that good?"

A small smile graced his face, "She retired as an assassin after two terms with the Justice Guild. Not many assassins retire from any guild. And the Justice Guild is one of two Honor Guilds." He started walking again as he let out a bark of laughter, "To be a woman in a man's career, working where men are often treated better and women are bullied because they're considered weaker. Your mom was an outrageously strong person." He smirked seeming to look back fondly on her mother. It made it a little easier for Kirra to deal with their deaths.

Pushing open a heavy metal door with no window, Zeke and Kirra entered a room where their backs were to that same obsidian stone, and another wall was nothing but glass. The hall was lit but the inside of the cell was dark, though Kirra could see inside it easily enough. Shredded remains of what appeared to be a bed was occupied by a large black wolf, only slightly smaller than that of an ancient wolf. The walls of the cell were adorned with deep gashes and fluids that looked like they could possibly be blood. It was too difficult to tell with the low light in the cell. The state of the cell caused Kirra to cover her mouth with surprise and horror.

Kirra's excitement turned to anger as she turned on Zeke, "What have you been doing to him!?"

Zeke was already holding his hands up as he calmly explained, "He took his wolf form after being here for a week and began destroying the room. There used to be more to the room but we had to remove them for his own safety." Zeke paused as though he didn't want to tell her before he began, "He turned back briefly and attempted to harm himself. Since this last time of him taking his form, he has refused to change back and even injured a few of my people who attempted to feed him." The news caused Kirra to scrub her face with her hands as she attempted to hold herself together. Giving her a moment to process this information, he gave her the last of the news, "We haven't allowed you to see him because of the difficulties in dealing with him and letting him recover from his attempts at harm. The other problem is that he has been in his wolf form for a while. The change could be permanent if he stays in his full form for too long. There will probably already be permanent traits given how long he has already been in it."

Wiping away the tears from her face, Kirra calmed, finally asking softly, "Can he see us?"

"Not yet. I wanted to give you time to process all of this first." He approached a control panel, asking, "Are you ready?" After she gave the okay, Zeke started changing the settings on the panel, causing the cell lights to turn on slowly. The darkened glass wall of the cell started to grow clearer as Kirra got the chance to see the real condition of his cell in the harshness of the brighter light. Zeke looked toward Kirra, giving a curt nod before leaning on the corridor's cool obsidian stone.

Taking a deep breath to steady herself, she stepped forward cautiously and called to him, "Justin?" The large furry head turned instantly, almost as if it were surprised at the voice it heard. Unfurling from the ball of fur, it rose, showing how emaciated the wolf was as it padded forward. Sickening cracks soon reverberated off the walls of the cell, making his transformation sound much harsher than it probably was. Slowly, his form started to shift back to that of his human appearance.

Justin pressed up against the glass and growled out towards the pair. Two sets of fangs had replaced his normal teeth, one set on the upper and one on the lower. His long hair had become a mix of dreads that weren't maintained mixed with shaggy lengths of long hair that partially covered the toffee-colored skin of his face. Finally, that growl gave way to accusing, harsh words, "Are you even going to fight back?! Or are you just going to stand there and become his prized little puppet?!"

"Justin..." His accusation made her step back from the glass as she stammered out, "You're the only family I have left and—"

"And you're the prophecy. Mom and Dad put their lives on the line for you to have a chance at life! And this is what you're doing with it?" A snort followed his sharp words as he shook his head in disbelief.

The sting of his words still hurt, causing the welling of tears in her eyes and her voice starting to shake with a mix of anger and sadness, "I'm trying to save your life because I have no one else!"

Stepping from the glass, he held his arms out from his sides, gesturing to his cell in grandiose, stating, "Some life I'm living here. A glass box as a caged animal." Turning his back to her and waving a hand dismissively he made his way towards the back of his cell, "You should have let him just kill me. Better than you being a puppet."

The sharp words from his last statement hit true and deep. Backing away from the glass of his cell, a soft sound of hurt came from her as the warmth of tears started to stream down her face. Covering her face with her hands, she shook, crying soundlessly but shaking all the same. Kirra in her mind, was doing everything she could on her end to get them out, and here he was accusing her of doing the exact opposite. She wondered why he had such little regard for his life and wished her to be alone on a strange planet that she knew so little about still. All the while, Zeke remained silent, his face a blank mask as he leaned on the wall with his eyes closed.

Turning to see his sister with her face buried in her hands, a soft look came to his face as he approached the glass wall and pressed against it. He called out softly to her, "Kirra..." He hadn't meant to cause her more pain than what she had already endured.

She didn't answer him. Taking a few calming breaths, she waited until they were more even, and the tears had stopped before looking up at him, asking, "Did you, Mom, and Dad all know I was the Prophecy and never tell me?"

A look of shock came across Justin's face, telling Kirra everything she needed to know. As he looked between Kirra and Zeke, he finally spoke in a low tone that hinted at his anger, "Kirra I don't know what he's been telling you about Mom and Dad, but don't listen to him!"

"So you knew... this whole time..." She hadn't wanted to believe it. All of it shocked her, replacing her somber mood with a quiet rage.

He pleaded with her in an almost begging tone, "Kirra, they made me swear an oath. I couldn't break it!" She turned from him as he started to pound at the glass trying to make her stop her from leaving, "Kirra, listen to me. They did it for your own good I swear..."

Pausing just inside the doorway without looking at him, that anger came through as she spoke, "You, Mom, and Dad... You all stopped me from hatching my spirit." With a shake of her head, the last was said with the same quiet fury she was feeling at that moment, "I was drugged for years, and you knew what I was and never told me!"

His pleading grew more desperate, "Kirra it's not what you think! They made me swear on my life. I couldn't tell you! I was supposed to protect you!" His banging on the glass grew more desperate as he watched her start walking out of the room out of sight.

Zeke finally pushed off the wall to follow Kirra as the boy's anger redirected to Zeke. String after string of curses were thrown at Zeke though he said nothing in return. He didn't even glance at Justin or look maliciously at him. Reaching the control panel, he flicked a few of the switches before his voice was no longer heard. A long sigh left him as a mixture of pain and hurt fell over his face. Prepping to face the upset teenager who had found out she'd been lied to her whole life, he put a mask back on.

As Zeke exited the cell, he noticed Kirra swiping at her eyes, seemingly attempting to compose herself. Reaching out, he attempted to touch her arm lightly which instantly withdrew as she stated firmly and stubbornly, "I'm fine... I'm fine... I just can't believe they've been lying to me my whole life...."

As she was still gathering her composure, Zeke thought about how to console her before he finally stated, "No training for the rest of the day." Kirra looked like she was about to argue but he insisted, "You have had a rough day. It would be better for you to rest and process what happened today. You can train to your heart's content tomorrow, but today, do whatever you want within reason." Taking a long breath, he said, "I have some situations that require my attention, but I will be taking over your energy control training from here out."

Kirra nodded, asking, "The dragons are getting closer to the border?"

He seemed to debate on how much to reveal to her before explaining, "They punched a hole through the border defense with the aid of the Soulwalker." He leaned in stating, "Do not take this as a good thing. The dragons are not good people Kirra. Some are, but most are not. Their council would sooner leave you untrained and hidden from the rest of the multiverse than teach you what you need to survive." Kirra didn't know how to respond and just nodded as he started to escort her out of the restricted area.

Once she was out of the prison area, Kirra wandered the Citadel before getting bored. Eventually, she went to the stables and took Snow on a ride while explaining the day's events to him. Seeking advice from her spirit and Snow simultaneously, the pair didn't know how to guide Kirra in her current predicament. Both felt the bite of betrayal at the information she'd been given that day, but this was a problem they'd decided she'd need to figure out on her own. Eventually, Kirra returned to her room for the day mentally exhausted.

Collapsing on the bed, thoughts of the day's events continued to swirl in her head, keeping her up as she lay there waiting for sleep to come. This day, of all days, had been rough. Her family knew about her being the Prophecy and had lied to her about it her entire life. Zeke had even known it before her, but his knowledge had only been suspicion based on information. Eventually, she forced her brain to concentrate on something else. She had other concerns to worry about, like trying to remember the maze that was the prison.

A young feminine voice called out to her in her sleep, "Pssssssst." Rolling over onto her back, Kirra pulled the covers up to her neck thinking it was just a dream. The poke she felt on her nose told her otherwise. Opening her eyes, Kirra screamed while throwing a punch at the person in her room. Easily sidestepping the punch like she was made of water, she glared at the offending punch like Kirra was crazy.

The girl looked about the same age as Kirra but was short, had long brown hair, and was staring at Kirra very curiously. The teen looked to be on the curvy side but wasn't rounded in a way that made her seem obese. After a few apprehensive moments, the girl finally stated with a mischievous smirk on her face, "You wanna get out of here?"

Kirra was still waking up and trying to figure out what was going on, "Uh.... What?" Rubbing her eyes as she adjusted in the bed, she stated, "I have a curfew." Squinting at the girl, she swore that the girl looked familiar.

A soft groan came from her, "Oh my goooooood. You, are so slow. I'm bustin' you out of here you dork."

"What?"

Sighing out, the girl moved to the door and opened it before looking back at Kirra, "You want to get out of here, or not?" She gestured at Kirra like she was an idiot.

Hesitantly, Kirra looked at her as her sleep started to wear off and recognition had finally kicked in. Both her spirit and herself made the connection at the same time, "You're... You're the Soulwalker?"

The girl gave her a questioning eyebrow and corrected her, "Uhhh... It's actually Planeswalker, but it's the same difference." She looked over her shoulder, taking a deep breath and letting it out before turning back to Kirra stating, "If we're gonna move, it's going to be now."

She held her hand out to Kirra and motioned for her to follow her. After a brief hesitation, Kirra gave in to the girl's demand and followed her as she led the way through the halls. While Kirra continuously looked around with nervousness at possibly being discovered at any moment, the Planeswalker moved with a confidence and surety she had only seen in others like her trainers and Zeke.

Kirra was constantly worried that at any moment, someone patrolling the halls would catch the pair of them moving through the halls, but it felt like they were taking turns just out of sightlines of everyone they were crossing. The girl was almost a full head shorter than Kirra but moved with the quickness of someone who would have been the same height as Kirra. Even Kirra had to jog a bit to keep up with the Planeswalker just to match speed with how fast she was navigating the halls.

The girl suddenly ducked around a corner lifting a finger to her lips as Kirra did the same. A light showed around the corner, letting the pair know that a soldier was about to pass their current location.

Kirra's heart about jumped into her throat as the Planeswalker made a few signs with her hands before waving a hand over the stretch of hallway from bottom to top. The entrance to where they were hiding shimmered like a curtain had fallen in place as the soldier stopped and examined the shimmering curtain of air.

Confusion ran over the soldier's face as he looked down the other hallways, confused as if he had made a wrong turn somewhere. The place he was standing should have been a hall, but there were only three ways to go instead of the four. After a brief moment of confusion, the soldier shrugged and proceeded down another hall as his footsteps echoed through the corridors.

When the soldier was out of sight, Kirra whispered, "How did he not see us?!"

The Planeswalker let out a muffled giggle before simply saying, "With Magic." Making a hand sign, she waved her hand once more, and the illusion of the wall she had put into place disappeared. Leading the way through the hall again, they came to a door that led outside. Opening it, she peered carefully around the corners before stating, "Alright, I'm going to turn into a wolf and you're going to hop on and hold on for dear life."

Before Kirra could say anything, the girl walked out into the night and with a soft burst of light shrouding her body, her form took the shape of a beautiful white wolf shaking out its fur. Turning towards Kirra, two brilliantly blue eyes peered at her, stating firmly, "*Hop on...*" The Planeswalker's voice echoed softly through her head with her new form.

Anxiety filled Kirra as she looked around for a moment before following the command at her spirit's encouragement as well. The wolf standing before her was tall and lanky but nowhere near the size of Snow as she clambered on top of it. It almost looked like she wasn't fully grown yet. The moment that Kirra gripped the fur of the wolf's neck, the wolf took off and was quickly maneuvering along the outskirts of the city. It was almost like she knew the full path of the terrain of the cave before even seeing it.

The thought occurred to her too late, that her brother was still trapped back there in the Citadel, *"Wait, what about my brother?!"* Worry started to clog her mind as images of him being tortured and used to get control of her back floated through her mind.

The wolf screeched to a halt and peered over its shoulder at Kirra, *"Your brother? I was only told to rescue you."* There was a moment of something soft brushing against her mind as the thought of her walking through the prison popped into her head and was fast-forwarded. The wolf looked down at the ground, seeming to be considering the situation.

Kirra pleaded softly, *"He's the only family I have left."*

The wolf looked over its shoulder at Kirra pausing before saying, *"I'm going to drop you off first. I can't carry two on my back at the same time."*

"No, no, no, no... we have to go back—" The wolf wasted no time in bounding away through the forest once more. She didn't even notice how far they had made it in such a short amount of time. As the pair approached a clearing, the wolf slowed to a trot as Kirra saw every teenager at the camp, causing her to stare in awe. It wasn't just them though. There were adults Kirra had never seen before as they spotted the wolf coming and started taking their full forms.

Dragons of every size, type, color, and age started to take their full forms around groups of kids. As the wolf approached the only white dragon in the group, Kirra stared up in awe. The wolf lowered its body slightly, saying, *"This is where I leave you ..."*

Kirra slid off the wolf, turning to face her as she pleaded desperately, *"You have to go back for my brother please, plea—"*

She felt a huff at her back as the sound of a melodic, serene voice called out to Kirra calmly, "Calm, child." As Kirra turned, she was face to face with a dragon head the same size, if not larger than her whole body, as the dragoness raised its head to look down at her. Before her stood a pure white dragon with scales that glimmered under the moonlight, peeking through the holes in the ceiling of the cave. Horns curled back slightly from her head and slightly out of the way of the long, slender, but muscular neck.

That serene voice called out again, *"For the moment we are here to rescue you and the ransomed dragonlings. It is too dangerous to linger for long now that we have you. At any moment our efforts could be discovered."* The dragon looked at the wolf, saying elegantly, *"Thank you for your help this day, Planeswalker. You will always be remembered for sav—"*

"You're just going to leave without rescuing her brother?" The wolf pointed out cutting the dragoness off, *"We're right here. Give me five minutes and I'll get him for you."*

The dragoness said, *"It is too dangerous to linger here for just one person. The longer we stand here, the longer we put the rest of these children in danger."*

Letting out a frustrated growl, the wolf's voice echoed through the air, *"I'm not going to sit here and debate this with you. If I can save one life... I'm doing it."* Turning to look at Kirra, the Planeswalker confidently spoke, *"I'm going to get your brother."* She added lastly, *"Wait for me. I won't be long. I promise."* The white wolf didn't bother waiting for a reply and ran towards the line of trees they had come from.

"We are leaving now!" A derisive snort came from the dragon before turning to address Kirra, "Climb on, little dragon. We must leave at once."

Kirra insisted once more, "But, my brother. We can wait for a little while lon—"

"We already waited for you... We cannot afford to wait longer." She leaned down and asked her softly trying to make Kirra see reason, "What is worse, one life... or that of a hundred?" The dragoness gestured with a wing to all the other teens around.

Kirra looked down at the ground as she thought. Looking at the crowd gathered in the clearing, she saw all of the young faces, some of which she recognized. The teenagers were climbing up on the dragons, attaching themselves to harnesses and belts that held them securely. So many more teens than those just at the camp left her feeling conflicted and overwhelmed. Zeke's voice floated through her mind as she remembered him saying one of many things she had found she agreed with him on. The needs of the many outweigh the needs of the few.

Giving in to the weight of all of the other teens present, Kirra approached the white dragoness and started climbing aboard. She was one of the last to get herself secured to the dragoness as she realized that not every dragon had teens on them. Her heart ached, and tears started to form on her cheeks, but she was doing what her brother wanted her to do either way. She whispered softly to herself and apologized for leaving her brother behind.

Everyone's movement stopped, and even the dragons were still like the predators they were. It felt like everyone was waiting for a signal to move. All of them stared in one particular direction. The top of the cave where the holes lay above. Kirra realized what was about to happen. Almost as if in unison, the dragons began to spread their wings as one and the sound of leathery flaps filled the night sky. The sound of an explosion pierced through the air as Kirra gripped the straps that held her to the white dragon for dear life. Suddenly, the dragon she was sitting on was moving quickly through the air. Looking upwards, the shimmering of the barrier over one of the holes in the cave roof was gone as bits of metal and rock started to fall.

The number of dragons that came to aid their escape became clear as the horde took to the sky. Those without riders on their backs were on the outsides of the formation. They clearly planned on a fight happening from all of the noise. Off in the distance, it appeared that a task force was already being sent after the group of dragons as the explosion had given away their presence. Several members of their guard began to peel from the group to deal with the forces heading their way to distract and hold them off.

Part of Kirra worried about the Planeswalker and the fact that she was getting left behind with her brother, but the dragoness had warned her that they were leaving. Letting her thoughts drift, she looked towards the Citadel and its stone city as the wind whipped her hair around her face. The sight of a squad of bats flying in their terrifying full forms drew her attention making her eyes go wide as she ducked close to the scaly hide of the dragoness. At the same time, the dragon she was riding started to perform evasive maneuvers as several bats flew through the grouping of dragons clearly searching for Kirra.

All around the group, different hues of fire started to shoot out from dragon's mouths as they fired their breaths at those they could fend off from a distance. Closer still, those who hadn't peeled off from the group started ripping bats from the mass of dragons and throwing them in the distance as far as possible.

As the last bit of bats was dealt with in the group, the dragons with teens flew headlong to the starry sky above. At a breakneck pace, all of the dragons were working overtime, doing everything in their power to save the teens as they made it to the open skies of the cool night through the roof of the cave. Continuing forward as the last attempts of bats fell behind from their greater speed at rising in the air, the chase for them was given up. Gaining a higher altitude, the group finally leveled off once their tails were clear.

All around calls of victory were heard from not only the dragons flying the teens safely out of Bat Colony, but the teens as well. Kirra seemed the only one who didn't cheer at the successful escape. Her eyes lay back on the mouth of the cave where her brother was still trapped as the Planeswalker was more than likely being captured for attempting to free him. She said a small prayer, hoping for his health and safety despite knowing it might be useless.

Despite the beautiful display of greenery and mountain forests all around, Kirra's mood was somber at the thoughts that plagued her mind. Her spirit tried to console her and assure her that she was making the correct choice, but it changed nothing about how she felt. Eventually, as the sun started to peak on the horizon, the desert started to come into view, lighting the barren wasteland beneath the horde.

Kirra had never heard nor seen anything like it before. It was a welcome distraction.

"What happened here? Why is there no life?"

An amused chuckle came from the white dragoness she was riding, "There is life here, but it is merely a desert. We refer to it as the Wyrm's Ocean. The vast desert spans the middle of the land from ocean to ocean. Miles and miles of nothing but sand and desert-dwelling creatures. One of which we call wyrms. Large burrowing creatures that do not see but feel and consume their unknowing prey from below. Even to dragons, they are dangerous unless you know where you can rest. This land's second most dangerous part is the lack of water."

The dragon's head towards the ground as though spotting something, "Look there little dragoness…" Below were dots of people riding on what appeared to be lizards. They looked like lizards you would find on Earth from this distance until she remembered how high up they were. She explained in that same calm voice, "A Sand Strider caravan. Not everyone can afford the luxuries of fuel for air transport, nor can they sprout wings and fly. The Sand Striders effortlessly glide across the sand and leave no trail behind. It allows them to travel across the Wyrm's domain without risk of becoming prey."

Kirra had only read about some of the creatures that inhabited Spiritoski. The descriptions did **not** do justice to the sight before her. Even with the wonderment of all of it, one thing bugged Kirra about everything that had happened, "What's going to happen to the dragons that helped us escape, who are still back in Bat Colony?"

The dragon's words were cold and blunt, "They knew what they were risking when they signed up for this. The entire effort was a volunteer force. Dragon Army doesn't force anyone to do anything they aren't willing to die for."

With those words, Kirra looked behind to see if any others had made it. There were no shapes in the distance towards the mountains that indicated that any others had made it back safely. All she could do was hope they made it out okay. It made her wonder how the Planeswalker was doing. She hadn't even asked where her brother was and charged blindly to get him. Her spirit had a comment about that, *"It was stupid and brash. That girl will more than likely die trying to save your brother."*

She retorted, *"I can still hope..."*

"Hope is a silly thing to have. It does not help you accomplish your tasks or goals. It is a flawed idea that only makes people feel they are worth something."

Kirra scolded, *"It helped me keep my sanity when all was lost. When I thought I would be stuck there in the Black Citadel serving under the Bat Lord for the rest of my life."*

An audible snort echoed through her head, *"And yet the dragons saved you in the end. Their forces, their plan, their people, and their power. Not ours. Hope didn't save you Kirra... Months of planning and the bravery of these people did."*

"Maybe you're right..." She didn't want to argue with her spirit after the time they had spent working with each other. They'd gotten far in their relationship, and she didn't see the point in arguing.

23
NOT THE PLAN

T he moment the Planeswalker had run off into the woods at top speed, a voice screamed in her head for her to turn around, *"This isn't the plan! Planeswalker! Listen to me! If you get captured—"* David had been guiding her from the start of their endeavors the moment they had started helping the dragons with their plight. She was in no way indebted to help them but wanted to make a difference for the better. David was her handler and her voice of reason. He'd been teaching her from day one after she found out what she was capable of.

"David stop. I'll be fine. I know how to lose them okay..." There was a pause before she replied, *"Kinda..."* With a shake of the wolf's head, she continued, *"The point is, I'm not going to get captured...."* She and him both knew it was almost impossible to capture her while she was in this state. Taking damage usually broke her concentration and brought her out of the universe she was walking in and back to her original. The problem with damaging her was that she was fast and it felt like she always either saw or felt the moves before they came her way.

Racing through the forest, David eventually calmed down and let her concentrate as she ran through Kirra's memories repeatedly. She was retracing her steps and the pathing as well as what she needed to do to get through the Citadel to rescue Kirra's brother. David knew the dragons well enough that she trusted his intuition, but the Planeswalker liked to hope that the dragons might not actually be all that bad. She knew he was concerned about her being abandoned while she was attempting to save as many as possible.

Distracting herself from the stress of the upcoming fighting, she started a conversation with David about some of the extra parts she had accidentally pulled from Kirra's open mind, *"So do you think Zeke is lying about all of this? Like trying to liberate the bats from their oppressed state? I know we've seen how the dragons can be, but it can't be all that bad, right?"*

A long sigh came from him before he stated, *"No I don't believe he is. A lot of the supposed lesser spiritosk have been treated like crap. If you're not a dragon, you're not special and not worth a damn. You're just like every other race through the multiverse if you don't have some kind of ability. Spiritosk without powers are only one step above humans and that's how we've always been viewed. Despite my own ability, I'm still seen as untrustworthy just because of my race within the spiritosk as well."*

"What about humans?" The next inquisitive question came as she powered through the forest, seeing the Citadel starting to come into sight.

"Humans are only a step above demons. They're considered nothing more than cattle and flesh to be sold for profit or blood... Sometimes, even meat. They have no powers, no abilities, aren't strong, short-lived, and they're easy to kill. And they're only above demons because no one trusts demons and their savage ways. That's why I'm trying to figure out why

you're off to rescue one silly little wolf boy when he possesses no powers, no abilities, and no reason to actually rescue him when the dragons got what..." David's words cut off as soon as he realized part of the reason why she was doing it.

"Figured that part out?" She let out a soft giggle, *"They'll use him as a potential threat against her, torture him, maim him, try and draw her out by using him as bait, and force him to stay alive until she surrenders to..."* Pausing only a moment, her voice deepened, mocking the ridiculous nickname, ***"The Bat Lord..."*** Before she returned to normal, *"... So, there is that. But most of all... no matter how small or unimportant a life is to everyone else, every life is valuable."* Her voice ended on a somber note, *"Trust me. I know how it feels to be forgotten."*

Finally reaching the edge of the forest, the plant life started to thin out as she reached the edge of farms and booked it through open areas towards the major city. As She reached the city's edge, the Planeswalker started to weave through the buildings carefully. All of her senses were on high alert, allowing her to maneuver easily through the city without being spotted. The sound of a loud explosion drew her attention to the cave's roof.

To get a better view of the situation, she hopped up on top of the closely connected buildings and sighed as David commented, *"You better take advantage of that because there goes your ride..."*

*"I do all this work to help them out, take out several Bat Spiritosk encampments, all of the territory research at all the risk to myself... and these jerks are probably still going to take full credit for everything, **AND** flippin' abandon me and the one person that can be used to manipulate the Prophecy. These dragons are frickin' genius."*

The raspy baritone of David's voice chuckled, *"I did warn you about the dragons before you continued to work with them. Come on kid, get a move on. You're on a time crunch now."*

Letting out a sigh, she let go of the slight, one of many from the dragons at this point, made her way to the edge of the Citadel, and ran through what she had pulled from Kirra's memory once more. The ground was abuzz with soldiers scrambling left and right as she slipped back into a human form before changing her outfit like a second skin to look like one of the Bat Colony's soldiers. Moving through a side door with no traffic, she worked her way into the Citadel again. Sucking in a breath, she let it out slowly and spread her senses wide, feeling out the halls just with her intuitive energy sense and creating a visual map in her own head to figure out where she needed to go. Once she was finished, she could feel David smiling from wherever he was monitoring her, *"Nicely done, you're getting really good at that. Far better than anyone your age."*

She giggled softly, *"Yeah, I do better under stress... And this is very freakin stressful dude."* Making her way through the halls, she was lucky until she stopped at the door with a badge reader. Letting out a snort, she held her hand over the badge reader and summoned a small bit of static to short the system. Opening the door, she pushed past as a small pop came from behind her on the badge reader causing her to grimace. Not only could she smell the fire from the panel, but she could hear and feel that she had destroyed the panel completely as she hurried down the hallway a little faster.

A snort came from David sarcastically, *"Very smooth Planeswalker. Very smooth."*

"Alright, so I let it go to my head a little bit…" She knew she had to hurry up because it wouldn't be long until the fighting thinned out or someone discovered her messing up with the panel. Working through the maze of halls confidently, the Planeswalker had gotten lucky so far. Either people were running to aid in the fight or were too concerned with the fighting to ask why she was going toward the restricted prison area. With all the luck she'd been having, she kept repeating in her mind:

Don't say it!

Don't say it!

Don't say it!

"Man I've gotten really lucky so far…" The second that those words came from her mouth, she came to a soldier standing guard as she rounded a corner to the main part of the prison block.

"What are you doing here?" The masked soldier slowly started to approach her while gripping his weapon but hadn't yet raised it fully.

David's snarky comment came, "*You had to say it, didn't you?*"

The Planeswalker didn't even try to hide that she wasn't supposed to be there. With a smile and a nervous laugh, she slowly lifted her hands. The moment the weapon started to raise to point at her, she reacted. Lowering a hand and lifting it in one swift movement, she concentrated on the obsidian under the soldier. She'd gotten good enough at magic that she didn't even have to make the signs but think of them and the wording for the simpler spells and it came to her easily. As the stone raised and began to encase the soldier in stone, she let out a sigh, stating, "I swear, I was trying not to say it." The only thing that greeted her was David's raspy laughter.

She grimaced while looking at the soldier encased in stone. The man was completely trapped and couldn't move an inch right along with the weapon being encased with stone, but allowed him to breathe. About to walk past the encased soldier, the sight of his personnel badge made her pause. Reaching out for it, she started to cackle evilly before snatching it from the man's uniform, which caused a series of muffled complaints from him. Tapping his head with the badge, she smirked, "I hope you were good to these prisoners because I'm about to release *all* of them."

Humming a playful little tune, the Planeswalker started making her way down the hall and, one by one, began opening every single cell she could with the badge. Most of them were all dragon spiritosk but David stopped her partway through releasing people practically screaming, *"WAIT!"* The badge hovered over the reader as he explained, *"That's a demon..."*

Peeking into the cell, she got a better look at the being inside. Ryse's face was shrouded by his hair as he curled up at the back corner of the cell, looking worse for wear. It took her a moment to identify the demonic features because the only real giveaway was the tail and his needle-like teeth. There was a momentary pause as she analyzed the man before she said, *"And?"*

David explained, *"All demons are bad..."*

David screamed as he saw her hand absently move to the reader and open the door. Ryse seemed confused at the act as he had heard others getting freed and thanking her, but he didn't expect it to happen to him. Opening the door, the demon practically towered over the Planeswalker as she gave him a friendly little wave and commented aloud to David and Ryse, "I think they might just be misunderstood, the same way everyone believes that bats are evil, wolves are savages, foxes are tricksters, and so on. I'm not going to let that same prejudice affect how I think."

As Ryse stepped out of his cage and gave a smile before realizing he could possibly scare her, he stated, "I'll remember this in the future..." Pointing to the collar around his throat, he asked politely, "Can you remove this infernal device as well by chance?"

Unaffected by his unsettling smile, she moved forward and smiled at him pleasantly before looking at the collar that seemed to hold no way to remove it naturally. Pursing her lips she seemed to think for a moment before making a few quick hand signs on either side of the collar. Concentrating on the material of it, she suddenly pulled her hands apart causing the thing to rip free and fall away as though someone had just ripped it in half. Ryse reached up and rubbed at his neck with a sigh before she smirked at him, chuckling, "Behave now... or don't..." She went to turn and leave before her arm was suddenly grasped.

Ryse's hold was tight as the girl turned back towards him, "I owe you a life debt, which I will pay back someday." He wanted to make sure that her favor hadn't gone unnoticed. His red eyes scanned over her intently before slowly releasing the hold, "I will be able to find you no matter what form you take now."

A curse echoed through her head as David's voice commented, *"Gods! He's got Energy Sight!"* She backed away from him still confused and slightly worried, *"The same blood ability you have, but very experienced. It means he can find you no matter what shape you take while you use your soulwalking ability."*

Backing away from him, she seemed slightly worried before nodding her head and moving down the hallway continuing to release people. If he was going to be a danger to her, it would be a day she'd have to worry about in the future. She needed to concentrate on the current mission. Reaching the end of the hall where Justin was supposed to be, she swiped the badge over the reader, but it continued to flash red. After what had just happened, she wasn't playing around anymore and resorted to Spartan kicking the entire door using Kidori as it smashed into the room before sliding to a stop.

Stepping through the door, she admitted to David softly, *"This is the part where I tell you that I know both Kirra and Justin..."*

David asked curiously, *"You do?"*

"Yup..." Moving to the side of the panel on the glass wall, she touched it, hitting a few buttons and causing the glass to become clearer and the room to light up as Justin rose from the destroyed remnants of the bed.

"You changed what you looked like right?" David asked.

"Yes and No..." She commented as Justin started walking forward and instantly snarled upon seeing the uniform. Looking down at herself, a small curse came from her as she resumed the normal look she had taken when she freed Kirra, apologizing, "Sorry, sorry, sorry. I forgot I was mimicking a guard... I'm here to save you." The Planeswalker was wearing ordinary jeans with her wavy brown hair pulled half back. Her torso was covered by a plain black loose t-shirt as she gave him a friendly wave.

"No, no, no... my sister. You have to get her out, she's the Prophecy." He said with concern etching every facet of his face, "Save her."

Already moving forward and inspecting the glass that separated them, she explained calmly, "She's already out. I didn't even know about you until Kirra said something. I don't think they even considered saving you to be quite frank. Ah-ha!" Locating a weak point in the glass, she smirked and started to make a few hand signs to manipulate the elements of the glass. Sending vibrations through the glass, the entire length of it shattered as she smiled victoriously and waved her hand to him, "Alright let's go. We're going to have to find our own way out since the dragons abandoned us and couldn't wait."

The mangy-haired and emaciated Justin was surprised and cautious at what she'd just done as he asked hesitantly, "Was that... magic?" She motioned for him to step out as he moved over the beam where the glass had been set in the floor while nodding at him before he asked, "You're not the Prophecy though..." This seemed to confuse him more than anything.

"I'm something else." She laughed before helping him over the beam and starting to lead the way back through the maze of halls, asking, "What abilities do you have?"

Justin didn't seem to want to look the gift horse in the mouth and just accepted what was happening as he followed her, "I just transform into a wolf. There's nothing special about me..." There was something odd about the girl, but for some odd reason, he trusted her. Something in his gut told him she was telling the truth.

"Pfft. Please... You don't need special abilities to be special. Trust me." Leading the way through the maze, she kept waiting for him to keep up because of his condition. All the while, she was going through several scenarios in her head about how they could get out of the place together and survive. She was combining the information that

Kirra knew about the place with her own. Pausing momentarily, the Planeswalker smirked, "I know exactly how to get out of here."

Picking up a bit of speed as she walked through the halls, Justin kept trying to get her attention as they passed the man entombed in stone. It seemed everyone had left the soldier alone causing her to let out a sigh as she tossed the badge back on the ground near his feet. Justin finally gripped her arm refusing to go further until she explained everything to him. With a sigh, she told him about the dragons rescuing all the teens, the Prophecy included. She explained her plan to him and how she planned to run them with a pack of ancient wolves out of there together since all of them would be about the same size given their age.

Once everything had been explained to him, he seemed okay and stable enough to follow her as he understood the plan. Moving through the halls all the way up until one of the side doors that led outside, she stopped and peered around. Telling him to follow behind her closely because of the sounds of fighting outside, the two stuck to the shadows as the skies above the city turned into an open battlefield where some dragons were fighting back. The Planeswalker couldn't help but think that those were the dragons she had just let out of their cells.

Leading the way to the side of the Citadel where the stables for the wolves were kept, the Planeswalker slowly made her way into the building and started opening pens. At first, a few of them started growling but seemed to calm as she motioned towards them. Moving through the stables and letting all of the wolves out, she started pulling the saddles off of each and every one before getting to the last stall. Opening it carefully, vicious growls greeted the pair.

The largest white wolf she had ever seen rushed at her, stopping just as its maw snapped out at her face. The girl merely reached up and gave its nose a boop, causing it to huff and shake its head with confusion. Justin had stood back while this was happening, ready to reach out and grab the girl, but she seemed unafraid as it appeared to be a feint. Giving a few sniffs to the girl, the massive white ancient wolf's eyes went wide with surprise before giving the Planeswalker an affectionate nuzzle.

Laughing out, she patted the wolf and nuzzled back against it before the pair went quiet. Turning towards Justin, she spoke in the first words in what seemed like forever, "They're going to run with us. It seems his entire pack had been captured and they've been using them to train either the kids or run through the cave." She started to take her wolf form and Justin followed suit as the pair shook their fur.

The Planeswalker was the smallest of the entire pack, but it was clear Snow seemed to pay some respect by giving a light head bow to her. As the wolves discussed the path they were going to take, they bolted as one fluid group and made for the forest despite all the fighting happening in the woods and sky around them. With all of the havoc, the pack and the extra pair were not even noticed exiting the stables.

While they ran, Justin ran up next to the Planeswalker asking, *"What did you say to him?"*

"I showed him where a hole in their entire barrier was. He told me he and Kirra were already aware of it. Seems your sister had been trying to formulate an escape plan this entire time but hadn't figured out how to get you from your cell since they hadn't let her see you yet."

Even in their primal communication, surprise leaked through, *"She'd been looking for a way to get out this entire time?"*

"Yep. Apparently, it's what kept her going. She was planning on getting strong, learning some tricks, and then using them to escape with you when she figured everything out. It gave her hope. Sometimes, that's all you need to get by."

Justin didn't know what to think of her statement. He'd not thought his sister had been looking for an escape at all as she'd always been the good kid, but perhaps the Planeswalker was right. A little hope had gotten Kirra through it in the end.

Despite a few hiccups, the group managed to navigate safely through the cave and the warzone that was going on without getting spotted. There were a few close calls, but they all trusted the large ancient wolf leading the way toward the exit.

As they started to approach the little clearing on one of the sides of the hollowed-out mountain, the collective group came to a halt as several huffs of frustration came from them. Before them in the clearing lay several downed dragons, a few groupings of bat colony soldiers, and the one and only Zeke. The distaste was shown without sound but the baring of fangs as several members wanted to fight them. The Planeswalker managed to convince them not to barrel into a fight though.

David commented sarcastically, *"Is this part of your plan?"*

"No, but I'll work with what I got..."

Curiosity and worry got the better of David, *"What are you going to do now Planeswalker?"*

Quickly scanning the area, her eyes went over everything happening. Several dragons were in their full forms, and several more were in their normal forms being secured as they spoke. Several of the soldiers, including Zeke, were near the wall where the hole was, working on attempting to set up a temporary barrier until they patched the hole that allowed anyone access into the cave that wasn't the main entrance.

A slow smile came to her lips as she took her human form once more and finally said softly to Justin, "Stay in your form for now. I'm going to try to distract them and free the other dragons. If things go awry, go with Snow."

"What about you?" Justin asked in a concerned voice, still using that primal dialect.

She merely smiled at him, reaching up for something around her neck, and tugged a silver chain that was hidden under her shirt. Realistically, she was pulling it from where it had been stored as something told her to give him the medallion, which would come in handy later. Pulling the medallion free from her shirt, it revealed its dull, silvery surface with a wolf etched upon its surface. The wolf itself was curled up as though it were sleeping, tail covering its eyes, though it looked as though it could still see past the fluffy tail.

Still holding the chain, she placed it around Justin's dark furry neck, stating, "Don't worry about me. I think you were meant to have this though. I don't know what it is just yet, but I think you'll need it in the future." She reached up, patting his neck before whispering, "And no, this isn't an I'm going to die speech."

With a sudden movement, she was gone from in front of the group of wolves. The movement was impossible for them to track. She had moved faster than even that of a vampire which was saying something as she appeared next to the group of soldiers. Despite that, the wolves bristled with nervousness at her being next to all of the soldiers, but they respected her wishes for them to remain hidden.

The soldiers didn't even see her standing out of place in what appeared to be a casual outfit for anyone in the multiverse. Finally, she cleared her throat which caused nothing to happen. After a few more moments, she loudly said, "Whatcha talkin' about?" In an almost synchronized motion, the group turned while raising guns at her as none of them recognized her voice, or her.

Before anyone even got the chance to fire, Zeke's voice rang out the command, **"Hold your fire!"** Stepping from behind the grouping of soldiers, he moved towards her and seemed to size her up. The only response he received was a polite smile and a small wave. A snort of amusement came from him as he asked softly, "Soulwalker?"

Letting out a soft laugh, she brushed off his words stating, "Actually, I prefer to be called Planeswalker."

Another amused snort came from him as he remarked, "That explains a lot." Leaning towards her, he stated confidently, "You're a descendant of the Guinini family." His eyes creased with his smile.

The pleasant smile that had been on her face faltered as she stammered softly, "How... do you..." She reached out with her senses and felt over Zeke and the area with as fear instantly entered her heart. There was a feeling of familiarity like their very souls resonated with each other. Zeke closed his eyes seeming to hone in on that feeling of familiarity. With it, she felt the sheer overwhelming strength and power emanating from him. The sheer feeling of raw power scared her, making her tense. Her whole being told her one thing. Run.

The already skittish Planeswalker tensed as she sensed someone move toward her with clear intent. With a few quick, sharp, speedy movements, she was next to the captured dragons. She had done what she needed to and Zeke realized it too late. A few of his soldiers had moved up to intercept her, which moved them closer to her location and where she had wanted most of them positioned.

He screamed out for her not to do what she was going to, but she had already started reaching towards the ground and started the spell. His scream was cut off as she controlled a thick wall of earth and created a bubble around the majority of the soldiers. The hole in the wall had been blocked off, cutting off their escape, but there were still dragon spiritosk she could save.

As a few soldiers leveled weapons on her location, she moved forward using her speed to her advantage. Even while fighting off the soldiers, she had started freeing the nearest dragon, which started a chain reaction. They worked quickly and efficiently as a team, freeing one dragon after the next. Soon, there were dozens of them, and very few bats left to fight against the force that was fighting back once more. Even as the sound of something hard hitting the stone bubble she had made around the soldiers, they'd find out that using just Kidori to free them from there would not be possible.

Approaching a small group of dragons, she ordered, "There's a pack of ancient wolves at the forest's edge. Grab them and fly them out to safety." The second she mentioned them, the wolves all started to walk out as they bowed their heads to her respectfully. The one pure black wolf of the group started to approach her as she commanded, "Transform..." As he did so a few more dragons started to rally on her as Justin took his normal form.

Turning toward the group, she commanded them, "One of you fly Justin to his sister. I'm going to do something really stupid and help the rest of your kin out of here." She raised her voice to those who were further away as she called out, "All of you who wish to stay and fight are free to do so, but let it be known I'm not asking you to. You've done enough this day. Return to your loved ones, friends, and families if you are too injured or tired."

A single dragon knelt down as it rumbled deeply right next to the Planeswalker and Justin. Without giving a second thought, Justin climbed on the back of the dragon that knelt down. The second he did, it started to rise as he secured himself as tightly as possible, calling out, "What about you?!"

She let out a bit of snort, "You'll see soon enough. Now go!" The last was said to the dragon more pointedly as the sound of an explosion rang out. The dragon, a leafy green dragon with plants and vines hanging all over its body, took its cue to leave and leaped into the air. A pair of dragons flanked its sides, ensuring her orders were followed.

The last thing the threesome of dragons would see was a very large white ghostly form starting to take shape. What started as a blob of pure white energy morphed into a wolf bigger than any dragon there or anywhere. As it started to form, the wolf lifted its head before tossing it skyward as a howl resonated through the air with sheer power. The song of the howl was tragic and beautiful all at the same time, but its effect on the bats was glorious. The song seemed to have targeted their particular frequency of hearing as bats started to drop from the air around them like flies.

The wolf's steps disturbed not a single tree or piece of life in the forest as it approached the Black Citadel. As their group rose up in the air, Justin could see behind him that more and more dragons were following as the Planeswalker covered their retreat. This was the last sight that the horde of dragons escaping through the still compromised barrier on the roof of Bat Colony would see as sounds of victory roared from them.

The feeling of freedom in Justin didn't last as he kept glancing back, his thoughts wandering to the girl whose powers had laid waste to Bat Colony. This should have been a moment of joy, but he couldn't help but keep wondering about the girl who possibly sacrificed herself for his life and several others. A sudden warmth in the medallion along his neck told a different story. Along with it came the feeling of pure joy as he looked behind to see something in the distance streaking towards them. The streak of pure white light was blazing through the air effortlessly, catching up to the group quickly.

None of the dragons seemed disturbed by the light as it listlessly floated up to Justin and kept pace. Finally, the light fell away, giving form to something Justin thought he'd never see in his lifetime. A six-winged creature with white feathers, a wolf tail, and ears attached to the girl that had given aid to him in his time of need. Her eyes were a bright, brilliant blue twinkling with the innocence of her youth. He'd only read of their existences and heard some descriptions of them, but he knew her for what she was now. An angel.

He'd been careful in his inspections, finding that the wings were completely transparent. They were the sole source of light that emanated from her very being. Eventually his eyes found her face to examine those brilliant blue eyes. For the first time after spending the last 30 minutes with her, recognition finally kicked in, causing his eyes to widen.

Raising a finger, she pressed it to his lips and spoke softly, "That medallion on your neck means you are something more than just a wolf. I don't know quite how it works, but I could feel in my core that it belonged to you because of your loyalty. Despite being in your situation and not being freed, you still thought of your sister first. You're the Guardian of Loyalty." She instead addressed the group, "Take care and ge—"

With a sudden loud snap, it was as though she had just faded out from the world, causing a laugh from another dragon, "Oi, did she just fade from the plane again?"

The dragon Justin was on even shook from his own laughter as it replied, "Yeah, she faded from this plane... again."

Several comments rang out afterward about being thankful that she didn't randomly disappear in the middle of the last fight. As their conversations continued, it appeared that her sudden disappearance was a repeat occurrence. Justin found as they continued speaking that she had been helping them for a while and that her efforts were pushing the war in their favor. Even with all of their abilities, the sheer number of bats and their tactical prowess were overpowering the dragons. Justin couldn't help but think that they merely rescued his sister to bolster their forces in their favor.

24

DRAGON COLONY

A s the last dragons in the fighting returned with the horde of dragons, they informed the group that the bats wouldn't be following. The Planeswalker had secured their escape by grounding their entire fleet of aero planes and copters. She'd taken out not only their fleet but their entire energy grid that powered the main city while managing not to destroy homes or cause damage to the environment. Bat Colony would be busy for a long while fixing what she had broken and had secured their escape in one fell swoop.

As Dragon Colony was a long flight from where they were, they had hours of travel ahead of them despite how tired all of them were from the fighting. Several dragons mentioned owing their lives to the Planeswalker for freeing them from the prison. Because of her actions, they were more than happy to escort Justin the great distance to the group further along. Their efforts in flying only strengthened as they finally saw the original rescue group ahead of them as dragons bellowed out to notify them of their presence.

Soon, the group merged as throaty bellows of excitement, surprise, and joy rang out at the arrival of the late-coming dragons. The forest dragon holding Justin snugly to his back with the vines along its body called out to the white dragoness, "Oi Shiro, you missed it."

Kirra looked up from her spot to the approaching green dragon as he continued, "The Planeswalker went berserk on the bats. Started smashing up all their aero planes and took out their energy grid as well. It was bleedin' crazy. We thought we were all doomed, and then she came raging through as a spectral wolf of some kind larger than even Jacob. Next we knew, bats were dropping out of the sky and she was wreaking havoc. And now we're here!"

Shiro turned her head towards the speaking to her, "Oh? Quite impressive timing that one has had recently." Her head turned a smidge further to the leaf-covered lump on his back, "Who is that Tempest?"

Looking towards his back, he shed the leaves away, allowing the vines to hold him in place. Justin woke up looking confused as Tempest said, "This one here is Justin. Planeswalker said to get him to his sister."

Kirra was exhausted, only half paying attention to what was going on, but the sound of her brother's name caused her head to shoot up. Looking to where both dragons were looking, she screamed out as the familiar dark hair of her brother could be seen, "Justin!" Confused and still sleepy, he turned his head toward the direction of the voice as she screamed out, "By the gods, Justin!"

The dragons exchanged a look momentarily before Shiro announced to the group, "We're going to rest at the Oasis coming up to let our passengers stretch their legs and spread the load out!" The horde took turns letting groups land so no one got accidentally trampled from the sheer number. It was odd seeing so many dragons of various types grouped together as they were. The show didn't last long as they started to form their little cliques and moved off to rest while they could.

The moment that Shiro landed, Kirra was already jumping off and running towards Justin. She couldn't help but think it was all a dream. That all of this was just some terrible amazing dream and she was going to wake back up in that room again. Running up to him, she threw her arms around him, squeezed him tight, and held on, afraid he might disappear if she let go. Shiro padded over and noticed the two embracing one another, before addressing the large gathering, "15 minutes and we are back in the air."

Kirra mentioned with a laugh, "That's not a whole lot of time." She finally pulled back from the embrace, wiping tears of joy from her eyes. She'd grown some in height and was almost the same size as him now.

Justin laughed at his sister's words before his eyes went wide and pointed to a figure in the sky, screaming, "BAT!"

Shiro's head turned in a split second where Justin was pointing. Sure enough there was a bat flying towards them as a dark streak could be seen in the sky. Shiro easily put herself between the bat and the group that had gotten off of her letting out a roar. A glow emanated from her throat, following a deep rumbling, letting the intruder know she wasn't an idle threat.

"Down girl... no friendly fire in these parts..." Shiro seemed to relax at what must have been a familiar voice to her. Giving him room to land, she backed up eyeing the dark brown bat warily.

As the bat landed taking their normal form, Shiro addressed him with disdain tinging her words, "I thought you stayed on the back lines where it was safe?"

Getting closer to the group, the details of the man became clearer. Dark clothes decorated his thin body. The man looked sick and pale, like he didn't eat enough. Much like Cash, there was a set of large fangs that were easily spotted when he spoke. His face was tired and worn with stress despite his youth. Dark, disheveled, and short hair lightly obscured purple intelligent eyes. He looked like he could have been in his late 20s if he were a human, but the tiredness in his eyes spoke measures about his real age.

He stopped in front of Shiro, apparently unafraid of her threats, "Yeah, and I usually do. Given everything that happened, I was checking to make sure she wasn't captured since my link to her was just suddenly cut. You seen her?"

A red dragon stepped up and spoke in a gravelly voice, "Disappeared from the plane like she was never here." A sigh of relief came as the dragon continued, "Must be nice being able to show up and disappear so easily. You know, staying out of harm's way and not risking your life." A growl and clear discontent was let out. It seemed he was the only dragon who felt that way towards them as they either hissed or growled lightly.

Letting out a snort, the bat replied, "Yeah. Right. So terrible. Having someone come out of nowhere to free your leader, turn the tide of some battles that were going poorly, save the Prophecy, save her brother, save the dragons that were left behind. So very terrible of her risking her own existence when she is supposed to be hiding."

"David... We're very appreciative of the efforts that your friend has applied to our side of the war. All we mean is that she has not risked anything given what she is. And neither have you." Shiro commented while eyeing him clearly not approving of what she considered cowardice.

David snorted, shaking his head, "Well, as long as she is okay. I'll be on my way..." He turned away to fly off in another direction he hadn't come from, but there was a clear look of disbelief on his face from the dragons' discontent.

Kirra asked curiously, "Who was that?"

"The Planeswalker's handler. He showed up right after she returned Jacob to the Colony in good health." Shiro commented, watching the bat fly off until he couldn't be seen anymore, "We almost jumped him when he showed up out of nowhere, but the fact that she said he was with her, or at least there for her, saved them both. It was all a little suspicious, but she has been nothing but helpful since she showed up that day."

"Who's Jacob?" Kirra asked as she looked up at Shiro.

She chuckled lightly before saying, "He's the leader of Dragon Colony. He got captured by the Bats months ago. We had been attempting to figure out how best to free him, then one day he came flying back with that girl who rescued you on his back. Since then, the tide of the war has changed. We were losing, now we are not." She nodded towards a group of people waiting nearby, "I believe they want to speak with you."

Kirra turned to see Death and Nicki waving at her excitedly, which made her light up. Running over to the group, she gave Death a hug which he reciprocated by picking her up and spinning her in a circle. Justin wandered up as the group recalled what happened after the energy thief fiasco. Not wanting to disturb their musings, Justin stood near, listening to the group talk. They recalled their own accords after Kirra had been taken and talked about how Black Dragon had seemingly disappeared without a trace. Then mentioned how Ryse had been dragged through the camp one day. It seemed that Zeke had kept his promise about letting them continue to be trained and taught by the trainers.

Even as they conversed, a few were giving Kirra's brother side-eyed looks of distrust, given how he looked. The only person who seemed even to acknowledge Justin at all was Death. Soon after, Shiro called for them to start grouping up to take off again. Given there were more dragons there than planned, especially with those who managed to escape the prison, they decided to spread the load.

The sun had risen by now, making the trip easier for the dragons as they crossed the desert. Once it started to turn into canyons, Kirra could tell that the dragons started to bristle with excitement. In the distance, a large wall of stone started to take shape. From the distance they were at, it didn't seem like much, just a wall starting in a canyon of windswept pillars. As they got closer, it grew to be so much more.

By now, the sun had risen to give way to the early noon of the day and bathed the city in a golden light under the greenish-blue sky above. Behind the city sat a forest with a small range of mountains and a volcano. Much like the Bat Colony, the city was built to flow with the land. This city spanned much larger than the other. Clear districts had been created from the walls that seemed to have been added through time as the Colony grew. Several could be identified just by the types of buildings around, market, apartments, houses, military, and so on. Even a stadium sat off on its own with pillars of stone spread all throughout it as dragons alike flew over or ran on the ground below.

At first, Kirra wondered why they weren't flying straight down into the city, but as they got closer, it became apparent. All along the walls, turrets were stationed at intervals, protecting the skies and intruders from coming in and attacking the city directly. The horde soared towards a large rectangle gate past several large hovering transport ships. As they passed through the gates, she watched as their group slowed through a set of scanners before speeding up once more. Laughter echoed from the dragons flying as collective sounds of awe came from most kids who'd grown up on Earth.

Ads floated across the sides of walls on the major skyways and roads of the crowded city. Traffic was divided in the air between aero vehicles and flying forms with mandated flight speeds for both. Roads below and in the skyways had mandatory lanes for emergencies, which the horde was using the air emergency lane with the teens in tow. Vehicles on the ground roads were comprised of hover carts and carriages pulled by animals or just single riders on their personal mounts. There was almost no noise pollution from vehicles despite how some areas could be populated. It was quite different from the traffic on Earth.

As the group progressed, they could see the more individualized sectors of the City. All sorts of other races appeared to have made up Dragon Colony despite the majority being draconic in nature. They even bordered what looked like an ocean or perhaps a sea of some kind, as the colony was one expansive city. Having lived on the Preserve most of her life, Kirra had never seen anything like it.

Walls sectioned off the City as it expanded. The outer edges were a mixture of Import, Export, Trade hubs, docks, and agriculture. The military had its own district as they skirted around the edge, still approaching the center. Signs for other districts marked Market Square, Residential, and University lined their travel, but the teens never got to see any of those. They were flying straight towards the Capital Square, which was wedged right against the base of a massive mountain.

The Capital Square seemed to be where the most varied groups of people were. The horde eventually split into smaller groups, flying towards the nicest set of looking buildings. The stark white of the buildings stuck out from the rough and woodsy-looking mountain. Gold-topped roofs shaped like onions complimented the white, giving the place the look of a sultan's palace. The entire area had been cleared of traffic of all kinds, whether on foot or wing, as they landed on marbled white tiles.

The sun sat higher in the sky now, reflecting the excitement of the bristling teens who looked around in awe despite how exhausted they must be. Those riding on dragons started to hop off with collective groans of soreness. As soon as their riders jumped off, dragons started taking their human forms as a mix of colored skin, horned heads, and various mixtures of class, poor or rich, started to give way. Most dragons kept their horns on display, and some of those there had tattered clothes, signifying their escape from the prison. Looking to her brother, she saw him in a similar uniform as he informed her that the Planeswalker had opened and freed quite a few of the prisoners in Bat Colony.

The clearing of a throat grabbed Kirra's attention from examining all of the ornate-looking details of the buildings. It seemed like everything was lined and detailed with gold or silver. Kirra turned to look at a woman dressed in an ornate gold and white dress robe, which caused her eyes to go wide. The woman looked like a goddess, though she stood at a height similar to that of her brother. Blonde hair was neatly pulled back like a golden halo on her head, alabaster skin free of scars, and the stature of someone who held themselves with elegance and confidence. Her robe-like dress was decorated ornately in swirling, delicate patterns. Kirra couldn't help but to admire her.

The rest of the rescued teens were being herded toward where Kirra and Justin were as the dragoness named Shiro waited in her normal form for them to regroup. Once they were all within hearing range and she had their attention, she called out, "Welcome to Dragon Colony. My name is Shiro. If you all will follow me, we will get the lot of you sorted out."

The kids all started to slowly voice their opinions and questions at once before Shiro quieted the group, "All will be explained soon. Please remain calm for the moment. If your families are here, they will have already been notified. First, we need to make sure the lot of you are taken care of medically. Most of you have spent your time on another planet for the entirety of your lives and need vaccinations for future life here."

As the worked-up teenagers started to calm down, Kirra fell back, speaking with her brother in a low whisper, "What do you think they are going to do with us?"

"I don't know. I'm not a dragon, and our parents...." He didn't need to finish his sentence as he grew quiet. Kirra had never considered it before, but he was in a tight spot, given his race and the war. The wolves hadn't picked a side. Something Kirra had learned during her time in the Citadel. She'd even seen diplomats from Wolf Colony sent to speak and work out trade deals.

Letting go of her thoughts, she leaned over and tried to touch him, "Hey... are you..." She'd never asked him about how he was doing with their parents' deaths.

Shrugging out of her reach, Justin voiced flatly, "I'm fine... I'll be fine... don't want to think about it right now."

Slowly, the group of teens were being cordoned into a single-file line that snaked inside the building. Several stations had been set up with what looked like nurses all wearing masks and gloves. Each of the stations was doing various things like taking blood, giving shots, asking questions, and so on. The noise from the multiple people talking was overwhelming for Kirra as she walked through the line and took it all in. She was used to the quiet of the forests in Bat Colony and the only noise around being either a teacher speaking or the sound of fighting.

As the line moved, one table called out, signaling her to approach. Looking up hesitantly, she took a few steps in that direction before stopping and reaching out towards Justin. Giving her a reaffirming squeeze, he went with her so she wouldn't be afraid of being separated again.

Approaching the table, the woman looked up, eying the pair before asking for her name. Kirra answered while clinging to her brother, and the woman said, "I just need to give you a few shots for vaccines, remove the chip that's in you, and take some blood samples for tests."

The sounds of struggle nearby caused Kirra to tense as most seemed either distrustful by nature or blatantly didn't want to go through what they were doing. The woman across from her seemed to have a straightforward, no-coddling method about her. She motioned to the seat next to the station, waiting for Kirra to take a seat, which made Kirra shake her head.

A frustrated sound escaped the woman, "Look, I am doing this on my own time to help you kids. You can choose to trust me or not, I don't care." All Kirra had to go off of for trust was a pair of uncaring eyes that looked tired and didn't seem to care. The ocean-blue orbs didn't hold any kindness in them, and the rest of her was obscured by medical clothing.

Kirra could feel her chest tightening as her breathing started to hasten before her brother stepped forward, "Here…" The woman grabbed a separate sheet and started jotting down his information. As he sat down in the chair, she took his arm, strapped it down, took some blood, and gave him a shot. Right after, she pulled out a scanner of some kind and ran it along the length of his body before giving him the okay. As soon as he was finished, he hopped out of the chair saying, "See… nothing bad…"

It took some coaxing on her brother's part, but eventually, Kirra sat down in the chair, and the woman worked over her quickly. The worst part about the entire process was the chip that had been placed at the base of her neck under the skin. Once the chip had been pulled out, Kirra jumped to her feet and covered her neck with her hand, having had enough, it seemed.

The woman's voice was pointed and harsh, "I need to bandage that wound."

Kirra pointed out very strictly to the woman, "I don't need it." As her brother tried to reach for her and coax her back into the chair, she swatted his hands away, stating, "I'm not being stubborn; I just don't need it." She was putting her foot down, which was something she'd never done with her brother before, and caused him to look at her with a questioning look.

"Quit being unreasonable and sit down so I can stitch you up. I am not getting accused and blamed for the Prophecy getting an infection because they are being a stubborn brat. Now **SIT**."

"What is going on here?" An older man with a raspy-sounding voice and long, straight white hair that flowed almost with a life of its own approached. Despite the humble-looking greyish robe that draped his body, there was an air of authority about him. As he waited for an answer, he leaned on an ornately carved white staff that held an amethyst inside of the intricately carved dome at the top.

The nurse seemed to hesitate now as she answered, "The Prophecy is declining further medical care and has an inch width of gaping skin on the back of her neck."

Kirra's retort was instant, "Lady, I just spent the better part of almost a year stuck in the outdoors, living in a cabin, forced to go through survival, martial, and Kidori training. I've been chased by blind hounds, hell hounds, and energy thieves in an enclosed forest and smashed my head open more times than I can count. I think I would know if I needed a few stitches or not."

The older man looked between the two momentarily before finally declaring, "She'll be fine." Kirra looked over at the older man as he seemed to be staring right at her soul saying, "She heals rapidly. She won't need stitches or healing."

A scream echoed through the air, making Kirra jump and glance around, ready for a fight. Her heart was pounding in her chest, and her breathing quickened as she tried to locate the danger. Unable to locate the danger, her eyes searched all around until a hand plopped down on her shoulder. Almost immediately, she wheeled around, throwing a punch that was halted as her breathing quickened and more screams rang out. Kirra pulled free of the grasp as people around her started looking at her like she was crazy.

Running her hands through her hair, she tried to slow her breathing as her spirit worked to get her to think rationally once more. Looking around, she came to the conclusion that the screams were of people getting reunited with family members. The realization smacked into her hard that she and her brother were all alone with no family. It caused her to collapse and break down into tears as she just started crying uncontrollably.

Something about no longer being in constant danger made her crack and break down in front of everyone. The old man knelt down next to her, trying to help her compose herself, but eventually, he picked her up and carried her somewhere more private. It was all overwhelming for her as the room around her spun. Kirra didn't remember much, but she did remember sitting in a quiet, dimly lit room with a cup of warm tea between her hands.

Fiddling with the cup of tea, the old man, her brother, and Shiro managed to get her to calm down. Justin kept looking at her, waiting for her to break down again. Shiro held a look of empathy, or was it sympathy for her? It was something she wasn't used to. For the moment, she was trying to remain calm and in control of her emotions.

As she became more aware of her surroundings, she looked around the small ornate side room they were all in. The entire room was bright, the walls were white with gold ornaments gracing the edges of walls here and there. At the same time, it was lit very lightly, so the room would be dim. It was definitely some kind of meeting room.

The older male asked in his raspy, quiet voice, "How are you feeling?"

"Lost... and broken..." She was quiet for a moment before asking, "What's going to happen with me and my brother?"

The old man replied instantly, "Your brother and you will be placed under the care of Shiro."

Justin, who wasn't one to beat around the bush, pointed out, "I'm not a dragon though. I don't belong here."

Shiro spoke bluntly, "You will remain here until you are of age. After that, we can't stop you from doing whatever your heart desires." Shiro paused briefly before considering her next words, "I would advise that you stay here for longer, given what your sister is."

There was a snort of disbelief as Kirra stated, "So what, I just traded one prison for another one?" Her brother seemed to mirror her own thoughts but didn't say anything since she'd said it for him.

Shiro took in a breath to speak, but instead, the old man asked, "Do you know who I am?"

Kirra looked at him and said plainly, "What does that have to do with anything?"

He spoke up right after she asked the question, explaining, "My name is Jacob James. I am the previous Prophecy and the High Councilor of Dragon Colony." Kirra quieted down, letting him continue, "No, this is not a prison. When you both come of age, you can do whatever you wish. When you start learning magic, I can attempt to help you learn a few spells from during my time as the Prophecy, but I make no promises that it will succeed."

Kirra had to ask, "What exactly does being the Prophecy entail? Everyone keeps telling me I'll be able to do magic and do all of these things, but..." her voice drowned out slowly as she tried to figure out what she wanted to say.

Jacob stepped forward as Kirra struggled for words and placed his hands on her shoulders, giving them an encouraging squeeze, "To be the Prophecy means to be a peacekeeper. You will be Judge, Jury, and Executioner in your decisions. You will decide the outcome of wars and can change the tides of wars in favor of one side or another. You will be the voice of reason when there is chaos. You will be destined to exact great change throughout the Multiverse." He gave her a foreboding look before smiling easily, "Just be a teenager for now. You will know your purpose when the time comes."

As she thought about his words seriously, some gears started turning in Kirra's head. Looking over to her brother, she asked his input, "What do you think?"

He had been fiddling with some medallion between his fingers before he looked up at her, "I think they're telling the truth. That and... we have nowhere else to go. I'm almost of age, so it won't matter much to me." Justin shrugged, "I think it's your choice on what to do either way...." Jacob seemed to be squinting towards the medallion Justin was fiddling with as he spoke.

After playing with the tea cup between her hands, Kirra finally answered, "Alright, I'll give it a go..."

Shiro smiled with relief and held her hands out to the pair of them, "Come now... I'll show you where you'll be living."

There was a pause from Kirra, "It's not at that big white building?"

The question seemed odd to Shiro, but she answered with a laugh, "The Council Center? By Cerinos no. I have my own house that I live in when I'm not on excavations or doing council meetings." She let out a chuckle and waited for them to stand and follow her. Shiro wasn't at all what Kirra was expecting, given how she acted when she first met her. Hopefully those concerns of Kirra's would be snuffed out over time. Perhaps it was because of her tendency to not trust given what happened or that she was expecting the worst given her time in Bat Colony. Time could only tell.

Shiro led them from the large building where the rest of the kids had been getting split up either with families that were related to them or into houses that were willing to take in kids without homes or families. There was tension in the siblings as they followed behind Jacob and Shiro as they led the way out of the large building. It looked like some sort of conference center that had been converted temporarily for the day.

As they exited the main large building, some sort of hover carriage was already waiting for them. Attached to the carriage were horse-like creatures with fins in various spots on their body. The creatures had four toes on each foot and fins that extended from the back of the necks and even tails instead of horse hair. They were a beautiful teal color with blue stripes that streaked their body. Kirra had never seen anything like it before, but it seemed to be a common creature used to pull the carts, according to Shiro, as the pair saw them.

The only sector they seemed to pass through was that of the Market Square. Once they passed through, mostly forest, road, and higher-class residential surrounded their ride. The group remained quiet on the travel to the house as Kirra and Justin took everything in. As the Carriage came to a stop, Kirra sat up and watched Shiro and Jacob both sit up, moving to exit. Reaching up, Shiro seemed to pull out a cube of some kind and hold it over the driver's own cube before the carriage driver spurned the odd creatures down the road.

Everyone seemed to pause and tense as they turned toward the large, almost colonial-style white house. On the steps of the wrap-around porch sat a person no one expected to see.

25
HOME

S hiro looked less than pleased to see the Planeswalker sitting on
the steps of her home, but there she was. A growl rumbled deep
in her throat at the unwelcome invasion. The Planeswalker sat on the
steps to the wrap-around porch of white, leaned back, and completely
relaxed.

The displeasure in Shiro's voice seemed impossible to hide as she
growled out, "What are you doing here?" The question was more
demanded than asked.

Jacob reached forward, gripping Shiro's arm, squeezing it before he
approached and questioned more respectfully, "To what do we owe
this pleasure, Planeswalker?" A hint of suspicion lingered in his voice.

The girl was idly making light dance with her fingers before she
looked over at them and said in a friendly, absent-minded voice, "I
came here as a favor to one of my own..." A soft chuckle came from
her, "Someone requested a personal escort, so I happily obliged." She
stopped playing with the dancing lights before hopping off of the
steps. Cupping her hands together while tipping her head back, she
let out a howl that mimicked a wolf perfectly. Moments later, a large
ancient white wolf came trotting around the edge of the building,
snorting several times.

Kirra instantly recognized the wolf as Snow and ran over to greet him with a hug that was returned in kind despite his lacking arms. Shiro watched with awe at the display of affection and slowly approached the Planeswalker. Jacob joined her, tilting his head towards the young Planeswalker. Not long after, Kirra, Justin, and Snow joined the group.

With a questioning look towards the Planeswalker, Kirra asked, "H-How did yo—"

The girl explained very bluntly before Kirra could even finish, "I found him wandering the forests with the pack Justin and I freed from Bat Colony. You should be lucky that I found him at all. Even luckier so that he wished to hold true to his partnership with you. So, I obliged his request and brought him here... Against my better judgment." Her lips pressed in a flat line said she had disapproved of Snow's wishes greatly.

Kirra walked forward, a bit hesitant, but said gratefully, "Thank you so much for this. You have no idea how much this means to me."

"I didn't do it for you. I did it for Snow." She bowed her head for a moment towards the wolf before continuing, "If you three don't mind, I need to speak with Jacob and Shiro." She looked over at the pair of older dragons with a frown before adding, "Privately."

Kirra looked to her brother and then to the older dragons before Shiro nodded her head to the house's doors. With a wave of Shiro's hand, the sound of a few clicks was heard at the front doors as she seemed to unlock it. Her voice was as Serene and calm as ever, "Go on, explore the house to your liking. The only rooms that are off limits are the ones that are locked." Kirra looked at the pair of elder dragons with unease before walking up the steps of the house. Justin followed, but he gave the Planeswalker a soft bow of respect before moving on, which she returned with a small smile.

As the door clicked shut, the Planeswalker turned towards Jacob and Shiro with a look of anger on her face, "You were going to let him die."

Jacob answered this time, "They had a clear mission and were not to stray from their instructions regardless of whose lives were at stake."

The much shorter girl walked up to the pair and glared at them, "You were willing to leave him behind, and so was she, despite all of you knowing he could be used against her in the future."

Jacob folded his hands neatly, looking down his nose at her, "I understand your concern in this matter, but the boy's life was inconsequential to that of the Prophecy's immediate evacuation."

Her anger quickened as she responded, "This isn't just about him. This is about myself as well. You would rather follow exact orders to the T than change something a little bit to save people's lives." She turned towards Shiro, anger still seething around her, "You would have rather let your people die in that prison than risk the chance that I offered at saving all of them. I had to go in myself and do what you lot were too cowardly to do. All for one person."

Shiro explained, "One person who could change the entire multiverse."

Letting out a laugh, the Planeswalker shook her head in disbelief, "You all are on your own from now on. I've heard how all of your kin talk about me, how they talk about David. You say we're cowards for not 'really' being in danger. But hey, you have your Prophecy now, right?" She let out a laugh, shaking her head.

Jacob frowned deeply at her words, "You're going to let the bats win this war?" He looked almost angry, "You would let that tyranny run us over and watch it happen?"

The Planeswalker was taken aback by those words as she moved forward and tapped Jacob on the chest with a single finger, "No, you will decide if the bats win or lose this war. Not me. This wasn't my fight, to begin with, and I only partially got involved because I accidentally stepped in the middle of it while I was learning what I was capable of. But your lot doesn't need me or want me, so I wish you the best of luck because you're not getting help from me after the crap you guys pulled." Before anyone could respond, there was a sudden loud snap as she suddenly disappeared. Several similar snaps were heard going off in the distance.

Shiro looked genuinely concerned as she said, "You think she is going to side with Bat Colony?"

Jacob shook his head, "I do not believe so. We will prepare for the worst just in case." With a sigh, he finally said, "Keep an eye on her, and start her training on creating mental blocks immediately."

"And what if she doesn't have the fortitude for it?" Shiro inquired as she watched the back of the retreating Jacob.

Stopping, he looked over to her, "She must..." He gave her one last look before turning to leave.

With a sigh, Shiro went inside, looking for the kids, wondering where they had wandered off to. Clasping her hands in front of her, she closed her eyes and let her energy spread out from her. Like tendrils, they fished through the very barriers of walls and ceilings, feeling out for any energies that gave off a beating heart. After a few moments of concentrating, she finally found them.

Leaving the expansive front room and going up the split staircase, she quickly worked through the halls of a home she knew well in search of her foster children. It seemed they had made it up to the bedrooms and explored the rooms together while conversing.

Overall, the house was ornate, but not opulently so. It was well maintained with wood or tile throughout the whole of it. There were finely stitched rugs where wood or tile didn't decorate the floors. As Kirra inspected one of the desks, she thought she recalled some décor that looked very familiar to the style. It reminded her of Zeke's office. The house gave off a feeling of homeliness while still being grand. As Kirra was caught eyeing the room's color, she snarled lightly. Justin questioned her about the look she was giving.

Her response was soft, "It reminds me of Zeke's office and the dining room. Just...." She didn't know how to word it, "It feels weird."

Shiro commented lightly, "If it is not to your liking, you are more than welcome to change how it looks." The comment caught both of them off guard as Kirra acted like she wasn't doing anything wrong, and Justin put down the object he had been inspecting, "I did not mean to startle either of you. Please take the day to explore. Just stay near the house. Tomorrow, we will go into the Market and get you both settled with something that doesn't look like you just stepped out of a prison encampment." Both Kirra and Justin looked down at their clothing, realizing that what she said was true before she commented further, "Uh Justin, can you put your wolf fangs away?"

The drolled-out comment came, "I can't." Shiro looked at him as though he was lying, "I can't hide them. Something is wrong."

Kirra piped up as she said, "Zeke... He warned me that something like that might have happened. You were in your wolf form for a long while, which sometimes affects your appearance."

Shiro nodded her head, "I see. Just a forewarning to you, Justin. People will treat you differently because of that. It usually means you are too poor to hunt normally, so you take your wolf form to do so." Justin looked at her like she was an idiot, "I am merely trying to—"

Justin didn't give her the chance to finish, making Kirra grimace at his tone, "I understand what you're trying to tell me. I already know."

There was a long and awkward silence as the three stood there staring at each other before Shiro clapped her hands together and said, "Well... I'll let the two of you settle in, and I'll call you for dinner when it is ready." She turned towards Kirra, "There is a large stable out back with saddles and halters, though I do not believe I have any for wolf-based mounts. I'll see about getting a fitter to make a custom one for your mount." Shiro started leaving as she paused, "Just stay near the house for now. We'll talk more after the both of you have gotten some decent rest and recovered." With that, she made her way out.

Justin left shortly after Shiro did, and soon Kirra was left alone with her thoughts as she talked with her spirit. A portion of her felt guilty at having left her brother and even Snow in that place, but Justin had told her to go initially. He was even furious at the fact that she hadn't fought back despite him being captured.

Days went by and Shiro was nothing but generous with her time in helping the pair, at least that was what Kirra thought. Shiro was always polite and courteous towards them and even went out of the way to make sure they were as comfortable as possible given everything they went through. Eventually, Kirra was sent back to school, but Justin was homeschooled given how close he was to coming of age and the fact that he was a wolf, not a dragon. It seemed the school only catered to those with draconic spirits.

Although Justin was a wolf, Shiro was always polite towards him. She saw that his own wants and desires were taken care of, even going so far as to hire a martial teacher who was a black wolf like him. It also turned out that the man training Justin was one of the best martial artists on Vashirosk. It had made things a bit easier for him. For once, he had someone around with common interests, and he was one of the tallest men Kirra had seen in her life, rivaling that of Black Dragon, which said something. Despite how large he was, he was extremely gentle.

Kirra discovered that both Ky and the twins had wound up going to the same family. Apparently, Ky had some family left over that was willing to take both of the boys, and they were getting on famously. She was in a couple of classes with the three and all of them seemed to be fairing okay despite what happened. Kirra had to catch up in her classes, given she hadn't been taught much about Spiritoski and all it offered, so she had extra classes on top of training with Shiro. Her foster mother had telekinetic abilities, so her powers lay in the mind portion of the Major Eight.

There were times when Kirra felt like Shiro was hiding something from her. She felt that Jacob and Shiro were hiding something grave from her as they sometimes treated her like a delicate eggshell that was cracked and ready to break. Sometimes she'd catch them looking at her like they were expecting her to suddenly explode, but she chalked that up to the fact of what she had gone through for almost a year. Sometimes, she wondered if Ky might have gotten the same looks. He had been in that camp for longer than her, but she never saw any of his extended family members staring at him like he was about to burst.

It seemed that everything was going about as normal as it could be. Things were going to be okay for her and her brother. Kirra had Snow, her Spirit, who she had nicknamed Wrath, her foster mother, Shiro, and her brother. Her parents weren't there, but she was learning plenty and realizing that the dragons weren't as bad as everyone had been painting them.

Even though things were going well, she still had a long way to go. Kirra hadn't yet learned what her power was exactly and still had to learn how to use and control magic. She had a long way to go if she compared herself to the Planeswalker and her magic use.

Getting up and doing her normal morning routine, Kirra was happy she had a break from school. Sleepily heading to the shared full bathroom, she showered and sighed at not having to deal with her studies for the day. It had been four months since they'd arrived, and things had returned to normal for her and her brother.

Wrapping a towel around her body, she went up to the fogged-over mirror, wiped it clean, and instantly let out a scream of terror, punching the mirror on reflex. Recognition took over as she realized the person in the mirror was actually her. Immediately, she cried out for Shiro, screaming for her to come.

"What is it?! What happ—" Shiro paused mid-sentence. A teenager with long silky white hair and icy blue eyes wrapped in a fluffy white towel stood before her. They were clutching their hand tightly, trying to stem the flow of blood while standing in front of a broken mirror.

The girl's lips moved, and Kirra's voice came out with confusion, "W-What... Why—" It took her a moment to formulate her question, "What happened to my hair and eyes?!"

Justin and his massive trainer followed the sound, rushing up the stairs as Shiro held out a hand for them to halt as she said softly, "Your parents..." She paused momentarily, "They had someone enchant your hair and eyes so you would look like their child." Kirra stammered over her words in the bathroom, hidden from view of the two men, as Shiro explained, "Jacob saw the enchantment the moment you arrived, but didn't want to alarm you."

Confusion etched the lines of Kirra's young face, "W-what?"

"We can—"

"Fix it..." Kirra looked at her on the brink of tears, "Please..."

With a long sigh, Shiro nodded her head, "I'll make a few calls..."

About the Author

Aubrey grew up struggling with dyslexia and learning to read at the late age of 7. She started creating a world to escape from her everyday life. She has been writing since the age of 12 and has continued to refine her world. Starting out writing on paper with pencil and moving to typing on the family home computer, the original idea was almost realized. Real life hit hard as the recession of 2007 hit, causing her to join the United States Air Force. The idea for her creation never died, but several corrupted files, lost data, broken computer hard drives, and corrupted flash drives later, her dream was all but forgotten. After a 10-year stipend of military service, she was honorably discharged and later diagnosed with chronic major depression, generalized social anxiety, and PTSD. Aubrey now lives happily in Oklahoma.